CROWNS OF RUST

CROWNS OF RUST

KINGDOMS OF SAND BOOK II

DANIEL ARENSON

The Frozen Sea

Elasia

Denegar

Gael

Berenia

Aelar

Kalintin

Leer

The Encircled Sea

Sekhadia

Zohar

Phedia

Tereen

Aken

Shenutep

Sekur

Nur

Suna

The Encircled Sea

Kalintia

Ma'oz

Gefen

Beth Eloh

Sekhadia

Zohar

Tarath El

Blando

The Known World

OFEER

On a warm spring morning, the birds singing and the flowers blooming, Ofeer stepped into the gardens to pull her father's corpse off the cross.

Jerael Sela, Lord of the Coast, hung there outside his villa, overlooking the hills and distant sea. The legionaries had dislocated his arms, twisting them like wet rags before nailing the palms into the wood. Three days in the sun had done the rest. Blood dripped down the ravaged body, and the crows were still working at the flesh, tugging off strips, burrowing down to bones. The eyes were already gone.

For three days and nights, Ofeer had heard it. For three days and nights, she had remained in the villa, lying in Jerael's own bed, letting Seneca—the man who had crucified him—fuck her over and over as Jerael moaned outside, as Seneca moaned above her, as the crows cawed, as the legionaries jeered. For three days, Ofeer had felt crucified herself, pinned to that bed, pinned under Prince Seneca, her half brother, pinned under all her guilt, her misery, her drunken stupor. And on this fourth dawn, his moans had died, and Ofeer had emerged from a state like death, come here into the garden to bury the only father she had ever known.

She stared at the corpse. It reminded Ofeer of the dog she had seen roaming these hills. By Eloh, it hadn't even been a month ago; it felt like a lifetime. The cur too had withered, rotted, dying for days before Seneca had put an arrow in its head. That had been the day this had all started, the day the Aelarians had come into their lives, the day the Sela family had shattered like their nation, like this body on the cross.

Ofeer's eyes dampened. She padded closer, hesitantly, the dewy grass squelching under her bare feet. Suddenly a great fear filled her that Jerael was still alive, that when she approached, he would moan, turn those empty eye sockets toward her, speak in a raspy voice, accusing her.

Your fault. Your fault. Traitor. Traitor.

Yet he simply hung there, and the only movement came from a crow that still stood on his shoulder, pecking at skin.

"Shoo!" Ofeer blurted out, and tears fled her eyes. "Shoo!"

She lifted a stone and tossed it, missing the bird, but it was enough to send it fleeing. As the crow flew, it glared down at her, cawing.

Caw, caw! was the sound, but Ofeer heard other words. *Traitor. Traitor.*

She trembled as she stood before the dead man on the cross, then fell to her knees.

"Father," she whispered. "Father, I'm sorry. I'm sorry."

Of course, Jerael was not her true father, not her father in blood. It had been Marcus Octavius, Emperor of Aelar, who had raped her mother in the war, who had planted Ofeer into her belly. For all her eighteen years, it seemed, Ofeer had railed against Jerael—against this man who had raised her, had loved her, had seen her as a true daughter.

"I betrayed you," she whispered, her tears salty on her lips. "I joined the invaders of Aelar. I watched them kill, destroy. And only now can I call you 'Father.'"

It was slow work, pulling Jerael free from the cross. A few men of the Magisterian Guard, who had been standing around the garden, approached to aid Ofeer. Perhaps some pity did fill their hearts, hidden deep within layers of iron armor and the iron will drilled into the soldiers of Aelar. Yet the grave Ofeer dug on her own. This was work she would allow no Aelarian to perform. Jerael had raised her, had called her "daughter," and she owed him this. A last honor. A last plea for redemption.

"I'm not a Sela by blood," she whispered, digging the grave. "But I am by name. A name you let me bear. No foreign invaders will profane your final rest. It's your daughter who lays you down."

Ofeer did not know how long it took to dig, perhaps just an hour, perhaps most of the day. She worked in silence, sweat dampening her cotton dress. She buried him under the pomegranate tree that he had loved, in view of the coast below that he had ruled. She rolled a boulder toward the grave, a makeshift tombstone, and she carved his name upon it, and gently she uprooted and replanted cyclamens upon his grave.

Beside the grave of Jerael Sela rose a smaller tombstone, an older grave. Here, in view of the sea, rested Mica Sela, Ofeer's younger brother. She still remembered the day he had died—the same day he had been born. Twelve years had passed, and now father and son lay side by side.

Ofeer looked away from the graves and gazed west. Past fields and vineyards lay the city of Gefen, and beyond it the sea. Even from here on Pine Hill, she could make out the foam on the waves, white lines upon the green water. The distant scent of salt filled her nostrils, and Ofeer remembered those days long ago, before the rage and pain of youth had filled her. Days when she and her family would ride their horses down to the sea, run along the sand, collect seashells, bathe, laugh. The boys and Atalia always went diving underwater, seeking sunken coins, and Ofeer would be so afraid that they would drown, so afraid to lose them.

And now our family is broken, she thought. *Now two among us are dead, and the others are lost.*

Mother and Maya—caught in the war in the east, perhaps trapped in Beth Eloh, the capital city on the mountain where Porcia Octavius fought. Koren and Atalia—slaves in chains, trapped in the bowels of those Aelarian ships that still anchored in the harbor. Epher—missing in the north, perhaps dead. Jerael and Mica—buried here at her feet.

And me, Ofeer thought, the wind blowing her long black hair. *A lost woman.*

For so many years, through the bitter days and wild nights of her youth, Ofeer had wandered along the port. Drinking. Gambling. Crying. Fucking. Dreaming. Gazing across the sea, praying to someday reach the land of Aelar. To join her true father there. To leave Zohar—this land she had thought so backward, so stifling—far behind, lost in distance and memory.

"Who am I now?" she whispered, gazing toward that sea again. "Where is my home and who do I serve?"

Hers was the blood of both eagles and lions, and she did not know.

"So the bugger finally died." The voice rose behind her. "About time. The son of a whore's groans were keeping me up at night."

Ofeer turned around. Her childhood home rose before her, shaded by pines and cypresses. The villa was built of pale sandstone, the doorframe painted azure, the windowsills blooming with flowers. The house where she had grown up. The house from which the Sela family had ruled over the port for generations. The house that now belonged to the conquerors from Aelar.

Prince Seneca stood in the doorway, dressed in a deep purple toga lined with gold. The fabric was wrinkled and stained, hanging loose to reveal half of Seneca's chest. His face was unshaven, his eyes still blurry, and he held a goblet of wine. Since conquering Gefen four days ago, the young prince—he was only nineteen, a year older than her—had been celebrating his victory in an orgy of booze, music, crucifixions, and sex. He had invaded this land clad in iron and gold, every one of his brown hairs perfectly combed. War had left him looking like a different man, a decade aged.

There was more than drunkenness in his eyes, Ofeer saw, gazing into them. There was haunting fear. He had seen things in battle he could not forget. And Ofeer knew then that the wine, the sex, the torture and death of Jerael—those had not been to celebrate his victory but to forget it.

She nodded. "Lord Jerael Sela is now at peace."

"*Lord* Jerael?" Seneca scoffed and stumbled across the garden, pausing to gulp more wine. "No, Ofeer, my sweet beauty of the east. He was no more a lord than a pig is king of a sty. He hurt you. All these years he hurt you." He reached out to stroke her hair, his fingers rough, his eyes red. "He can no longer hurt you. Nobody will hurt you again."

Sudden rage flared in Ofeer. For too long, she had allowed this. Allowed him to stroke her, to fuck her, to toy with her, to lie to her. She shoved his hand away.

"I begged you for his life," she hissed. "I did not ask for this. Do not dare pin this on me."

Yet even as she spoke those words, Jerael's blood stained her hands. She had run from Jerael when he had needed her most. She had joined those besieging his city. She had entered the bed of Seneca, the man who had murdered him. Did she truly think that burying Jerael, that lashing out against Seneca, could cleanse her soul? No. Ofeer gazed down at her hands, at the dirt and dried flecks of blood, and she knew that she could never clean them.

She expected Seneca to rage at this, perhaps even to strike her. But instead his eyes softened, and he took her hands in his.

"Your heart is gentle," he said. "And death is such a terrible thing when you first behold it. I'm a great warrior, and I've slain many men, and my heart is hardened. I often forget how traumatic death can be to those young and soft." He winced. "The way the guts hang from sliced bellies. The way the crows peck at the eyes. The stench of it. Gods, the stench of blood and shit and rotting flesh. You never hear about those in the great epics. You never see those from the high seats in an amphitheater. But here …"

Again his eyes took on that haunted look, staring beyond her, staring parsa'ot away, and Ofeer knew that he wasn't talking about her.

"You poor, proud, stupid boy," she whispered. "You have no idea, do you?"

He had no idea what war meant. He had no idea that they shared a father. He had no idea that all those times in his tent, in her mother's bed, he had lain with his half sister. He had no idea that she scorned him, that she was afraid—perhaps not even that he himself was afraid.

And I'm just as foolish as he is.

Seneca drained his goblet and tossed it aside. "You grow bold, Ofeer. And I like that. I have no use for meek women. The meek die in this world. The meek are worms for us rulers to stomp on. I conquered the coast of Zohar for the glory of Aelar, but my conquest is not complete." He turned to stare toward the eastern hills. They spread for parsa'ot, leafy with pines and wild grass. "There are mountains east of here. Jagged dry mountains that guard the desert. And on them rises a city called Beth Eloh, the capital of this kingdom. The spring whence lume flows. We head there now, Ofeer. All three legions. My sister will already be there, bloodying her forces while ours prepare for glory. Once I conquer the capital, my father will name me his heir." He grabbed Ofeer's arm and bared his teeth, and a wild light burned in his eyes. "And you will be my concubine, my pet of the east, a dark beauty for all the lords and ladies of Aelar to see and desire. They will envy me for my prize."

She let him hold her arm. She let him brag, let him sneer. She stared into his eyes, lips tight.

I am your sister. I too am a child of Marcus Octavius. I will not be a war trophy for you, Seneca. I will talk to the emperor. I will demand his surname. And I will be a princess of an empire.

Movement caught her eye. She stared over Seneca's shoulder, back toward the eastern hills, and squinted.

Horses. A hundred horses or more came galloping toward them, their riders raising the eagle standards of Aelar.

Seneca turned to stare too, and his face paled.

"Porcia," he whispered.

SHILOH

The rider came at dawn, coated with dust and sweat and blood, to tell her of her family's ruin.

The day was sweltering, even this early. The sun lashed Beth Eloh with a fury, like a second invader, determined to burn the city down. Across the cobbled streets that snaked between brick homes, the people scurried from shadow to shadow, finding some relief beneath the awnings of shops or palm tree fronds. Hundreds crowded around the city wells, and many children wandered the streets, leading donkeys laden with gourds full of water, selling sips for copper coins. Even the legionaries who stood across the city, guarding gates and courtyards, slumped in the heat, their armor searing and reflecting the sun.

It's too early for this heat, Shiloh thought, standing outside the palace and gazing at the city. *Too early for this ruin. Too early for me to lose my daughter.*

With trembling hands, she unfolded the papyrus, read the letter again. She had read this letter over and over all day, weeping at first, but since then her eyes had gone dry. A letter from Maya. From her sweetest child.

Zohar can no longer be a home to me.

Shiloh had read those words so many times they lost meaning.

I must walk the paths that Luminosity lays out before me, paths of light through shadow. Where they take me, I don't know. I only know that tonight is farewell. That tonight I must part from the woman I love most in the world. From my mother.

Words that cut Shiloh like a blade in darkness, carving out all that she was, that she had been, that she could hope to be. Words cruel like a dagger of dull iron.

You are my light in the darkness. You are the beacon of my soul. You are always the prayer on my lips, my guiding star. I love you always, with all my heart, no matter where I go.

Shiloh folded the papyrus. She walked across the courtyard of smooth flagstones. The palace of Zohar rose at her side, soaring into the blinding white sky, its columns surrounding its dome. When she reached the eastern balustrade, she stared into the desert, and the sandy wind stung her face.

"Are you out there, Maya?" she whispered. "Please come back. I won't scold you. I won't be angry. I just want you back here. Please."

Footfalls sounded behind her, and Shiloh turned to see Prince Shefael walking toward her. She supposed he was King Shefael now—King of Zohar, puppet of Aelar. He still wore his royal raiment—an ultramarine tunic, fine leather sandals, and a lavender cloak pinned with a pomegranate fibula. A crown of gold rested upon his head, and many rings gleamed on his fingers. The scrawny boy Shiloh had known had grown into a heavyset, bearded man, fattened on feasts and wine during a siege that had seen his people dwindle to skin and bones.

And yet, despite his kingly appearance, his old soldiers—men of Zohar, clad in scales, sickle swords upon their thighs—guarded him no more. Legionaries now marched alongside Shefael, men of Aelar. They wore lorica segmentata across their torsos, while strips of bolted leather hung down to their knees. Red crests flared from their helms. To these guards, Shefael was more prisoner than king.

"Aunt Shiloh." When Shefael finally reached her, his face was red, his breath heavy, and he held her with moist hands. "I've sent out four hundred riders. They scour the land in all the directions of the wind. We'll find Maya. I promise you."

Shiloh stared at her nephew. The boy who had once picked a hundred figs from the tree in her garden, gorging himself until he had thrown up. The prince who, they said, had forged a letter from his mother—Shiloh's own sister—naming himself heir to Zohar. The man who had let the Aelarians butcher his brother, who had let the enemy into this very city.

A fool, Shiloh thought. *A traitor. And perhaps the only man who can find my daughter.*

"I should be out there," she whispered. "Searching with them."

Shefael shook his head. "No. We've discussed this. I need you here, with me. I need your wisdom." He looked downhill at the city streets, where thousands of legionaries stood. He leaned closer to Shiloh, dropping his voice so that his guards could not hear. "I don't know when this army will leave, Aunt. Sometimes I think they'll stay forever."

Yes, she thought. *A fool. But a fool who shares my blood. Who now rules Zohar. Who now serves Emperor Marcus Octavius, the man who raped me, the man who will rape this kingdom if I cannot pull my nephew's strings as well.*

Shiloh had sailed around the Encircled Sea with her husband years ago, when no pale hairs had silvered her braid, when no crow's feet had tugged at her eyes. She had sailed by kingdoms like Nur, provinces that survived as they paid tribute to their masters, as they accepted the chains of Aelar. And she had sailed by coasts where cities lay in ruin, where bones baked in the sun, where millions had perished, where the eagles of Aelar had not been appeased with enough meat to guzzle.

If the price of our life—life for Maya when she's found, life for my family, life for all in Zohar—is a foolish client king, then we must pay this price. For all other roads lead to bones and fallen halls.

"You allowed the eagles into the lions' den," Shiloh said. "Now you must deal with their talons."

And I must deal with a lion club who fled. With a piece of my heart torn out. With a fear that will not leave me.

It was then that Shiloh saw the rider.

At first he was but a speck on the horizon, still outside the city walls, raising a cloud of dust, traveling from the west. As he drew closer, Shiloh could make out a horse, still too far to show color. The rider entered the city—for the first time in a year, the gates were open to pilgrims, farmers, and other travelers. The horse galloped along the city streets, heading here, toward the Mount of Cedars and the palace on its crest. And as she watched the rider approach, her heart sank, and Shiloh knew—whether from divine insight, from some hidden sense of lume, or simply from a wisdom inside her—that he came bearing ill tidings. Cold sweat trickled down her back.

Finally the rider reached her, dust coating his cloak, beard, and tanned skin. In this courtyard beneath the golden palace, the highest point of the city, he dismounted and knelt before her and Shefael. He panted, seeming so weary he could barely breathe, and blood stained bandages across his arm and side.

"My lord," he rasped. "My lady."

Shiloh inhaled sharply. She knew him.

"Hanan." She knelt by him. "Are you hurt?" She turned toward the legionaries. "Bring water! Bring milk and honey!"

The legionaries only smirked. Shiloh returned her attention toward Hanan. The tall, bearded man had served as a bodyguard in their villa on Pine Hill, had been a family friend for twenty years.

"My lady," he said, and his eyes dampened. He held her hand in his trembling, callused grip. "I am sorry."

No. Tears flooded Shiloh's eyes. *No. Oh Lord of Light, no, please, no.*

"Tell me," she said, struggling to keep the tremble from her voice, not to show weakness to the legionaries who watched, who smirked. "Are they all ...?"

"Lord Jerael has fallen." Hanan lowered his head. "The city of Gefen has fallen too, its defenders slain."

Her world crumbled.

A thousand thoughts stormed through her mind, crumbling.

Only one remained.

"What of my children?" Shiloh whispered.

"Atalia and Koren live, but … my lady, it grieves me to speak these words."

Still kneeling, she dug her fingers into his shoulders. "Speak them nonetheless."

Hanan placed his hands on her arms and stared into her eyes. "Taken captive. Placed in chains. The legionaries say they will be shipped to Aelar as prisoners."

As slaves, Shiloh knew.

"What of Epher?" she whispered. "What of Ofeer?"

Hanan shook his head. "I don't know, my lady. They say that Epher fought with the hillsfolk outside Beth Eloh."

All the hillsfolk had died outside Beth Eloh, Shiloh knew. She had watched them all die from the wall.

Slowly, she rose to her feet.

She turned toward Shefael.

"My king, send out a hundred more riders. We need more people searching for Maya. And send a hundred priests, a hundred masons and engineers, and a hundred wagons of supplies to Gefen. The wounded will need healing, the walls will need repairs, the people will need medicine and food and blankets." She nodded. "And give Hanan a place at your table tonight. He deserves to feast with a king."

Shefael only stared at her, mouth hanging open. Two of the legionaries who guarded him took steps forward, frowning under their iron helms.

"You are not to issue commands, whore of Zohar—" one legionary began.

She met the man's eyes and interrupted him. "And you will not interfere with how we manage the daily affairs of our kingdom, legionary. Porcia Octavius has ridden out of this city. Until your emperor officially names Zohar a province of Aelar, and until he appoints a governor to command us, I *will* issue my own commands."

She was playing a dangerous game here, she knew. A game whose rules were not yet set. Until the pieces arranged themselves in their final positions, she could not predict each movement's outcome, and as she stared down this legionary, memories of those fallen lands—of the ruins and corpses around the Encircled Sea—filled her mind.

But a few things she knew.

My husband is dead. My children are missing or sold into slavery. But a hundred thousand souls still live in this city, and many more live across the land of Zohar. And if I cannot protect them now, if I cannot walk this tightrope between subservience and autonomy, all these people will join my husband underground.

Finally the legionary nodded. One battle won.

"My lady." Hanan approached her again, head lowered. "We will pray in the Temple tonight. We will pray for Lord Jerael's soul, for—"

"Tonight we will walk through the city," Shiloh said, "and distribute food and water to the poor. The heat is sweltering, dangerous for those weakened by siege. Then we will write a letter to Emperor Marcus in Aelar, offering him our servitude in exchange for our lives; a messenger will carry it to the port. We will continue to oversee the search efforts for the missing, and we will continue to bury the dead outside our walls. Now go, Hanan. Wash and change your clothes and drink and eat. Then join me again. We have much to do."

He nodded and left her, perhaps wondering at how her heart could be so calloused. What he did not see was the pain inside her, was the heart that threatened to shatter, to leave her a ruin, a dead soul in a dying body.

There were a million lives in Zohar to save. A million lives who needed her, whose need might just save her.

She got to work.

EPHER

ummmm.
Buzzzz.

For a long time, darkness and sound.

Shadows and a dark labyrinth.

Epher wandered through a shadowy city, knowing he had to find something, to reach a destination, knowing that if he failed, his family would die. But he was lost. He moved faster, soon running, but the streets kept twisting around him, reshaping, leading to dead ends. He ran faster, trying to find what he needed—to find his home. To find his family, to protect them. They were dying. They were dying and he was lost, and the streets narrowed, and—

It flew before him. A great eagle, black, its wings dripping rot, its talons coated in blood. Its head was a human skull, bustling with crows, maggots in the eye sockets. It grew closer, and Epher realized it was massive, large as the city, its black wings hiding the sky.

"Go!" the eagle cried, voice impossibly deep, thundering.

Epher ran through the city streets, trying to flee it, to flee those talons, but it flew everywhere, mocking him.

"Go! Go away!"

Epher raced up a craggy black staircase, ran down an alleyway, trying to find an exit, a way out, and those talons grabbed him, shook him, dug into him.

"Go away, whore?"

There. He saw it. An archway. An archway and light beyond it, finally sunlight, searing, hurting his eyeballs. He gasped for air. The talons tightened around his shoulders.

"Get lost, cunt," the voice whispered, but it was no longer deep and booming. It was soft, feminine, flowing through that archway of light. He tried to see, but it was so bright.

"Hungry?" he whispered.

"Hungry," the voice answered. "Hungry!"

He blinked, trying to see. Her face appeared before him, framed with wild red hair, haloed with light. Her eyes were soft, and she stroked his cheek.

"Hungry," she whispered.

The light faded.

The shadows wrapped around him.

He wandered strange fields in the sunset. He wore the armor of a legionary, iron strips across his torso, a skirt of leather straps, a crested helm. The fields turned from green to gold, harvested, leaving barren soil to plow, then growing again, reaped again, the seasons churning with every step as he walked. Before him, he beheld a great city upon hills, ten times larger than Beth Eloh. Its white gateways led to many towers, to statues of gold, and he beheld a woman there, her head lowered. A woman all in white, her skin, her hair, all of her the color of milk, and above her head floated five golden triangles like a crown. In her one hand she held a feather of gold, in the other the skull of a feline. The woman raised her head, revealing empty eye sockets.

"She will enter through the Gate of Tears," the woman said, lips not moving. "She will walk through the city of God, bring healing to the hurt, prayers to the weary. Her light will burn us."

Epher tried to reach her, to ask what she meant, but he fell. He was falling from the walls of Gefen, falling down toward the sea, falling, falling, knowing that he had to wake up, he had to open his eyes before he hit the bottom.

He gasped for air and stared above.

He saw the stars.

He took slow breaths, trying to orient himself. He was no longer in the labyrinth of stone. He no longer wore armor. No pale women, haloed with golden triangles, hovered before him in gateways of white stone. He heard a soft trickling sound like wine pouring into a cup.

I'm awake.

He pushed himself to his elbows, wincing in pain. In the moonlight, he saw that he wore only his undergarments, and that tattered strips of cotton bound his wounds. He lay on a hill, and many other hills and valleys spread around him. He could just make out the moonlight on boulders, olive trees, and a human figure that crouched ahead.

"Hungry?" he whispered, voice raspy.

The trickling sound stopped. She spun around, eyes wide, and quickly stood up and tugged down her tunic—the very tunic he had given her long ago. He saw that strips had been cut from it, matching the fabric that bound his wounds.

"Cunt!" She grinned. "Go away!"

She bounded uphill toward him, knelt, and fussed over him—placing a hand on his brow, examining his bandages, peering into his eyes, opening his mouth to scrutinize his tongue. All the while, she kept chattering, mingling a few choice human curses with random clicks and clucks and squeaks. She reminded Epher of some nervous mother bird dotting over her hatchling. He thought back to what Benshalom had told him.

Simpleminded. We call her Red.

Epher dropped onto his back, too weak to keep himself propped on his elbows.

"Red," he whispered. "Your name is Red."

The young, red-haired woman cocked her head, kneeling above him. "Red?"

He slept again.

When finally his eyes reopened, it was morning. The sun revealed dry tan mountains in the north, rising toward a city on a plateau. Beth Eloh. It seemed a parasa away, maybe two—just a smudge in the distance. Moosh and Teresh, the horses Epher had taken from Gefen, stood nearby, tethered to a palm tree and munching on wild grass. The woman from the beach crouched by a campfire, cooking oats in an iron helmet. *His* iron helmet.

Epher finally felt well enough to sit up. He spent a moment looking at the young woman. Scrapes and bruises covered her body. Her skin was pale, strewn with freckles, and mud and dry leaves filled her matted tangles of hair. He had given her a fine, newly woven tunic, and already it looked decades old, tattered down to strips. He was twenty-three years old, and she seemed no older, but it was hard to tell her age; too much grime covered her, smeared across her face.

When she saw that he was awake, she hopped toward him, carrying the helmet of oats. She held it out to him.

"Hungry?" she asked, then winced and dropped the hot iron onto the ground.

He nodded. She wrapped cloth around her hands, lifted the helmet again, and held it up to him. He drank the oatmeal, feeling some strength return to him.

"How long has it been?" he asked, his voice a little stronger. "Since the battle?"

She blinked at him. "Go away? Get lost. Go away, whore."

He sighed. "That's all you can say, isn't it?"

She nodded emphatically. "Hungry. Red! Ur nim is Red."

"Your name is Red," he corrected her, pointing at her.

She grinned and jabbed him with her finger. "*Your* nim is Red." She launched into a stream of nonsense; it sounded like baby talk, simply sounds and clicks and coos, not words in a true language.

Epher rose to his feet. His legs shook and his head spun, and he leaned against an olive tree. He stared north toward the distant city. He couldn't see its fate from here. When he squinted, he could just make out glints of metal on the wall—sunlight on armor. Whether it was the armor of legionaries or Zoharites, he couldn't say.

"My mother and sister are still there," he said. "The battle might still be raging. Porcia might still be besieging the city." He lifted his armor, which Red had tossed aside, and pulled the suit of scales over his head. He saw his sword tossed several amot away by some bushes, and he walked downhill toward it. "I have to go back."

Before he could clasp his sword to his belt, Red raced up toward him.

"Go away?" she said, frowning.

He nodded, working at attaching his sword. "Yes, I—"

"Get lost!" she said, eyes dampening. She shook her head wildly, grabbed his sword from him, and tossed it aside. "Cunt. Cunt! Whore. Your nim is Red. Your nim is Red!" She panted, grabbing at him. "Go away!"

Epher sighed and pried her hands off. "Red, listen to me. I have to go back to the city. To fight the legionaries. You know the legionaries?" He tugged up his hair, mimicking the crest of a centurion's helmet. "They're bad people. I have to fight them."

Tears flowed down her cheeks. She wouldn't release him. When he tried to walk toward his sword, she grabbed him and pulled him toward her, embracing him. "Go away," she whispered, still shaking her head. "Lenaries?"

"Legionaries," he said, nodding.

Fear filled her eyes, and she pointed at his wounds. "Lenaries nim is Red." She tried to pull him back toward the campfire. "Lenaries go away."

"Red!" He touched her cheek, lifting her tears onto his finger. "I know you're scared. But I can't abandon my city. If the battle still rages, I—"

"Ballel go away!" She tugged up her hair, mimicking her own crest. "Lenaries nim is Red. Lenaries Red." She pointed at the city. "Lenaries. Lenaries!"

Epher sighed. It was no use. He couldn't understand what she meant—had the legionaries taken the city, or was she merely afraid because the enemy was still outside the walls? He finally managed to hang his sword from his belt, then mount his horse.

"I'm sorry, Red," he said. "I have to go."

"Go away!" Now anger filled her eyes. She grabbed her makeshift bow and arrows, climbed onto the second horse, and glared at him. "Sorry go away? Hungry go away."

He smiled wanly. "My name is Epher. Not Sorry." He pointed at himself. "Epher. Do you have a name? A real name?"

She blinked at him. "Nim? Nim is Red?"

No. No, her name was not Red. The hillsfolk had given her that name. He had thought of her as Hungry at first because she had mistaken it for her name, back on the beach, when he had offered her food. But she needed a true name, and perhaps nobody had ever given her one.

Epher looked around him at the hills, the olive trees, the campfire, the distant city, then back at the young woman.

"Olive." He moved his horse closer to hers, leaned across the saddle, and poked her arm. "Olive. Your name is Olive."

She pointed at herself. "Olive?"

He nodded.

She bit her lip, then grinned. "Olive, Olive!" She pointed at him. "Pher."

"Epher," he corrected her.

"Epher." She pointed him, then at herself. "Olive."

He dug his heels into Moosh, his chestnut gelding, and began riding downhill. Olive followed, riding on Teresh, the slender white mare.

They made their way into a valley strewn with yellow grass, its last few flowers wilting. It was not yet summer, but the day was sweltering. Sweat dripped down Epher's back and brow. His wounds began to hurt now, a throbbing pain beneath his bandages. He didn't want to imagine what they looked like. His head felt too tight, as if the skull were squeezing the brain, but even worse was the thirst. He found his canteen still in his pack, half full. He drank some and gave the rest to Olive.

"You're thirsty too, Moosh." He ruffled his horse's mane. "I know. We're going to find you a nice stable with water and hay and apples."

The gelding neighed appreciatively.

How long was I asleep? Staring ahead at the distant city, Epher could see no signs of battle. No catapult projectiles flew. He could hear no screams or clanging metal. The battle had ended. Whoever won, he couldn't say.

"Are you still in that city, Mother and Maya?" he asked softly.

When they passed by a persimmon tree, they paused to pick the fruit, and they ate as they kept riding, giving fruit to the horses too. The orange flesh was incredibly sweet, soothing his throat, but seemed to worsen his thirst. He would find no water out here, but there would be wells in the city—and hopefully still a lion on the throne.

The sun had reached its zenith when ten horses came thundering their way, moving from the city. Epher reached for his sword, heart leaping. Olive hissed and bared her teeth and grabbed her bow. But these were no legionaries riding toward them. The riders wore robes, and veils hid their heads and faces from the sunlight. They seemed to wear no armor and bear no weapons. Zoharites.

"Friends!" Epher called to them, raising his hand.

The horses curved their path, thundering across the valley toward them, then rode in rings around Epher and Olive. Olive spun from side to side, hissing and spitting, and nocked an arrow.

"Go away! Get lost, whore! Go away, cunt!"

"Olive, easy." Epher pushed down her bow, then turned toward the riders. "What news do you bring from Beth Eloh?"

One of the men pulled back his scarf, revealing a gaunt, bearded face, the dark eyes staring from under thick brows. Those eyes widened.

"Epheriah?" the man said. "Epheriah Sela!"

Epher gasped. Both men dismounted their horses, stepped toward each other, and embraced.

"Hanan!" Epher said. "What are you doing so far east? What happened in Gefen? Do you ride from Beth Eloh?"

His father's bodyguard lowered his head. His eyes darkened.

"Only a day ago, I shared grim news with your mother," Hanan said. "Now a second time I must deliver the tidings."

For a long time, Hanan spoke, and Epher listened.

My kingdom, fallen.

Epher fell to his knees.

Koren and Atalia, taken captive. Maya missing.

His heart seemed to shatter.

My father, dead.

Epher wanted to remain strong. He wanted to stand tall, to raise his chin, to nod, to speak proud words, vowing vengeance. But instead he wept.

My world is gone.

The tears flowed, and his body shook. Vaguely he was aware of Olive kneeling at his side, stroking his hair, whispering soothing nothings into his ear.

Hanan placed a hand on his shoulder. "I'm sorry, Epher. I loved your father dearly. My heart breaks. I must ride on now— ride on to find Maya, to bring her home. Will you join us?"

Epher looked up through his tears, not knowing what to do, where to go.

"Maya has always spoken of seeking a Luminosity teacher." Slowly his hands curled into fists. "And I know who would have spoken to her of such things. Keep riding, Hanan, but I cannot go with you. I travel to Beth Eloh. To speak to the only lumer there. To Avinasi."

SENECA

He stood on Pine Hill, watching Porcia approach, and felt his world burn.

Fire. Fire, hot, all consuming, flared inside Seneca. His hands curled into fists. Hatred. Pure, unadulterated hatred. It blazed inside him, tightening his chest, squeezing his head.

She still rode in the distance, but even from here, Seneca knew that his older sister was smirking at him, mocking him, planning ways to grind him into the dirt.

The fog of booze dispersed. His fury burned it away. He stepped into the villa, grabbed his armor, and strapped it on. He fastened his gladius to his side. He ran a hand through his hair and stepped back outside.

"My prince?" Ofeer said. "You seem frightened."

He glared at the girl. The half-breed stared back at him. There was something different about her this morning. Burying that brute Jerael had placed a defiance in Ofeer's brown eyes. She was still beautiful—achingly so—with olive skin, long black hair, taunting lips, her body slender yet curved. For three days now, she had lain in bed, meek, barely alive as he took her again and again. Something about the new boldness in her eyes, her wakefulness from stupor, set Seneca's blood boiling, made her even more desirable than before.

He wanted to take her again. To strip off her dress. To fuck her right on Jerael's grave. To make her always his, to show her who he was, to conquer her, to break that defiance in her eyes as he had broken the city of Gefen. That was what conquerors did. They took something fair and they broke it.

"I'm never frightened," he told her. "I'm a conqueror." He drew his sword. "My sister will learn this. Stand back, Ofeer. I'll protect you from her."

He turned back toward the east. Porcia was closer now. Two hundred horsemen or more rode behind her. Her lumer rode at her side, that pathetic, sniveling little wretch named Worm. They all wore armor and bore spears and swords—aside from the lumer—and the hooves thundered. Soon they reached the villa, spreading across the hill.

"Baby brother!" Porcia called from her horse.

She dismounted and walked toward him. The princess wore a breastplate of dark iron. While his breastplate bore golden filigree, hers was bare of any ornament, no finer than a beggar's chamber pot. She pulled off her helmet and shook free her waves of chestnut hair.

"Nice place you got here." Porcia looked around, nodding appreciatively. "Lovely little country villa. Some beautiful flowers for you to sniff. A beautiful girl." She glanced over at Ofeer. "Nice tits on that one. Did you stick your cock between them yet?"

"What are you doing here?" Seneca snapped, stepping toward his sister. "Father told you to invade from the north. The west is mine."

Porcia raised her eyebrow and patted his cheek. "My, my, baby brother. Such a temper. You always did have a tantrum whenever I played with your toys. Here." She reached into her pack. "I brought you a new toy to play with."

She slapped something red and wet against his chest.

"Gods!" Seneca screamed, stepping back.

A severed manhood slid off his breastplate and thumped onto the grass. Ofeer covered her mouth and fled into the villa. Porcia only laughed.

"What?" Porcia gave him a cockeyed look. "You've always loved playing with your own cock. I figured I'd bring you one back from the war."

"Get this shit out of here!" he shouted at one of his men. The legionary nodded and stepped forward, wincing as he lifted the gruesome gift. Seneca spun back toward his sister. "Porcia, I've had enough of your rubbish." He felt his eyes stinging, and he refused to let himself cry, refused to let her see his turmoil. "Get out of here. Now! The coast is mine. I'm going to tell Father."

Porcia laughed. "Oh, please do, baby brother. In fact, let us 'tell him' together. I've come here so we can sail back home, you and I, brother and sister." She slung an arm around his neck. "We'll tell Father how you conquered a little house on a hill, spending your days drinking and whoring, while I conquered Beth Eloh."

Seneca shoved her off him. "You did not. It hasn't even been a month since you invaded Zohar. That city's walls soar a hundred feet into the sky. They're wider than a man is tall." He trembled with rage, with terror that she was speaking truth. His eyes stung anew. "You're a fucking liar. You couldn't have conquered that city within a month."

"A month? I only needed a day, sweet brother." She patted his cheek. "Do you know how Aelar grew great? How we subjugated the land of Nur, how we rule every port around the Encircled Sea, how one city—Aelar, a mere city!—rules the known world?" She leaned closer to him and licked her teeth. "Because we make deals. I made the rat king an offer he couldn't refuse. I disposed of one enemy—no more troubling than a flea on a dog's ass—and in return, he gave me a city. But, oh …" She glanced down toward the city of Gefen, which nestled the sea a league away. "I suppose wasting three legions trying to smash the walls of a little seaside town—walls that will be quite costly for the Empire to repair—will impress Father too."

Seneca's hands trembled. He needed a drink. Damn it. He needed more wine. Porcia seemed to vanish before him. Corpses danced in his vision, stripped of skin, dripping blood—the battle reanimated, taunting him.

For nothing. For nothing. Blood for nothing. Their skinless faces split into grins. *You invited us in, for nothing, nothing but bones.*

"You lie!" Seneca screamed, drawing his sword.

This wasn't supposed to happen. Porcia was supposed to exhaust her forces in the northern hills, then to languish outside

Beth Eloh, the princes' hosts grinding at her, wearing her down, until he—Seneca Octavius, the Eagle of Aelar—marched in with his legions to capture the city and deliver her from death.

Porcia sighed and looked at the fallen goblet in the grass. She stepped back toward her horse and mounted it. "I'll be taking a ship back to Aelar. I left a few good men in Beth Eloh to run things while Father names me his heir. Do feel free to stay here drinking and whoring, though. It does seem to be what you're best at."

With that, Porcia dug her heels into her horse and rode on, trampling over Jerael's grave on the way to the sea. Her men followed, their horses leaving their steaming waste across the garden.

Seneca stood for a moment, staring after them. He realized that he had strapped his armor on wrong, using the shin guards on his forearms. No doubt Porcia had noticed.

For nothing. For nothing.

Again those corpses danced.

His eyes dampened with tears.

I lost. I should never have lingered here. Father will grant her my inheritance.

His world seemed to burn around Seneca. He needed more wine. He needed to pound those ghosts out from his head. He needed Ofeer. Head spinning, he stumbled into the villa.

OFEER

S he lay in her parents' bed, knees pulled up to her chin, listening to the horses' hooves fade outside. She screwed her eyes shut, and she bit her lip so hard she tasted blood.

"Please let me wake up," Ofeer whispered. "Please, God. Let me wake up, let this all be a dream."

How could this be real? How could her life have shattered? How could this terror be true?

"I want to go back." Tears burned down her cheeks like rivers of fire. "I want to go back to how things were. I'm so sorry, God. I'm so sorry for everything I did. For hating my family. For running away. For joining the eagles. I'm sorry. I'm sorry. Please forgive me. Please let this just be a dream. I want to go back."

Ofeer trembled. She thought back to how she had been years ago, when she was very small. Sometimes at winter nights, the thunder would boom, and she would get frightened. She would run through the halls of this house—it had seemed as large as a palace then—and leap into her parents' bed. She had not then known that Jerael wasn't her father. She had only known that she loved them, loved the burly man with the thick black beard, loved the kind woman with the long braid and wise eyes. Ofeer would nestle between them, and they would dry her tears, and she would sleep here—in this very bed—comforted by their warmth. She had known then, cuddled between them, that nothing could hurt her, no thunder in the sky, no waves from the sea, no monsters in shadow.

And yet monsters had come here. The waves had washed over their city. And now they were gone. Jerael—dead. Her siblings—kidnapped. Her mother—lost in Beth Eloh, maybe dead, the city fallen.

And my true father is the emperor. Ofeer thought back to her mother's words, later confirmed by Taeer the lumer. *Seneca and Porcia battle for their inheritance, and I'm their sister.*

She thought back to how Seneca had fucked her, again and again, here in this very bed—the bed where she had sheltered from thunder between her parents. He did not know who she was. To Seneca, she was nothing but an exotic beauty of the east, a concubine, but when Ofeer thought back to what they had done here …

She stumbled out from the bed. She made it to the window just in time to vomit outside, a twisting, wrenching thing that emerged from her with a horrible sound, the inhuman sound of a beast, squeezing her innards with a demonic force. She felt as if a demon had possessed her.

Finally, drained, Ofeer wandered through the house. She grabbed a jug of wine from a table—wine was everywhere here these days—sloshed it in her mouth, spat it out, then drank. Drank again. Drank more than she had ever drunk back in her wild youth in the port. She walked through her home. In the dining hall, where Ofeer had spent so many evenings with her family, praying and laughing and singing, legionaries were playing dice on the table. In her old bedroom, a legionary was bouncing a city whore on his lap.

She found Seneca in the library. He stood silently, his hand against the wall, head lowered. Shelves of scrolls rose around him, and mottles of light passed through burgundy curtains.

There he is, Ofeer thought, staring at him. *A scared boy. A murderer. A monster who murdered the man I had once thought of as a father. My half brother.*

Seneca did not look at her as he spoke.

"When I was very young, Porcia once caught me playing with one of her dolls," he said, voice soft. "Just a little wooden soldier with a blade of real iron. She broke my arm. As I screamed on the floor, she only laughed, and she told me that I would never be a soldier, that I would always be weak, as weak as little Valentina. My arm still hurts in winters. I don't think it'll ever stop hurting." He raised his head and looked at Ofeer, and she saw that tears filled his eyes. "I thought that if I came here to Zohar, if I proved myself in battle, if I won Father's legacy ... that the pain would end."

"Some pain never ends," Ofeer said, thinking of the pain between her legs, thinking of the pain in her heart, of that vision she could not erase. Jerael hanging on the cross. Crows eating him.

"I wanted to be a warrior, Ofeer." He stepped toward her and held her hands. "But I'm a coward. I … I saw things in the city. Things you can't imagine. Men burned, the skin peeling, but still they lived, screaming. I can still hear those screams. Organs spilling. I saw a legionary tear the heart out of an enemy and hold it up as a trophy. I saw a man with no legs running from fire. He ran on the stumps before a javelin tore him down. I don't know what I will be when I return to Aelar. Not a conqueror, just … something broken."

"You are a conqueror," Ofeer said, her own tears dry now, staring into his eyes. "You conquered the coast. You conquered me. You saw men killed, but oh, sweet Seneca … how many of them you killed yourself! You nailed Jerael to the cross and left him to rot. My sweet, sweet Seneca. You've always been a conqueror. And you've always been broken."

He stared at her, eyes narrowed, as if not sure if she was complimenting or mocking him.

"What do I do now?" he whispered. "Tell me, Ofeer. Tell me. I'm scared. If Porcia becomes empress …"

Ofeer looked around her at the library, the place where Maya had loved to spend hours reading until Mother forced her to bed. She thought about the legionaries in her bedroom. She thought about the graves outside. She thought about Beth Eloh fallen, the city of Gefen destroyed. She thought about her old dreams, when she had stood at the port, gazing west, dreaming of Aelar, of that land of towers and heroes and endless joy, the land of her father.

Zohar holds nothing for me now. Our house has fallen. My family is scattered, maybe all dead. She took a shuddering breath. *It's time to follow my old dream. It's time to go home.*

"You return to Aelar." She touched Seneca's cheek. "You tell Emperor Marcus all that you did here. That you breached the thick walls of a fortified city and claimed it, street by street. That you conquered the port—the last port in the Encircled Sea that Aelar had not yet ruled. That you proved yourself in battle, seizing many slaves and treasures. All while your sister simply struck a deal with a fat, drunken king who had sat upon the throne when she got there, and who still sits there now." She wrapped her fingers around his arm. "You tell your father these things, Seneca Octavius, without tears in your eyes, without fear in your voice, but with a raised chin, with squared shoulders. And you take me there with you. We sail to Aelar. Together."

ATALIA

"Let me out of here, you piss-guzzling sons of pigs!" Atalia thrashed against her chains, screaming, ignoring the pain of her wounds. "Let me out and face me like men, you cock-loving whores! Put a sword in my hand and fight me, or you're nothing but cowardly dogs who piss on walls!"

She panted, weak with weariness. Nearly four hundred other galley slaves filled the ship around her, chained to their posts, clad in rags. Some were ragged and scarred from many beatings—slaves who had rowed the ships here. Others had been captured only days ago in Gefen; Atalia recognized many of their faces. She kept trying to peer to the back of the ship, to seek Koren, but no matter how many times she called his name, she heard no answer.

It was dark here, the ceiling low above them, and no portholes broke the hull. The only light came from the narrow holes the oars slid through. The place was crowded. The knees of the slave behind her hit her back. The slave at her side pressed against her, their elbows banging. Hundreds of rowers, crammed here like worms in a rotten apple, and they hadn't even left port, not during all the three days Atalia had languished here. The place stank of sweat, shit, blood, and disease.

"Let me out!" she cried again. "Wall-pissers! Let me out!"

An overseer lolloped her way, a beefy man with a bald head and wide belly. He grinned, a missing tooth gaping in his mouth, and looked at the sticky floor of the ship. "Looks like you're the one pissing all over now." He lashed his crop, and the leather slammed into Atalia's back, tearing the skin. "Now be silent. Another word from you, and I'll beat you till I'm cracking your spine."

His crop lashed again, and Atalia roared with pain. Her hands tightened around her oar. More than anything, she wished she could tear this oar free, could kick off the chain that bound her ankle, could swing the wood as a weapon and kill the overseer, kill them all. But the bald man merely trundled off, seeking another slave to subdue.

"It's no use, Atalia," said the galley slave at her side, the one who shared her oar. "Save your strength for the journey. I heard the men say we'll be leaving port soon."

She turned her head to glare at the fool. Daor was a young man, only a year shy of her own nineteen summers. Dark stubble covered his face, and the marks of whips lined his back—many of those originally aimed at her. Chains bound his ankle to the floor. They sat together on a wooden slat, the space so constricted their bodies pressed together, sweat mingling in the heat. Back in Gefen, he had served in her phalanx. A potter's son. A young fool.

"You will refer to me as 'Commander.' You are still a soldier of Zohar." Atalia squeezed his arm—painfully, she hoped. "Is that clear?"

"The war is over," Daor said. "We lost. We—"

"—are still warriors. Are still lions." She bared her teeth at him. "And I'm still your military commander. This war isn't over until every last Zoharite is dead underground or under the sea."

Inwardly, Atalia winced at her choice of words.

My own father is dead.

She lowered her head, jaw tight. She couldn't stop seeing it in her mind. Seneca Octavius, smirking and drunk, swinging his hammer, driving the nails into Father's hands and feet, nailing him to the cross. She couldn't stop seeing all the dead, the thousands of them, soldiers who had fallen around her in Gefen. Perhaps Daor, this young fool, was the only other soldier left. Perhaps all of Zohar, from the port to Beth Eloh on the mountains, had fallen, and perhaps all her family was dead.

I will find you someday, Prince Seneca Octavius, Atalia vowed silently, teeth grinding. *And I will kill you. And I will kill you, Emperor Marcus Octavius.* Her tears burned. *I will kill every last Aelarian who ever set foot in Zohar.*

"Commander," Daor said, voice softer now. "I'm sorry about what happened. To your father. I admired him greatly. He would often visit my family's pottery shop, break bread with us. He was a great lord, yet not too great to spend time with those who served him, who loved him. We'll always remember him, all those across Zohar, from sea to desert."

If there's anyone left in Zohar, Atalia thought. With Gefen fallen, the gateway to their ancient kingdom was open. If lucky, Atalia knew, Zohar would become a province in the Aelarian Empire. If unlucky, every man, woman, and child would be killed and the cities ground to dust.

"Thank you, soldier," she said. "We will avenge him. We will avenge all those whom we lost. I don't know if any others from our phalanx survived. Maybe none other in all the hosts of Zohar still survive. But I promise you, Daor Ben Bashan the potter—you and I are still soldiers. So long as we live, we will fight."

No sooner had she finished speaking when the drums began to beat.

The galley slaves fell silent and stared around the shadowy hold. Chains clanked. Wood creaked. At the back of the ship, framed by tin lanterns, a beefy man, shirtless and gleaming with sweat, sat before a drum stretched with leather. He gave it another two beats, the drumsticks thick as clubs.

"Galley slaves!" the man bellowed. "We set sail! Left oars, row!"

The bald overseer—the one who had whipped Atalia— marched down the deck. "Port oars, row!" he cried, swinging his lash.

Atalia's jaw locked. Her hands tightened around the oar. Finally, after days in chains, they were heading out. They were leaving Zohar.

"Row!" the overseer cried, and the lash swung, hitting her shoulders.

The drum beat.

"Port oars, row!"

Along the portside, buried deep in the bowels of the ship, a hundred and eighty galley slaves moved their oars.

Wood creaking, lash flying, drum beating, the ship began to turn.

"Starboard oars, row!" the overseer cried, and a second drum beat—this one with a more metallic sound.

The starboard slaves rowed. The ship adjudged.

"Row, row!" The drums beat together. "Port and starboard, row!"

Atalia sat by the hull, pressed against the wood, refusing to oar with the others. Through the hole her oar passed through, she could just make out glimpses of the harbor. The ship was moving faster now, heading toward open sea. She could see other ships moving around hers, their own oars splashing through the waters like the legs of great caterpillars.

"Damn it, slave, row!" The overseer lolloped toward her and swung his lash, bloodying her back.

Atalia spun around and glowered at him. She couldn't rise, not with the chain binding her ankle, but she could still defy him. She released the oar and raised her chin.

"I will not."

"Commander!" Daor whispered.

The overseer smiled thinly. He drew a curved dagger from his belt, leaned down, and pressed the blade against Atalia's cheek. She stiffened and hissed.

"You don't need eyes to oar." The overseer licked his lips. "I'd enjoy cutting them out. Maybe I'll keep them in a jar as a souvenir. You see that old rat over there, a few benches away?" He gestured at an old man, a cloth wrapped around his head, hiding his eyes. "I took his eyes five years ago. He oars nicely now." He pressed his dagger a bit closer, and a bead of blood trickled down Atalia's cheek. "Now, will you row like a nice little slave?"

Atalia hissed and screwed her eyes shut. Her heart beat against her ribs.

I am a soldier. A warrior of Zohar. A lioness. I will not serve the eagles. I am no slave. I will be brave, I will—

"She'll row!" Daor said. "Please, master, I'll make sure she rows, or I'll row twice as hard."

The drums still beat. "Row, slaves, row!"

The dagger trailed down her skin, and Atalia sucked in air between clenched teeth, trembling.

"Commander, please," Daor said. "We'll get out of here. I promise you. And you'll need your eyes to fight. We're rowing to Aelar. To the emperor. How can you fight him without eyes?"

Damn him. Damn the boy.

Atalia groaned, gripped the oar, and began to row to the beat.

Boom. Boom. The drums beat. The oars splashed. The benches creaked. The whips lashed. The great Aelarian ship, bearing hundreds of soldiers on the deck above, gained speed. The overseer grunted and trundled away, whip swinging at other slaves.

"Stay brave, soldier," Atalia whispered to Daor, her breath shaking. "Stay strong. We are warriors. I'm with you, lion of Zohar. We must be brave."

"I fight with you, Commander," he said. "Always. We are still lions."

As she rowed, Atalia stared through the space between oar and hole. She could only see the smallest slice of the outside, but it was enough. She could make out the breakwater of mossy boulders. The other ships. The sandy beach spreading north and the green hills beyond.

And then water. Nothing but water.

Goodbye, Zohar, she thought. *Goodbye, my homeland. Goodbye, my family. I will avenge you. I promise. I swear this, Father. I will avenge you.*

The drums beat and the oars moved and the ships sailed onward, leaving Zohar behind.

MAYA

T he desert seemed endless.

The sandy hills spread into the horizons, beige and lifeless. Boulders, canyons, and cliffs made for slow passage, and the sun beat down, so hot Maya thought it could melt the sand. Her camel snorted beneath her, saddlebags jangling. Maya swayed in the saddle, feeling weak. She had wrapped her prayer shawl over her head—the one her father had given her, the shawl he had sewn for Mica years ago—but it couldn't block the searing sunlight. Whenever she touched her hair, it felt hot like molten metal. Her dagger hung at her side, her gift from Atalia. Whenever Maya's hand brushed against the weapon, she yelped with pain, for it had grown so hot she could have cooked meat on the blade.

"Did we make a mistake, Beelam?" she said, voice hoarse. "Are we doing to die out here?"

The camel twisted his head around, snorted, and sniffed her sandal. She patted his scruffy head, and he licked her fingers.

"Keep going forward, Beelam! You're moving in circles."

The camel snorted, straightened his neck, and kept walking forward. Maya bounced on the hump. Pebbles and sand spread below them, and the hills, canyons, and valleys sprawled ahead, and no matter how hard Maya squinted, she could see no end to them. Was she still in Zohar, or had she crossed the border into Sekadia, the great eastern kingdom? She didn't know. She was a child of the coast. She had grown up on verdant hills lush with olive, fig, and palm trees, never far from the sea. Here was a different sort of sea, yet while the Encircled Sea was full of life—thousands of ships regularly traversed its waters—Maya saw no signs of life here. Nothing but her and her camel in the endless beige.

"Maybe we should go back." She wiped sweat off her brow. "I brought ten whole skins of water, and not much food, but I don't know how long that'll last."

She sighed and looked behind her, but she could no longer see Beth Eloh. During the first two days of her journey, she had seen riders in the distance, seeking her. Sent by her mother, no doubt. She had lost them in the canyons and caves, and she had not seen pursuit for a day now. Even if she turned back, Maya didn't know if she could find her way back. With the sun at its zenith, she knew not north from south, east from west.

"Let's rest, Beelam."

She rode for a while longer, trying to find a cave—she had seen several yesterday—but found none. Finally Maya dismounted in a sandy valley and set camp. The sand was too hot to lie on, so she unrolled both her blankets, placed one on the ground, and the other atop herself, forming a makeshift hovel. She drank, finishing another waterskin; only five were now left, half of what she had brought. She dared not eat. In her rush to flee Beth Eloh, she hadn't packed enough food. She was down to only a fig cake, a few dry dates, and a loaf of bread.

She tried to sleep, but the heat was sweltering, keeping her awake. The sun soon warmed her blanket so much that Maya felt like she was sleeping under embers. She couldn't stop sweating, losing precious water. She wished she herself had a hump like Beelam, storing the energy she needed for this journey.

Finally night fell. No sooner had the sun set than the temperature dropped. Maya found herself shivering. Back in Gefen, between the trees by the sea, nights were always warm this time of year, but the desert became cold as winter with the sun gone. She shivered and wrapped herself in both blankets. She rode her camel again, only the moon lighting her way. She navigated by the stars. The Evening Star, brightest in the night, always shone in the west. The Lodestar, pale blue, shone in the north, the tip of the Lion's Claw constellation.

The sun rose again, and she kept riding but soon had to stop. It seemed even hotter today, and she drained her last waterskin. Soon her tongue was parched, her lips cracked, and her skin burnt. And still the desert did not end. Another mil, and Maya saw bleached bones, half-buried in the sand. Human bones.

"I'm a fool, Beelam." She hung her head low. "I fled Beth Eloh with no map, no plan, chasing a dream. Avinasi told me that there's a center of Luminosity across the desert, but what if she lied? What if she just wanted me to die out here?"

She rode onward, cursing herself. She should have stayed behind, even if the Aelarians had caught her, had shipped her off to their land across the sea. At least she would have lived, could have used her Luminosity in the Empire. Out here, she would soon fade to nothing but bones.

Along with the heat and thirst and exhaustion, fear for her family filled Maya, perhaps worse than all.

"Please, Eloh," she whispered, gazing up at the sky. "I don't know if you can hear me. I don't know if you answer prayers. But if you're there, and if you care for me, please forgive me. Forgive me for running away, for abandoning my family. Forgive me for all those times I was mad at Mother, all those times I scolded Ofeer. Forgive me please." Tears she could not afford to shed filled her eyes. "Look after them, Eloh. Keep my family safe. I've never prayed much before, but this is the most important prayer of my life. If you hear me, and if you never listen to my words again, please, Eloh, hear me this one time, and keep my family safe. I'm scared. I'm so scared of the Aelarians, scared what will happen to my family. Let me die if you must, but let my family live."

She searched the sky and land, seeking a sign that Eloh had heard her—a burning bush, a comet from the heavens, a voice from above. She saw nothing but the desert, the sand and boulders and hills spreading endlessly. And still the sun beat down, baking her hair.

She kept riding, soon out of water. Her head began to ache, and nausea grew in her belly. She ate her last fig cake, but it soured in her belly, and she leaned over the camel and vomited. Her head swam. It was all she could do to stay in the saddle.

When the sun returned to its zenith, beating down with full force, Maya set camp again.

She lay on her blanket, barely strong enough to breathe. She tasted blood in her mouth and sucked it greedily.

I'm a fool. A fool. A dead fool. Bones, nothing but bones. Why did I set on this quest?

She lay on the blanket, lost in this desert, trembling. She let herself breathe deeply. To feel the wind. To gaze at the blue sky, the dunes beyond.

To feel the world.

The wind breathed.

The desert lived.

She felt the sand, endlessly blowing, forming and reforming. She felt the sun, the stars, the moon, rising and falling, forever dancing around the world. She felt tiny lives, scorpions and beetles, moving beneath her, deep underground. She felt the life of clouds.

The wind breathed.

The desert lived.

Maya rose.

The light flowed across her, illuminating her fingers, bright in her eyes. There was still lume here. She was far from Beth Eloh, but lume still filled this desert, and she could light it. She wove it around herself, healing her cracked lips, soothing her burned skin, calming the turmoil in her belly.

The light grew stronger, threatening to overwhelm her. She remembered what Avinasi had told her, and she managed to contain the fire, to weave the strands, bending them to her will, then disperse them. The luminescence faded. Maya could see the desert again.

Ahead, on a hill, stood a goat.

Maya blinked.

A goat!

"Life," she whispered.

Her belly rumbled. She had lost her last meal, and she had no more food. A goat could refill her belly. She reached for her dagger and drew the blade.

The goat stared down at her.

Maya slowly rose to her feet, blade in hand.

I can pounce. I can be like Epher and Atalia, a warrior, a huntress. She took a step toward the goat. *I can survive out here.*

Strangely, the goat did not attempt to flee her. When she approached, the animal sniffed at her pockets, perhaps smelling crumbs of the bread she had held there yesterday.

Maya raised her dagger.

I can do this. I can hunt. I can survive.

The goat licked her fingers, and Maya sighed and lowered her blade. Perhaps she was not a survivor after all.

"Get out of here," she said. "Go. Go!"

The goat turned and left.

Maya climbed back onto her camel. "Follow him, Beelam. Follow that goat. Where there are goats, there will be water."

They rode. They rode for what felt like hours. Sometimes the goat seemed to vanish, but then, moments later, would reappear on a distant hilltop. The land grew rockier, the hills soon growing to mountains. Canyons snaked below, and boulders dotted valleys. The goat always scurried ahead, climbing paths the camel couldn't follow. Beelam was a master at surviving the desert for days without water, but his hooves were clumsy here.

"Slow down!" Maya cried to the goat. "Wait ..."

Her voice cracked. Again the blood filled her mouth. She swayed in her saddle and fell. She hit the ground, skinning her knee. She cried out in pain, pulled her knee to her face, and licked the blood.

Maya hung her head low.

"It's no use, Beelam. We can't catch him. The goat is probably just a feverish vision. Even Luminosity can only ease my pain for so long." She hugged the camel's leg. "We're going to die here. Die far from everyone. You and I."

A soft spray hit her face. Beelam's breath was soothing, cool, wet. She savored it, a last respite from the heat.

But when she turned toward his breath, she found Beelam's neck raised. He was staring eastward. And still she felt that damp spray.

Maya frowned. *That's not his breath.*

Beelam began to run. Maya followed, sandals kicking pebbles and sand. The spray grew stronger, and she could hear it—water! Falling water!

She raced up a hilltop, then fell to her bloody knees, tears falling.

"Thank you, Eloh," she whispered. "Thank you."

Life. Beautiful life.

A waterfall cascaded down a cliff ahead, feeding a pool in a canyon. Greenery sprouted around the water—palm trees, bushes, fig trees, grass. Birds fluttered from branch to branch, and the goat stood below, drinking from the pool. Maya found a path that descended toward the pool—carved by men. She led Beelam down, ran across the hot stones, and leaped into the water. She cried as she drank, and she swam, splashing about.

Eloh had sent the goat, she knew. The light of God shone upon her. Her quest was blessed.

She was laughing under the waterfall, and chewing dates she had picked from a tree, when the thief grabbed her camel.

Maya gasped.

The man was wrapped in a white robe and hood, and a sickle sword hung from his belt. While Beelam was drinking from the pool, the thief grabbed the camel's reins and leaped onto the saddle. He dug his heels into the beast, and Beelam took off, racing away from the water.

"Stop!" Maya cried, eyes wide. "Thief!"

New fear filled her. Without Beelam, she couldn't cross the rest of the desert. Cursing, she swam across the pool, every stroke lasting an eternity. By the time she emerged onto the bank, the camel and thief were gone.

Maya sucked in air. Her wet dress slapping her legs, she ran.

EPHER

As soon as he entered the royal palace, Epher marched across the mosaic toward King Shefael, grabbed the man's throat, and squeezed.

"Damn you, you traitor." Epher glared at the beefy, bearded man, hand tightening.

"Son, enough!" Shiloh shouted.

"Release him!" cried the palace guards, Zoharites in scale armor, weaponless, their swords confiscated by the Empire.

Even the three legionaries in the palace stepped forward, raising their javelins. Men grabbed Epher, tugging him back. A legionary swung his javelin, slamming the shaft behind Epher's knees, forcing him to kneel. The other legionaries grabbed his arms.

Olive screamed and raced across the hall, leaped onto a legionary, and began tugging the man's arm, biting and scratching.

"Go away, cunt!" the wild, redheaded woman shouted at the legionaries. "Get lost, whore!"

"What did they pay you?" Epher shouted at the king, struggling in the legionaries' grip. "What did you get to open the city gates?"

Shiloh rushed forth, speaking in soothing tones to the legionaries. The Aelarian soldiers released Epher, muttering about hot-blooded desert rats. Epher ignored them. Panting, he stared at his cousin on the throne. Shefael sat there, face red beneath his beard. He had been drinking from a goblet of wine; drops of the crimson liquid now stained his purple cloak. The crown of Zohar, shaped as the crown of a pomegranate, sat on his head.

"What did I get?" Shefael gingerly touched his throat. Finger marks still wrapped around it. "My life. Your life. The lives of a million people, every last one in Zohar."

Epher spat. "You're lucky the legionaries confiscated my sword at the city gates, cousin. I'd skewer you if I could, and our shared blood be damned. I fought outside the walls. I almost died outside the walls. Ten thousand men and women died there, butchered while you cowered here. You could have joined us, fought with us—"

"And died with you!" Shefael shouted. His voice echoed through the throne room. He rose to his feet. Both men were tall and broad, and years ago, they would ride together, duel with swords, and swim against the hard currents in the sea. In the past few years, however, since claiming the throne, Shefael had let his body go soft. Fat now coated the old muscles, and veins covered the nose, the remnants of too many empty wine bottles. The king stared at Epher from under sweaty eyebrows.

"And died with you," Shefael repeated, softer now. "Three legions had come upon our city. I could not have defeated them, not with all my men here. And even if, by a miracle, Yohanan and

I could have cast back Porcia's forces, her brother waited in the west, leading three more legions. No, Epher. This war could never have been won. So I made the only deal I could make."

"A deal that cost your brother's life." Epher would not tear his stare away. "You let Porcia kill Yohanan and his warriors— nearly kill me too. You sold our very kingdom. You let my father die on the cross. All so you could keep your ass on this throne—a throne you made a mockery of."

Shefael's face flushed a deeper shade of crimson. He pointed at Epher, finger shaking. "You'll see, Epher, that I'm still a king. I can have you thrown into the dungeon for your insolence."

Epher snorted. "Better insolence than treachery. I do not recognize your claim to this throne. I do not recognize that we have a throne anymore—just a chair. Just a chair for a drunken fool."

"Fool!" Olive repeated and spat at Shefael's feet. "Fool, fool. Go away, fool."

The palace guards stepped forward again, reaching toward Epher. The legionaries raised their weapons. Epher snarled, prepared to grab a javelin or sword from a legionary and fight— fight Shefael like Yohanan had.

But a voice rang through the hall, stopping him cold.

"Enough! Epher, he's right. Shefael did the right thing."

They turned around. Both cousins' eyes widened. It was Shiloh who had spoken.

"Mother," Epher whispered.

She stood with hands on her hips. Her braid hung across her shoulder. She was a slender woman, quick and graceful as a gazelle, but standing here, she seemed as fierce as a lioness.

"Your cousin did the right thing, Epher," she repeated. "He made a horrible choice. The only choice he could make. The choice that saved our lives. Your father died, Epher, because he chose to fight. Yohanan died because he chose to fight. Benshalom died because he chose to fight. Shefael surrendered, and so my firstborn son now lives."

"I live because of Olive." Epher took hold of the redheaded woman's hand. She cooed and laid her head against his shoulder. "She's the one who saved me from the battle."

Shiloh's face hardened. "And if Shefael had not opened the gates of the city, do you think that you and Olive would still live? No, son. The Empire would do to us what it did to Leer. It would smash every wall, every tower, every house. It would slay every man, woman, and child. Zohar would not have become a province of Aelar. It would have become a wasteland, mere desolation where once cities had stood. Your father was brave, Epher, and I loved him dearly, and I will never stop loving him. But he chose death, and Shefael chose life."

Epher narrowed his eyes, staring at his mother, and it was as if he didn't recognize her. It was the same Shiloh on the surface—the same brown eyes, same braid, same cotton dress. But something had changed in her. There was a new pain to Shiloh Sela, but a new strength too.

Epher turned away. He couldn't stand to be here. Not a minute longer. His father—dead. Yohanan and Benshalom and all their forces—slaughtered outside the walls, himself the only survivor. Atalia and Koren—shipped off to slavery. Maya—missing. Ofeer—joined with the enemy. Tears threatened to fill Epher's eyes. He could find no air. He couldn't speak.

He turned and marched out from the hall, leaving his cousin, his mother, and the legionaries behind. With a squeak, Olive hurried after him. The rest did not follow.

He marched through the palace. As a child, Epher would run through these halls, playing with his siblings. They would visit Aunt Sifora, Queen of Zohar, every year for the fall harvest. The Sela children would fill these corridors and chambers with laughter, and Epher had spent many hours wrestling with Yohanan and Shefael, his older cousins, in the gardens. Now the laughter was gone. Now this was no longer a palace, not truly, but a great prison. Now Aunt Sifora was dead, now Shefael ruled as a puppet to Marcus Octavius, and all lay in ruin. His family. His kingdom. His life.

"Epher," Olive said softly, hurrying to keep up with him. "Epher, go away? Olive go away?"

Epher paused and turned toward her. They stood in a corridor between columns, arches rising above them. To the west, between the columns, spread a view of Beth Eloh. Thousands of brick homes, cemeteries, domes, silos, steeples, and workshops crowded the hills, and cobbled roads coiled between them like strands of thread, leaving barely any room for a few scattered palm and olive trees. The ancient city was three thousand years old, a source of lume, of pride, of light for all of Zohar, now a corpse for eagles to feed on.

He looked back at Olive. She gazed at him with huge, frightened eyes. She was trembling, he noticed. Her face, beneath the mud that still covered her, was pale.

"No, Olive." He took her hands in his. "You don't have to go away. I'd like you to stay here with me."

"Stay," she whispered. She turned to look between the columns at the city, and her trembling increased. The legionaries at the gates had taken her bow and arrows, but she kept glancing over her back as if still seeking her weapons. She pulled one hand free and pointed at the city, and she began to chatter, gushing out nonsensical words like a baby just learning to talk.

"You're scared," Epher said. "I know. Maybe you've never seen a city before, never seen houses, streets, walls. But I'm here with you. You saved my life twice already, first in the hills of Erez and then outside this city. I'm going to do whatever I can to protect you." He pulled a dry leaf from her hair. "I don't know where you come from, and I don't know what happened to you. But I'm going to help you. I'm not going away, and neither are you."

He wasn't sure she could understand him, but perhaps she understood the tone more than the words. She pulled him into an embrace and laid her cheek against his shoulder.

"Epher," she whispered. "Olive. Epher Olive."

"Epher and Olive," he said.

"Epher an Olive." She nodded, holding him close. "Epher an Olive."

Holding her hand, Epher kept walking. He knew where to find the one he sought. He had spent enough hours in this palace to know. He walked down the corridor until he reached the palace's central tower. Here he climbed a spiraling staircase, moving between columns. With every iteration around the tower, he could see other views of the city. When he faced the north, he saw the Temple nearby, the only structure in Zohar larger than the palace, a building of white stone and gold. Like the palace, the Temple rose on the Mount of Cedars, a walled hill that formed an acropolis within Beth Eloh. The western view revealed domed houses leading toward the city's outer walls, and beyond them the sun setting over the remains of the battle. Facing south, he saw the wild hills where Olive had nursed him. When the staircase faced east, he saw the desert spreading into the distance.

Finally, still holding Olive's hand, Epher reached the top of the tower. A dome rose here, as large as the villa on Pine Hill. A walkway surrounded it, ringed with pale columns capped with gold. He felt like an ant crawling along a crown upon a bald man's head.

There she stood, staring eastward, the sandy wind fluttering her white robes. Avinasi. Bracelets jangled around the lumer's scrawny arms, and golden rings hung from her ears. The scent of myrrh wafted from her. She seemed ancient beyond measure, as old as this very city, and Epher had the strange feeling that she had been waiting for him.

He approached her, fingers tingling, aching to grab a sword. "You sent her away."

Slowly, Avinasi turned toward him. Her neck creaked. Her withered face twisted into a slight, knowing smile. The wind billowed her shawl, jangling the coins sewn along its hem.

"Your sister has taken the path of light, son of Zohar," said the ancient lumer. "I did not send her on this path, merely illuminated her first step."

"Where did Maya go?" Epher couldn't hide the anger in his voice. "Her letter talked of Luminosity." He grabbed the old woman's wrist. "What path did she take?"

Avinasi raised an eyebrow, and her smile widened. She raised a hand, the fingers tipped with nails like claws, and stroked his cheek. "So much rage in you. So much pain. So little light. You are a child of shadow, Epheriah Sela, son of Jerael. The darkness will continue to rise inside you, like bitumen bubbling up in a pit, as it rises across your land." Her fingers moved down, and her fingernails ran along his throat. "I fear for you, child. Twice already have you skirted death, but keep walking the shadowy path and no light will save you."

He shoved her hand away. "Where is Maya?"

"Beyond your reach. She must seek truths that can no longer be found in Zohar, not under the shadow of eagle wings. But she will return, son of Zohar, before the end. She will enter this city again. Whether you live to see her depends on the path you choose, a path of darkness or a path of luminescence."

With that, Avinasi spun around and walked along the walkway, robes fluttering. The lumer seemed almost to hover, and within an instant, she vanished around the dome. Epher snorted out breath, the rage still inside him. He hurried after her.

"Avinasi, stop!"

Yet he could no longer see her. He ran along the walkway, racing around the dome until he came full circle, reaching Olive again. Avinasi was gone.

"Avinasi go away," Olive said. She thought for a moment, then nodded. "Cunt."

Epher nodded weakly. He stared between the columns toward the west. The sunlight was fading, and the stars emerged. The Dancer's Coin shone before him, the brightest star in the east, a lantern in the sky over the desert.

Are you looking at that star now too, Maya? Can you see the stars wherever you are, Atalia and Koren? Do you still look to the sky, Ofeer, and do you think of us too?

Epher did not know the answers to those questions, and the pain seemed too great to bear. His shoulders slumped.

"Epher an Olive go away," Olive whispered and touched his cheek. Her hands were grimy, the nails bitten down to stubs, but her touch was far softer and more pleasant than Avinasi's.

Epher nodded. They stepped off the roof, climbed downstairs, and Epher found one of the palace guestrooms—the room he would stay in as a child, visiting Beth Eloh with his family. Alcoves dotted the walls, some holding candles, others holding jugs of water. A bed lay by a window. At once, Olive lay down on the floor and yawned.

"Bed," Epher said, pointing. "Sleep on the bed. I'll take the floor."

She blinked up at him. "Bed?"

He nodded. "Yes, there's only one. I'll find you your own room tomorrow. You can sleep here tonight."

"Ur nim is Red," she said, nodding sagely. She climbed onto the bed and sat cross-legged. "Olive an bed."

"Olive *in* bed," he corrected her.

She grabbed his hands, grinning, and tugged him onto the bed too. He stumbled over the edge and thumped onto the mattress.

"Epher an Olive in bed," she said.

He blinked. "God's beard, that was almost a proper sentence. Epher *and* Olive in bed."

She nodded excitedly, hair bouncing. "Epher *and* Olive in bed. Avinasi go away." She yawned, lay down, and pulled him down beside her. "Bed. Bed."

He had wanted to lie on the floor, not share the bed with her. When her body pressed against him, he realized how—under the layers of filth—she was still a fair young woman. He didn't need those feelings in his life now. He had vowed not to feel anything for another woman, not after what had happened with Claudia, not after—

Olive kissed his cheek. "Bed," she whispered. She closed her eyes, cuddled against him, and slept.

Epher sighed and stroked her tangled hair. "Goodnight, Olive."

He held her in his arms, but he could not find sleep. Too many visions filled the darkness—visions of the dead outside the city, of his siblings in chains, of his father on a cross. The world seemed woven of shadows, and he could find no light. Is that what Avinasi had meant? That he would let grief, anger, and pain consume him?

Then let Olive be my light, he thought, holding her against him. He kissed the top of her head, and she mumbled and stirred but did not wake. *Let Olive guide me in the darkness as the Dancer's Coin guides travelers in the night. Let Olive be my desert dancer, my beacon in shadow.*

That star shone outside the window, and finally Epher slept, holding Olive in his arms.

OFEER

S he stood at the stern of the *Aquila Aureum*, flagship of the Aelarian fleet, staring back toward the east, but she could no longer see Zohar. The water spread into all horizons.

"Farewell," Ofeer whispered. "Farewell, Zohar, land of my mother."

A sudden urge filled her to spit toward the east, to shake her fist, to laugh. She was finally free! Free from that land that had stifled her. Free from that house that had trapped her. Never more would Ofeer—the daughter of an Aelarian—be forced to live among the savages. Never more would she skulk along the port, drowning her misery in booze and sex and spice. Never more would she live among brutish Zoharites, with their beards and coarse clothes, barbarians who mocked her, who had never been her true people. That old land—the backward province that had crushed her soul—was gone forever from her life.

Yes, Ofeer wanted to rejoice at leaving. She wanted to look away and never look back.

And yet she could not.

As she stared east, she remembered her tears of pain, but she also remembered joy, remembered light. She remembered herself from before her childhood, playing on the beach with her siblings. Restday meals around the table, feasting on fruits and breads, then playing mancala in candlelight. Harvest trips to Beth Eloh and songs in the halls of kings. Her mother hugging her. Epher teaching her to use a sword. Ofeer even missed Maya ... a little.

Tears stung her eyes, and Ofeer knuckled them away.

"No," she whispered through clenched teeth. "No! They hated me. All of them hated me, and I was never one of them. Besides, it's too late to go back. Zohar is gone. My family is gone." She squared her shoulders. "I am now Ofeer of Aelar, nothing more."

She spun away from the stern and walked across the deck. The *Aquila Aureum* was massive, a floating castle. The masts rose high, sails unfurled, dyed white with red stripes. Many sailors rushed about the polished deck, tugging ropes, turning winches, and climbing ladders. On the way to Zohar, the deck must have been crammed full of soldiers, but few legionaries stood here now; most had remained in Zohar, and Seneca had told her that many would remain there for years.

Other ships sailed around them, and in their holds they held spoils from Zohar—gold, gemstones, artwork, and mostly slaves. Most of the ships had remained behind with their legionaries, their new home in Zohar's port, but even this skeleton fleet seemed massive to Ofeer—an entire floating city.

When she leaned over the railing, Ofeer could see the ship's oars churning the water. The galley slaves were chained below the deck, buried within the ship. They would not see sunlight until the *Aureum* reached Aelar, eighteen days if the winds favored them and the sails gave them extra speed. As Ofeer walked, she tried to count the oars, but she kept losing count.

He holds one of those oars. Her breath shuddered. *He's there, beneath my feet, right now.*

The pain was too great. Ofeer shoved the thought aside. So what? Who cared if he was there? That no longer mattered. That was no longer her family. Her fingers shook, and she hated that those people still had power over her. She wouldn't let the Sela family ruin this for her—her dream, finally sailing to Aelar. She wouldn't let that thought, that pain below the deck, spoil the culmination of all her work.

She made her way past an iron winch that held the anchor on a chain, past the central mast, and around a wooden tower that rose thrice her height, topped with battlements for archers. She reached the prow, climbed three steps, and leaned across the nose of the ship. An iron figurehead thrust forward, shaped as an eagle's head, a weapon to ram into enemy ships.

Zohar never had enemy ships, Ofeer thought. *Not since the war nineteen years ago, when Marcus Octavius—my real father—sank them all. Back when he took Zohar's island, back when he slept with my mother, when he made me.*

Ofeer cringed. Mother's words returned to her, the last words the woman had spoken to her.

Marcus Octavius, then a general in the legions, sank our fleet, invaded our island of Cadom. He took your brothers captive, Ofeer. He would have killed them had I not let him into my bed.

Ofeer found herself trembling. She had known for years that Jerael wasn't her father, that her father was an Aelarian. Shiloh had always refused to reveal more details. Ofeer had always imagined that her father was a handsome sailor, perhaps a wealthy merchant, that he had wooed Shiloh, that Shiloh had succumbed to his charms for a night of infidelity.

But he wasn't some sailor or merchant, Ofeer thought. *He was Marcus Octavius, Emperor of Aelar. And he didn't woo my mother.*

Ofeer clenched her fists and lowered her head. She had not wanted to hear at first, had ignored Mother's words until Taeer the lumer had confirmed them. Now the horror of it shook her body.

I was not created on a night of passion. I was created with brutality, with terror, with war.

She took a shuddering breath, staring northwest across the sea. Somewhere, many days of sailing away, Aelar waited. The land she had so often dreamed of, the land from the fairy tales, the songs. A land of white towers, of lords and ladies in silk, of beautiful music, of art, of civilization. A land so unlike crude Zohar. A land where, in her dreams, her father was a wise, handsome lord.

The land that slew thousands in Gefen, Ofeer thought. *The land that spawned Seneca, a man who nailed Jerael to a cross and fucked me to the sounds of dying groans. The land of Marcus Octavius, a man who kidnapped my brothers and raped my mother.* Her eyes teared up.

"What am I doing?" Ofeer whispered, clasping her hands so tightly they ached. "Why am I here?"

A hand touched her shoulder, and Ofeer jumped. She spun around to see Seneca standing on the deck.

"You startled me," she said.

"I'm sorry. I'm sorry for everything, Ofeer." He handed her a small obsidian box. "I brought you something."

She took the box from him and opened it. Inside shone a golden ring with an indigo stone. She raised her eyes and looked at Seneca, silent.

"It's lapis lazuli," he said. "We found it in Gefen. It's not the most precious stone, I know. In Aelar, I promise you finer gems—rubies and diamonds and sapphires the color of sky. But I wanted you to have this for now." He took her hand and slipped the ring onto her finger. "To say I'm sorry. I showed weakness in Gefen. I angered you. The burden of command is sometimes heavy to bear. Please accept this gift of my conquest."

A gift you plundered, Ofeer thought, staring at him.

She knew the woman who had worn this ring, the wealthy wife of a merchant who had owned a fabric shop on the coast, a place where Ofeer would shop for silk scarves. She wondered if that shop still stood, if the ring's original owner still lived.

She turned back toward the prow, stared again across the water.

"You don't like it," Seneca said. "I know. You don't just want Zoharite jewels. You want the treasures of Aelar, and they will be yours. I'm the prince of an empire, Ofeer. If we can convince my father to name me heir, if we can get rid of Porcia, I'll be emperor someday. And then the wealth and glory of Aelar will be yours."

And then I will be the whore of Aelar, Ofeer thought. *Concubine to my own brother.*

She lowered her head. This is not what Ofeer had wanted. She had wanted treasures, yes. She had wanted to see an empire. But not like this.

"All I ever wanted," she whispered, "is to belong."

"You do belong." Seneca squeezed her hands in his. "You belong with me."

He tried to kiss her, but she turned her head aside. He placed a hand on the small of her back, and his touch disgusted her. She couldn't help but grimace.

"I'm sorry, my prince," she said. "The sea doesn't agree with me. My stomach churns."

For an instant, rage twisted his face—burning rage that he did not get what he wanted. She knew that very, very rarely Seneca did not get what he wanted. But the moment passed, quick as it had come. He nodded.

"You're seasick. You've spent your life on land, but you'll gain your sea legs before the journey is over." He kissed her cheek, reached up, and squeezed her breast. "Come to my cabin when you feel better. I'll make you forget all those memories of home."

Tell him, spoke a voice deep inside Ofeer. *Tell him the truth. Tell him that he's your half brother. Tell him that you can no longer kiss him, no longer warm his bed. Tell him that you've sinned, formed an unclean, incestuous bond. Tell him the truth!*

Yet Ofeer could not, even as he held her breast, as his eyes lusted for her, as his hardness pressed against her thigh.

If I tell him, he'll be enraged, she thought. *He'll refuse to believe me. He'll toss me overboard. He'll murder me, as surely as he murdered Jerael.*

And so she only smiled wanly, then shuddered in disgust once he had left. She remained on the prow, staring across the sea.

What will I find when we reach you, Aelar? she thought. *Will I find myself trapped in Seneca's talons, as I had been trapped in Zohar? Will I dare confront my father, demand he acknowledge me as his daughter? Will I finally dare tell the truth to Seneca, and when I do, will I dare face his wrath?*

Ofeer did not know the answers. She did not know what land she would find beyond the sea. She did not know what life awaited her—a life in the court of an emperor, or a life surviving on her own, fleeing Seneca and their sin.

A voice spoke beside her, and again Ofeer started.

"It's strange, daughter of Zohar, how your seasickness turns your face green only when the prince is nearby."

Ofeer spun around to see Taeer, Seneca's lumer. The Zoharite was taller than Ofeer, at least a decade older, and far wiser. That wisdom shone in her dark eyes and curled her full, painted lips into a mysterious smile. A cloak of crimson silk fluttered around Taeer's body, and the dress beneath plunged low, revealing a golden lion amulet that hung between her breasts. Golden bracelets, shaped as snakes, curled around her wrists, and her fingernails were painted the color of blood. A scent of frankincense clung to her, flowing into Ofeer's nostrils even as the sea wind blew.

Ofeer stared at this woman, eyes narrowed.

Who are you, Taeer? she thought. *You paint your face and clad yourself in silk like a courtesan, yet you wield powerful magic—powerful enough to serve a prince.*

Staring into those dark eyes, Ofeer had the uncomfortable sense that Taeer's gaze was undressing her, peeling back her cloak and skin and muscles, gazing into her very soul, mocking her innermost secrets.

"What do you want?" Ofeer said.

"To help a fellow daughter of Zohar," said the lumer, a small smile still on her lips. A mocking smile.

She thinks me a fool.

"I am a daughter of Aelar just as much," Ofeer said.

One of Taeer's arched eyebrows rose. "Yet you've never been to Aelar. And yet you wander this ship like a lioness trapped in a cage. And yet you cringe when my prince touches you."

"He's my brother," Ofeer said, not bothering to mask the bitterness in her voice. "You told me that on the beach. My half brother, at least." Ofeer lowered her head, and the wind gusted, billowing her hair and cloak. "Sometimes I wish you and my mother had never told me the truth." When she raised her eyes, they were damp. "Does my pain amuse you, Taeer Bat Ami?"

"The folly of humanity amuses me," the lumer replied, still smiling thinly. "Men and women battling over ports and cities, killing, conquering, fucking, birthing, dying ... the endless dance of humanity, all for nothing but sand. The true kingdom of glory lies in Luminosity, in the light of Eloh, not in stones and water and flesh."

"And yet my flesh is what Seneca desires," Ofeer said. "And the stones and sand of Zohar are what he claimed. Taeer, I'm afraid. I told him I'm seasick, but that angered him. His lust knows no bounds. Perhaps I can spurn his advances on this ship, feigning sickness. But once I reach Aelar, what should I do? If I tell him the truth—tell him that I'm his sister, that his desire is incestuous—he'd be mad. So mad." Her voice dropped to a whisper. "He would kill me, Taeer. Just like he killed so many in Zohar, like he killed Jerael. What do I do? If you truly care for me, truly want to help me ... grant me your wisdom."

Ofeer didn't know why she was telling Taeer these things. She didn't know if she could trust the lumer—*any* lumer. And after all, Taeer was Seneca's closest companion and confidant, bonded to him since he'd been a child.

Perhaps I'm just scared, Ofeer thought. *And I just need an older, wiser woman from home to help me on this ship of Aelarian men.*

"Wisdom?" Taeer said. The wind jangled her golden earrings, and the sun shone in the emerald eyes of her serpentine bracelets. "Wisdom is what one grows from pain. Wisdom is a light that shines in darkness. I cannot grant you wisdom nor counsel; you must find your own luminous path to their gates. But I will aid you still. Seneca is lustful, that is true, and prideful, and wrathful. Over our years together, I've served him with light, but with flesh too; he craves my flesh more than my luminescence. I will go to his bed this night, and he will release his lust into me, and every night until we reach Aelar." Taeer smiled thinly. "I will drain his desire, sparing it from you."

Only days ago, Ofeer would have felt jealous, would have raged at the thought of Seneca in bed with another woman. Now she felt nothing but relief.

"And once we reach Aelar?" Ofeer whispered.

Taeer stroked Ofeer's cheek, those long bloodred nails whispering across the skin. "There are four pillars to Luminosity, child. Healing. Muse. Sight. Foresight. That last pillar would reveal your future to me, but I choose not to summon this magic. I've guided generals and princes along paths of fire and blood, and I watched their own pride twist the paths I had foreseen, leading them to doom. Remembering the past can be a burden; knowing the future can be a curse. Find your own paths. Follow your own light. I will be there, not guiding your way, but shining in darkest shadows."

Ofeer blinked, her eyes suddenly tearing up. When she could see again, Taeer was gone. Once more she stood alone at the prow. With a deep sigh, Ofeer stared at the sea, trying to imagine the towers, temples, and secrets that lay beyond the horizon.

Ofeer lowered her eyes and looked down at her feet. The thought kept niggling, calling to her, a force she could no longer resist.

For not only Ofeer Sela now sails to a new empire. He is there, beneath my feet.

Ofeer turned around. She sucked in breath and clenched her fists. It was time to enter the darkness.

KOREN

*B*oom. *Boom.*

The drum beat.

"Oar! Oar!" the overseer cried.

Sweat drenched Koren, and his manacles chafed his ankles and wrists. His muscles cramped, but whenever he slowed from oaring, the whip lashed again, cutting into his back.

Boom, boom, pounded the drums.

Whish, crack! cried the whip.

"So what time do they bring us wine and cheese?" Koren asked the slave at his side. "Or do they serve ale and lamb? I'd take ale and lamb too, ideally with some nice mint sauce." He smacked his lips. "I'm not picky—ow!"

The whip lashed again. "Keep rowing, slave, and keep silent."

The overseer was a leathery man with one eye. They whispered that the brute had been a galley slave himself once, had lost his eye after striking a master. Whether the story was true or not, Koren couldn't say. What was certain was that the one-eyed overseer delighted in his current role.

"It's nice to see a man take such satisfaction in his work," Koren said, grimacing as the blood dripped down his back. "Passion! Makes the day go by much faster."

His chains clanked as Koren kept oaring, trying to summon as much vigor as the overseer showed when whipping slaves. The brute spat, grumbled, and walked on. The oars kept pounding.

"You know," Koren said to the slave at his side, "he's rather a conversationalist, that overseer. He gave me an actual grunt! More than I've heard from you in a while."

His fellow rower sat on the wooden bench so close their bodies touched. He was an older fellow, his beard long and gray—a Zoharite by the looks of him, perhaps one captured in the war nineteen years ago. The old man gave Koren a sad look, then stared back at his oar. He rowed onward.

Koren sighed. "So, old boy, tell me." He talked as he rowed. "Which do you prefer—the single-humped dromedary, or are you a champion of the two-humped variety? Wars have been fought over humps, you know."

The slave still said nothing.

"So you're not interested in conversation," Koren said. "Would you like to sing then? All right, we'll sing 'The Maiden of Gael.'" Koren cleared his throat. "One, two, three—"

Before Koren could launch into a song, the whip lashed again. "Silence! Row!"

Koren bit down on his tongue, cursing the pain. His back was a raw mess by now, but damn it, he couldn't just row silently. He had to talk, to sing, to find some distraction from this pain, this fear. Anytime Koren fell silent, he could see it again—his father on the cross. With every breath, Koren worried about his family. About Atalia, who was taken captive with him, but was not on this ship. About Ofeer, who had joined the Aelarians. About Mother and Maya who had traveled to Beth Eloh. About Epher who fought with the hillsfolk. Were they still alive? Was he the last Sela?

No. Koren could not allow this terror to consume him. Physical pain was nothing compared to the pain inside him.

"It's no use, Zoharite," rose a deep voice behind him, a voice like thunder and wind in caves. "Old Graybeard won't speak a word. We don't even know his name."

Koren glanced over his shoulder at the slave behind him. He was a man from Nur, the southern empire that had fallen to Aelar. His skin was so dark it was nearly black, bleeding where the whip had lashed him. His head was bald, his eyes weary. The man had spoken in Aelarian—the *lingua franca* of the Encircled Sea—his accent heavy.

"What happened to him?" Koren said.

"They say his wife and sons burned before his eyes," said the Nurian. "He's been rowing here since then, nineteen years now. Poor bastard."

"How long have you been rowing?" Koren asked.

"Three years myself," said the Nurian. "Feels like three hundred. I killed a legionary in Nur. I did it for Queen Imani, bless her name. Stabbed the man right between the shoulder blades." The slave laughed, a laughter that soon turned to coughing. Blood speckled his lips. "Was worth it."

Koren cringed. He did not crave to row here for three years himself, let alone decades like his neighbor. Was this his fate now—to remain here until he grew a long white beard, until he finally died of old age or the beatings of the whip, still chained to the oar?

Damn it, I wish Atalia were with me at least, he thought. *She'd sing with me.*

He had not seen his sister since the day Father had died. On Seneca's orders, they were kept separated. If Atalia too was now a galley slave, she was rowing in a different ship. Sometimes Koren would look through his oar hole, trying to see the other Aelarian galleys that sailed there, trying to spot Atalia or Ofeer or Seneca on them. But they always sailed too far away, their passengers too small to recognize.

Movement ahead caught his eye. Koren raised his head. A figure was climbing down into the ship's hold. As the figure kept descending the stairs, Koren saw sandaled feet, then a cotton dress, and finally black hair framing a tanned face.

Koren had never been quick to anger, but now rage flared through him. His fists trembled around the oar.

"Ofeer," he hissed.

She walked through the hold, her footsteps hesitant. Koren couldn't fault her for her look of disgust. On the outside, the ship was a work of beauty—its sails striped white and red, its hull painted with green and gold motifs, its balustrade engraved with figures of gods, its figurehead a decorative eagle. Belowdecks, however, lurked a different world. Here was a place of sweat, blood, human waste, and misery. A place of lashing whips, of jangling chains, of men and women reduced to animals, praying only for death.

Ofeer walked over the filth, coming to stand beside Koren. She was still beautiful as always, her skin clean, her hair neatly brushed, her dress fine cotton. Her pendant—the eagle of Aelar—hung around her neck. Koren, meanwhile, must have looked like some swamp creature, covered in blood, sweat, and filth.

"Koren," she whispered.

Suddenly he no longer felt like talking. He looked away, still oaring.

Ofeer placed a hand on his shoulder—his shoulder cut by the whip.

"Koren, I'm sorry." Her voice shook. "I ... I'm going to talk to Seneca. I'm going to get you out of here—as soon as we reach Aelar. Atalia too. I'll speak to the emperor if I must. I—"

"You killed him." Koren ground his teeth, unable to stop the venom. "You killed my father."

Ofeer's tears splashed him. "I begged for his life. I begged Seneca to spare Jerael. I ... I buried him myself, I—"

"Leave me." Koren wouldn't look at her. "You made your choice. You chose to live among the Aelarians. You chose Seneca over the family that raised you. Go to him. Get out of this place.

You are Ofeer the Aelarian, too fine a lady for the bowels of a ship."

"Koren, please." She grabbed his knee. "I beg you. Please forgive me. I can help you. I can still make this right. I'm your sister, please—"

"You are not my sister." Koren put all his might into the oar. "I have two sisters: Atalia, whom you put in chains too, and Maya, who thankfully fled you. You and I are no longer family."

Tears streamed down Ofeer's cheeks. She trembled. "I love you, Koren."

"Leave!" he shouted.

Her face hardened. Her eyes narrowed, still leaking tears. Her mouth thinned into a line. Ofeer nodded, turned, and left the hold.

Koren continued to row, silent, staring at the scarred back of the slave before him.

MAYA

"**S**top!" she shouted. "Thief, stop!"

Maya raced through the oasis, her wet dress clinging to her torso and slapping against her legs. Her heart thrashed, and she panted.

"Bring back my camel!"

The palm trees rustled ahead, and she glimpsed the thief making his way down the canyon. He was riding Beelam, her poor camel. Without her mount, Maya knew, she was doomed to remain in this oasis, trapped here as surely as a castaway on an island.

As Maya ran between the fig and palm trees, she drew her dagger with the pomegranate pommel, the one Atalia had given her. Soon the camel and thief vanished from view. The ground became rocky, the trees sparse, leaving no tracks.

He's going to take the camel into the desert, Maya thought, breath shaking in her lungs. *He's going to leave me stranded here.*

She cursed the thief. She cursed herself for ever coming here. Why hadn't she asked Shefael to send guards with her? Her cousin might have given her a royal escort. Why hadn't she asked Mother to come with her? Perhaps Shiloh would have agreed.

Instead Maya had slunk out in the night, terrified of the Aelarians. All because of what Avinasi had said. All because of words from some old lumer who had probably worked for Aelar. The lumer's words echoed in Maya's mind.

This city of Beth Eloh is the world's greatest fountain of myst, but there is another spring, child … a hidden light. A place where lumers can be free. You must travel there, child. You must cross the desert, and you must seek my sisters.

And so Maya had come here, traveling east with no map or plan, only with her camel, with fear in her heart. Only to find herself stranded, lost, dying.

Finally she stopped running, placed her hands on her knees, and breathed deeply. Her head spun. She was still sick with too much sunlight, with hunger and thirst. The spring water flowed to her left, down to a mere trickle over stones. To her right, a rough staircase had been carved into the canyon wall. Maya climbed. Perhaps from above, she would find a better view of the canyon and the desert beyond, could still find her camel.

When she emerged from the canyon, she stood for a moment, panting. She shielded her eyes from the sunlight and stared around, squinting. The oasis filled the canyon with greenery and spread around its rim, a cluster of palms and dates and grass. All around rolled the dunes and rocky hills of the desert. Across the canyon, the waterfall sprouted from the spring, cascading into the pool where she had bathed.

No camel. No thief. But there—near the spring's source—a flash of red caught her eye, soon vanishing between the trees.

It was a long walk around the canyon. The sun baked her hair and dried her dress. Finally she circled the crevice, headed over hot stones, and reached a cluster of trees. She stepped between them to find water gushing from between stones, cascading down into the pool.

A voice rose behind her. "You know, I could just kill you now. Nice arrow to the back."

Maya spun around, heart leaping into her throat. There! She saw him high in the branches of a fig tree, mostly hidden between the leaves. He held a bow, an arrow nocked and aimed at her. The camel thief.

He was a young man, no older than her brothers. A shock of black hair covered his head, and stubble grew over his cheeks. His skin was tanned deep bronze, and he wore a cotton tunic.

"And I can see up your tunic," she said. She could think of nothing else to say.

The young thief glanced down, flushed, and wobbled on the branch. He tried to pull the tunic down, swayed, and tumbled off the branch.

He slammed into a second branch, tried to steady himself, and kept falling. His arrow fired, whizzed through the air, and sank into a palm tree. With a thump, he hit the ground.

Maya ran. She leaped. She pounced onto the thief, driving her knees into his belly. The air left his lungs with an *oof*. Before he could toss her off, Maya placed her dagger against his throat.

"One move and I open your neck." She sneered down at him. Her hand trembled, and her heart threatened to leap from her throat, but she kept the dagger pressed against him. "I'm serious."

The young man dutifully froze. "You couldn't really see up my tunic, could you?"

Maya shook her head. "Thankfully not, or I'd probably have run away in fright. Now where's my camel?"

The thief sighed beneath her. "I should have just shot you. By Eloh, I should have just shot you in the back."

Maya frowned, staring down at him, her dagger still against his neck. "You ... worship Eloh?" For the first time, she realized that the young man spoke fluent Zoharite, that a lion pendant hung around his neck. "I'm still in Zohar, aren't I?"

"Zohar? Oh, no. This is Aelar! And I'm the emperor. Didn't you see the palaces?"

Maya sighed, climbed off him, and sheathed her dagger. She looked around her. "I was traveling for so long. I was sure that I was in Sekadia by now."

The thief rose to his feet too, rubbing a scrape on his neck. He jerked his thumb over his shoulder. "Sekadia is that way. Just across those dunes, actually. Behold, the eastern might of Zohar!" He swept his arm around him. "Not much to look at." He reached out his palm for her to shake. "Name's Leven."

She stared at him, not taking his hand. "Where is my camel?"

Leven shook his head. "Not telling. You can't have him back. See, anything and anyone that wanders into this oasis belongs to us."

"I don't belong to anyone." Maya glared.

Leven scoffed. "Be thankful you belong to us now. Farther east, the Sekadian slave traders would slap you in chains, drag you off to the slave markets, and sell you to the highest bidder. Here you just had to give up a camel."

"Where is my camel?" she shouted, drawing her dagger again.

Leven grabbed his fallen bow and arrow, and it seemed blood would spill when a harsh voice rose from beyond the trees.

"Leven? Leven, damn you, boy, what are you doing out there?"

The young thief cringed at Maya. "Oh, now you've done it." He sighed and lowered his bow. "Well, come on with you. Come meet the family. Might as well."

Leven turned and walked between the trees. Frowning, Maya followed. Past the palms, she saw a camp, well hidden between boulders and trees. Three tents rose here, and a pot lay on a smoldering embers. Several children hopped around a bearded old man in crimson robes, who sat reading from a scroll. A middle-aged woman stood here too, hands on her hips, clad in white robes and a shawl.

Among the people stood several goats, sheep, and camels— her own camel, dear Beelam, among them.

Maya was about to run to her camel when the stern woman shouted, "Leven! Leven, you fool of a boy. You told me that camel just wandered in on its own." The woman sighed and turned toward Maya. "Please forgive my son. I've spared him the rod too often." She grabbed a branch and brandished it. "It's not too late to beat some sense into him."

Maya thought back to her own mother, how Shiloh had always seemed so stern. Suddenly Shiloh didn't seem so bad after all. Maya's eyes dampened to remember her mother, the woman's kind eyes, warm embrace, and loving smile.

"Darling!" said Leven's mother. "He made you cry! Oh by God, I'm going to beat him tonight." She stepped closer and pulled Maya into an embrace. "Hush now, child. Are you lost?"

Maya shook her head, suddenly letting all those tears—tears she could not shed in the desert—fall into this woman's warm embrace. The other camp dwellers gathered around her, even the animals. They introduced themselves. The woman was Zehav, Leven's mother, and the old man was Keremyah, his grandfather. The children were Leven's younger siblings, a little horde of them.

As they named the last child who hopped about, a moan rose from ahead. Maya frowned and stared. For the first time, she noticed that another child lived in the camp. The boy lay on a rug beneath the trees. He was pale and shivering, and a damp cloth lay on his forehead. Maya approached slowly.

"Stay away from my brother," Leven said, reaching out to stop her.

"Leave her alone," said Zehav. "You already stole her camel. Let her see." The stern-looking woman stared at Maya and nodded. "This one has a touch of Luminosity to her. I can see it in her eyes."

Maya walked toward the trees and knelt by the boy. He lay on a rug, moaning, feverish. Flies bustled around him. When Maya pulled back his blanket, she winced. An ugly wound split open his leg, full of pus and maggots. Maya looked back at Zehav.

"He fell." Zehav's eyes dampened. "My youngest son. He fell into the canyon a week ago."

Maya turned back toward the boy. "What's your name?"

The child couldn't reply, only moan. When Maya touched his arm, she pulled back her hand in alarm. He was burning up.

"My uncle went to Beth Eloh, seeking a healer," said Leven. "He was supposed to be back by now."

But he would not return, Maya knew. Not with a healer. Maybe not with his life.

She inhaled deeply. She tried to ignore those who crowded around her, ignore the moans, the fever, the stench of the wound.

She listened to the trees rustle. To the waterfall flowing. To the wind in the sand.

The oasis was alive. A soul, pulsing, breathing in a living desert, in a world that ever spun between sun and moon. In her mind, she saw ancient travelers, lines of camels, bells chinking and women dancing and prayers rising into the sky. The stars shone above, spinning, and the sun baked the land, and flowers bloomed across the desert.

Eras and histories and a single moment, a breath of life of a world.

A world of lume.

Her hands shone as she wove that lume, forming luminescence, magic alight. She still lived in Zohar. She still could draw this light from the eternal spring. The world was all in silver and gold, and she placed her hands upon the boy.

"What are you doing to him?" Leven said, but he sounded so distant, a mere echo from long gone era. All was eternal. All was the grace of Eloh.

Her hands worked over the boy, weaving the light into the wound, pulling out the disease, cooling the fever. She let her light fade. She leaned back, breathing heavily, bringing the world back into focus.

Once more, Maya was here, in a moment of time, in an oasis, a mere girl again.

Before her, the boy sat up and blinked. The damp cloth fell off his brow. The rot had left his leg. The wound was still there, still bleeding, but free of the disease.

"Now he can heal," Maya whispered.

Slowly, the boy rose to his feet.

Zehav ran forward, tears in her eyes, and embraced her youngest son, then embraced Maya. Grandfather Keremyah wept too and prayed and praised Maya's name, and even Leven—that accursed camel thief—lowered his head and begged for Maya's forgiveness.

She let them embrace her, feeling drained.

So much lume filled me in Beth Eloh, she thought. *But I've been using too much, seeping away my strength.*

She felt as if she had just lost a jug full of blood, and she longed to return to Beth Eloh, to soak in the lume, to refill her reserves. Maya understood now why the lumers of Aelar, servants of that distant city in the heart of the Empire, traveled to Beth Eloh on a pilgrimage every year.

Food is the fuel of the body, Maya realized. *Lume is the fuel of the soul, and my soul feels dry.*

"She's pale!" Zehav said. "She's trembling. Quick, children, go put the food on the fire. Get wine. We must let Maya rest."

Zehav—whom Maya had at first thought so stern and frightening—bustled around the camp, concern in her eyes. Soon everyone sat around the campfire, where Zehav cooked flat breads and skewers of lamb. The young ones rushed about, pouring Maya a glass of wine, washing her feet with a damp cloth, and rubbing ointment onto her burnt skin. Grandfather Keremyah prayed from his scroll, blessing her with ancient words. Even the youngest son, his wound freshly bandaged, hopped about and laughed with his siblings, his life returned.

A mug of wine in her hand, a steaming plate of lamb and bread on her lap, Maya slowly told her story. She spoke of fleeing war in Gefen, of Porcia Octavius arriving in Beth Eloh, of the kingdom falling, of her father dying. She spoke of Zohar, their proud and ancient kingdom, falling to Aelar, now a province of an empire.

"And so I'm traveling east," Maya said. "As far east as east goes, until I reach the sea. Avinasi told me that I'd find a center of Luminosity there, beyond the reach of the Empire."

The oasis family looked at one another, silently. Finally it was Keremyah who spoke.

"Child, stay here with us." The elder reached out a wrinkled hand and patted her knee. "I'll teach you to pray, to grow herbs, to raise the animals. You'll be safe here, for we are surrounded by sand, an island in the desert. I brought my family here to flee the corruption of Zohar, the women who walked with bare legs in Beth Eloh, profaning their god, and the princes and kings who bickered and fought, and the Aelarian scrolls and theater and poetry that had been invading our land long before their hosts arrived. Here is not only an oasis of life, but an oasis of light, of the light of Eloh. You are a lumer, a child blessed by God. Stay here with us. Stay and bless us, and let us bless you."

Maya lowered her head. "I thank you, Keremyah. Truly I do. But I can't stay. I'm not yet a lumer. I can feel lume, and I can harvest it into luminescence, and Avinasi taught me a little. But there's much I must learn. Only in the east, across the lands of Sekadia, can I find lumers who will teach me."

"Will you stay the night, at least?" asked Zehav.

Maya nodded. "I thank you."

That night, Maya slept under the stars, and in the morning, Zehav served her a meal of dates, figs, and flat breads dipped in olive oil. Once more, Zehav tried to convince her to remain, and once more, Maya was tempted. This was a good place. A safe place. A place of home, of family, of light.

But she could not. Avinasi had told her to seek a path of light, and that path stretched east.

Zehav sighed. "Very well, Maya Sela. If you must travel east to find your fate, I won't stop you. But I will send my son with you, part of the way at least. He'll accompany you to Sekur, a great city in the heart of Sekadia, where you can join a caravan for the rest of your journey."

Leven was busy climbing a palm tree for dates. When he heard his mother's words, he fell from the tree and groaned.

"What, Mother?" He leaped to his feet. "No. Why must I go?"

Zehav swung her branch at him. "Because if you stay, I'll clobber you. You robbed Maya, and in return, she healed your brother. We owe her his life. Take three camels, and protect Maya on her way east." She turned back toward Maya. "The city of Sekur is a long ride from here, a great metropolis in the heart of Sekadia. Many merchants and pilgrims travel back and forth from that city. You'll find transportation from there to the eastern sea." She handed Maya a rolled-up scroll. "Take this with you. It'll guide your way."

Maya unrolled the scroll and gasped. A map! A beautiful map illustrated with an artist's hand. Maya had seen many maps of the Encircled Sea before, but here was a new map, showing the eastern realms of the world—from Zohar in the west all the way through the deserts of Sekadia to the distant eastern sea.

"Thank you," she whispered.

"What is a map for the life of my child?" Zehav embraced her. "Bless you, Maya. You are a daughter of light, and you will grow into a great priestess. Farewell, daughter of Zohar. Wherever you go, I will pray for you, and we will always tell your tale."

Three camels rode out from the oasis that morning. Maya rode on Beelam, while Leven rode on his own animal. A third camel carried their supplies. The oasis grew smaller and smaller behind them, until it was just a green speck on the horizon, then a memory. The desert spread ahead, golden and hot and unforgiving.

SHILOH

S
he stood in the courtyard among thousands, tears in her eyes, watching the desecration of her kingdom.

The palace of Zohar rose before her, carved of pale stone. Shiloh's ancestor, King Elshalom, had built this palace a thousand years ago, uniting the tribes of coast, hills, and desert. Shiloh's own father had reigned here, her sister after him.

I left this palace to marry Jerael, she thought, gazing at the white walls and golden columns. *But this will always be my home. A home stolen from me. A home profaned.*

The Aelarians covered the palace like maggots on a corpse. Legionaries stood guard on the towers, a man between each pair of columns, javelins in hands. Hundreds of legionaries surrounded the courtyard, armor bright, eagles painted onto their shields. More stood on the palace balcony—the place whence Shiloh's sister, father, grandfather, and monarchs for a thousand years would address the people of Zohar. The place where Shiloh herself had stood so many times as a child, gazing upon her city and the adoring crowds.

Now the crowds simmered. Around Shiloh, men and women, clad in rough homespun, grumbled and spat. Many uttered curses. One bearded man grabbed his crotch, speaking of what Zohar should do to Emperor Marcus. Standing among them, Shiloh remembered the ruins she had seen along the beaches of the Encircled Sea—the remnants of kingdoms which had rebelled against Aelar, which now lay as stones and bones, cities for crabs.

"This war is not over," Epher said, standing at her side among the crowd. His hands balled into fists. "Find me a hundred good men and a hundred iron swords, and we will retake this palace."

Shiloh shook her head. Wind billowed her silken veil. "I already lost my husband. I will not lose my firstborn son. We lost, Epher. Now let us live."

Three legionaries on the balcony raised silver trumpets, and the wails rolled across the city. The crowd of Zoharites turned to stare.

An Aelarian man emerged from the palace onto the balcony. While most legionaries wore lorica segmentata—iron strips across the torso—this man wore a fine iron breastplate emblazoned with golden filigree. A crimson cloak draped off his pauldrons, and a crest of red horsehair sprouted from his helm. He was a tall man, towering over his guards, his face as craggy and hard as the palace bricks. Shiloh stood below in the courtyard, a mere commoner now, thousands of Beth Eloh's people around her. Even from here, it seemed to her that this general on the balcony met her gaze. That he knew her name. That he craved to hurt her.

Shiloh knew this one. She had been to Aelar in her youth. She had seen this face before—a cruel face even then.

"General Remus Marcellus," she whispered, fingernails digging into her palms. The Dark Eagle. The man who had crucified a hundred children in Leer. The man who had led the legions in Gefen, who had taken Shiloh's children captive.

On the balcony, Remus raised his arms and cried out, voice ringing across the courtyard.

"People of Zohar! Aelar is your friend."

The crowd stared. Many muttered. A few cursed under their breath and spat.

Remus continued speaking. "My name is Remus Marcellus! In his wisdom and glory, my emperor—the beloved Marcus Octavius—has named me governor of this province. Welcome, Zoharites! Welcome to the light and civilization of the Aelarian Empire."

The grumbles rose louder now across the crowd.

"Your king, Shefael Elior, shall remain your king," said Remus. "Your city, Beth Eloh, shall remain your home. Bend the knee to Aelar, and serve her glorious emperor, and you will live in peace and prosperity, and Aelar's glory will be your glory. Resist the Empire, and ..."

The general nodded.

Below the balcony, the palace gates creaked open. Legionaries emerged from within, dragging chained prisoners.

Shiloh covered her mouth, her eyes dampening.

Dozens of beaten Zoharites emerged onto a sunlit dais. They wore only loincloths, and their backs bled. Chains hobbled their ankles, and crowns of thorns dug into their brows. Each prisoner held a cross, bent under the weight. Their blood dripped onto the palace stones.

The crowd in the courtyard shouted, and some tried to rush forward, to save their comrades, but a hundred legionaries stood in their way, forming a wall with their shields. The crowd cried out in rage and fear. Epher himself cursed and tried to barrel through the crowd, but Shiloh held her son back.

Men of Gefen, she knew, staring at the beaten prisoners. Their faces were swollen and bloody, but she knew them. Most were warriors. Men and women who had broken bread at her table, who had played with her children. Among them stood Master Malaci, the kindly old Sage of the Sea, the man who had taught Shiloh's children their numbers and letters, who had taught Jerael himself decades ago.

The crowd seethed. A few Zoharites tried to shove their way between legionaries, only to be beaten back. A javelin thrust, impaling a Zoharite's thigh. A shield knocked down a woman.

"Behold those who fought Aelar upon the coast!" Remus cried from the balcony. "They sought to cast Aelar back into the sea, and they cursed our emperor. Shefael bent the knee and lived! Now, Zoharites, you will see the fate of those who resisted."

The crowd roiled. Men cried out in rage, cried for vengeance, cried in hatred of Aelar, cried the names of those prisoners they knew.

100

Shiloh cried out above them all. "Mercy!"

The legionaries stood still, shields raised, as behind them the prisoners bled, backs bent under the crosses they bore. At Shiloh's side, a man picked up the cry. "Mercy!"

Soon a thousand were chanting across the crowd. "Mercy!"

Remus Marcellus stood on the balcony, staring down at the crowd. His eyes were hard, but Shiloh thought that, even from this distance, she could see a thin smile on his face.

"Mercy! Mercy!"

Remus stepped closer to the edge of the balcony and raised his arms. The crowd hushed.

"I have heard your cry!" said Remus. "Aelar is not without mercy. As a gift to Zohar, I will release a single prisoner. Choose, Zoharites! Choose one among the rebels."

In the crowd, people began calling out names. Zohar was a small kingdom, and many of these soldiers of Gefen had family and friends here in the capital.

"Free Baras!" shouted an old man. "He's my son."

"Free Amalia!" cried another man. "She's a woman. She should not die in blood. Free Amalia!"

"Free Malaci!" rose another voice, and soon other voices repeated the chant. "Free Malaci! Free Malaci!"

Shiloh counted seventy-three prisoners on the dais, but only nine or ten names were being called, and soon the cries of "Free Malaci!" drowned out all other voices. The chant rose across the crowd, for Master Malaci was renowned across Zohar, a great thinker and teacher, as beloved as any king.

Remus nodded, and legionaries pulled the cross off Malaci, then began unlocking the old man's chains.

"No!" Malaci cried. "Not me. I'm old. I'm old!" The sage hobbled forward and stared up at the balcony. "Prefect Remus! Spare my grandchild. Spare Ramael. He is young. Spare his life and let me take his spot upon the cross."

Pain twisted Shiloh's heart, and she lowered her head.

You've always been noble, Malaci. You've always been Zohar's finest.

The legionaries tugged Malaci back to the line of prisoners, and soon the sage was holding a cross again, nearly crumpling under the weight. His grandson was tossed forward, freed from his burden. The young soldier fell to his knees, crying out wordlessly for his grandfather.

Shiloh raised her chin. Tears on her cheeks, she stepped through the crowd. At the foot of the dais, legionaries stood, blocking her passage. Shiloh stared up at Remus Marcellus. The prefect stared down from the balcony.

"Hear me, Prefect Remus Marcellus of Aelar!" Shiloh called out, her voice ringing across the courtyard. "I am Shiloh Sela, born to House Elior, aunt to Shefael Elior, the King of Zohar." Her chest ached, and her knees shook, but still she spoke, summoning all the strength inside her. "You let Malaci exchange his freedom for his grandson. Let me exchange my life too. Spare another lion of Zohar! Spare a man or woman, and let me take their place upon the cross."

"Mother!" Epher cried behind her, reaching out to grab her.

Shiloh was shocked at her own words, that she would make this sacrifice. Yet how could she not? How could she live, linger on in guilt, as these sons and daughters—these lions whose only sin had been to roar for Jerael—perished in agony? She could not. She would die a thousand deaths for them.

"Mother!" Epher cried again, and the crowd roared out its dismay, crying for Shiloh to turn back, calling for Remus to reject the offer.

For I too am loved among the people, Shiloh realized. *Though I do not deserve their love, for it was my family—the line of Elior—that led them to servitude.*

"Mother Shiloh, come back to us!" cried men behind her.

"Spare Mother Shiloh!" rose another cry.

"Mercy, mercy!" rose voices in the crowd.

"Grandfather!" cried Ramael, reaching toward Malaci.

A man in the crowd tossed a stone. It hit a legionary's shield. Other men tried to push between the soldiers, to reach the prisoners, and cries of rage and terror rose, and the legionaries drew their swords. More stones flew.

"Enough!" roared Remus from the balcony. "Shiloh Sela, return to the bosom of your people. You did not sin, and so you will live. Legionaries! March them out!"

With wails, with blood, with tears, the march of grief began.

Through the city of Beth Eloh the condemned walked. Whips tore into their backs. Crowns of thorns dug into their brows. On shaking feet, they walked the cobbled streets, between homes and workshops, past temples and towers, through markets and cemeteries. Hundreds of legionaries guarded their way, shields raised, whips lashing.

From rooftops, windows, towers, alleyways, the people of Beth Eloh watched the procession. A mother wept for her condemned child, reaching out to him, shoved back. Prostitutes hung their heads low. A priest ran forward with a jug of honeyed milk, tried to feed a trembling prisoner, was knocked down. On and on, the procession marched, leaving a trail of blood. A trail of grief. A trail of suffering.

Forever this blood will stain our city, Shiloh thought, following the procession. *Ever this shall be a path of tears.*

She wanted to turn away. She did not want to witness this torture, this desecration of her ancient, holy city. Yet she couldn't turn away. All these men and women under the cross, they were all her sons and daughters. Her sister was dead. Her husband was dead. Shefael sat upon a mockery of a throne, the strings of the Empire tugging him as a puppet.

Perhaps Zohar is now entrusted to me, Shiloh thought. *Yet how can I save her from this blood?*

"Mercy!" cried some.

"Aelarian dogs, go home!" shouted another man, his voice dying as a javelin thrust into his chest.

The march of grief continued. The sun beat down, cruel as the whips. Stray dogs, skeletal and feral, lapped the blood off the cobblestones. Donkeys and camels fled. The condemned walked down alleyways, brick walls rising so close at their sides the crosses scraped across them. Arches rose above, crumbling and ancient. These stones had seen three thousand years of travelers; now they witnessed the death of a nation. Past bleached domes splotched with bird droppings, around an olive grove, past the tomb of King Elshalom, along the Old City walls where palm trees grew, they marched on. Dying already. Flayed, dripping blood, crying out in pain, their crosses red—onward they marched.

Remus led the way, riding a splendid white stallion, his armor brilliant in the sunlight, his cloak billowing—a deity of iron and gold. Finally, after what seemed like eras, like generations, the prefect led the procession into the Valley of Ash. Thousands of years ago, before Elshalom, idolaters had sacrificed their children here to the cruel god Baal. They would burn the young ones inside great bronze idols, cooking their flesh, dancing as the screams rose. Today new life would be sacrificed here to new gods.

The legionaries led the condemned into the valley, and the hammers rose.

Shiloh knelt on the hot soil. "Mercy," she whispered.

The voices rose across the crowd of onlookers. "Mercy. Mercy."

Yet still the hammers fell. Still the crosses rose. Seventy-two lions. Sons. Daughters.

Shiloh rose to her feet. She raised her head and stared to the sky, tears on her cheeks.

"Hear, O Zohar!" she cried in a trembling voice—the ancient prayer of her people. "Ours is the light."

Across the valley, the thousands raised their hands to the heavens. "Ours is the light!"

Shiloh remained in the valley long after Remus Marcellus rode off, long after the rest of the crowd dispersed. She wanted to give the dying milk and honey, to soothe them, to shoo away the crows, but Shiloh would not, and her prayer for mercy changed to a new prayer.

"Let them die, Eloh," she whispered. "Please, let them die."

They hung on the crosses before her, old Master Malaci among them, and they lived. Through the night, nailed to the wood, arms dislocated and twisted, they lived. And Shiloh remained, kneeling before them, praying, waiting through searing sunlight and night again, and still they lived.

On the third day, legionaries came to the hill, laughing and drinking and spitting, to tug the corpses down. That day, a second march began. The priests of the city led the way, as they carried the fallen through the streets, as the people prayed, as the legionaries laughed. Shiloh buried the fallen among kings and queens and prophets, and she placed stones upon their graves.

Let them be the last, she prayed between the tombstones. *Let us kneel, serve, suffer if we must, but let no more die.*

She looked at her son. Epher stood at her side, staring at the graves, and more than grief in his eyes, she saw rage. His fists trembled, and Shiloh trembled too, and she knew that more would die.

ATALIA

In the belly of the ship, the galley slaves oared.

Stroke after stroke.

Day after day, night after night.

Whipping after whipping.

The hours, the days, the weeks blended together. Atalia no longer knew darkness from light, pain from sleep, life from death. She had become but a creature. Oaring. Oaring. Her muscles stiff, aching, screaming. The whip on her back. Gruel in her belly. Brief hours of sleep, chained to her bench. Then rowing again, and the drum beating, and the stench of piss and shit and blood and sweat, and every few days a dead rower left to rot for hours before they dragged out his corpse.

Thus was her life as a galley slave—not a life at all but a nightmare, crushing, twisting her, melting her into a beast, a creature as pathetic as a stray dog.

"Soon, Commander," Daor whispered over and over. "Soon we'll be at Aelar."

Yet what did the boy know? What awaited them at Aelar?

"Who says they'll even let us off?" Atalia snapped at him once. "Maybe we'll never set foot on land again. Maybe this is our life now—oaring back and forth across the Encircled Sea."

Daor turned to look at her, and a thin smile tugged at his thin face. "You are the daughter of Sela. They'll want to parade you in the streets of Aelar. You'll get out of here."

Those words were not comforting.

Sometimes, when the wind filled the ship's sails, the masters let the rowers sleep. The slaves never left the hold of the ship. They never saw those sails, never saw the sky or sea, never smelled the salty air. But when the wind was right, when the ships sailed smoothly upon the water, when the drum beat stopped, when the whips rested, the galley slaves slept.

They lay on the floor during those hours—sometimes only moments—stuffed between the wooden benches like corpses in graves. Their chains twisted their ankles, and the benches dug into their sides, and they woke more pained and weary than ever.

Atalia lost count of how many nights she had spent like this. She spent them with Daor between two benches, pressed against him, her nose against his cheek, his knees against her belly, both of them filthy and stinking and so weary it seemed likely they would die before they woke.

She tried to be strong for him. She was his commander. She had trained him for war. She had fought with him, had watched their phalanx perish. She had to lead him, even here. Yet it was on one of these nights, crowded with him on the floor, their oar atop them, that Atalia finally wept.

She couldn't stop herself. Her tears just flowed, and her lips shook, and her body trembled. She thought that Daor was asleep. She had waited for him to sleep before weeping. Yet at the sound of her sobs, he opened his eyes, and he stroked her hair.

"Commander," he whispered.

She tried to look away, to hide her tears, but there was no room here. She was never apart from him, their bodies always pressed together, the other galley slaves pressed against their sides.

"Go back to sleep, soldier," she said, tears on her cheeks.

"Commander, it's all right to cry." He touched her hair. "I cry. We all cry here in the belly of this ship."

"I don't!" Yet her fresh tears still fell. "I can't. I'm a *segen* in the army of Zohar, a commander of a phalanx. I must still fight. Still be strong."

Daor exhaled slowly. "Maybe the war is over, Atalia, maybe—"

"You will call me 'Commander.'" She glared at him through her tears. "Is that understood, soldier?"

He stiffened, and his eyes hardened, and he looked ready to argue ... but then he only nodded. "Understood, Commander."

He placed his arm around her, pulling her close, so that she nuzzled his neck.

"Why are you like this anyway?" Atalia whispered, her lips pressed against his skin.

"Like what?" Daor asked.

"So ... so calm. You don't tremble. You don't shout. You don't talk about killing or escaping." Lying pressed against him, she stared into his eyes. "Who are you, Daor? Back in my phalanx, you were just my soldier. But who are you? Who were you?"

"A potter's boy," he said. "You know that."

"I don't give a fuck who your dad was." She wrapped her fingers around his arm. "Who are *you*? Did you ever play with wooden swords? How many times did you sneak out of temple during Restday services? Which girls in Gefen did you fuck?"

He raised an eyebrow. "Does a commander need to know all this about her soldier?"

"Yes." She nodded. "Standard military procedure, asking these questions."

Daor smiled wanly. Footsteps sounded, and Daor hushed, waiting until the overseer walked by. Once the burly man had passed them, Daor spoke again, his voice but a whisper.

"I never played with wooden swords. But I played mancala with my brothers quite often. I was rather good at it. I played with the fellow soldiers too. And I sneaked out of temple services almost every Restday."

"I knew it!" Atalia couldn't help but grin. "Naughty soldier was a naughty temple boy."

He smiled too. "My brothers and I would crouch low and skulk between the pews so that the priests couldn't see. We'd go outside into the yard, and you know those fruit trees there, the ones that grow those little hard, green fruit that look like grapes, but are rock hard? What are those fruit anyway?"

Atalia bit her lip. "I was going to ask you the same thing. What *were* those trees?"

"I don't know, but those little grapes were like marbles, whatever they are. Some kind of round olives maybe? Could break all your teeth, but we never ate them. My brothers and I would collect them, hide between trees, and toss them at one another in mock wars. Right there outside of Gefen's temple, right in the yard, while everyone else prayed inside."

Atalia's laughter snorted out of her. She forced herself to bite her lip, to stifle the sound lest the overseer heard. "God, I'm jealous. My mother never let me sneak out. Every Restday, we all had to go, we all had to sit there in the pews all morning, just to set an example. Just because we're the Sela family, lords of Gefen." Her eyes dampened anew to remember those days. "Daor, do you remember that time when the chandelier broke in the temple, and some servant tossed it out into the yard, and it completely shattered? And all the crystals—hundreds of them—scattered under the fallen leaves and pine needles?"

"Of course I do," Daor said. "God, we were digging up crystals for a year. I used to think them a treasure. I had collected a few of them, kept them at home on my windowsill. I was sure they were giant diamonds, worth a fortune, but they were only glass."

Atalia laughed. "I had three on my windowsill too. I used to pretend they were magical, that I could see the future in them. My sister Maya always told me that magic only comes from Luminosity, but I liked to pretend." She poked Daor's ribs. "What about my other question?"

He tilted his head. "Which one?"

She bit his chin—hard. "You know!"

He winced. "About which girls I …"

She nodded. "Which ones did you deflower? Or which ones deflowered you? Or …" Atalia's eyes lit up. "Are you still waiting to be deflowered?"

The young man sighed. "No longer waiting. There was one girl." His voice dropped, so low she could barely hear. "Did you know Odaleet?"

Atalia frowned, thinking. "Who's her father?"

"Benta, the baker."

Atalia nodded. "I know Benta. Big man with a big wife. Odaleet …" She gasped. "I know! A skinny little girl, the opposite of her parents."

"Not so skinny!" Daor said. "I used to buy bread there sometimes. At first. Then a lot. Then every day. Just to see her."

"Until one day you came for bread rolls and ended up with a pair of nice tits in your hands instead."

Daor looked away. "I love her, Atalia. Don't talk of her like that."

"Call me 'Commander,' soldier."

"I love her, Commander. And … I'm scared. I don't know what happened to her." Suddenly he was shaking. "I don't know if she lives. If any of them live. If—"

"She lives." Atalia nodded. "The Aelarians like bread too. They won't kill the bakers. Just the soldiers. She's still there, baking breads, thinking of you, soldier. One day we'll return there. And we'll visit that bakery again. And we'll hunt for crystals outside of Gefen's temple, and we'll argue about what kind of fruit those are, and we'll toss them at each other, and you'll come dine with us in the villa on Pine Hill, and ..."

Suddenly Atalia was crying again, and now Daor was shedding tears too. They cried together between the benches of the ship, holding each other, their tears mingling.

"I miss home," Daor whispered.

"Me too." She stroked his cheek. "I promise you, soldier. I promise you. We will see Zohar again. We will see our families again."

She kissed him—a peck on the cheek, then on the lips, then something deeper, a kiss that was warm, salty, tasting of their tears, that lasted forever but ended too soon.

"Is that standard military procedure too, Commander?" he asked.

She nodded. "You performed admirably, soldier."

She closed her eyes, nestling against him. She was falling asleep when the shriek rose, tearing through the hold, rousing her.

"Slaves! Up! Are you lazy bastards here to sleep or to row?"

Atalia opened her eyes and rose from the floor. She stared, blinking in the shadows. A woman was stepping down into the hold from the upper deck, holding a spear. She wore a dark breastplate, a skirt of studded leather strips hung halfway down her thighs, and a leather pack hung at her side. Her hair was long, wavy, and brown. Her face was sharp, almost jagged—the chin pointed, the cheekbones high, the grin tapering to daggerlike points. A grin that could cut iron.

Atalia had never seen this woman before, but she had heard that shrill voice shrieking above deck. She had heard countless tales of this woman. Her cruelty was infamous across the world. The Aelarian Assassin. The cannibal who ate the hearts of her victims.

"Porcia Octavius," Atalia hissed.

The princess of Aelar walked through the hold between the rowers. Every man she passed, Porcia swung her spear like a staff. Cutting flesh. Raising screams. Spilling blood.

"Up!" she screamed. "Lazy worms. You're not here to rest. Row!"

Atalia grunted. They had been rowing for hours without rest. But as Porcia drove her spear into a man's foot ahead, Atalia reluctantly returned to the bench and grabbed the oar. Daor rose with her.

The oars moved again, propelling the ship onward. Porcia kept walking down the hold, inspecting slave by slave. A cruel smile tugged back her lips, revealing teeth like those of a wolf, the fangs unnaturally long.

When Porcia got closer, she slowed down, and her eyes narrowed.

Keep walking, Atalia thought, staring at the whipped back of the slave before her. *Just keep walking, princess.*

But Porcia stopped. She stared. Atalia refused to look at her, kept staring at that whipped back, kept rowing. Yet Porcia would not walk on.

"It's you, isn't it?" Porcia's voice slithered, as smooth as a snake over hot stones. "The Sela whelp."

Atalia couldn't help it. She leaped to her feet, released the oar, and raised her fists with a snarl.

"Commander!" Daor said, trying to pull her back down, but Atalia shoved him off. She stood, her ankle chained to the floor, glaring at Porcia.

I'm taller than her. Atalia's snarl turned into a savage grin. *I'm stronger. I can break her.*

Porcia perhaps was shorter, but she wore iron armor, and she held a spear. The princess tilted her head and raised an eyebrow.

"You've got fire to you." Porcia nodded. "I like that. I respect a strong woman. Around the Encircled Sea, too many women are meek cowards who submit to their men."

"I submit to no one," Atalia said.

Porcia raised her spear, bringing the blade toward Atalia's cheek. Atalia winced as the spear drew a thin line. She felt her blood drip.

"You will submit to me," Porcia whispered, eyes ablaze with a strange fire, her grin widening. It was an inhuman grin, her lips tapering into points, revealing nearly all her teeth. A demon grin. "Once we're in Aelar, you will be mine. Mine to torment. Mine to break. My slaves last a long time in the arena, Atalia Sela. I choose the best, and I train them hard, and they do not die easily. But oh … they suffer. You will suffer the fangs of lions and the claws of

Daniel Arenson

the tigers. You will suffer the swords of the Empire's cruelest gladiators. And you will *live*."

The princess pulled back her spear, brought the blade to her mouth, and licked the blood.

Yes, I will live, Porcia, Atalia thought, staring at the princess. *I will live long enough to rip out your throat.*

"I brought you a gift." Porcia reached into her pack and pulled out something round and malodorous. "Somebody you knew, I think?"

Porcia tossed the severed head at Atalia's feet.

Atalia screamed.

She looked away. She retched, losing the gruel she had eaten hours ago. Daor cried out at her side. She had seen it for only a second, but Atalia knew the image would never leave her.

Yohanan's head. Her cousin. Fallen prince of Zohar.

"I preserved it for you," Porcia said. "I used just the right chemicals. It'll last a long time and keep you company. I thought you might miss your family down here." Porcia laughed. "In time, I'll bring you the rest of them."

The princess's footfalls thumped as she left the hold. The ship tilted and the head rolled, vanishing into the shadows. Atalia kept gagging, eyes stinging, blood dripping.

I will kill you, Porcia, she vowed. *Put a sword in my hand, put me in the arena, and I will raise every gladiator in Aelar against you.*

"I will kill you," she whispered, tasting her bile and blood. "I swear this. I swear on my father. I swear on my god. I will kill you, Porcia Octavius."

116

The ship sailed on through the night. With every stroke of the oars, Atalia imagined that she was swinging a blade, cutting Porcia's mocking face.

VALENTINA

D ozens of lords and ladies splashed in the water, and laughter rang through the bathhouse, but Princess Valentina Octavius felt frozen, and she could think only one thought, over and over.

He's my father. The fool. The wretched slave. This bearded brute. I'm his daughter.

Frescoes covered the walls around the heated pool, depicting dolphins, fish, and sea nymphs, while a mosaic adorned the pool floor, its tiles forming seashells and starfish. An aqueduct supplied water from a hot spring, steaming and aromatic. Columns surrounded the bathhouse, topped with marble statues of nude gods.

Many of the patrons, just as naked, were far less godly, yet there was no shame here, for Aelarians believed that all flesh was but a tribute to the heavens. Generals, returned from the wars in Gael, proudly displayed their scars. Their wives chatted on the pool's rim, feet splashing in the water, their bellies and breasts stretched from childbirth and nursing.

Valentina remained submerged, the water up to her chin. She had always felt ashamed here, her body exposed to the bathers—the body of an albino, a body she had never let anyone but Iris, her lover, see.

But Iris is dead now, Valentina thought. *You murdered her.*

The pain of Iris's death grew daily. Valentina did not think it would ever leave her. Every morning, when Valentina woke, the bed felt cold and empty without Iris by her side. Every night, when Valentina lay down to sleep, she could not bear to lie there without Iris—her lumer, her lover—in her arms. She dreamed of Iris most nights, wonderful dreams, dreams that the lumer was still alive. Dreams of Iris's dark eyes, bright smile, brave soul. And darker dreams—memories of Iris's corpse in the grass, strangled at Emperor Marcus's feet.

Valentina lowered her head. Part of her raged at Iris. *You knew! You were a lumer. You must have known that Septimus is my father! Why did you lie?*

But of course, Valentina knew why. She knew that Marcus would act to keep the secret safe. That he must have threatened Iris—knowing she would see the truth with her magic—forcing her to lie about Valentina's parentage.

So you poisoned him, Iris, Valentina thought. *You poisoned him so that you could finally tell me the truth. So that we could finally escape him. But now you're gone, and now I feel so lost.*

The water up to her neck, Valentina raised her eyes in the pool, and she stared at Marcus.

The emperor and his memento mori bathed together. They always bathed together—Marcus and Mingo, emperor and fool, her false father and her true father.

Emperor Marcus, though already fifty years old, still had the body of a young man, wide and muscular and bearing the scars of battle. Always Marcus brought with him his memento mori, a slave to remind the emperor of his own mortality—that all mortals, even emperors, were not truly like gods of marble but mere withering flesh. Mingo looked the part, appropriately withered. His frame was scrawny, almost skeletal, the skin wrinkled. His gray beard hung low, and his hair was a wild mess of tangles. Both men were of an age, but while Marcus lived in a palace, dining on fine fare, Mingo lived in the kennels, feeding on whatever the other slaves tossed him, often only apple cores and bread crust.

But he's not really named Mingo, Valentina thought. *His name is Septimus Cassius. The senator who once fought Marcus, who tried to keep Aelar a republic. The man whose family I was stolen from. My father.*

Emperor Marcus stood on the rim of the pool, the steam hiding his nakedness. He raised a sponge on a stick like a scepter.

"My friends!" the emperor called out. "We are here to celebrate the fall of Zohar!"

Across the bathhouse, the nobles of Aelar cheered and laughed. Valentina remained silent. Lumers, she knew, could communicate over great distances, sending messages through their luminescence; the news of Zohar's fall had traveled quickly.

The thought of Luminosity twisted Valentina's heart. To most Aelarians, lumers were like horses or mules or slaves, simple beasts to serve them. Porcia beat her lumer, the meek girl she called Worm. Seneca treated his own lumer, the mysterious Taeer, as no more than a whore.

But I loved my lumer, Valentina thought. How must these lumers have felt—Worm, Taeer, a hundred others across Aelar—to learn that their homeland had fallen?

"Princess Porcia and Prince Seneca will return to Aelar within a fortnight," said Marcus, "and we will hold a victorious march in their honor. As they sail across the sea, we celebrate here in a little sea of our own."

"Hail Princess Porcia, whose sword thrusts into the hearts of her enemies, whose cruelty knows no bound!" cried Mingo the fool. He stood on the pool's edge and gave a little pirouette. "And hail Prince Seneca, whose prick thrusts into the loins of foreign whores, and whose pride is even larger!"

The crowd roared with laughter, and Valentine felt herself blush. She hated blushing. With her pale cheeks, she always turned bright red.

"Forgive my fool!" said the emperor, laughing. Marcus only ever laughed around Mingo. "He's honest to a fault."

He's honest, but he's no fool, Valentina thought, looking at the pair. The truth still shocked her. The truth Iris had hidden from her. The truth Mingo had finally revealed.

Valentina found herself trembling. All her life, she had felt different from the Octavius family. Her face rounder. Her heart gentler. No statues of Valentina rose in the city, while statues of Marcus, Porcia, and Seneca soared in the Acropolis, watching over the Empire. So yes, the truth shocked her … and yet felt as true and comforting as a mother's embrace.

And if Marcus discovers that I know, he will strangle me. He will kill me like he killed Iris. Like he killed my true brothers.

Yes, Valentina had heard those stories. The nobles and soldiers no longer spoke of them—they dared not—but servants and slaves dared, whispering in halls and deep chambers beneath the palaces, places where Valentina often sought refuge from the court, often heard the secrets that echoed.

It had been nearly two decades ago that General Marcus Octavius, the hero who had conquered many lands, had finally conquered his own land. That day, he had marched into the Senate, announced himself the Emperor of Aelar, demanded the senators serve him … and plunged Aelar into a bitter civil war.

The war had raged for years. Septimus Cassius, consul of the Senate, had refused to bend the knee to Marcus, had summoned armies to his call. The Cassius family fought bravely, nearly freed Aelar from Marcus's grasp. But its armies fell. The House of Cassius shattered. When the war ended, the Senate remained standing—half its senators slain, the others sworn to serve Emperor Marcus Octavius, to run his empire for him while he conquered all lands still remaining around the Encircled Sea.

Septimus Cassius remained too—his toga replaced with a loincloth, his back bent, his beard long, his mind and body broken—now a fool named Mingo. Forced to linger on while his sons lay buried. Forced to forever see his old enemy shine, his beloved Republic gone.

And forced to see me, Valentina thought. *Septimus's youngest daughter.* Her eyes teared up. *Marcus not only wanted my father to see his glory. He wanted him to see me—to see me raised as his enemy's daughter. For nobody else to know the horrible truth. But I know the truth now.* Anger flared inside her as she stared at Marcus through the mist of the bathhouse. *I know who you are, Marcus Octavius. I know that you murdered my lover. I know that you murdered my true brothers. I know that you think Mingo is but a fool, but he's not. His spirit is not yet broken. He is still Septimus Cassius, the senator who defied you, and he is still my father.*

"Behold!" cried Mingo-who-was-Septimus, interrupting her thoughts. "I am the great Emperor Marcus! See my magnificence!"

The bearded, naked slave was standing on the aqueduct that delivered heated water to the pool. On tiptoes, arms windmilling, the fool walked along the stone rim of the aqueduct.

"Be careful, Emperor Marcus!" cried a lady from the pool, tittering. "You will fall and split your imperial head!"

"Nonsense!" Mingo cried. "I am crossing the Ponatius Bridge over the rushing Volaga River, on my way to crush the barbarians of Gael." He took another few steps along the aqueduct, moving toward the pool. "I am as immortal as the gods, my body made of iron, my piss molten gold." He gave a pirouette. "Behold my glory, I—"

With a yelp, Mingo fell. Valentina's heart leaped. The slave nearly hit the rim of the pool. By a miracle, he missed the hard stones and crashed into the water. The crowd of bathers roared with laughter and clapped their hands.

"Be careful, O Glorious Emperor Marcus!" said the true Marcus.

The bearded slave nodded in the water. "The stones are slippery, dominus. Far more dangerous than a horde of Gaelian barbarians."

"Far more dangerous indeed!" agreed Marcus, laughing. "Now go swim, my fool, for you still stink of the dogs you lie with. Go bathe while I speak to my generals."

Mingo swam on his back, spurting out water like a fountain. Bathers laughed and fled from his advance. Some of the younger women cringed in disgust, and their lovers—rugged, laughing men—protected them in their arms from the withered creature swimming by.

My father, Valentina thought. *The fool. The creature. A pathetic wretch to fear and mock. And I would prefer him as a father over Marcus— any day.*

She noticed that he was swimming toward her, arms flailing and splashing. Valentina remained frozen in the bathhouse, the hot water rising up to her chin. She wanted to flee. If the emperor saw her talking to Mingo, he would suspect. He would kill Mingo, perhaps kill Valentina herself. She knew this. Marcus couldn't know that Valentina had learned the truth; it was impossible. Yet as the fool swam toward her, she found herself frozen.

He swam by her, then paused for just a breath. When he gazed at her, his face changed—for just a heartbeat. The folly left his eyes. Suddenly, even bearded and wild as he was, Mingo was

Senator Septimus Cassius again. The man who had governed the Republic. The man who had resisted the Empire.

"Midnight," he whispered. "The wharfs."

His eyes stared into hers—somber, serious, intelligent eyes … then once more the eyes of a fool. He spurted water upward, then swam on, sending a group of young bathers fleeing.

That evening, Valentina lay in her bed, feeling so alone, so cold. She hugged her pillows, tucked her blankets under her feet, but still felt so empty. She missed Iris. She tried to imagine her lumer—her kind brown eyes, smooth black hair, smiling lips—but she kept seeing the corpse on the grass, naked and strangled, Emperor Marcus standing above.

Finally Valentina rose from bed and donned her simplest stola, a mere sheet of white linen bound with a silver fibula. Over it, she wrapped a gray cloak. She tiptoed out of her chambers, made her way down the corridor, and into the gardens. As she passed that place—the place where Iris had died—Valentina quickened her step. Soon she left the palace grounds.

The Aelarian Acropolis spread around her across the hills, the center of the city, of the Empire's glory. Triumphal arches, columned temples, the great library, the amphitheater, the colossal statues of Marcus and his children—all rose across the Acropolis, the greatest buildings in the world. Stories told that Nur had towering pyramids, taller than buildings here, but that they were crude, ugly things. They said that Zohar had palaces of wonder, but that they were ancient, craggy, crumbling, mere relics of lost glory. Here was the true heart of the civilized world, here in the center of Aelar, yet Valentina felt trapped.

She reached into her pocket and felt Iris's letter there. Its words echoed in her mind.

Find a swift ship. Sail to Zohar, and come to a city called Gefen on the coast. You will walk along the beach there, admiring the seashells and smooth stones and palm trees, and you will feel great peace, the peace of lume flowing across you, soothing all your fear, all your pain. And as you walk there, you will see a girl ...

The pain seemed too great for Valentina to bear. She had come so close to fleeing. To sailing to Zohar with Iris. To escaping this place of lies, poison, secrets, so much fear. But Iris was gone now, and Valentina would never walk along that eastern beach with the woman she loved.

She walked between temples, making her way downhill, until she left the Acropolis. She moved through the city. Aelar was large, and it was a long walk to the wharfs. She could have taken her horse, but horses drew attention. This night Valentina moved like a shadow, wrapped in her cloak, disguised as a mere commoner. She tugged her hood low, hiding her white face, white hair, and colorless eyes, a countenance all in Aelar would recognize. Clouds hid the moon, and the oil street lamps could not penetrate the shadows of her hood.

She walked for hours. She walked down street after street, between brick homes with tiled roofs, past columned temples, along the river, through a grove of cypresses. With every step, fear grew in her heart, and she wanted to run back to the palace, or

126

hide in an alleyway, or flee the city altogether. Yet she forced
herself to keep going. To find him. Her father.

Finally, in the darkness, she reached Aelaria Maritima, the
port of Aelar.

At once Valentina realized the folly of her journey here.
Aelaria Maritima was massive. Of course it was. She had been
here before, several times, but in her distress and fear, she had not
paused to consider its size. The boardwalk stretched for a league
or longer. Great breakwaters thrust into the sea, lined with towers
and colonnades. Hundreds of buildings rose here, maybe
thousands—taverns, houses, workshops, temples, bathhouses,
gymnasiums, even theaters. Just the port of Aelar was a city in its
own right, bustling with activity even at midnight. Prostitutes
leaned against statues of old heroes, breasts exposed. Legionaries
gambled in taverns, and drunkards swayed along the boardwalk.
Beggars lurked in shadows, and youths were playing with wooden
swords. The smell of fish, tar, sweat, and ale filled Aelaria
Maritima, and lanterns swung on the masts of a thousand
anchored ships.

How will I find you here, Father? Valentina wondered. She
would have an easier time finding a piece of hay in a pile of
needles.

She walked along the boardwalk, cloak wrapped around her.
A feral cat hissed from a shadowy alleyway, eyes shining. A few
more steps, and she passed a brothel where prostitutes stood in
the windows, clad in togas—outfits for distinguished men and the
lowest of women—and drunkards stumbled in and out the door.

127

Valentina recognized Senator Quintus, one of the city's most esteemed citizens, slip into the shadowy house, and she hurried by, terrified that he would recognize her. She kept walking, passing along piers where countless boats docked.

"Where are you, Father?" she whispered. Even at this late hour, thousands of people crowded the port. She would never find him here. Never—

"Spare a denarius, domina?" A cloaked beggar reached out from the shadows. "A denarius for a poor old veteran of the wars?"

Pity filled Valentina's heart to see the beggar. He was a scrawny man, limping on a wooden leg. His hood shadowed a bushy brown beard and a leathery face. He stank of old booze. No doubt the man had been wounded in one of her father's wars against the kingdoms around the Encircled Sea.

No, not my father, Valentina thought. *Emperor Marcus is the man who kidnapped me. The man who lied to me. The man who murdered the one I love.*

She reached into her pocket for a coin. "Here, friend." She placed it in the beggar's palm. "Spend it on a hot meal or a tavern bed or ..."

As the beggar stared at her, Valentina's voice trailed off. She gasped.

Septimus winked at her. "Thank you, domina." His voice dropped to a whisper. "My daughter."

Valentina stared in wonder. Truly Septimus was a fine actor. The fool Mingo, to him, was just a disguise; here was another performance.

"Father!" she whispered.

He glanced around, then cackled. "Thank you, domina! Thank you for your kindness." He slunk back into an alley. "I would be glad to sell you one of my homemade flutes for your coin. Come, come."

Glancing around too, dreading to see somebody else she recognized, Valentina stepped into the dark alleyway. The old beggar—her father—hobbled there, coins rattling in his tin mug.

"Your leg," she whispered, pointing at the wooden peg.

"Aye, domina, my poor old leg, lost in the wars ..." He winked at her. "Things are not what they seem in the docks, are they? Nor in the palace. Both are places of lies and shadows."

"So what is the truth?" Valentina asked.

He limped closer, and he whispered into her ear, his voice different now—not the high-pitched voice of Mingo the fool, nor the rasp of the beggar, but a deep, soft, kind voice. "That I love you. That I've always loved you, always watched over you, always been proud of you—proud that you remained kind, pure, and good, even in the nest of vultures. You are truly my daughter."

She wiped tears from her eyes. "You were always there, all my life. And I ignored you. Feared you. Forced myself to laugh when everyone else laughed—when Porcia would trip you, or Seneca toss bones at you and make you eat off the floor. I just watched, and ... I didn't know. I'm so sorry." She embraced him.

"I want to say that I love you too, but I feel like I don't know the real you."

He nodded and stroked her hair. "Aye, child. That was not me in that palace, eating off the floor like a dog. That is who Marcus thinks I am, whom he thinks he turned me into. It was his task, his revenge, to turn Septimus Cassius into Mingo the fool. So I put on a show for him, pretending to lose my mind, my dignity, but always I was playing a character, that is all. A puppet who danced for him, like the puppet kings he installs in those lands he conquers." He sighed. "I didn't mind my own humiliation. Let them laugh at poor Mingo! But every day and night, I regretted that I could not be a father to you."

Valentina lowered her head. "Marcus Octavius was never much of a father to me. Seneca has always been the only one in the family who seemed to love me. Oh, Father." She looked back up at him. "How I wish we could make up for those lost years! How old was I when … when …"

"A newborn," Septimus said, eyes damp. "Marcus's men murdered my wife—your mother—when she was still pregnant with you. They … they took you from her. They cut you out." His voice shook. "You emerged into the world already motherless, so frightened, so precious. Marcus's own wife had died in the war only days earlier, pregnant herself, her babe lost. And so Marcus stole you, replacing his slain child with my living one. At least I got to watch you grow up, never far. At least I got to see you safe and happy."

Happy? Had she ever been happy? She had never known a mother. Marcus had always been cold and stern, Porcia cruel. Seneca had been kind to her—he had always loved her—but as Valentina had grown older, she had begun to fear the prince, that darkness she sometimes saw in his eyes, seeds of Porcia's madness she worried would grow into twisted forests.

"I've only ever been happy with my scrolls, with my birds, with my lumer," she said. "Never with the Octavius family. But I want to be happy with you, Father. These meetings between us feel so short, so fleeting, so dangerous."

Septimus's voice dropped lower. He glanced around the alleyway, then back to her. "Lies are always comforting. Truth is always a thing of danger. And here is another truth, child. Marcus Octavius's reign will not last forever."

Valentina took a step back. Her breath shook in her lungs. "What do you mean, Father?" She thought back to the night Marcus had been poisoned, how Iris had blamed the memento mori for the crime. In Iris's letter, she had confessed her own guilt, but now Valentina wondered. Even if Iris had slipped the poison into the meal, had she acted alone? Or was she part of a web Valentina had never seen, no more than she had seen the truth of her parentage?

"First I must know, Valentina," Septimus said, somber now. "First I must know your loyalty. Know if we have your trust."

We.

Valentina trembled. A web. A web of lies, a web of spiders, all crawling nearer and nearer, invisible, weaving their gossamer, waiting to strike.

"I trust you," she whispered, remembering Iris's corpse. "And you can trust me. You have my loyalty, Father."

He stepped closer toward her. He held her arm, leaned forward, and whispered into her ear. Valentina listened and felt as if the world collapsed around her.

MAYA

The desert sprawled out before them, endless under the sun, the dunes rolling to all horizons.

"Sekadia," Maya whispered from her camel, gazing at this ancient, eastern kingdom. "Ancient land of bones, of light, of gold, of beauty and of cruelty."

Leven rode his own camel beside her. He squinted at the distance. "Really? I see only sand."

"There's more here than sand," Maya said softly.

The young thief scratched his stubble and pushed his black hair back from his brow. His dark eyes narrowed further. "I still see only sand."

Yet Maya saw more. There were rocks and boulders, hills and valleys, metal and crystal. There was the sky above, the beating sun. There was the rocky path their three camels walked down—a camel for her, a camel for Leven, and a camel that carried their supplies in jangling saddlebags. And there were memories here, an ancient history Maya felt all around her.

There wasn't much lume here. They had left Zohar behind, and the spring of light had faded. Yet Maya still carried lume within her, and she didn't even need to luminate it to *see* this place—to truly see it. In her mind, thousands of camels traversed this desert, carrying spice merchants back and forth. Armies thundered by on horses, soldiers in white cloaks and shawls, swinging sabers. She saw monuments rise—statues, obelisks, great cities—only to fall back into the sand and vanish.

Sekadia. A vast land, a hundred times the size of Zohar. The land that six hundred years ago had enslaved the Zoharites, forcing them to build great monuments that had long since crumbled. The land that first invented writing, irrigation, astrology, war. The vast land, nearly as large as the Aelarian Empire, that Maya had to cross before she could reach her destination: a second spring of lume, and a Luminosity center by the sea.

She unrolled her map, the one Leven's mother had given her. Zohar seemed so small on the parchment, a mere stretch of coast and a few hills, a kingdom she could hide under her fingertip. To the east spread most of the parchment—Sekadia going on and on, finally reaching the distant sea. And there, on the eastern coast, a small symbol. A candelabrum with four candles. Symbol of Luminosity.

The place I seek, she thought. *Light by the eastern sea.*

"The sea seems so far," she said. "We've barely covered any distance."

"So far for you." Leven—that damn camel thief—uncorked his waterskin. "I'm only taking you as far as Sekur. Then it's back to my oasis." He drank deeply and passed her the skin.

Maya took it gratefully. She drank. It was hot here, so hot it felt like traveling through soup. The sun blasted them, blinding, beating like whips. If not for her cloak and shawl—the prayer shawl Father had given her, sewn years ago for Mica—the lashing sunrays would have burnt her skin. She and Leven were desert children, their skin brown, their hair black and thick, bred to survive the heat, but this desert seemed cruel enough to melt iron. Even their camels grumbled with every step.

"Let's rest and pitch the tent," Maya said. "It's almost noon and getting too hot. We'll keep traveling in the evening."

Leven snorted. "You coastal girls. Can't handle the heat?"

She glared at him. "Is that why you spent your life hiding in an oasis, O great desert warrior?"

He bristled. "I spent years traveling this desert, fighting off brigands, sometimes going for days without water. Meanwhile you grew up in a villa by the sea, pampered and spoiled, a proper princess."

"That villa is gone now," Maya said softly. "And that sea is swarming with eagles. Life on the coast is no easier than the desert, and we are both Zoharites, and both stubborn, and both need to rest." She halted her camel in a valley between two dunes. "Here."

They raised their tent, driving the poles into the sand, and rested in the shade. More than anything, Maya longed to wash her feet—to feel that healing water flow over them, soothing her, cooling her. Yet they only had a few waterskins left, barely enough to drink until they reached Sekur, capital of Sekadia. She rolled out a rug, and Leven took dry figs, dates, and nuts from his pack. They shared the meal. It was so hot, even in the tent, that Maya could barely stomach eating. She forced herself, knowing she needed the energy.

She lay down on the rug and closed her eyes, trying to sleep, only to be roused by music.

She peeked to see that Leven had pulled a flute from his pack. She recognized the tune he played. It was "The Shepherd of Zohar," an old hymn.

"I'm trying to sleep," she told him.

"I'm trying to play music."

She tried to snatch the flute from him, but he pulled it back. "Any requests?"

She nodded. "I request that you put that flute away."

"No respect for an artist." Leven sighed and placed down the flute.

"I lost respect for you when you stole my camel." Maya rolled over, facing the tent wall.

She heard Leven lie down beside her. The tent was too small. She could *smell* him, a smell of some strange spice she didn't recognize, and sand, and dry fruit, and a lingering scent of the oasis.

She rolled back toward him. "Stop that."

"Stop what?" He lay beside her, frowning.

"Stop stinking."

He blinked at her, then laughed. "I don't stink. I put on a special blend of myrrh and musk and olive oil, precisely to prevent stinking."

She nodded. "So that's what stinks. Your perfume."

"It's not perfume!" He stiffened. "I don't wear perfume. I'm not a lady."

She leaned closer and sniffed his neck. She nodded. "Perfume. There was a fine lady in Gefen, a real beauty in pink silks, who wore the same scent."

"Well, you smell like a camel's ass."

She raised her eyebrow. "How do you know? Do you often sniff camel asses?"

Now it was his turn to roll away from her. "I thought you were going to sleep."

Maya closed her eyes again, but sleep eluded her. It was too damn hot. The air was too thick, flowing around her, caressing her skin. Somewhere outside something was clicking or chirping—some insect or snake. She tried to ignore it. When still she couldn't sleep, she poked Leven in the back.

"Leven," she whispered. "Leven, are you asleep?"

He groaned.

"Leven!" she said again, louder now.

He flopped onto his back. "What?"

Maya stared at him. "Why did you steal my camel?"

"Still on about the camel!" He raised his hands in indignation. "I'm a thief, that's why. I steal things. That's what I do. The way you're a princess, and you can't help being one, I can't help being a thief."

"I'm not a princess," she said. "I'm King Shefael's cousin."

"That makes you a princess."

She shook her head, her black curls swaying. "No it doesn't. That's not how the lines of succession work. I'd have to be Shefael's sister or daughter to be a princess. You'd know this if you were more than an uneducated thief." She frowned. "Did you get to steal much at the oasis? What, did you snatch drops of water from the pool, maybe leaves from the palm trees? What kind of thief lives in an oasis?"

He sighed. "An exiled one."

"Exiled from where, a perfume shop?"

He nodded. "I was."

She frowned. "Hush, you."

"It's true."

She groaned and looked away. "You're not funny."

"I'm serious. It's where they finally caught me." Leven stared up at the ceiling, seeming lost in memory. "I was born in Beth Eloh. At least, I think I was. I can't remember anything before I was two or three. But I was always a thief. My mother was a beggar, soft in the head, the sort of woman who yells at pigeons, thinking them demons." His voice softened. "I was mostly on my own as a child, scampering through the streets with other urchins. I stole from everyone. Everyone, Maya! I nicked rings off the fingers of priests. I snatched gold from the purses of merchants. I grabbed coins from the fingers of lechers paying their whores. It was perfume that finally got me."

"The smell gave you away while you were sneaking up on some fine lady with a purse of gold?"

He shook his head. "I tried to rob a perfumery. You know Palmari's Paradise?"

Maya nodded. It was a perfume shop in Beth Eloh, a place where the wealthy shopped for their fragrances. Queen Sifora herself would buy perfumes there. Ofeer even had a bottle from Palmari's Paradise back in the villa on Pine Hill.

"I tried to snatch a vial from the shop," Leven said. "It was called Angels' Meadow. A scent of flowers and resin, spicy and sweet. I was so nervous to hold it, so careful, that I slipped. I let the vial drop from under my cloak. It smashed right on the perfumery floor. Next thing I know, the city guards had me in chains, and I was about to be stoned to death. Me, stoned to death! With my beautiful face and all."

Maya cringed, turning back toward him. "Stoned to death for stealing a single vial of perfume?"

"Well ... the perfume and a whole collection of rings, bracelets, necklaces, and holy artifacts they found in my pockets. It was your aunt who spared my life. Queen Sifora herself. She was a kind woman, Maya. A good queen. I was spared the stones, instead given a good whipping and cast out from the city, sent to travel east into the desert."

He pulled off his tunic, exposing his bare torso, and turned to show her his back. Maya could still see the scars. She passed her finger along one scar; it was thin, pale, and slightly elevated.

"But ..." She frowned. "I thought Zehav is your mother. That Keremyah is your grandfather. That all those boys scampering around the oasis are your brothers."

"They are!" Leven said. "Well, in a way. They adopted me. I arrived at their oasis two years ago, thin, thirsty, almost dying, beaten, and cast out from the city. They took me in, nursed me back to health. Zehav now calls me her son. Grandpa Keremyah vowed to return me to the path of righteousness, and he's been teaching me prayers, trying to instill Eloh's values in me. But I don't think it's been working. Once a thief, always a thief."

"So that's why you stole my camel?" Maya asked. "Because one exile wasn't enough?"

He stared at the tent wall for a long moment, then back at her. "Do you know the story of the scorpion and the frog?"

She shook her head. "Tell me."

"A scorpion once wanted to cross the lake, so he asked a frog for a ride. The frog refused, saying, 'You will sting me.' The scorpion denied that, explaining that if he stung the frog while they were crossing the lake, they would both drown. The frog saw the sense in that, so he let the scorpion climb onto his back, then began to swim across the lake. Halfway toward the opposite shore, the scorpion stung the frog. As they were drowning, the frog asked, 'Why did you sting me?' The scorpion replied, just before they both vanished underwater, 'Because it's my nature.'"

"So you're a scorpion and I'm a frog," Maya said.

He poked her with his finger. "Sting."

"Ouch." She pouted and poked him back, right in the chest. "Sting you back."

He poked her nose. "Sting," he whispered ... and suddenly he was stroking her hair, gently passing his fingers through her mane of black curls. Maya had always hated her hair—it wasn't nice and smooth like Atalia's or Ofeer's—but this damn thief seemed to like it well enough, judging by how determined he seemed to keep stroking it. She let him. That stupid thief.

"Are you riding me across the pond?" she whispered. "Are you trying to steal my heart before you steal my camel again?"

He nodded. "You're on to me."

He leaned closer, until their noses almost touched, and she gazed into his dark eyes. Maya had never kissed a boy—unless you counted Eriz Ben Akadia outside Gefen's bakery, but that had barely been a peck. She thought that here it was, here it was coming—her first kiss, and she trembled, and—

Hooves.

Hooves sounded outside.

A wail rose through the desert.

Leven leaped to his feet and drew his sickle sword. Maya grabbed the dagger Atalia had given her. They raced out the tent into the blinding light of the desert.

On the dune above, she saw them. Six camels bearing six riders, all charging down toward them.

Sekadians, Maya realized.

She could barely see their faces. They wore long white robes, and hoods hid their heads. They wore masks formed from great skulls, vaguely humanoid, and startlingly blue eyes peered through the sockets. Those were eyes like sapphires, shining in the sun, staring at her. In their gloved hands, they raised curved blades, longer than any swords Maya had ever seen. Aelarian swords were the length and width of a man's forearm, and Zoharite swords weren't much longer, curved like sickles. But these blades were twice the length and thin, reminding her of the beaks of cranes, and their pommels were shaped as talons. At their sides, the men held whips of braided leather.

"Bone-raiders!" Leven spat and raised his sword before him. "God damn bone-raiders."

The camels reached the valley and began galloping around Maya and Leven, raising clouds of dust.

"What are bone-raiders?" she cried.

"Much worse than scorpions," Leven said. "Desert scum. Outlaws."

"Sort of like thieves?" she shouted over the storm.

The raiders halted their camels and leaped onto the sand. One of the men, his skull mask clattering, rushed over to grab Maya and Leven's camels. The other robed figures advanced, closing in around them, swords and whips raised. One man began to curse and yell. Maya spoke a smattering of Sekadian; Master Malaci had taught her some of the language back in Gefen.

"Drop your knives!" the man seemed to be saying. "Drop them!"

142

"Your mother's cunt!" Leven shouted and leaped forward, blade lashing.

"Leven, no!" Maya cried.

But the thief ignored her. He soared into the air, then plunged down, his curved sword gleaming. The raider cursed and swung his own blade, and the swords crashed together. No sooner had Leven hit the sand than he thrust his blade upward. For an instant, Maya wasn't sure what happened. Then she saw the raider's white cloak turn red, and when Leven tugged his blade back, the outlaw's innards spilled onto the sand.

The other robed men howled and charged, blades swinging.

Maya cried out as a man reached toward her. His whip flew. Maya lashed her dagger, trying to cut the whip, but the thong wrapped around her arm. She cried out as the man yanked her forward. Another man cracked his whip behind her, and it coiled around Maya's torso, cutting her belly, tightening around her.

Ahead of her, she saw other bone-raiders lashing their whips against Leven. The thief fell, still swinging his sword. He managed to sever one whip, but the others slammed against him. A whip hit Leven's cheek, and his blood spilled.

A third whip wrapped around Maya, this one around her legs, pulling her ankles together. She fell onto the sand. A man leaned above her, eyes like blue lanterns, and Maya lashed her dagger wildly. She managed to cut him. Her blade drove through his forearm, cutting down to the bone, peeling back the flesh, and horrible fear and horrible satisfaction filled Maya.

The man roared, and another raider kicked her. The boot drove into Maya's side, and the breath was knocked out of her. She couldn't even scream. The whip yanked down her arm, and another boot slammed onto her hand, crushing her fingers. She found her voice and screamed, and her dagger fell.

"Leven!" she managed to cry out, but she couldn't see him. The robed figures loomed above her, the skull masks leering, those horrible blue eyes burning her, bright as suns. The blows rained onto her, hands yanked her to her feet, and ropes wrapped around her. The raiders pulled her arms behind her back and tied them, and Maya glimpsed Leven lying in the sand, bleeding, maybe dead. Then a man shoved a sack over her head, and all the world went dark.

She screamed but nobody seemed to hear. She felt them grab her, lift her, and toss her across a saddle. A camel snorted below, and the men talked in their language. One hawked and spat.

"Leven!" she cried. "Le—"

A whip slammed into her back, knocking the air out of her, and the men laughed. Another whip cracked, and the camel she lay across brayed and began to move. She heard the other beasts walking around her. Maya bounced across the saddle, wounded, blind, tied up.

The eagles did not grab me, and the scorpion did not sting me, Maya thought. *But the desert is full of many beasts.*

The bone-raiders carried her onward—perhaps to slavery, perhaps to death, riding through the heat and light of a foreign land.

ATALIA

S he was rowing in the bowels of the ship, her rage fueling her weary bones, when the world exploded with fire, screams, and blood.

The night had begun like any other. A bowl of gruel for each galley slave, a sickening sludge thick with hairs and grains of dirt. Hushed conversation and tears and prayers. Old Zekeria whispered about his slain sons. Joyada, once a priest in Zohar, led a few slaves in prayer, while Tuja, an old Nurian, whispered to the spirits of forebears. And more rowing. Always rowing. Moving ever onward toward Aelar, day after night, week after week.

They said the journey would take twenty days, but already Atalia felt as if she had been chained here for eras, the passing of seasons and the rise and fall of empires. She could barely remember her life outside this ship. Once she had been a warrior. Once she had been the daughter of a great lord. Once she had stood on the walls of a city, defending her homeland with sword and sling. Once she had been part of a family, had eaten lavish meals in a villa under a painting of elephants, had been loved.

That Atalia was dead. That Atalia seemed but a dream, a faded memory of a memory.

Now she was nothing but a slave.

No. She ground her teeth, and her knuckles whitened around the oar. *Not a slave. Never a slave. Still a fighter.*

She looked over at Daor who sat at her side. His beard was still short but tangled into a shaggy, sweaty mess. His hair hung across his brow, matted with dirt. The stripes of whips still bled across his back, and the chains had bloodied his ankle. He looked like she must have looked—a haggard, beaten, dying wretch. But he was still her soldier.

"We are lions, soldier," she whispered to him, tasting sweat and blood on her lips.

He nodded, moving the oar they shared. "We are lions, Commander."

She was going to reach over, to touch his hand before an overseer could walk by, to show him that she still cared for her soldiers. That she cared for him. She had released her oar, for just that breath, when the world crashed.

Screams.

Blood.

A beast of iron and shattering wood, filling the air.

Blazing fire.

The ram slammed into the hull, shattering slats of wood, snapping oars, snapping men. Shaped like a dragon's head, the iron plowed through galley slaves, a great beast of metal, eyes ablaze with fire. A man fell, skull crushed. A woman screamed, knocked down, her skin and flesh tearing off as the iron dragon pulled back.

"Commander!" Daor cried.

The bench they sat on shattered. They fell, covering their eyes against the showering chips of wood. Their chains rattled, dragging against the floor, and slaves screamed around them.

The ship tilted madly. It seemed to rear in the water like a breaching whale. For an instant, a horrible instant of terror, Atalia gazed through the hole the iron dragon had left in the hull.

And she saw war. She saw death.

Dozens of enemy ships were sailing through the night, dragon rams thrusting out from their prows. On their decks stood burly, bearded soldiers in fur, wielding axes and torches, their hair golden and their faces painted.

"War!" roared a legionary somewhere above. "Archers, fi—!"

Before Atalia could hear more, the ship slammed down, and water gushed into the hull.

The stream was black, cold, stinging her wounds. Atalia screamed and tugged at her chains, but they were still fastened to the floor. Men and women cried out around her. Above her head, she heard feet thump across the deck, heard the muffled cry of legionaries.

We're going to drown. Terror constricted Atalia's chest. She couldn't breathe. She couldn't see. *We're going to die.*

"Commander!" Daor grabbed her arm.

She gasped for air. The water rushed around her feet, tugging her down, making the chains even heavier. A slat of wood dug into her shoulder.

I can't. I can't breathe. I'm going to die. I can't move.

The ram slammed into the ship again, tearing through slaves only *amot* away from her. A man fell before her, ribs snapped, skull shattered. An oar drove forth like a javelin, impaling another slave through the belly.

Again that terror seized Atalia. That terror she had felt upon the walls of Gefen. Overwhelming. Sweat drenched her. Water splashed over her. The blood of her fellow slaves coated her.

A coward. A coward. I'm a coward. I can't breathe.

There was fire. Fire in the ship. But she could barely see. Blackness spread across her vision, and Atalia realized she was going to faint, and in the shadows she saw it again: Gefen falling. Her soldiers dying. Her father on the cross.

"Commander!" Daor cried again, grabbing her, tugging on her chains.

She stared at him, blinking. His face floated before her through the darkness.

No. Not all my soldiers are dead.

She sucked in air, and she leaped to her feet.

"Come on, soldier!" she cried. "Out of these chains! Tug, tug!"

They yanked at their chains together. The water kept rushing in. With the hull shattering around them, a few slaves had managed to free themselves, only for the ram to slam into the ship, crushing them. They fell. Other slaves trampled them. Through holes in the hull, Atalia could see the battle: dozens of ships slamming into one another, and soldiers leaping from deck to deck, and flaming arrows filling the night.

She wrapped the chains around her wrist. She stared at Daor.

They gave a mighty yank. Underwater, the floorboards creaked.

The water kept rushing in. The ship rocked madly. Fire blazed. Smoke filled the hull. Above deck, she heard men scream, smelled burning flesh. Flaming arrows streaked through the air outside, and one flew into the hold, hitting a chained slave.

The ram slammed into the ship again, and wood and fire and iron filled the air.

The ship shattered.

Atalia screamed and tugged the chains.

The floorboards collapsed beneath her, and water gushed upward, frothing. She kicked her legs, and she was swimming.

"Soldier, swim!" Atalia cried. "That's an order!"

She grabbed Daor, pulling him, tugging his chains until they too came free from the shattering floor. They swam. What remained of the ship spun around them, and corpses floated, thumping into them.

They plowed through the dead. Chains still dangled from their ankles, dragging through the water. Atalia swung her oar before her, clearing a path through the corpses. With deafening cracks, wooden slats shattered, one by one, thrusting into the hold like the teeth of a giant. The water kept gushing from below. With a roar and grumble like a drowning god, the ship tilted, the stern thrusting into the air. The water churned in a maelstrom as the galley began to sink.

Atalia swam.

She swam through the dark, bloody water.

She swam through the blood washing Gefen.

She swam through a nightmare of dead, of falling kingdoms, of deserts burning, of sand, endless sand and eagles above.

She reached out her hand. The beasts below pulled her legs, hungry gods of waterdepth, chewing, pulling, eating her alive. The chain on her ankle became as a living thing, a serpent of metal, chewing, pulling, drowning her.

But still Atalia swam and still she reached upward, a single hand rising from the inferno.

We are lions.

She roared, unable to hear her own cry over the din.

Hear, O Zohar! Ours is the light.

Darkness fell. Shadows enveloped her. The water tugged her, black as memory.

Join us. Join our kingdoms of water. Rest. Sleep.

Through the darkness, light. The light of fire. The light of Zohar. Light above. A moon wreathed in fire.

Atalia Sela, daughter of Zohar, warrior of sand, reached up and grabbed the shattering hull.

The jagged wood cut her hand. Her blood dripped down her arm. Still she tugged, screaming, holding onto Daor with her other hand. She pulled herself up, using all her strength, all the strength she had mustered in the battle of Gefen, for here was the great battle of her life. She rose toward the light.

She crawled out from the crumbling hold, out into the sea, out into water and salt and flame and ten thousand screaming men.

Fire. Light. Screams.

All around her spread the darkness. Bodies sank. Arrows pierced the sea, their flames extinguishing, leaving trails of steam. A ship's ram, a great iron eagle the size of a man, plunged down before her, churning the water.

Atalia danced in the realm of the dead. In the water, they sank. The corpses of galley slaves. The corpses of legionaries. In every face, she thought she saw Koren. Every face became her father's. A dance macabre in black and red water. Kingdoms washed under the waves of war.

Join us. Dance with us.

Atalia screamed, water in her mouth. She kicked, her chain rattling.

Not this night. I am a lioness. I will roar.

Her head rose from the surface, and she gulped down smoke and foam. She swam.

She stared around her, trying to see, to make sense of the chaos. The naval battle raged around her. Slick galleys were charging against the Aelarian fleet. They were shaped as dragons, complete with snarling rams of iron, and dragons reared upon their sails and standards. Their many oars rose and fell, and their warriors were tall, burly, and pale, their hair long and blond, their eyes blue.

"Gaelians," Atalia whispered, eyes wide.

She had rarely seen Gaelians. Sometimes they visited the port in Gefen, traders from the snowy northern lands, come to swap furs, iron ore, and strong spicy spirits in exchange for Zoharite perfumes, vellum, and silverwork. Atalia—with her olive skin, black hair, and dark eyes—had always marveled at these travelers with their snowy skin, golden hair, and sapphire eyes. Aelarians tended to be paler than Zoharites, but they appeared downright swarthy by the Gaelians. The northerners had always seemed beautiful to Atalia, mystical creatures like spirits from a tale.

But she had never seen Gaelians like these. Here were no enchanted traders from distant lands of magic. Here were *warriors,* brutish, barbaric. Blue and orange paint coiled across their faces, and they roared, baring sharp teeth. Tattoos rippled across their muscles, and their axes swung into legionaries, tearing open armor, cracking shields. The men sported flowing yellow beards, chinking with bone beads, and women fought among them, golden demons with horned helms, shrieking, swinging axes and hammers, terrible to behold. They were tall, beefy people, the largest Atalia had ever seen, and suddenly she thought Gaelians more like beastly giants than kindly spirits.

No wonder Aelar failed to subjugate them, Atalia thought. *Here are true warriors. And I'm a warrior too.*

"Come on, soldier!" She grabbed Daor. "Swim. To those dragons! Swim!"

They swam, navigating through the battle. Around them, soldiers and slaves drowned. Arrows flew everywhere. Legionaries blew horns, beat drums, and tossed javelins toward the enemy ships. Barbarians and legionaries battled on the deck of a *quinquereme* galley. Atalia saw a Gaelian woman, blond braids swinging, slice her axe across an Aelarian's belly, sending entrails flying like serpents from a basket. A legionary drove his sword upward, piercing a Gaelian's chin, driving the blade out the top of his head. Atalia kept swimming, heading away from the Aelarian vessels. Smoke hid the stars and moon, and the burning sails lit the night.

She was weak, wounded, weary. She was too thin, too famished, too haunted. The sea kept tugging her, and an arrow scraped across her hip. But Atalia kept swimming. Her arms kept rowing. She was inside the hull again, moving that oar. Rowing forward. Rowing with her arms. Stroke by stroke. Ignoring the pain. Pain was irrelevant. Pain could no longer stop her. She would keep stroking. She would live. She was a lioness.

And all the while, Daor swam at her side. Bleeding, his breath rattling, but never leaving his commander. Always her soldier.

They swam around a sinking ship. Corpses floated around them. Other survivors swam here too, arrows picking them out. Atalia kept searching for Koren, trying to see him, calling his name. But he never answered. Several Aelarian ships were still afloat; did he row inside them?

"Koren!" she cried. "Damn you, Koren, where are you?"

The only answers were the cries of legionaries and Gaelians.

"The galley slaves escape!" The voice rose from above, shrill, twisted with rage. "Shoot them down! Sink the slaves!"

Atalia turned toward the voice. Past sinking corpses and floating jetsam, she saw him. He stood on the deck of the *Aquila Aureum*, the flagship of the fleet. Seneca Octavius.

The man who murdered my father.

Atalia was tempted to swim toward him, to climb the deck, to pummel the smirking princeling. But around Seneca, legionaries raised their bows. A hailstorm of arrows flew.

"Commander, down!" Daor said, grabbing her.

They sank underwater. Arrows pierced the surface and sank around them. One arrow scraped across her. Atalia swam lower, then kicked her legs. The chain kept tugging her ankle, dragging her down, but she forced herself to keep swimming underwater. Daor swam with her. An arrow slammed into his own chain and shattered.

They rose over the surface, gasped for air, and saw the battle around them in the night, the ships burning, the arrows flying. Ahead, Atalia spotted one of the dragon galleys. She sank again.

She swam, nudging Daor onward. He swam with her.

The dragon ship loomed above them. Its figurehead was forged of dark iron, forming the head of the dragon, complete with horns and blazing red eyes. On the ship's deck rose the barbarians, wreathed in shadows and flame like demons of Ashael. Dragons snarled on their shields, and even their axe heads were shaped like the beasts. Several of their archers, clad in furs, raised their bows.

Atalia hissed, trapped between Seneca on one side and the Gaelians on the other. Daor swam beside her, blood seeping.

The northern warriors tugged back their bowstrings, aiming at Atalia and her soldier.

"Fuck Aelar!" Atalia shouted, waving her hands in the water. "Sons of Gael, hear me! Fuck Aelar and fuck Emperor Marcus Octavius!"

She spoke in Aelarian, a language understood around the Encircled Sea by anyone with a pinch of education. She took grim satisfaction knowing that Seneca, approaching from behind her, could hear too.

"Fuck Aelar!" Daor shouted at her side.

"And fuck Prince Seneca right in his ass!" Atalia cried, voice hoarse. "Gaelians, I am Atalia Sela of Zohar! I fight with you. Pull me aboard, and I'll slay Aelarians for you!"

Arrows whistled behind her. Atalia glanced over her shoulder to see the *Aquila Aureum* charging, firing at her. She sank, pulling Daor down with her, narrowly dodging the hailstorm. Even in the water, she heard the barbarians roar, saw their oars stroke, propelling their dragon galley onward.

When she raised her head again from the water, the ships slammed together.

The eagle ram of Aelar's ship crashed into the Gaelian hull, shattering wood, snapping oars. The blond barbarians roared, ran across their deck, and leaped onto the imperial galley. While the Gaelians fought wildly, every man for himself, the Aelarians fought as a single being. Across their deck, they formed a wall of shields, spears thrusting out from the enclosure. A wooden fortress rose upon the deck, and from its battlements flew arrows.

Atalia kept swimming. She reached the Gaelian hull, dragging Daor behind her.

"Gaelians!" she cried. "Pull me up! We fight with you!"

One of the barbarians stood on the deck above, a scruffy man with a golden beard. He tossed a rope down to her, calling out in his language, which Atalia didn't understand. She grabbed the rope, and Daor—wounded, panting Daor, her loyal soldier—clung on with her.

Hope swelled in Atalia for the first time since Gefen had fallen. She began to climb.

I will fight again. She grinned savagely. *I will kill legionaries. I will end what I began in Gefen.* She pulled herself up the rope, feet clambering against the hull. *I found a new army to fight with.*

"Atalia, you fucking bitch!" rose a voice behind her, twisted with mad laughter. "Atalia Sela, the Whore of Zohar!"

Clinging to the roof, halfway up the hull, Atalia turned her head.

She saw him there, standing at the prow of his ship, charging toward her, grinning an insane grin.

"Seneca," she hissed.

He cackled madly, arms spread out, the oars of his ship stroking like the legs of a demonic millipede. The vessel came charging toward her, its eagle-head ram gleaming. There was death and madness in Seneca's eyes.

Behind the prince stood Ofeer.

Atalia's rage exploded. She glared past Seneca, focusing all her hatred upon her sister. Ofeer, the traitor, stood clad in an Aelarian stola, her eagle pendant shining.

"Traitor!" Atalia screamed, still dangling from the rope. "You killed him! You killed Father! You—"

"Commander!" Daor cried, grabbing her.

Seneca's ship charged, and its iron ram drove toward them.

Daor kicked off the hull of the Gaelian ship they were climbing, pulling Atalia with him. They swung on the rope.

"Atalia!" Ofeer cried.

"Die, whore!" Seneca cackled.

The eagle ram slammed into the dragon galley with an explosion of wood and water.

Atalia and Daor swung on their rope.

The galley shattered. Gaelians cried out and fell. Oars snapped. The ram pulled back, drove forward again, and crashed through the Gaelian hull. The sailor who had tossed down the rope screamed and fell overboard. The rope snapped. Atalia and Daor fell.

The dragon galley—their hope for rescue—collapsed and sank.

Gaelians screamed, drowning. The arrows of legionaries filled the water. More imperial ships kept storming forth, plowing into the northern barbarians. Legionaries tossed their javelins.

"Damn you, Ofeer!" Atalia cried, back in the water. "Curse you, Seneca!"

She tried to swim toward them, to board the *Aquila Aureum*, to kill them both with her bare hands. But Daor was pulling her away from the wreckage. They kicked madly, sinking, rising again. The water foamed and ash rained.

All around, in the water, the Gaelian ships sank. The golden-haired warriors floundered, clumsy, heavy, drowning. Above the din, Seneca laughed—a mad, inhuman laughter.

"Commander, we have to go," Daor said. "Swim! With me!"

He tried to pull her away from Seneca and Ofeer. Atalia thrashed, trying to free herself, to swim toward them. "I'm not done fighting! We are lions! We—"

"We are done!" Daor said. "Look around you, Commander. The Gaelians are being slaughtered. There's no hope here. Swim with me!"

She looked around her. She saw that he was right. The Gaelians were collapsing under the onslaught. On the Aelarian decks, the northern raiders fell before the shields and spears of the legions. Their dragon galleys, though fearsome in appearance, shattered before the eagle rams. Only two Aelarian ships had sunk. Twenty or more Gaelian galleys were listing, burning, and sinking into the black sea.

"There's no force that can resist the Empire," Daor said, bobbing in the water. "Not in the Encircled Sea. A hundred nations of the coasts fought them, but the fleet of Aelar wins every battle. Come, Commander. Swim! To safety."

"I will not flee from battle." Tears filled her eyes. The wreckage of the dragon galley—her hope for salvation—burned before her, sinking. Beyond the flames and smoke, they still waited. Seneca, the man who had murdered her father. Ofeer, her half sister, who had betrayed them all, who had doomed Zohar. Atalia had to reach them, to kill them. And she had to find Koren, who must still be imprisoned in one of these ships.

More arrows flew, and Daor tugged her, pulling her underwater.

Atalia swam with him.

They sank in the darkness. They rose, gasped for air, sank again. They swam onward.

I'm sorry. I'm sorry, Koren. Her tears flowed into the sea. *I'm sorry.*

It seemed hours that they floundered in the water, their strength waning, before they moved far from the light of the fires, swimming into deep, enveloping darkness. Smoke and clouds hid the moon, and the only light came from the distant ships, moving farther away.

A slab of a ship's hull, large as a raft, floated before them. Atalia and Daor climbed onto the wood, shuddering, coughing, chains still dangling from their ankles. They huddled together.

"Commander, we're safe now," Daor said. "We're safe."

Atalia lay on the makeshift raft, coughing, barely able to breathe. With what remained of her strength, she held Daor's hand.

"We're safe, soldier," she whispered.

But she knew that she was lying. In the darkness, she watched the lights sail away—sail west, sail toward Aelar, leaving behind the wreckage of the Gaelian assault.

For just a few moments, hope rose, Atalia thought. *For just a few heartbeats, I thought that I could fight again, that I found a new army. Now that hope sinks around me with thousands of corpses. Now we're truly alone.*

Daor wrapped his arms around her, and Atalia lowered her head, lost at sea and in shadow.

EPHER

They stood in the garden, staring at the tomb, contemplating the death or rebirth of a nation.

Epher had never been to Aelar, but his parents had, and Epher had heard the stories. They said that in Aelar, on the northern coast of the Encircled Sea, gardens were lush pieces of paradise. Grass rustled across them, and flowers of every kind grew from rich, moist soil.

Here, in the heart of Beth Eloh, sand covered the garden rather than grass. No flowering shrubs grew here but only scattered thistles, thorny and hard like the people of this desert city. Even the tomb was not some grand, marble mausoleum like a place where Aelar would bury a king, a marvel of architecture boasting columns and engravings and statues. No. This tomb was a simple cave on the hillside, a great round stone stoppering its yawn.

Yet here, Epher thought, was one of the holiest places in Zohar—indeed in the world. Here was the tomb of King Elshalom himself, first monarch of Zohar—his ancestor.

Elshalom was not the founder of the nation. That honor went back to Adom himself, the first man to have heard the word of Eloh, to have seen the light of Luminosity in the desert, to have gathered followers, forging the nation of Zohar. Yet Adom was a figure of ancient myth, a prophet who had lived thousands of years before Elshalom, and none knew of his burial place; some claimed that Adom was merely a legend. This tomb of Elshalom, the first monarch, the man who had united the tribes of Zohar into a kingdom—here lay true bones, a thousand years old. Here had begun the dynasty that flowed down into Epher's own blood.

Shiloh stood at Epher's side, gazing with him at the tomb. She was only forty years old, still young, still beautiful. Epher thought her the most beautiful woman in Zohar. Yet sadness lay upon Shiloh Sela, a great weight, almost a physical thing that seemed to crush her. The hint of wrinkles tugged at her tanned skin, and the first strands of white had invaded her braid. A widow. One of her children dead, the others missing—all but him.

How does she go on? Epher thought, looking at his mother. *How does she find this strength?*

She was a small woman. Epher must have weighed twice as much or nearly so. Yet he felt that his mother was stronger than them all, than any soldier who still lived in this city.

"Did you know," she said, standing here in the garden, "this city was already two thousand years old when King Elshalom united the tribes of Zohar, when he made us a kingdom. Since his reign, we've lived united, but before that the tribes fought, killed, burned, destroyed. We were weak. We nearly vanished, just another nation falling to sand like so many others. King Elshalom brought us peace. Epher, I know you seek more war. I know you seek to resist the eagles. But the time for peace is here."

"The time for peace ended when Seneca Octavius murdered Father," Epher said.

Warblers chirruped in a nearby fig tree, picking at the fruit. Epher had a horrible memory of the crows picking at the corpses after Yohanan's battle. Shiloh turned toward him.

"We've been conquered before," she said. "The Sekadians sacked this city six hundred years ago, took the tribes of Zohar captive, and enslaved us for a century. A thousand years before that, we were slaves in Nur. Only a century ago, the Kalintians invaded our land, butchered us, forced us to worship their idols. Yet we survived. Whenever we were exiled, we returned home. Whenever our land was destroyed, we rebuilt. A dozen times, Beth Eloh fell to an invader, century after century. And we're still here. The nation of Zohar still stands, eternal."

"We're stubborn bastards," Epher agreed. "And hard to kill."

Shiloh lowered her head. "We are very easy to kill. Epher, we're dealing with something different this time. An enemy such as our ancestors have never faced. Before you were born, I sailed around the Encircled Sea. I saw what remained of those kingdoms that defied Aelar."

"Ruins." Epher couldn't help but shudder.

"Sand," said Shiloh. "Nothing but sand on the coast. Ruins would be something—a memory at least. The Aelarians left *nothing.* Entire kingdoms crumbled into grains of sand, lost to history. If we resist Aelar, that will be our fate too."

Epher squared his shoulders. "You yourself said that we've survived the Nurians, the Sekadians, the Kalintians, the—"

"All nations that sought to enslave, to steal, to destroy."

"And what does Aelar seek?"

"To *govern*," Shiloh said. "To *civilize*. That's how they see it. They envision a single empire across the world. They will make us part of this empire, whether we wish it or not. They will build aqueducts, bathhouses, paved roads, schools, amphitheaters—"

"Schools to teach their own stories," Epher said. "Amphitheaters where gladiators fight and die in human cockfights."

"Better than all of us dying. And if you do what I fear—if you take that dagger I've seen you hide, if you raise it against Aelar—that is what will happen. All of us dying. And in a year or two, some other girl will sail by our coast, and she will see nothing but sand, and she will not know our name. Aelar wants us to *live*, Epher. To live on our knees, yes. To speak Aelarian, watch their plays and gladiators, maybe even fight in their wars. But is a life of servitude not better than the fall of a nation?"

"Maybe not," Epher said.

She glared at him. "Then you're a fool. Then you're not the son I raised. It is life—life itself!—that is holy, that matters, not whom we bow to."

"I bow to no one," Epher said.

"Only emperors and dead men bow to no one. Which do you think more likely that you'll become?" Shiloh's voice softened, and she embraced him. "Please, Epher. Bend the knee to Shefael and Governor Remus. Serve the Empire and abandon your thoughts of rebellion. Bury that dagger that you smuggled into Beth Eloh—yes, I know of it—and encourage all others to bow too. I already lost one son to the grave, and all my other children are dispersed. I cannot lose you too."

She was weeping now, and Epher held her in his arms.

"You won't lose me, Mother," he said. "I promise."

It was not what she wanted to hear. He knew that. But it was all he could say to her this day.

He left her in the sand garden, and he walked through the city. Life was slowly returning to Beth Eloh. A boy rode a camel down a cobbled street, brass pots and pans jangling in the saddlebags. An old man led two donkeys down the road, the beasts carrying rolls of fabric. A few children were playing with apricot seeds, competing to toss them into a clay box drilled with holes.

Epher made his way through the marketplace. Alleyways snaked between brick homes, holding a bustling hive. Vendors sat on tasseled rugs, selling their wares from tin platters. The smells of cardamom and cumin tickled the nostrils, and an old lady was roasting spiced fava beans, selling them in cloth packets. Little shops peered alongside the alley like caves, glittering with brass pots, silver statuettes, colored glass beads, geodes, bracelets and earrings shaped as serpents, olivewood camels with zirconia eyes, and countless other trifles and treasures.

Past the marketplace, Epher walked down a cobbled road under the Mount of Cedars, a hill green with olive and cedar trees. He stared up at the vast, glittering acropolis upon the hill. Walls surrounded the complex, and beyond them soared the Temple, the center of Zohar's faith in Eloh, the Lord of Light. The building was the largest in Zohar, dwarfing even the palace beside it, carved of white stone and topped with a crown of gold. Even from down here, Epher could hear the priests chanting and blowing ram horns.

Is Mother right? Epher thought. *If we rise up, if we fight again, will all this city—thousands of houses, the marketplace, the palace, the Temple— all fall, all be ground to sand?*

Everywhere Epher walked here—from humble residential streets to markets to the holy Mount of Cedars—he saw the legionaries. They stood in armor, even in the sweltering sun, spears in hand, swords hanging from their belts. Their shields bore the names and symbols of their units: Legio VII *Feratta*, the Ironclad, their sigil a bull; Legio V *Victrix*, the Victorious, the crowned eagles; Legio XIII *Lamina*, the blades, eagles clutching swords.

Most of the legionaries seemed to be ethnic Aelarians. They stood taller than most Zoharites, and fairer too. Their skin ranged from olive-toned to a rich cream, their hair from black to light brown. Most had brown eyes, but many had gray, green, and even blue eyes, colors rare among Zoharites. Meanwhile, the soldiers from Legio XIII—eagles holding blades on their shields—didn't seem to be native Aelarians. Some had the dark brown skin of Nurians, others the tall carriage, blue eyes, and blond hair of those who dwelled in the northern provinces of Denegar and Elania.

Auxiliaries, Epher realized. *Men conscripted from conquered lands.*

He wondered how long before Zoharites too served in this military machine, before Shefael's own troops—ten thousand warriors who had fought against Yohanan—would don the lorica segmentata and bear the gladius swords of the Empire. The Zoharites had been disarmed, their armor and swords confiscated, but how long before they were forced to wear new armor, to bear new blades, to swear fealty to Marcus Octavius—to go conquer foreign lands in his name? The thought sickened Epher.

Every autumn in his childhood, Epher and his family would make a pilgrimage to Beth Eloh for the harvest festival—all but Maya, who was forbidden to approach this fountain of lume. They would stay in the palace with Aunt Sifora, Queen of Zohar, and walk across the hills, all in white, to pray in the Temple. His mother still dwelled in the palace, even now, but Epher did not crave to set foot there ever again. Shefael now ruled there—cowardly, treacherous Shefael. His cousin perhaps now wore a crown and sat on Sifora's throne, but he was nothing but a slave to Governor Remus Marcellus.

Instead of walking to the palace, Epher traveled down quiet streets of stone. Houses rose around him, built of limestone bricks and topped with domes. A donkey walked across a courtyard, carrying a wagon, its wheels rattling against the cobblestones. Doves pecked for seeds, and a few palm trees rose from rings of stone. Epher made his way toward a house, a small and simple abode with pale brick walls and a white dome. He had paid the owner in gold, renting the house—a private place, far from Shefael, far from Remus Marcellus, far from Avinasi.

A place to hide away. To plan. To nurse his anger.

Epher stepped inside to find Olive lying on the tabletop, blowing on a feather, struggling to keep it afloat just above her mouth. She was naked, her skin golden in the light that shone between the curtains, and her hair was a pyre of flame.

When she heard him enter, she leaped up, blowing the feather aside. She bounded toward him. "Epher and Olive!" she said proudly. "Epher … Epher …" She frowning and chewed her lip, then grinned. "Epher back come!"

"Epher came back," he corrected her.

"Epher came back, Epher came back!" She ran in circles, hooting. "Epher go away. Now Epher came back."

He groaned. "Olive, remember what I told you about being naked? Part of belonging to civilization means wearing clothes."

She paused from running and pointed out the window. "Civization. There." She pointed at the floor. "Here no civization. Here naked."

He couldn't help but spend a moment admiring her. After many threats and cajoling, he had finally—only this morning—convinced Olive to wash herself. She had put up a fight, squealing when he brought in the basin of water, escaping naked down the street, and finally coming back only when he threatened to toss

169

out her bow and arrow. It had been another battle to brush her hair. She had cursed every foul word she knew, snapped one hairbrush in half, and nearly bit off his arm, but finally he had managed to untangle her wild red mane.

Right now, cleaned and brushed, Olive was a new person. No longer Hungry, the wild beast he had met on the beach. No longer Red, the crazy rambler the hillsfolk spoke of. Finally—a true woman of Zohar.

When he had met her, years of filth had covered her. Mud had hidden her skin, and leaves and dust had caked her hair into a matted paste. But now ... now she appeared as a young, beautiful woman. Her skin was pale as a Gaelian's, almost white, and strewn with countless freckles. Her orange hair hung down to her chin; he had been forced to cut off the rest, unable to remove the worst of the tangles. Her nose was small and upturned, her eyes green. With her pale skin, fiery hair, and emerald eyes, she didn't look much like a typical Zoharite. Epher sometimes wondered whether she had come from a distant land, perhaps the daughter of a foreign merchant, lost here in infancy. Perhaps Olive's origin would forever remain a mystery, but her future they could mold together. A future here, in the land of Eloh.

"You're not a wild beast," he said softly. "You're a human. A real human. A smart one, aren't you?"

She nodded. "Olive smart."

He found the tunic he had given her, lifted it from the floor, and pulled it over her arms. "We might not have civilization indoors, but I won't be able to concentrate on teaching you if you're naked." It was a struggle to not keep looking. "Now, are you ready to learn more words?"

She nodded, the tunic pulled down to her knees. "Ready."

Over the past few days, Epher had been teaching her, and she had been learning fast. Every day her vocabulary grew. He was surprised by her intelligence. She wasn't only learning a new language. She was learning her *first* language, learning the very concept of what language was. Epher looked forward to the day—even if it was months away—when she knew enough words to tell her story, tell him where she had grown up, why she had never learned how to speak.

Over the past few days, he had taken her through the city, pointing out everything they passed—dogs, cats, donkeys, camels, horses, houses, trees, boys, girls ... teaching her every word. She had learned much, forgotten much, relearned, and kept practicing, kept prattling.

But the outside world—this civilization—had become unpleasant to Epher. He had seen how the people looked at her, heard them scoff.

"Halfwit," a man once said, shaking his head.

"Wild beast," a legionary had called her.

When Olive had begun to repeat those words—proudly calling herself a halfwit and beast—Epher had decided to spend a day indoors.

They walked into the second chamber and sat on the bed, and Epher pointed at her hand.

"Hand," he said.

She nodded. "And. Epher and Olive!"

"No." He shook his head and pointed at her hand again. "*Ha*nd. With an H. Hand."

She lifted her hand and examined it, brow furrowed, then looked up at him quizzically. "Hand?"

He nodded and pointed at her leg. "Leg."

She pointed at his leg. "Leg. Epherleg." Back to herself. "Oliveleg."

He touched her hair. "Hair."

She pointed at her head. "Air."

"No. Not your head. Your hair. Here." He stroked her hair. "Hair. With an H again. Hair."

She leaned closer to him and touched his hair. "Hair."

He brought his fingers down to her cheek. "Cheek."

She caressed his beard. "Cheek," she whispered.

"Lips," he said.

She moved closer. "Lips," she whispered. Suddenly she blushed and looked away. "Olive scared."

He found that he couldn't stop stroking her hair. He wanted to stop. This was wrong. He forced his hand back. It felt like ripping off a part of him.

"Why are you scared?" he asked.

She looked back at him and lifted his hand. "Hand," she whispered, raised it, and pulled his fingers to her hair. "Hand and hair." Her voice was barely a whisper. "Lips."

He did not know who initiated it. He did not know if he leaned toward her, she toward him, or both together. But before he could understand how, he was kissing her. Just softly at first, a mere peck on the lips, then a deeper kiss, his hands in her hair, her arms wrapped around him.

"Lips," she repeated. "Epher and Olive lips."

"Kiss," he said.

She frowned. "What is kiss?"

"This." He kissed her again.

Staring into his eyes, she pulled her tunic off again and tossed it aside. She sat naked beside him on the bed, their bodies pressed together. "Teach more." She pulled his hands down to her breasts. "Teach Olive."

That evening, he taught her all the words of their bodies, over and over as they made love, moving naked in the bed as the sun set.

Epher had made love to women before—to Claudia Valerius, daughter of Aelar's old ambassador, and once to Karin, the daughter of a chandler in Gefen. Olive made him forget those other women. Her lovemaking was a wild thing, like fire, burning across him, an animal act. She cried out loudly, not caring that neighbors might hear. She bit his shoulder, nearly tearing the skin, and wrapped her legs around him, squeezing him, calling out all those words he had taught her.

It seemed hours that they made love. When they were done, they lay in the darkness together, coated in sweat, panting, the room sweltering. He lay on his back, and she nestled against him, cooing, her fingers exploring his body.

"Chest," she whispered, stroking him. "Belly." She reached farther down and closed her fingers around him. She frowned and looked at him quizzically. "Stick?"

He laughed. He had taught her that word yesterday when finding a branch on the street. He nodded. "Stick."

She laid her cheek on his chest and closed her eyes. "Olive tired. Olive sleep now."

"*I* am tired," he corrected her.

She nodded. "Epher sleep."

Soon she was sleeping, her breath tickling his chest. He stroked back locks of her damp hair and kissed her forehead.

I want to stay here forever with you, he thought. *I never want to leave this bed.*

Maybe his mother had been right. Maybe it was best to bend the knee, to live under Aelar's rule, to send children to the Empire's schools, to see their marble idols rise in the city, to serve in the legions. To survive. To live. To spend his life with Olive, here in this home. Part of a cruel empire, yes—but still alive. Still with her.

But in the darkness, Epher still saw it. The death outside the walls. The slaughter of Yohanan and his men. In his mind, he still heard the words: the news of his father dying, of Koren and Atalia shipped off to slavery, of Maya fleeing the legions into the desert. How could he submit now? How could he forget thousands slaughtered here, their blood crying out from the earth?

He could not. Even as he held Olive in his arms, Epher knew that he could not abandon this fight. He was still a warrior of Zohar, his father's heir, heir to a land stolen from him. With Jerael dead, it was Epher who now ruled the Sela house—a house fragmented and scattered across the world. He would not forget his duty. He would fight on—whatever way he still could.

Still lying with Olive against him, Epher reached one hand down, lifted the edge of the mattress, and touched the hilt of the dagger he hid there—a dagger that would mean his body on the cross should the legionaries find it.

"The road is still dark," he whispered to Olive. She mumbled and stirred in her sleep, and he kissed her. "I'm glad you're with me."

ATALIA

The sea rose and fell. Twilight spilled across sky and water, and a million stars shone, and dawn gilded the sea. The lights of the heavens danced, and all the world became as it had been at creation. Chaos and water. Light and darkness. The moon and sun and the stars. And here, adrift—two small lights. Two specks of consciousness lost in the eternity.

"It is …" Daor coughed and licked his dry lips. Another sunset dripped around them, and the stars emerged. "It is rather beautiful out here, at least."

Clinging to their makeshift raft, Atalia glared at him. "Daor, sweetling?"

"Yes, Commander?"

"Fuck you."

He sighed. "I'm trying to find something positive, Commander."

"In that case, find us some land." She punched him with whatever strength was still in her. "Now keep paddling. North is that way."

Both lay across a chunk of deck, bellies against the wood, legs in the water. It was barely larger than a door, and the only piece left from their sunken ship. They paddled, moving onward across the sea. If any gull had flown above them, the bird would be forgiven for mistaking them for mere slabs of old meat. Their backs still stung with lashes. Their skin peeled, burnt by the sun. Daor's beard was filling out, and their hair hung across their faces, salty and ragged. Atalia couldn't remember how long had passed since the battle. One day? Two? A week? She was too weak to count time, too hungry, too thirsty. She could think only of finding fresh water, finding food, finding solid land to lie on. She kept paddling, kicking through the water. A chain still dangled from her ankle, always threatening to drag her down.

Let go, the chain told her.

Sink into the water, said the hunger in her belly.

Drink the sea, said the thirst.

Atalia wanted to listen to them. She wanted to end this. To sink, to find relief from pain. But whenever she slipped, she ground her teeth, and she brought two faces to mind: Seneca and Porcia.

I will survive this, she vowed. *And I will kill you.*

"How do you know we're moving north?" Daor said, feet splashing in the water.

Atalia pointed. Her voice was hoarse, and every word cracked her lips. "There, soldier. See those stars, the ones shaped like a claw? That's the Lion's Claw constellation."

Daor squinted. "It looks more like a hydra."

"Fine, it's a hydra." She groaned. "See that blue star? The one on top? That's the Lodestar. That always points north. And if

I know anything of the routes of ships, they always sail near the northern coast of the Encircled Sea. Something to do with currents. That means we're near land."

He blinked. "I thought the Lodestar always points east."

Atalia glared at him. "North! I think." She tilted her head. "Wait. Or was it the Evening Star that points north?"

Daor groaned. "Commander! If we're going back east, the distance to land ... by God, it took us two weeks by ship to sail from the eastern port."

"Calm yourself, soldier. We're going north." She looked back at that blue star. "I'm certain. Almost certain. Reasonably sure." She paused. "There's a good chance."

They paddled onward. Atalia kept paddling harder than Daor, spinning them off course, and she had to punch the soldier and get him to keep kicking. She could not tell how fast they moved, how long passed, how far they were. All her life had become pain, thirst, hunger, and paddling. Rowing forward. As the night stretched on, she was back in the belly of the ship, chained to the oar again.

Row, she thought, eyes narrowed. *Row. Row, slave!*

The whips cracked. The ship stank.

Row!

She rowed onward, kicking in the water, lost in the shadows.

Row!

She stood on the wall of Gefen, facing the legions, the soldiers storming up the ramp.

Swing your sword!

She swung her blade.

Stand your ground! Do not fall. Do not die!

With every kick of her legs, with every stroke of her arms, she still fought those legions. She still fought for Zohar. She still fought for her life. Dawn rose, and they swam onward, clinging to their raft, skin raw, lips bleeding.

"Commander?" Daor rasped, eyes red. "I'm going to stop paddling soon."

She turned toward him. "Do not lose hope now, soldier. Never lose hope!" Her voice shook. "I know you're scared. I know you're hopeless. That is when you must fight the hardest. When all hope is lost, you must roar the loudest. Never stop fighting, soldier. So long as you live, never give up. If you can draw another breath, you can fight."

He nodded. "That's nice, Commander, but I'm still going to stop once we're on that beach."

She stared at him, frowning, then whipped her head around. She gasped. Her eyes dampened.

"You bastard," she whispered, then kicked with more vigor. "Come on! Faster! Swim, soldier! Forward!"

They paddled, driving the raft toward the shore. The waves soon caught them, propelling them onward. They rose and fell, nearly losing their raft. The land spread ahead—a rocky beach and beyond it dark forests. They washed onto the shore like two rags, barely strong enough to crawl across the sand. For a long time, Atalia lay on the beach, her face in the sand, coughing, laughing. Daor lay at her side.

"Atalia, look," he whispered.

"It's Commander." She coughed. "We're still at war, soldier."

"Commander, look."

She raised her head from the sand, and she saw it. All across the beach, it lay—the wreckage of the naval battle. A chunk of a mast. An oar. A shattered piece of balustrade. Several barrels and pieces of rope. And two weak, shivering soldiers far from their home, swept ashore with the rest of the remains. Shaking, Atalia struggled to her feet. The world spun around her. Her head pounded. Her lips still bled. A chain still connected to her ankle. But she began to walk, moving across the beach, swaying, falling, rising again.

"Come on, soldier!" she said. "Up! Onward! We need to find some water here, and some food too. Come, we march!"

He struggled to his feet, swaying, and limped after her. "Where are we marching to, Commander?"

She turned toward him and gripped his arms. They stood among the wreckage, gulls cawing overhead, the forest rustling across the sand. "We're still going north, soldier. We'll still follow that blue star. We're going through this forest, through whatever stands in our way. We're going to find the land of Gael. We're going to tell the Gaelians what happened to their comrades at sea." A smile tugged at her lips. "And we're going to fight with them."

Two more steps and she found a barrel in the sand. When she smashed it open, apples spilled out, green and red—Zoharite apples, plundered by the legions. Atalia bit into one and tossed another to Daor. They walked toward the forest, leaving the sea behind, seeking water, seeking hope, seeking war.

OFEER

A
fter twenty days at sea, the victorious fleet returned home.
"Aelar," Ofeer whispered, standing at the prow of
the imperial flagship, tears in her eyes.

For so long, she had dreamed of this. For as long as she
could remember, she had spoken to everyone of sailing to Aelar,
had whispered of Aelar to her dolls, had drawn and sculpted and
sung of Aelar. And here it was. Here, after so long, here was the
land of her father. Here was the home she had craved all her life.

Here was the land she feared.

Ofeer was a daughter of the sea. She had been born and
raised in Gefen, the greatest port city of the east, a thriving
metropolis of many ships and high walls. Standing here at the
prow, approaching Aelar, she realized how tiny Gefen truly was—
no more than a village, a backwater. Here, before her, rose a city
to dwarf all other cities. Here was the heart of an empire. In her
dreams, the city of Aelar—center of the Aelarian Empire—had
always been large, but those dreams had not done it justice.
Before her rose a monster.

Breakwaters thrust into the sea like enveloping arms.
Gefen's harbor had breakwaters too, constructed of many

boulders piled together, forming ridges in the water; Atalia and Koren used to dare each other to walk upon the slippery, mossy stones. But Aelar's breakwaters were marvels of architecture, built of smooth bricks and topped with porticos of columns, and atop each column rose a marble statue, welcoming travelers. Lighthouses rose on artificial islands, and countless ships navigated the waters: merchant barges with red and white sails, military galleys lined with oars, fishermen's boats, and luxury vessels shaded by colorful curtains.

Here, before her, was the fabled Aelaria Maritima, the port of Aelar, the greatest port in the world, the inspiration for a thousand songs and tales, the beating heart of civilization.

And beyond the port, on the shore … Ofeer had never imagined such a place. She had always thought Beth Eloh massive, but Aelar was ten times the size, and not nearly as old and crumbling. Countless buildings rose there, lined with columns, topped with red tiles. Some were villas that rose above gardens and pools; others were more like palaces. Many apartment buildings stood six or seven stories tall, their windows arched. Towers, amphitheaters, statues as tall as mountains—they all soared here, spreading for leagues.

"She's beautiful, isn't she?" Seneca came to stand at her side, dressed in his polished armor of iron and gold. "All that I do, I do for her. For Aelar."

"She's beautiful," Ofeer agreed, unable to speak louder than a whisper. She turned toward Seneca. "Beautiful."

She trembled. So many emotions filled her. Fear for her old family. Fear of being so close to her true father. Fear that she was dreaming, or that this city of wonders held an ugliness she couldn't see from here, the way Seneca's beautiful form hid an ugly heart. She was excited, elated, happier than she'd ever been—but so afraid.

What life will I find here? Ofeer wondered. Would Emperor Marcus—her true father—welcome her into his arms? Or would she have to find her own path, a path of hardship and loneliness? Would she see Atalia here, or had the Gaelians sunk her ship? Was Koren still rowing below this deck, or had he succumbed to disease and exhaustion like so many galley slaves?

Ofeer did not know. She had not dreamed of coming here like this. A thousand times, she had imagined sailing to Aelar, seeking her father—perhaps a famous general, or maybe a wealthy merchant or lord. She had never imagined it like this.

The ship Ofeer and Seneca stood on—the *Aquila Aureum*—led twenty other galleys, all laden with the treasures of conquest: gold, jewels, artwork, and slaves from Zohar. They sailed past the breakwaters and into the cove. Countless ships sailed between them, bearing treasures from other distant lands. The curses and songs of sailors filled the air, gulls cawed, and fish flitted through the water. The statues of the gods rose alongside, and Seneca spoke to Ofeer, telling her the name of each god and goddess. But Ofeer barely listened, and her legs trembled.

So many questions. So much fear. Ofeer clutched the balustrade, never wanting to let go, not sure if she'd dare climb off this ship and set foot on this new land, the land she had dreamed of all her life.

The *Aquila Aureum* docked at a boardwalk lined with marble columns. A statue of a warrior stood atop each pillar, hand raised in salute. Thousands of Aelarians stood along the boardwalk, in the courtyards and streets beyond, and on the balconies of homes, taverns, and workshops. The men wore togas, the women wore flowing stolas, while children and slaves wore tunics. The plebeians could afford only simple fabric, unadorned white linen, but the wealthier citizens sported dyed, embroidered fabrics and wore golden jewels. Both commoners and the wealthy cheered as the ships docked, welcoming home their heroes.

Ofeer herself wore a fine stola now, a gift from Seneca. The flowing linens were dyed mustard and azure, colors Seneca had claimed contrasted well with her olive skin, dark eyes, and black hair. Her platinum eagle pendant hung around her neck—the same pendant she had worn in Gefen to remind her of her true homeland. Yet now, as Ofeer stood here on the prow, seeing the people of Aelar, she felt out of place, self-conscious, even in her new stola. What was her true homeland? Did her eagle pendant still symbolize Aelar, or was it now a symbol of Gefen, where she had first worn it?

I don't look like an Aelarian, she thought. *I'm too dark. My features are too sharp. I look like a Zoharite, dressed in clothes not my own.*

Seneca took her hand. He looked resplendent in the sunlight, the gold gleaming on his breastplate, his cloak woven of rich crimson embroidered with eagle motifs, and his sword hung at his side. A laurel of golden leaves rested upon his brown hair, and a ruby pin hung around his neck.

"See how they cheer for us. Wave to them, Ofeer! Let them see your eastern beauty."

He waved to the crowd, and the cheers rose louder. Hesitantly, hand trembling, Ofeer gave a wave, then quickly lowered her hand.

"Now we will let the city bask in our glory," Seneca said. "We return home victorious with the spoils of war. Our triumphal march begins." He kissed Ofeer's cheek to rising cheers. "Welcome home, Ofeer of Aelar."

The sailors lowered a gangplank, and legionaries disembarked first onto the boardwalk, forming two protective lines, holding back the crowd. Seneca and Ofeer followed. A chariot rolled forth, gilded and jeweled, pulled by four snowy horses with braided manes. Seneca climbed into the chariot, lowered his hand, and helped Ofeer rise and stand beside him.

"Prepared to display your whore?" The voice rose from across the boardwalk. "Lovely spoils of war you have there, brother! You should strip her bare and fuck her for the crowd."

Some in the crowd tittered and jeered. Ofeer's belly curdled. She looked across the boardwalk to see Porcia climb off a second ship. The princess winked at her.

My older sister, Ofeer thought, shuddering.

Porcia's armor was so dark it was almost black. A laurel rested on her head, and she held a shield and spear. She climbed into her own chariot, this one painted black and trimmed with gold. The severed heads of her enemies—soldiers of Zohar—dragged behind the chariot on ropes. Farther back, Porcia's soldiers were manhandling chained slaves off the ship, whipping their backs, and arranging them into lines. Ofeer sought Koren and Atalia among the prisoners but couldn't see them.

Growing up, Ofeer had always thought Atalia intimidating—an older, warlike sister with rage in her eyes. But *this* older sister, this princess of an empire, made Atalia seem no more threatening than a pup. Looking at the leering Porcia, the severed heads, and the whipped slaves, Ofeer suddenly missed Zohar, wanted to return to the ship, wanted to sail back to her home on Pine Hill.

"Ignore her." Seneca's eyes hardened. "Once Father names me his heir, Porcia won't be worthy of kissing your feet. You're mine now, Ofeer. Mine to protect." He squeezed her hand. "We'll tell Father what you said. How I conquered Gefen with blood and iron, while Porcia just forged a deal with a puppet king. He'll name me heir to this empire, and soon it will be Porcia in chains."

He cracked his whip, and his horses took to a trot. The triumphal march began.

The conquerors traveled through the city in two processions: Seneca leading his legionaries and spoils, and Porcia leading hers.

Ofeer stood in the chariot as Seneca waved to the crowds. They moved down a wide boulevard—so wide that both processions easily moved side by side with room to spare. Behind the two chariots marched the legionaries, their armor burnished, bearing the standards of Aelar—golden eagles on staffs. Wagons rolled behind the soldiers, holding the spoils of war: jewels, coins, and artwork plundered from Gefen, from the northern hills, from the vanquished hosts of Yohanan.

Living spoils were displayed too: captives of war. Hundreds of Zoharites walked between the legionaries, wearing loincloths, bleeding, beaten, chains hobbling their ankles. Thousands of people lined the roadsides, cheering as the victors marched by and booing the captives.

"Zoharite rats!" shouted a woman in the crowd, tossing mud onto the slaves.

"Desert whores!" a bald man cried and hurled a stone at the slaves, hitting a Zoharite woman.

Others in the crowd joined them, tossing rocks, rotten fruit, and excrement at the chained slaves. One Zoharite fell, and legionaries whipped him, tearing open his back, then yanked him up and shoved him onward.

Ofeer winced and turned toward Seneca, wanting him to stop this. But the prince didn't even seem to notice the violence. He was still waving, smiling at the crowd as behind the chariot the slaves bled. In the second chariot, Porcia was waving too as the severed heads dragged behind her. The princess noticed Ofeer looking and winked.

Help them, Eloh, Ofeer silently prayed. *Let this city be smaller than it seems. Let this march of bloodshed end quickly.*

She looked ahead again, gazing at the city before her, the heart of an empire. Ofeer was used to large cities; she had spent many harvest festivals in Beth Eloh, a city of a hundred thousand souls. But she had never seen a place of such splendor. Here was everything she had always dreamed of. Soaring temples on grassy hills, their columns white as snow, golden statues on their roofs. Palaces that rose from lush gardens of flowers and cypresses. Countless elegant homes—each a mansion by Zoharite standards—topped with red tiles, not just clay domes like back home. Even the poor lived in apartment blocks that rose seven stories tall; Ofeer had never seen buildings this tall aside from Zohar's palace and Temple in Beth Eloh. Aqueducts snaked through the city, three tiers high, delivering water to homes, bathhouses, and gardens. Pillars soared from courtyards, holding aloft statues of winged gods. On a hill ahead, Ofeer saw the Amphitheatrum—a great amphitheater, large enough to enclose a town. Golden statues, taller than the walls of Gefen, gazed down from another hill—one of Marcus Octavius, one of Seneca, one of Porcia.

A city of might and wonder. A city of a million people. The city she had always dreamed of. Here—here right now!—Ofeer was living her dream. She was riding in a golden chariot, a handsome prince holding her hand, as a crowd adored her.

And Ofeer could not take it.

She cared not for this wonder, this gold, these marvels of architecture. She kept looking behind her at the slaves. And finally, as the triumphal march was passing through a courtyard full of statues, Ofeer saw him.

Koren.

Her half brother, son of Jerael and Shiloh, walked among the other slaves. She hadn't been able to see him before, only now as the procession curved to circle a fountain in the courtyard. She barely recognized him. Ofeer had always known Koren to grin, laugh, and hop around like an excited pup. Today he dragged his chained feet. His beard had thickened, and his hair hung across his sweaty brow. Blood and sand still covered him—it must have covered him all the way from Zohar.

She could not see Atalia.

A legionary whipped his back, and Koren fell. His blood spilled. He struggled to his feet and kept walking, coughing, shoulders stooped.

"I have to go to him," Ofeer whispered.

Beside her on the chariot, Seneca was still waving to the crowd. The people surrounded the courtyard and stood on their balconies, cheering for the heroes' return. The prince couldn't hear her over the roar.

Koren fell again, and Ofeer's eyes dampened. Koren—the young man she had once scorned, thinking him nothing but a crude Zoharite, thinking herself a fine Aelarian superior to him. Koren—the boy who had once bandaged her skinned knee, making silly faces until she laughed and forgot the pain. Koren—the brother she had grown up with, wrestled with in the sand, swam with in the sea, laughed with so many times.

Blinking the tears from her eyes, Ofeer leaped off the chariot.

"Ofeer?" Seneca said.

She fell, banging her knees hard on the flagstones, then pushed herself up and ran.

"Ofeer!" Seneca cried, and somewhere in the background, Porcia laughed.

Ofeer ignored them. She ran back through the procession, elbowing her way between legionaries. She had torn her fine stola garment at the knees; she didn't care. She kept running, tears on her cheeks, until she reached him.

"Koren!"

A legionary stood above him, lash raised. Ofeer cried out and raised her hand. The whip slammed into her arm, cutting the skin, but she barely felt the pain. She knelt above her brother. Koren was on his knees, breathing raggedly, coughing, his back torn.

Gently, Ofeer helped him rise and wiped the sweat on his brow with her sleeve. "I'm here, Koren. I'm here with you."

"Where is Atalia?" His voice was raspy. Blood speckled his lips.

"I don't know." Ofeer shuddered. "Maybe she drowned, or maybe she escaped, or—"

"Move, slaves!" The legionary's whip cracked again. Ofeer cried out as the lash hit her back, tearing her stola and skin. The pain was worse than she had imagined. It claimed her, shot through her entire body, rattled her teeth. She had never imagined such pain could exist.

"Come, Koren," she whispered, guiding him onward, her arms wrapped around him. "It's almost over."

They shuffled down the courtyard, past a statue of a god that rose from a fountain, and onto another boulevard. Hundreds of Zoharite captives moved around them, chains rattling. Ofeer knew many by name, more by face; they were the people of Gefen, the people she had grown up with. Hundreds of legionaries moved ahead and behind them, some afoot, others on horseback or riding chariots.

Seneca and Porcia still rode ahead. As Ofeer walked with the captives, letting Koren lean against her, Seneca turned around only once. He stared at her. There was rage in his eyes, but a cold, icy, hard rage. His mouth was a thin line, and he was no longer waving to the crowd. His fists were tight around the reins. Then he turned forward again and kept riding, and he did not turn back again.

The triumphal march continued for hours. The city celebrated—a new land conquered, a new province for the Empire, its spoils displayed for the crowd. Musicians, dancers, and jugglers performed along the roads. A masked man walked on stilts, puppeteers performed for children, and boys dueled with sticks. Vendors sold cheap wine, fruit, and cakes from carts.

The prince, princess, and legionaries were met with cheers, worshiped as gods. "Hail Aelar!" rose the cries from the commoners. "Hail Seneca, hail Porcia!"

The adulation turned to scorn as the slaves walked by. The faces swam around Ofeer. Cruel, red, demonic masks. A pock-faced man tossed a stone. It hit Ofeer's shoulder, drawing blood. A young girl ran alongside, younger than Maya, shouting and cursing Ofeer, pelting her with filth. Boys laughed atop a roof. One dropped his pants and pissed her way, and Ofeer barely dodged the shower. A man spat from a balcony, and this projectile hit her, splashing her hair. Thousands of people. A million of them. All cursing, catcalling, pelting her with refuse.

"Come to me, Zoharite whore!" shouted a man from a chandlery doorway, grabbing his crotch.

"Show us your tits!" cried a youth, and his friends roared with laughter.

From a balcony, a woman upended her chamber pot. The nightsoil fell onto the slaves, a foul rain.

Ofeer kept walking, dripping filth. She kept her lips tight, her fists clenched, her chin raised. Her people. Her own people. The Aelarians—the people she had dreamed of so often. The people she had always known were civilized, genteel, beautiful, educated—the people she had thought so superior to Zoharites. The people she had always dreamed of joining. Now they mocked her, hurt her, shouted at her.

"Nice place, this Aelar," Koren rasped as they moved through the poorer quarters where masons, washerwomen, and slaves watched from their balconies and roadsides. "Lovely tour we're getting too. Just needs scorpions all over the streets to be perfect."

Ofeer would have given the world to walk on scorpions right now, if it meant washing off the filth, washing off the guilt, if it meant being back home. Her eyes watered.

"I wish we were home," she whispered, lips trembling. "In Zohar. In our villa on the hill. With Mother. With everyone else."

Koren rolled his eyes. "Oh, you say that every time we go on holiday. But as soon as we come back home, you want another trip."

"Not another trip like this." Ofeer groaned. "I'm covered with shit, Koren."

"Good. Usually you're full of it. Now it's full of you."

The sun was low in the sky when the triumphal march reached the city center. Walls surrounded several hills here, and upon the hilltops rose the Aelarian Acropolis—the pulsing heart of the Empire. Here was a city within a city, the center of Aelar's power. From her place among the slaves, Ofeer couldn't see much. A few gilded domes, shining in the sunset. The upper tiers of an amphitheater. The columns of temples.

He's there, beyond these walls, on those hills, Ofeer thought. *Emperor Marcus Octavius. My father.*

She narrowed her eyes and tightened her lips. She couldn't wait to see him. Once they brought her before the emperor, she would rush forth, coated with filth as she was, and cry out, *I'm your daughter! I'm a princess!*

Ofeer nodded. It was time to confront him, to finally let the truth come forth.

An archway towered ahead, breaking the wall, leading into the Acropolis. Many engravings appeared on it. Ofeer couldn't see them too clearly from here, but they seemed to depict various triumphs of the Empire, showing legionaries conquering lands around the Encircled Sea. The gateway doors were forged of bronze, and engravings appeared on them too, depicting legionaries in armor slaying half-naked, ugly barbarians. Three golden eagles, larger than horses, perched atop the archway, guarding the realm beyond.

As Seneca and Porcia approached the Acropolis gates, guards pulled the doors open, revealing a road lined with cypresses which led toward palaces and temples. But before Ofeer could get a better look, a legionary shoved her with his shield.

"Move, slaves!" the man shouted. "What do you think, that the emperor will welcome you filthy lot into his hall? Move, you sniveling maggots! Go!"

The whips swung. One lash hit Koren's shoulder. Another slammed into Ofeer's back, tearing her stola. With whips, shields, and spears, the legionaries herded the Zoharite captives away from the archway and down a side road, moving away from the Acropolis. Ofeer walked, hunched over and bleeding, leaning against Koren. Hundreds of other captives walked around them— the men and women Ofeer had grown up with in Zohar, people she had once scorned.

I've never been one of them, she thought. *Not until today. I had to come to Aelar to become fully Zoharite.*

The sun vanished behind the houses, and Aelarian boys climbed ladders, lighting oil lanterns that hung from poles along the road. The captives kept walking until they reached a towering stone building topped with a dome. An archway led into its shadowy interior.

"Go on, scum!" shouted a legionary. "Move."

Legionaries began goading the captives through the doorway into the domed hall. As Ofeer and Koren shuffled forward, approaching the building, she made out words engraved above the archway.

Oh God. No. Oh, Eloh, please no.

Koren saw the words too and grunted. He made a half-hearted attempt to escape, only for legionaries to shove him back in line and slam their spears against his back.

Leaning against each other, whipped and bleeding and covered in filth, Ofeer and Koren joined the other captives, walking through the doorway into the hall, passing under those engraved words.

Slave Market.

SENECA

After two months in the wretched east, Seneca rode his chariot toward his home, the imperial palace of Aelar.

He was the son of an emperor, and all the lands around the Encircled Sea were his by birthright—from the eastern deserts of Zohar to the southern savanna of Nur and to the snowy lands of northern Gael. Yet here, the Acropolis, this city within a city—this was his home.

He rode up the cobbled road, passing by the Circus—the expanse of packed earth where chariots raced for sport. To his left loomed the Amphitheatrum where gladiators fought, where lions fed on criminals, where wooden ships sailed in mock naval battles for a crowd of myriads. Golden goddesses gazed from the domed roofs of columned temples. Larger statues—of himself and his family—soared on a hilltop, so large their toes were like chariots.

And ahead of him—there, rising in the darkness, lit with many lanterns—the palace.

From here I will rule the Empire, Seneca thought. *From here I will crush any who oppose me. From here I will watch as Ofeer weeps and begs me to save her. From here I will cast out Porcia in shame, laughing as she flees my wrath.*

He looked to his side. Porcia still rode her chariot there. She held a lantern, and its light painted her armor a demonic red. The severed heads, the ones she had brought from Zohar and tied to the back of her chariot, had not fared well along the triumphal march. Preserved meticulously on the journey to Aelar, they had since crumbled along the city cobblestones, dwindling to broken skulls patched with skin and hair. Porcia saw Seneca staring. She grinned, made a loop with one finger, and thrust her other finger through it.

You're fucked, she worded and winked.

Seneca looked away. The fear leaped inside him. Two months ago, Father had given them each three legions, had sent them to bring Zohar to its knees. Whoever won Zohar, Marcus had said, would inherit the Empire.

If Porcia won the emperor's blessings, Seneca knew what his fate would be. He looked again at what remained of the heads trailing behind Porcia's chariot.

If she's ever empress, I'll be one of those heads.

They rode on toward the palace. His heart thrashed, his fingers trembled, and Seneca suddenly wished he had chased Ofeer, had brought her here with him, not let her get carted off to the slave market. Ofeer would know what to do, what to say. He gulped and sweat beaded on his brow.

What was it that Ofeer had told him back in Zohar? They had stood together in the villa's library. He had cried, and she had coached him, had told him what to tell Marcus Octavius. Something about ... Porcia training a puppet? And ... himself killing people? Or was it about how Gefen was a greater prize than a desert throne? Seneca couldn't remember. Damn it! The words all tangled in his mind. When Ofeer had spoken those words, her eyes boring into his, she had seemed so confident, so eloquent.

What the fuck am I supposed to tell you, Father?

His breath was shaking. They were reaching the palace. Damn it! Seneca wanted to flee, to hide, to find Ofeer and ask her again what to say. But he had no time. Damn it, no time! Porcia's chariot reached the palace first, and Seneca reached the courtyard only a moment later and halted his horses.

The palace portico rose before them, braziers lighting its columns. When viewed in the daylight, this was a place of white marble, golden statues, and classical peace and beauty. Now, in the night, it appeared to Seneca like the twisted gatehouse to the abyss. The statues, far above, blended into shadow, staring down at him like demons. Iron eagles perched atop the roof, glowering. In daylight, they shone for leagues, but in the night they looked to Seneca like vultures, waiting to pick at his carcass.

Be strong, he told himself. *You vanquished the Zoharites. You crucified Lord Jerael Sela, and you captured his port—the last port around the Encircled Sea. You can do this.*

"Are you ready to kneel before me, Seneca, when Father names me his heiress?" Porcia began climbing the stairs toward the portico.

"I'm ready to kneel when he names me heir. I mean—you will kneel. Before me."

He cursed himself and his thick tongue. Porcia laughed and kept climbing.

They stepped between the columns onto a platform. A hundred soldiers of the Magisterian Guard stood here, holding spears and lanterns. They knelt before their prince and princess, and two guards opened the palace doors. Porcia entered first, and Seneca followed at her heels.

A hall of splendor awaited them. Marble columns rose, capped with golden capitals shaped as eagles. Between each column rose a statue of a god or goddess, nude and unpainted. Frescoes of mythological scenes covered the rounded ceiling, while a mosaic sprawled across the floor, forming a great map— the Aelarian Empire in all its glory, encircling the sea, stretching deep south into Nur and far north, all the way into Elania in the northern ocean. The largest, mightiest empire the world had and would ever know.

A throne rose ahead atop a dais, but the emperor was not there. Marcus Octavius rarely sat on his throne. He had built this hall to cow the senators, those dogs who still thought themselves masters of the Empire. The only time Marcus sat on his throne was when a senator visited this hall, forcing the old goat to gaze up upon imperial glory. Any other time, Marcus scorned pomp and grandeur. He had been born to a soldier, raised a soldier, served as a soldier for years before crushing the Senate and turning Aelar from Republic into Empire.

Seneca knew where to find him tonight.

He walked across the hall and through a back door. Porcia walked with him. A dark corridor led to the back half of the palace, opening up into a grand hall, the same size as the throne room.

This hall was a tomb.

Few people ever entered this second half of Aelar's palace. While the front hall glittered with gold, mosaics, frescoes, and jewels, this place was austere, formed all of white marble, no precious metals or gemstones shattering the white monochrome. Only a single statue rose here, tall as a cypress, depicting Seneca's mother.

Luciana Octavius had been a beautiful woman, her nose straight, her hair curled. The marble statue depicted her as Dia, the goddess of spring. A wreath of ivy crowned her brow, and a stola draped across her, exposing the left breast, the marble so smooth it looked like real fabric. Under one arm, she held a stone jug, as if the statue were pouring forth blessings of wine.

The Cassius family murdered her, Seneca thought, staring at the statue. He had been only a baby during the great civil war, when Father had bent the Senate to his will—but not before the legions of Septimus Cassius had slain thousands, Luciana Octavius among them. Seneca had been too young to remember much of his mother; Valentina had been only a newborn, too young to remember anything. All they had of Luciana Octavius now was this statue, her mausoleum. Her body now rested within the hill, right under the statue's feet. A holy place. A place of memory, of loss.

It was here that Seneca found his father.

"She was strong," Marcus said, staring at the statue. "It's what few people realize. They come here—those who still remember—and they call her beautiful, and they call her wise, and they call her pious. They forget her strength." The emperor turned to look at his children. "It was her strength that lured me to her. Her strength that I hoped to teach you, her children."

Porcia took a step closer, knelt, and bowed her head. "My emperor."

Ass-kissing bitch.

Seneca followed suit, kneeling on the cold marble floor. "My emperor."

Marcus gestured for them to rise. The emperor wore a simple white toga this night, eschewing the rich, deep purple fabrics he wore in public, and his head was bare of crown or laurel. Yet he was still every inch a conqueror. It was in his face— a hard face, chiseled, cruel, the mouth thin, the nose aquiline, the forehead high and the jaw wide. If Seneca's mother was carved of flowing marble, Marcus was all iron.

Marcus spoke to his children, voice deep, echoing in the chamber. "My lumer has been speaking to Worm and Taeer from across the sea."

Seneca gulped. He had suspected that Taeer, during all those hours that she stood alone on the ship's stern, had been using her Luminosity to converse with her sisters. Gossiping bitches! A moment of panic flooded him. What had Taeer said?

What had Worm, Porcia's sniveling little lumer, said to her sisters here in the capital?

Seneca had never seen his father's lumer. Nobody had. Not Porcia. Not the lords and ladies. Not the senators. Not Valentina. Often Seneca had wondered whether his father had a lumer at all. No matter how often Seneca asked, Emperor Marcus refused to divulge the location of his lumer, yet surely he was hiding the witch somewhere. Marcus always knew far more than a lumerless man ever could.

"Father!" Seneca said, steeling himself. He had fought bravely in Gefen, had conquered, had killed, and now he faced a battle of a different sort. "Father, the port of Gefen is yours. The last port around the Encircled Sea that, until my conquest, eluded our empire. The Encircled Sea is now ours, an uninterrupted ring of coast."

Good, he thought, breathing shakily. *Good*. Those words had come out right, just like Ofeer had taught him.

Porcia seemed unimpressed. She yawned theatrically. "I always thought it was lume that Aelar cared for more than a pisspot scrap of beach. Lume—found only in Zohar. Lume—springing forth from Beth Eloh. The capital of Zohar is yours, Father. I conquered it for you—a city of a hundred thousand souls, the ancient capital of the Zoharites, the city that gives lumers their power."

Terror dug through Seneca, icy and all-consuming.

"She's lying!" he blurted out. "She didn't conquer anything! She just ... just left King Shefael on his throne. The same throne he sat on before Porcia ever arrived. I *conquered*, Father!" He sprayed saliva as he talked. "I *killed*, Father! I killed men. I killed Jerael Sela himself, a legendary warrior. I crushed the walls of Gefen. Porcia just made some deal, like a whore negotiating the price of a poke."

He panted, sweat on his brow, as his father stared at him. Emperor Marcus's frown deepened.

"Tell me, son," the emperor said. "You would speak of whores here in the tomb of your mother?"

Fuck. Seneca sweated. *Goddamn fucking whores.*

He bowed his head. "Forgive me, Father. I speak from passion, for I am passionate about my victories, of—"

"Of your victories?" Marcus said. "Are not all our conquests in the name of Aelar, not for personal vainglory?"

Seneca trembled. More sweat dripped down his forehead. All the other words he had planned fled his mind. Why wasn't Ofeer here? Why could he say nothing right? He glanced toward Porcia.

Oh gods, she's going to kill me. She's going to become empress and fucking kill me.

Porcia stretched. "When I arrived in Gefen, Father, I found Seneca drunk on a hilltop, a Zoharite woman in his bed. I think he conquered more bottles and local beauties than land." She laughed. "While he was busy drinking and bedding, I smashed the forces of Prince Yohanan Elior outside the walls of Beth Eloh. He commanded ten thousand men. I kept a hundred to sell as slaves. The rest still rot outside Beth Eloh, I reckon. I lost fewer than a thousand of my own men, most of them from the auxiliary forces. I sent the Nurian and Leerian conscripts to the front line. Good fodder. As for Shefael Elior—he's on our leash. I disarmed his men for now, but I left them alive. They knelt. In a year or two, they'll make a good addition to our auxiliaries. We can use them well in Gael."

Seneca stared at her, eyes wide, then back at his father. "But—but—Shefael ruled there before her! Porcia didn't *change* anything!"

Porcia raised an eyebrow. "Didn't I? I ended the turmoil in Zohar. Within a day, I settled the civil war that had been raging there for three years. I had Shefael kneel before me, swear his allegiance to Aelar, and pay us coffers of gold. That gold is being delivered into the palace treasuries as we speak, Father. Come inspect it tonight! It will fund a great triumphal arch in the Empire's honor. The lume will now flow uninterrupted from Zohar, while the desert folk remain docile. You see ..." She turned toward Seneca. "When you crucify their lord and fuck his daughter, the locals tend to rebel. When you keep their king on his throne, but attach strings to his crown, the people remain subservient while we reap our rewards." She patted his head. "You have much to learn of how to run an empire, little brother."

I've lost.

Seneca stared at his sister, frozen, unable to speak.

It's over.

Porcia smiled at him sweetly, her eyes flashing with mirth. She gave him the slightest of winks.

Seneca turned back toward his father. He had done all that he could. He had nothing more to say. He simply stared, silent.

Emperor Marcus shook his head in disgust. "Leave this tomb. Go wash yourselves, both of you. You still stink of the desert. Then sleep. In four days, it will be ten years since we vanquished the land of Phedia. We'll hold great games in the Amphitheatrum, and we'll dress a hundred prisoners in Phedian armor and feed them to the lions. At those games, I will announce my heir. Until then, I will meditate, I will pray, I will speak to my lumer, and I will decide. Now go."

"Hail Aelar!" Porcia said, spun, and left the tomb.

"Hail Aelar," Seneca said, voice so hoarse it was barely audible. He spun around, nearly tripped, and stumbled out of the hall.

Once outside in the night, trembles seized him. He fell to his knees on the flagstones, gasping for breath. Blackness spread around him. He could barely see. His head spun, and sweat drenched him, even in the cool night.

I stumbled. I spoke nonsense. She won. She won. He'll name her heiress. She'll kill me. My head will drag behind her chariot.

Seneca's eyes watered. He managed to rise, to stumble through the night. Statues rose around in the darkness, and each one became a Zoharite warrior, screaming, swinging a sickle blade. Seneca could still hear the clatter of swords, the roar of catapults, the screams, so many screams, of dying, of killing. Men died all around him in the night, limbs torn free, organs spilling, spines shattering against walls. Again he saw himself driving down the hammer, the nails piercing Jerael, and how the crows had feasted.

I killed him. I murdered him. I murdered a man. I swung the hammer and I felt it, felt the nails go through flesh. For nothing. For nothing ...

He fell again, shoved himself up, stumbled onward. He needed to drink. He needed his wine. He needed Ofeer. Oh gods, he needed Ofeer with him, needed to hold her, needed her arms around him, needed his head on her breast, her fingers in his hair, soothing him, needed to hear her tell him it would be all right. But she was gone, trapped in the slave market with her brother, his doing, all his doing again.

The temples seemed to tilt around him. Seneca ran. He ran through the Acropolis, sandals clattering, until he reached the archway and burst out into the city. And still he ran, racing down the streets, still wearing his imperial armor. People were staring. They would recognize him, try to assassinate him—like the Zoharites had tried, like Atalia had tried when pointing her blade at him at the dinner table. When you were a prince, everyone wanted to kill you—your enemies, your people, your own sister.

As he ran, Seneca tugged the straps of his breastplate and tossed it off. It was a priceless work of art, custom made. Let the mobs have it! As he ran, he tossed off his greaves, then his vambraces, remaining in his tunic. He didn't need armor anymore. Nothing more could protect him now, not if his father named Porcia his heiress. As soon as her ass hit the throne, his life was forfeit.

Finally Seneca reached his destination.

The Lunapar stood on a street corner, two stories tall, the largest building on the block. Warm light shone in the windows, and laughter, moans, and screams of pleasure rose from within. Seneca almost ripped the front door off its hinges and stumbled inside.

He stood for a moment, breathing, trying to calm himself, taking in this comforting, familiar place, his home away from home, the place where he had spent so many nights forgetting his pain.

It was an expensive brothel, among the best in the city. Not a seedy, foul place like the brothels the commoners visited. Here was a place for fine clientele—wealthy merchants, nobles, senators, even priests. Incense burned in silver braziers, and a hundred glass lanterns hung from the ceiling, shaped as phalli. Murals covered the walls, depicting every way to fuck a woman, dozens of paintings of dozens of positions, all painted in bright pastels.

Live women were here too, lounging on divans, leaning against counters, and drinking wine. They were not naked; only slaves or Kalintians were ever naked outside of bathhouses. Here were free women, citizens of Aelar. They wore togas, normally the garments of men, denoting their profession. Seneca remembered how, a few years ago, Porcia had once dressed Valentina in a toga, then roared with laughter until Father had ended the game. Seneca had not understood the jest until, as a youth, he had discovered the comfort of prostitutes.

"Prince Seneca!" said Mariana, a beauty with flowing brown hair and green eyes. She approached him and kissed his cheek. "Welcome home, hero of Aelar, conqueror of Zohar."

The other women rushed toward him, showering him with their affections. He shoved them aside.

"Wine," he said. "Wine! Where's the goddamn wine?"

A girl rushed forth, a virgin still in training, and served him a drink. Seneca guzzled down the cup. "More."

She poured him a second cup. He drained it. "Again."

With three cups of wine in his belly, his anxiety began to fade, his shaking to subside. Something bad had happened. He knew that. He was in danger. But the fear was hidden now, numb, buried under the wine.

"You." He pointed at Calina, a beautiful Nurian, her skin so dark it was almost black. "And you." He pointed at Mariana, an old favorite.

He had to lean on them as they walked upstairs. They went down a corridor, passing by many rooms. The sounds of sex rose all around. Some doors were opened, revealing the patrons and their mistresses within. Mariana and Calina took Seneca to the back room, the one that overlooked the garden, his favorite room.

"We kept this room empty during your absence," Mariana said; Seneca knew she was lying. "We saved it for your return."

Calina kissed his ear. "You are our hero of the desert."

Tears in his eyes, he began to pull off his clothes, but his fingers trembled, and he couldn't undo the lacings. Mariana and Calina helped him, laid him on the bed, and lay at his sides. One of the women—Seneca's head spun too much to tell which—reached down her hand to stroke his manhood.

"My prince?" she asked, raising her eyes in concern.

Her fingers worked, but nothing happened, and Seneca closed his eyes.

"Hold me," he whispered.

They held him, one at each side, their arms wrapped around him.

"Just hold me," he whispered. "Please. Please. Just tell me it will be all right."

"It will be all right," Mariana said softly, stroking his hair.

Calina kissed his cheek. "My desert hero."

He screwed his eyes shut, unable to stop the tears from flowing, unable to stop seeing the dead, unable to stop seeing himself swinging the hammer. He missed Ofeer. He missed being a boy, a boy unaware of war, of the war in Zohar, of the war here in Aelar. He wept.

I'm sorry, he thought. *I'm sorry, Jerael. I'm sorry, Ofeer. I'm sorry. I'm sorry. I'm sorry.*

He couldn't stop shaking, couldn't stop crying, even as Mariana and Calina held him, until finally he slept in their arms, and he dreamed that he lay with Ofeer back in a villa overlooking the sea.

VALENTINA

Valentina approached her sister slowly, hands clasped behind her back, breath trembling.

No, Valentina thought. *No, not my sister. She's the daughter of Marcus, and I'm the daughter of Septimus, and I fear her more than ever.*

"Porcia?" she whispered, her voice shaking. Her heart seemed ready to leap from her chest.

Five years her senior, Porcia stood at the stone altar in the dark bowels of the Temple of Camulus, the god of war. The stench of blood and raw meat filled the stone chamber. Flies buzzed. When Valentina stepped closer, she saw what Porcia was doing, and she nearly gagged. The princess was kneeling over a corpse—a human corpse—digging her knife through its chest.

"Valentina!" Porcia raised her eyes from her work, smiling. Blood stained her hands.

Valentina stood frozen, wanting to flee. The blood dripped across the stone altar, reflecting the light of the lanterns that hung on the walls, then ran in rivulets across the mosaic on the floor.

"I ... Porcia, what ..." Valentina stammered.

The princess placed down her knife. The body gave a twitch—still alive!—then lay still. Valentina could barely tell if the body was old or young, man or woman; it had been mutilated beyond recognition, the organs pulled out and arranged across the altar, as a soothsayer might seek the future in the organs of a hen.

"One of the captives from Zohar," Porcia said. "An old man. Weak with disease. Would have been useless in the slave market." She looked toward an obsidian statue of the God of War, towering and dark, glaring with stone eyes across the temple. "A good sacrifice for Camulus, though."

Valentina couldn't bear to look at the grisly scene. All her life, she had feared Porcia. The girl who would stone cats and behead them for sport. Who would laugh as lions devoured gladiators in the arena. Who herself would fight prisoners, slaying them for the crowds, then rip out their hearts. Valentina had often feared that this cruel blood flowed through her own veins.

Thank the gods I'm a daughter of Cassius, Valentina thought. *But Porcia doesn't know. She must never know. If she knows I'm not her sister, she'll sacrifice me on this altar too.*

Porcia stepped toward her and embraced her, bloodying Valentina's stola. The woman still wore her dark armor, the breastplate dented and scratched and flecked with old blood, and her blades still hung from her belt.

"Sister!" Porcia said and kissed Valentina's cheek. "Where were you today? Why didn't you come see your older sister return victorious from war? You should have come see the Triumphal Parade! Seneca and I paraded the captives through the entire city. A few died on the way. It was glorious."

Valentina had seen one Triumphal Parade before—her father leading the captives of Phedia a decade ago, when she had been only a child. Valentina had refused to witness those marches of splendor and death since.

She forced herself to embrace Porcia, to kiss her cheek.

I must play this game for a while longer. Until we're ready. Until the spiders strike.

"Where is Seneca?" Valentina asked. "I thought I'd find him here too."

In truth, it was Seneca she had come to see, Seneca she had always loved. Throughout her childhood, Valentina had always feared Porcia. She had seen Porcia's madness, even then—seen the youth strike her servants, brutalize her little brother, even condemn a cook to crucifixion for burning her favorite dish. True, Valentina herself had never suffered this wrath; Porcia had always seen her as a pet, a precious little thing to protect, to possess. Yet if Porcia showed her some twisted love, Valentina could not return it; she could feel no tenderness to the woman she'd seen skin a dog alive for the *Robigalia*, laughing as the animal screamed. But Seneca—he had always been the only family Valentina loved, a love not born of duty nor fear but true affection. Seneca had always been kind to her, had always played with her in the gardens, listened to her sing her songs, even played dolls with her. To Marcus and Porcia, Valentina had always been a possession; to Seneca she was a sister.

I'm not your true sister, Seneca, Valentina thought, *but I still love you.*

Porcia scoffed. "Our cowardly brother has no time to pray to the god of war, not even after a campaign. For centuries, the victors of Aelar, after a Triumphal Parade, would come here, to this place—to worship Camulus, to sacrifice blood to him. But Seneca is weak. Seneca is a sniveling pup, not a conqueror. I saw him flee the Acropolis, tears in his eyes. He's probably spending the night in a brothel." Shaking her head in disgust, Porcia returned to the altar. She drove her blade back into the corpse, carving out another organ. "Will you pray with me, Valentina? I can fetch another slave for you to sacrifice. It's a great honor to Camulus."

Valentina shook her head. "I'm no warrior, Porcia. I know how to sing, to play the lyre, to recite poetry, not to kill." She bowed her head. "I'll go find Seneca. I'll bring him home."

Porcia snorted. "Let him rot, wherever he is. You spend too much time with the boy. You're a woman now, Valentina. No longer a child. You must learn the ways of death and conquest."

I will learn, Valentina thought, *and I will kill, but not like you think.*

She bowed her head and retreated from the temple.

Valentina walked through the dark Acropolis, moving among temples, the palace, the amphitheater, the Senate. Wrapped in a cloak and hood, she stepped through the Imperium Gate, entering the outer city. The Acropolis—the inner city where those in power dwelled—was a place of marble columns, golden statues, of splendor and glory and knives that stabbed in the dark. The rest of Aelar, spreading around the Acropolis's hills, was a different place—a place of narrow streets, of apartment buildings that rose seven or eight stories tall, of taverns full of drunkards, of brothels full of lechers, of pickpockets and gamblers and ten-denarii whores.

Valentina knew where to find Seneca. The same place she had dragged him back from a dozen times. She walked through the night, wrapped in her cloak. When she passed by a pair of drunken, rowdy men, her heart leaped, and she hurried down the street. A legionary stood at a street corner, ignoring a legless beggar. A few people leaned off their balconies, staring down as they smoked hintan pipes. If anyone recognized her, Valentina knew, they wouldn't hesitate to kidnap, even to kill her; she was a princess of Aelar, worth a fortune in ransom, alive or dead. But she had become an expert at hiding her white hair under her hood, for choosing the right shadows to slink through.

It was here, in this warren, that Valentina had been meeting her father—her true father—for several nights in a row now. Whispering. Planning in the shadows. Sharpening their blades. Here she was a shadow herself.

Soon the houses grew larger, and Valentina passed down rows of small villas—the homes of Aelar's more prosperous merchants, officials, and tradesmen. Simple porticos, four columns a piece, rose along their patios, and many had humble gardens and even private pools. Down a few more streets, Valentina came across it—the Lunapar.

The brothel rose two stories tall, its windows made of costly glass, its door elaborately carved with phalli and dancing nude women. It was one of the nicest of such establishments in the city. Valentina had seen her share of senators and generals slink through this carved doorway. Some claimed that it was from the Lunapar, not the palace or the Senate, that Aelar was governed.

Valentina entered the brothel and pulled back her hood. The women at the door recognized her, embraced her, kissed her cheek; she had come here often enough to pick up her drunken brother. Valentina made her way across the common room, stepping across lush rugs between murals depicting all the ways to make love, murals that made her blush and look away. She climbed upstairs, trailing her hand across a balustrade carved into the shape of nude men and women, and made her way to the room down the corridor—his usual room.

When she stepped inside, she found Seneca asleep in bed. Two prostitutes lay at his sides, naked, blinking and rising from slumber. It was still dark outside, but several oil lanterns glowed on the walls. At a gesture from Valentina, the pair of women rose from the bed, pulled sheets over themselves, and left the chamber.

Valentina walked closer to the bed and stood over Seneca. He lay on his back, still asleep, the lamplight on his face. Valentina sighed.

You poor boy, she thought.

During the days, Seneca wore elaborate armor, carried sword and spear, rode in fine chariots, and boasted of his prowess in battle and bed. Lying here, naked, he seemed so small to Valentina, so weak. Only a young man, not yet twenty. Thin—too thin, she thought. His face soft, his hair fawn brown.

Just a child.

"Seneca," she said.

He blinked and moaned. "Wine."

She sat on the bed and placed her hand on his chest. "Brother, wake up."

"Wine!" he said. "Damn it, bring me wine. I need wine before I fuck you. I—" His eyes finally focused, and he blinked at Valentina, then gasped and tugged the blanket up his chest. "Valentina! What the fuck are you doing here?"

She glared at him. "I've come to drag you home. You're drunk. Or hungover." She sniffed. He stank of old wine. "I think you're both drunk and hungover at the same time, and I didn't even know that was possible."

He tried to rise onto his elbows, swayed, and fell onto his back. He reached toward a side table, pawing at a flagon of wine, and knocked it over. The crimson wine soaked the rug.

"Gods damn it!" Seneca said, tears in his eyes. "Wine! I want win—"

Valentina slapped him. "Enough wine."

He hissed and clutched his red cheek, staring at her with frightened, bloodshot eyes. "You hit me."

She raised her palm. "And I'll hit you again. And again. Until you come to your senses. Seneca, you returned to Aelar a war hero. Porcia is receiving adulation in the Acropolis. And you cower here with wine and sex and self-pity."

A tear now ran down his cheek. He looked away from her, still lying in bed. "You don't understand, Valentina," he whispered. "I ... I saw things. I saw men burning, still alive, running in flames. I saw a man with his legs cut off, running on the stumps. I killed people." He looked back at her, eyes haunted, and his voice dropped to a whisper. "I crucified somebody."

His tears were falling freely now, and Valentina's rage ebbed. She pulled him up and embraced him.

"It's over now," she said. "It's over, sweet brother. The war is over. You won. I'm here with you now, to take care of you, to love you."

Seneca sobbed, holding her close. "Thank you. My sweet Valentina." He caressed her milk-white hair, his fingers trembling. "What would I be without my little sister?"

You have only an older sister, Valentina thought, *and she is a murderous monster. I'm just one who still loves you.*

She kissed his cheek. "Come, Seneca. Put on some clothes. Return with me to the palace."

He rose from bed, grabbed a tunic, and pulled it over his body. It was no proper attire for a prince, merely what soldiers wore beneath their armor, but evidently he had come here wearing nothing else. He stared ruefully at the spilled wine, then back at Valentina.

"Not yet. I did something bad, Valentina. Something I need to fix." He took a shuddering breath. "Go home and wait for me. My war is not yet done."

MAYA

S he thought the journey would never end. She thought that this was her life now—a sack of beaten meat, burnt in the sun, withering away and praying for death. She thought that this was death. She thought this was an eternity of torment, an unending sacrifice to a cruel god.

The shamans far in northern Gael, Maya had once read in a scroll, believed that the souls of sinners froze forever in an underworld of ice, but Maya could not believe that. A torturous afterlife could not be cold. Torture was *hot*. It was the sun. It was the unending desert of sand.

And it was rope—rope that dug into her wrists and ankles.

And it was stench—the stench of the men who surrounded her, of the camel that bore her.

And it was the sound of them, the horrible sound of their hawking, their spitting, their guttural laughter as they taunted her, the sound of their leather whips as they cracked in the air, as they slammed into her.

Another day began—another day after an eternity of days. A day of captivity, stolen by the bone-raiders.

Maya dared open her eyes, dared stare into the searing light, though as always the sight made her shiver, made her stomach writhe. She lay slung across a camel like a sack, bound and gagged. The bone-raiders rode around her on their own camels. She couldn't tell how many rode here; she had tried to count them, sometimes counting eight, other times a dozen. The men never removed their white robes and hoods, and masks formed of skulls hid their faces. Only their eyes were visible, bright blue like fires of the sky. Their camels too wore their own masks, theirs made from the skulls of fallen camels, strapped across their faces with leather thongs. Sometimes Maya thought the bone-raiders mortal men, their mounts mere camels, but often she thought them undead chimeras, fused together, risen from the sand and tasked with tormenting the living.

She was trussed up like a lamb to the slaughter, bouncing on her camel, her body whipped, burnt in the sunlight, weary with thirst and hunger. She could barely muster the strength to raise her head. She looked around her, squinting in the sunlight. Dawn had only just risen, but already it was banishing the cold of night, replacing it with scorching heat. She had lost count of how many days and nights they had ridden. The bone-raiders never set camp. If they ate and slept, they did so in their saddles, an existence of ever moving onward, cutting across the dunes.

Maya twisted her neck from side to side, and finally she saw him. Leven hung across a camel farther back. The animal was a haggard beast, wearing its bone mask, a ghastly countenance painted with dry blood. The young thief who had once stolen

Maya's camel was now a camel's captive. The irony did not escape Maya, weary as she was. Leven too was bound and gagged, tied to the camel like just another sack of supplies. He met her gaze and winked, and he seemed to grin around his gag. Maya decided that nothing could dampen Leven's spirits, not if the demon Dagon himself rose from the sand to brand him with fiery rods.

"Drink." The guttural voice spoke beside her. "Drink."

She turned her head to see one of the bone-raiders approach on foot. The wind gusted around him, billowing his robes and raising demons of sand. His blue eyes blazed through the sockets of his skull mask. He held a drinking skin, which he uncorked and held up to her mouth. He tore off her gag.

"Drink," he repeated. His voice was boulders grinding together. "Drink."

She remembered the last time he had forced the liquid into her mouth. It had left her body as soon as it had entered, and her belly had roiled for hours. When she shook her head, the raider grabbed her jaw, prying it open, and forced the liquid into her mouth. It was a viscous stew, hot and thick with meat and oil, like drinking raw death. Maya gagged, but the raider kept the liquid pouring as she sputtered, struggling to swallow.

Finally the man pulled the skin free from her mouth. He laughed. "*Khasan!* Good for you. Keep you alive."

He spoke in Sekadian, the language of the east, but Maya understood him. She had read many scrolls in Sekadian back home, and several Elohist songs were chanted in this tongue, for the children of Zohar had once been slaves here in the eastern desert. *Khasan* meant *strength*, she thought—liquid strength.

"It tastes like a buzzard's ass," she told the bone-raider, hoping she was speaking Sekadian correctly. When the man laughed, she assumed she was.

I can make them laugh, Maya thought, wincing to remember the beatings she had endured. *If I can make them laugh, maybe they won't hurt me anymore.*

They rode onward. They always rode onward. At first Maya had thought the desert the same every day. She had been wrong. The desert was like the sea—different whenever you looked at it. One day, as they rode atop a great dune the size of a mountain, Maya beheld ruins below, half-buried in the sand. Rows of columns rose, their capitals shaped as snarling bats. Statues lay fallen, growling silently, shaped as chimeras of lions, serpents, goats, and other creatures morphed together. Another day, Maya saw the bones of great creatures in the sand—massive creatures, as large as the whales from the stories. Their ribs rose like porticos of columns, and their skulls lay in the sand, teeth like swords. She wondered if a sea had once covered this desert, if whales had died here, but when she saw bones stretch out from the spines, she wondered if these had been wings, if she gazed upon the remains of dragons.

At nights the temperature dropped so low Maya shivered on the camel. When she twisted her head around, she could see the stars—countless stars, great blankets of them, rivers of them flowing above. One morning, clouds gathered and a drizzle fell, and a rainbow spread across the sky, arching from horizon to horizon. Millions of white flowers bloomed from the sand, roused by the rain, a carpet of white that coated the desert, then wilted, gone within an hour.

Some days the camels rode closer together to pass through a gorge. One time, traversing the narrow passageway, Maya found herself riding near Leven—both slumped across their camels like sacks. Soon they were so close Maya could touch her cheek to his. They whispered to each other through their gags, voices muffled, words slurred—a little bit of companionship, a little bit of home.

As they rode, Maya had plenty of time to think. She knew that these bone-raiders, whoever they were, had some purpose for her. Why were they keeping her alive? At first, remembering the stories of war she had heard, Maya had feared they would rape her, but they had left her untouched. She eventually concluded that they intended to sell her. Perhaps at the great slave market of Sekur, perhaps to some traveling caravan encountered in another land.

Sooner or later, Maya thought, *they'll have to untie me. Nobody would buy a trussed-up sack. The bone-raiders will untie me, clean me, brush my hair, try to make me presentable, as beautiful as they can.* She inhaled deeply through her nostrils. *And then I'll have to run.*

She didn't know where she would run to. Most likely, running meant death in the desert. Then let it be so. She would rather die in sand than live as a brothel slave, a concubine, or a miner. Her bones would join those of the dragons in the desert. It was not a bad place to rest.

She was thinking these thoughts when finally, after what seemed like eras of traveling, the caravan reached the fortress in the cliff.

A great escarpment split the desert, a shelf of sandstone rising across the horizon like a wall, taller than the mightiest tower. A fortress had been carved right into the cliff—complete with columns, decorative archways, and statues of men and women with bat wings and demonic faces. It seemed to her vaguely Aelarian—not the statues, but the portico and pediment were clearly in Aelarian style.

Has the Aelarian Empire stretched so far east? she wondered. No, it couldn't be. No Aelarian would carve demons onto their structure; their gods were human in form, beautiful to behold. And this wasn't truly an Aelarian building. It wasn't a building at all; it was simply a great engraving, as tall as a palace, surrounding a cave. A mimicry, that was all. Somebody here in Sekadia had been to the Aelarian Empire, had seen the grand structures of that civilization, and had mimicked them here, a thousand parsa'ot in the east.

The caravan of camels made its way along a rocky path, heading toward the mock fortress. As they drew closer, Maya forgot her pain, her weariness, her fear, just stared in wonder. The structure was massive, perhaps even as tall as the Temple back in Zohar. She could not imagine how men had ever climbed so high to carve the hundreds of statues that stood on its pediment and columns. Surely there would be no way to build scaffolds in the desert, unless one hauled wagons and wagons full of wood for days on end across the sand. And surely men dangling from ropes on the cliff would never be able to carve work so elaborate.

Lumers carved this fortress in the cliff, Maya thought. Muse, one of the Four Pillars of Luminosity, had built this wonder in the desert.

She thought back again to Avinasi's words. The ancient lumer of Beth Eloh had told her that a second stream of lume flowed in the east, that lumers studied their art in a city by the sea. Perhaps lumers from that distant land had built this temple. Perhaps Maya was close to them now—close to a sanctuary far from Aelar, where she could learn her art.

The bone-raiders halted their camels by a staircase that climbed toward an archway in the fortress. They dismounted, grabbed Maya and Leven, and tugged them off their camels. The rough hands released Maya, and she fell down hard, banging her hip against the ground.

"Pahjahn!" barked a man. "Don't hurt the female. She'll fetch a higher price without bruises. Healthy young virgins fetch gold."

Pahjahn—a tall man with thick white eyebrows over his blue eyes—spat. "Go fuck your mother's cunt. I'll bruise her if I like. I'll slit her neck if I like. The girl's a fucking Zoharite. Their women have strange powers. Lumers, all of them."

The first man stepped closer and drew his saber. He was shorter and slimmer, but his eyes were no less fierce. "She's worth gold, you son of a whore. Covered in bruises, she won't even fetch silver."

Pahjahn snorted. "Fuck gold. Fuck silver. Useless to a bone-raider. You've become soft like a city dweller, Suraph." He drew his own saber. "I'm still a raider. I live for sand, for iron, for blood. I don't trust Zoharites. I say we slice off her head, leave her to rot here outside Aken Treasury."

The shorter man—Suraph—growled. "A rotting corpse won't fetch gold."

Pahjahn laughed. "Are you scared of her? I'm not. I'll slice her throat and fuck her corpse if I want. I—"

Suraph swung his saber. The movement was so quick, so smooth, Maya barely saw it. The blade sliced through the taller raider's neck as if cutting through silk.

The severed head hit the ground and rolled. Suraph spat and kicked it aside.

The bone-raider cleaned his blade on a piece of cloth, tucked it back into his belt, then grabbed Maya and yanked her to her feet. His eyes bored into hers. Maya's heart fluttered and cold sweat drenched her. There was cruelty in those eyes—no soul to them. She couldn't see his face; the bone mask still hid it, and he seemed to her more demonic than ever. He had saved her, but not from compassion, simply for greed.

"You can dance for us in the evenings," Suraph said. "You can prove your worth before we find you a master, one who'll pay gold." He drew a dagger and sawed at the ropes binding her ankles, then those around her wrists. "Don't bother running. Nothing but desert for days around us. We'll find you if you run, and then I'll let my companions do what poor Pahjahn suggested."

She winced when she brought her arms to the front of her body. Her muscles screamed as the blood flowed back through them. Maya had never felt such pain, and when she took a step, she nearly collapsed. It felt as if her body had atrophied, and her head spun. When Suraph tore the gag from her mouth, she gasped for air.

Not far away, another bone-raider was yanking Leven to his feet. The young man swayed, still bound and gagged. His skin was ashen, and sand filled his hair.

"Untie him too," Maya said. "He won't run."

Suraph returned his dagger to his belt and shook his head. "Not him. He stays bound. He's strong, that one, and quick. Got the look of a thief to him. Could make a good miner, fetch a few silver coins."

The bone-raiders began climbing the stairs and entering the fortress in the cliff. One of them manhandled Leven forward. Maya glanced behind her, seeing only parsa'ot of desert. She could run, she knew. Perhaps she could even steal one of the camels and ride. For a while, at least, she would taste freedom.

But they would catch me. They would kill me. She looked back toward Leven, but he had already vanished into the fortress. *And I can't leave Leven. That damn thief might have stolen my camel, but he's still a fellow Zoharite.*

Under the glare of the bone-raiders, Maya walked upstairs, through the archway, and into the shadows.

Seeing the beautiful, breathtaking columns and statues outside, Maya had expected a glittering hall of marvels, a place to rival the greatest palaces in the world. Instead she found a crude chamber carved into the cliff, not much larger than her villa on Pine Hill, simply a square cave.

Even as a captive, about to be sold into slavery, beaten and famished, disappointment curdled Maya's belly. Perhaps all grandness was like that. A facade hiding mere emptiness. Perhaps the greatest empires were but shells, perhaps the mightiest nations were but kingdoms of sand. Temples devoid of gods. Kings and priests revealed as but plain flesh when stripped of their vestments. All just gold and dust, splendor and shadows, crowns of rust and thrones of ash.

The bone-raiders moved about the room, setting camp. Still they wore their skull masks. One shoved Leven down into the corner, three moved to guard the doorway, and two others built a campfire on the rough floor. One man worked at skinning a goat he had hunted that morning. Finally Maya was able to count them properly: eleven men.

"If it's ransom you want," Maya said, mouth still aching after so long with a gag, "my mother will pay. She's a wealthy woman."

Suraph, the bone-raider who had beheaded his companion, scoffed. "Your bitch mother is halfway across the desert, back in Zohar, trapped in the talons of eagles. No, little one. We'll find you a good buyer from the passing caravans along the salt road." His blue eyes seemed almost to glow here in the shadows of the cave. "You'll fetch a high price, I wager. Ten gold coins or more for a young pretty virgin like you. Can you dance?"

Of course Maya could dance. She was the granddaughter of King Rahamyah Elior, descended from the line of Elshalom. She was the daughter of Jerael Sela, Lord of the Coast. All daughters in her family learned to dance and play music and sing. As children, Maya and Ofeer had spent many hours practicing these arts. Atalia too, at first, until she had snapped her flute over her knee and grabbed a sword, torn up her dresses, put on armor, and gone instead to fight with her brothers.

"A little." She glanced toward the fire, where the men were now roasting the goat. "Give me a choice cut of meat, and another cut to Leven, and I'll show you."

Those blazing blue eyes narrowed within the skull's eye sockets. Suraph stepped closer to her and drew his saber with a hiss. She didn't cringe as he placed the blade against her neck.

"Do you command the bone-raiders, girl?" Suraph said.

The metal was hot against her neck. "No. Do you? Or do you simply behead those who challenge you?" She wouldn't flinch, not even as the blade pressed closer. "Go ahead. I doubt you'll earn gold for a beheaded girl."

A flicker of approval filled Suraph's eyes. "You'd make a good bone-raider." He lowered his blade … then backhanded her. Hard. Maya gasped and fell to the floor, head ringing. Leven screamed through his gag.

"Fetch her a choice cut of meat!" said Suraph. "She'll dance for us after she eats. Remove the boy's gag and feed him too."

Maya rose to her feet, her cheek stinging. She stared at Suraph, rage burning inside her, and she wished she still had her dagger, wished she were a warrior like Atalia, wished she could plunge her blade into this man.

One of the bone-raiders began carving the meat. Only the outer layer was cooked; the insides were still raw and bleeding. The scent of the meat filled the cavern. Finally, after days in the desert, the raiders removed their skull masks.

They're only men, Maya thought. Just men like any others. Not even particularly impressive men—some with scars, some with large noses, one with a weak chin, another bald. Perhaps they too were like this fortress in the cliff—just sand behind the curtains.

They ate. The piece they gave Maya was mostly raw, only its crust cooked, but still she devoured the meat. She hadn't eaten a true meal in days. Juices and blood dripped down her chin and stained her clothes, and she realized that she still wore the same dress she had left Beth Eloh with. It felt like ages ago—a different life. Maya could remember her homeland, could remember her family, could remember herself there, an innocent girl. But that seemed a mere dream, a different life, not truly her in those memories.

Leven sat beside her, and when the bone-raiders tore off his gag, it revealed raw cheeks and bleeding lips. Still Leven managed to smile at her.

"A meal and a dance!" the thief said. "Maybe if we're lucky, we'll get foot rubs too."

The bone-raiders answered him with a cuff to his head. Leven grunted, grabbed the piece of meat tossed toward him, and focused on eating.

As she ate, Maya watched the sun set outside over the desert, painting the sky all orange and copper and red, finally vanishing behind the dunes. The stars emerged and the camels settled down to sleep. Inside the cavern, the campfire still burned, and the bone-raiders passed around skins of *khasan*. Maya was allowed to sip the meaty drink—not enough to quench the thirst inside her, but enough perhaps to ward off death for another few hours.

Suraph, lord of the bone-raiders, leaned back against a wall. He drank from a different skin, and Maya smelled spirits. His bone mask was gone, and his face was hard, leathery, lined with a network of scars.

"Now dance." He pointed at Maya. "Dance for us. There will be caravans passing here tomorrow, and I want to know what you're worth."

Maya stared at him, and she saw hatred, cruelty, and lust in his eyes. She wondered if he truly wanted to appraise her price or appraise her body.

He needs me to be a virgin, she reminded herself. *He said so himself. He can't sell me for gold if I'm not a virgin.*

Yet there was little comfort in that thought. Even if these men didn't rape her, what about whoever bought her? Would she end up a brothel slave? Perhaps forced into marriage, sold to some cruel warlord, made to dance in his hall? She was too weak to be a farmer or miner. In a city, she could hope to be sold to a family home, to become a tutor or maid. But here in the desert? Here there was only one purpose for a young woman.

"Dance!" Suraph said.

"Dance!" repeated the others.

Leven stared at her, and she saw pity in his eyes. He turned toward Suraph.

"I'll dance for you, my friend!" the thief said, puffing out his chest. "I'm a fine, alluring dancer, a true desert rose. I—"

A bone-raider slammed his fist into Leven, knocking him down. Other men kicked him and laughed as he bled.

"Dance or we keep beating him," Suraph said to Maya. "We don't need him to be pretty."

Maya rose to her feet. They all stared at her. Her dress was tattered and damp with sweat, not the fine dress of a dancer. Her body was weak and filthy, her hair a great matted mess.

And yet she danced. Danced like her tutors had taught her in Gefen, danced like she had danced with Ofeer, danced like all daughters of Zohar danced in the days of harvest upon the grapes.

The bone-raiders howled and clapped their hands in a beat. One pounded a drum.

Again Maya wished she were tall and strong like Atalia, not short and weak and meek. Atalia would grab one of the men's sabers, swing it, slay them all. Maya had never been a warrior, only a healer, a child of Luminosity.

As she danced, as the men watched her, a voice spoke in Maya's mind.

You are blessed, child. You are of greater strength than any warrior. The light flows through you.

Maya gasped and nearly lost her step in the dance. She knew that voice.

Avinasi.

Was the lumer truly speaking in her mind now, or was Maya merely imagining the wise old woman, the lumer of Zohar's court, speaking to her?

"Sing for us, Zoharite!" one bone-raider said.

"Sing, sing!" called the others.

Maya stared at them. Cruel men who had stolen her, beaten her, who would sell her to the highest bidder. Just men without masks. Just crude, simple, lost souls. She needn't fear them. They were darkness. They were sand. But she was the light of Luminosity. And that light gave her strength.

She thought of home.

In her mind, she saw them: the walls of Beth Eloh, kindled in sunset. The Temple on the Mount of Cedars, bathed in gold. Groves of olives and ancient tombstones draped across the hills, and the sun rose and fell, and the scent of the city filled her nostrils, a scent of myrrh, of olive oil, of desert wind. The turtle doves sang, and the hinds raced across the hills, and as Maya danced, the daughters of Beth Eloh danced with her. They wore white dresses, and their bare feet crushed grapes, squeezing the juice for the wine. All across the cities and villages of her land, the sons of Zohar emerged to watch the dance, to choose brides from among the maidens. Priests blew into rams' horns, and the song of lyres and timbrels flowed across the land. They were freed slaves, captive in Nur, captive in Sekadia, returned to their land between desert and sea. The waves whispered across the sand, and there on the piney hill, it rose. A villa. A home. Lantanas and cyclamens in the gardens and a pomegranate tree and a painting of elephants, and the light filled her.

Maya's hands glowed.

The lume rose inside her, and she luminated it, weaving it around her fingers, up her arms. The luminescence shone in her eyes.

I'm in a foreign land, but I'm still the light of my home.

The bone-raiders stared at her, some leaping to their feet, some drawing sabers. Leven gaped at her, eyes wide, jaw unhinged.

Four pillars of Luminosity, Maya thought. *Sight. Foresight. Healing. And Muse.*

Muse—the facade of columns and statues outside a cave. Muse—the marble statues for false gods. Muse—beauty woven from nothingness, all the works of men and women, kingdoms of sand shining for a moment, then gone in the wind.

Muse—the wonder and magic of the desert.

She danced.

No longer hesitant steps but a flowing dance of the wind, a column of smoke rising from the desert. She danced—not as a girl, not as a slave, but as living flame. She sang—a song of turtle doves in pomegranate trees, a song of waves on sand, a song of an ancient people and of young love. A song of golden columns and humble bricks of limestone. A song of copper, of bronze, of gold, of light. The song of her homeland, the song of her life by the sea, a song of luminescence.

They wept. Grown men, warriors of the desert, they dropped their blades, and they wept before her. She danced for them, faster now, eyes closed, feet barely touching the floor. She sang of a fallen brother, a fallen kingdom, of beauty still in her heart. She danced like the waves, like leaves in the wind, a song of pines and cedars, a song of the sea and sand. A song of starlight. A song of grace and memory.

The song of Zohar. A song of Luminosity.

"Beauty," Suraph whispered, tears on his leathery cheeks. "Sorry. I'm sorry. I'm sorry." He sobbed. "So beautiful."

The other bone-raiders were on their knees, weeping at the beauty of her dance and song. She let the muse flow into them, let them see in their minds the cedars and olive groves of her homeland, the sunset on the waves, the joy of home, the beauty of lume.

Leven knelt before her, arms raised, tears flowing. "It's so beautiful!" he squeaked. "I can hear the birds! I should have become a poet! A poet!" He rose and flapped his arms. "I can dance like a *bird*!"

Maya rolled her eyes. She stopped her dance, grabbed the young thief, and dragged him across the chamber.

"Fly this way, birdie," she said, pulling him out of the cavern.

They emerged into the night. The bone-raiders didn't follow. Maya could hear them still weeping inside the cave. She raced downstairs, dragging Leven with her until they stood on the sand again. The cliff loomed behind them, and the camels slept ahead—fourteen of them, all bound together with rope.

On the camels, she found the bone-raiders' treasures: decorative blades with jeweled hilts, sacks of coins, amulets and bracelets, gilded vessels, statuettes with gemstone eyes, and countless other pretty things that shone in the saddle bags. There was food here too—dry figs and salted meat—and water and wine. Her own belongings—the dagger Atalia had given her, the horn from Epher, the scarf from Father—were here too. Maya drew her dagger and cut Leven free from his bonds.

"Onto the camel," she said, pulling him toward one of the seated animals.

He flapped his arms, tears still on his cheeks. "But I can fly!"

"Good, so fly right onto that camel." She shoved him into the saddle, then mounted another camel, the one at the front of the line.

For days now, she had heard the bone-raiders issue their commands to the animals. She knew how to ride him.

"*Hasha!*" she said. "Hasha! Hasha!"

The camels grunted and rose to their feet. Maya and Leven swayed in their saddles.

"Hasha!" she said. "Go, go!"

The caravan of camels began to walk through the night, tied together in a line. When Maya turned toward the fortress in the cliff, she saw the bone-raiders emerge. They blinked and rubbed their eyes as if roused from a dream. Slowly they came to their senses, their eyes widened, and they drew their swords.

Maya cringed.

"Hasha!" she shouted. "Faster, faster!" She dug her heels into the camel. "Hasha!"

The camels began to run.

The bone-raiders ran in pursuit, roaring.

Maya cringed. "Faster!" she said. "Hasha! Go, go!"

The camels picked up speed, thundering across the desert. The bone-raiders cried out in rage. One tossed his saber, and the blade spun, flying past Maya, nearly cutting her. She kept kneeing her camel, driving him onward. Riding his own camel, Leven was busy flapping his arms and cawing. A dozen other camels ran with them, tied to one another, raising clouds of sand.

The bone-raiders began to fall back. The distance widened between hunters and prey.

Maya allowed herself a little bit of hope.

Atalia fights with her sword, she thought, *but I fight with Luminosity.*

Finally the sounds of pursuit faded, and she slowed her camels to a comfortable walk. The animals walked single file, still roped together. The clouds of dust settled, the stars spread across the sky, and the moon shone. Maya climbed off her camel and walked beside the animals.

Leven hopped off his own camel and approached her. "You know, those raiders back there ... we took their rides, their food, their water. They'll die back there."

Maya shook her head, looking back toward the cliff, but she could no longer see it. "No. As they said, a caravan will be passing through at dawn, men looking for slaves." She allowed herself a thin smile. "Maybe they'll find eleven of them."

She looked up at the stars. She had been watching these stars every night. The Lodestar shone in the north, the tip of the Lion's Claw constellation. The Evening Star, brightest in the night, shone a pale blue, marking the west. In the east shone the Dancer, swaying across the sky, and in her hand shone the Dancer's Coin, the fairest among her stars. As children, Ofeer had always adored the eastern Dancer, while Maya had preferred the Lion's Claw in the north. This night Maya felt a kinship with that celestial dancer of darkness and light.

"We left the cliffs of Aken," she said. "That means that the city of Sekur is north from here. We're close, Leven." Her eyes shone. "Close to Sekur, the great city in the heart of Sekadia. We can find more maps there. And a road to the eastern sea, and ..." She bit her lip. "I mean, *I* can. You're going back to Zohar. Once you take me there. Like you promised."

He tucked an errant strand of her hair behind her ear. "Do you remember when the bone-raiders captured us?"

She nodded. Of course she did. "We were in the tent, and—"

"And they rudely interrupted me."

She remembered his story of the frog and the scorpion. She stopped walking and stood on the warm sand. "You were about to sting me."

He kept stroking her hair, leaned down, and kissed her lips. "Something like that."

He kissed her again, and Maya closed her eyes and kissed him back. They stood in the desert, the stars above, kissing for a long time. The camels grunted around them.

When finally their kiss ended, she poked him. "Sting."

They walked on through the desert, taking the camels and treasure with them. After so long slung across the camels, they needed to walk. They needed to feel the sand beneath their feet, to feel the desert around them.

As they walked, Maya felt joy, relief, hope … but a demon still coiled inside her. She would not forget the beatings, the thirst, the ropes cutting into her limbs. She would not forget the eyes of the men upon her, the terror in her heart. She had hurt too much, and knew this pain would not soon leave her.

But I still have the light of Zohar inside me, she thought. *And I have Leven.*

She looked at him, that stupid thief, that scorpion of the desert. Perhaps he too was like a masked man, a fortress on a cliff, and beneath his smirk there was a soul as hurt as hers. She slipped her hand into his, and they walked through the desert together, leading their camels toward the northern star.

OFEER

It was a long cold night in the hall of slaves. The chamber wasn't much larger than the deck of a ship, yet a thousand slaves or more crowded here.

Ofeer huddled on the floor, knees pulled to her chest, unable to sleep. There was barely any room here to even lie down. Bats fluttered in the rafters, and three legionaries stood at the door, armed and armored. The slaves spread around her, some lying on the floor, others curled into balls. Many were Zoharites, most of them from Gefen, a few from the forces of Yohanan. But other slaves here came from across the world. Ofeer saw Nurians huddled in the corner, their dark skin nearly invisible in the shadows, and Gaelian captives of war, their skin pale and hair blond, and many people from nations she did not recognize: some with brown skin and large eyes, others with wide faces and slanted eyes, and a few with flaming red hair and freckled skin. Captives from around the Encircled Sea and far beyond filled the hall, the daily catch to bolster Aelar's population of slaves.

And I'm one of them.

Ofeer lowered her head to her knees, letting her hair curtain the view.

"How has this happened?" she whispered.

Koren shifted at her side, joints creaking. Chains still hobbled his ankles. "What, hitting puberty?" he said. "Well, Ofeer, when a girl grows up, she begins to see changes in her body and—"

She elbowed him hard in the ribs. "Quiet. I'm trying to sleep."

He cracked his neck, staring around at the thousand slaves covering the floor. "No you weren't. You were moping. Very different thing from sleep. Sleep is when you travel to wonderful lands full of honey cakes with wings and dancing elephants playing harps."

"Maybe those are your dreams," Ofeer said. "But my dreams are always about, well ..." She sighed. "About what happened yesterday. Sailing on a beautiful ship into Aelar—a city of magic, the center of the world, my father's homeland. Of traveling in a golden chariot with a prince, the crowds cheering around me. It's what I've dreamed of for years, what finally came true. But the dream has become a nightmare."

Koren frowned. "Are you sure you never dreamed of winged honey cakes?" He winced when Ofeer elbowed him again. "All right, all right. Look, Ofeer old girl, this was never my plan for life either."

She scoffed. "You never had any plans for your life."

He bristled. "Of course I did! I was going to marry Queen Imani of Nur. You know, the fabled beauty of the south, the one the poets sing of? And I was going to discover hidden treasure buried undersea, tame a demon using a magical ring, and raise a golem out of clay to fight our enemies. Lots of big plans."

"I think you'd have better luck raising a golem than having Queen Imani Koteeka marry you." Ofeer sighed and leaned against him. "Maybe my dreams were no more realistic than yours."

Koren was silent for a long time, staring at the shadowy mass of sleeping, praying, and shivering slaves that filled the dark hall. Finally he spoke softly. "Was it really that bad?"

She looked at him. "What?"

"Living in Zohar. With us."

Ofeer too was silent for a long time. Finally, "I don't know. I thought it was. I was in pain, Koren. Not because of you. Not because of Father or Mother or even Atalia, no matter how much she scorned me. The pain was inside me, a demon nobody else could see, nobody else could understand. It's why I always ran away from the villa, spent nights at the port in Gefen, gambling and drinking and dreaming of sailing here to Aelar. To a place where I could belong. I felt like an Aelarian in Zohar, and here in Aelar I feel like a Zoharite. I don't know who I am anymore."

"A Sela," he said.

She raised an eyebrow. "But Jerael Sela was not my father."

"Of course he was. Not by blood, maybe. But he raised you from your birth, didn't he? And you grew up with us Sela children. And you bear the Sela surname. That's what matters. Not who planted the seed, but who raised the sapling. We're your real family, and I'm your real brother. Not that shit-stained Seneca."

Ofeer lowered her head. "Koren, do you think Atalia is still alive? I haven't seen her since ... since the Gaelian attack. Do you think she drowned?"

"I think," Koren said, "that Atalia is the toughest hunk of meat in the Encircled Sea. If she had to swim back to Zohar, she did. If she had to wrestle a hundred sharks on the way back, she did. She's not that easy to kill."

Yet Ofeer heard the doubt in his voice. She wanted to believe that—that Atalia was alive somewhere, that she had clung to a shard of ship, maybe climbed into a landing craft, maybe even made her way onto another Aelarian ship and was somewhere here in this city right now. But it was hard to believe.

Please, Eloh, if you can hear me, protect Atalia. Let her be alive. Please.

Ofeer had often clashed with Atalia while growing up. The two were only a year apart, closest in age among the Sela children. Yet they couldn't have been more different. Atalia was tall, strong, brave, and crass. She cut her hair the length of her chin—not long and flowing like a proper woman's hair—wore armor even to the dinner table, and spat and cussed and dreamed of glory. Ofeer was shorter, daintier, far more frightened; she had always felt cowed in the presence of her bluff older sister. Many times, she had thought she hated Atalia.

But I love you, sister, Ofeer now thought. *Please be alive. Please keep fighting.*

She vowed that if she ever saw Atalia again, she would embrace her, tell her that she loved her, and never let go.

"Koren," Ofeer said, "do you remember that time we tried to bake fig cakes?"

Laughter snorted out from his nose. "Those things were half salt, half sand, what with you dropping them—twice."

She nodded, laughing too now. "But Father ate an entire cake, just to make us happy. Epher threw his out, and Atalia used hers for target practice."

Koren was laughing so hard he was waking up other slaves. "Maya tried to cobble our front pathway with them. Even the horses wouldn't touch them."

Ofeer leaned her head against his shoulder. "Mother could always cook so wonderfully. Those salads she made, the ones with flowers and pomegranate beads in them. Real flowers—in a salad! And fried fish with lemon and pepper." She licked her lips. "And the sweet bread with sesame seeds."

She found herself crying now. She had shed so many tears this spring she was surprised she hadn't lost half her weight. Koren began to tell another story—this one of the time Atalia had mistaken a roaming jackal for a barbarian assault—when a slave tossed a sandal at them.

"Hush and let us sleep!" said the man. "Bloody desert pups."

Koren and Ofeer fell silent. They struggled to find room to lie on the floor. Finally Ofeer managed to lie down, leaning her head on a sleeping woman's thighs, her legs across a slumbering man. Koren placed his head on her lap, his legs entangled with another slave's. For a few hours, they drifted in and out of sleep,

waking every few moments, trapped between nightmare and
reality.

Their second day in Aelar dawned stark and cold, streaming
through an oculus in the coffered dome above. No sooner had
the light roused Ofeer than the doors slammed open, and a group
of men bustled inside, clad in gray togas. Five pushed
wheelbarrows full of wooden slats, while five others carried scrolls
and quills. Here were hard men, Ofeer saw at once, faces leathery,
eyes stony, and rolled-up whips hung from their hips.

"Slaves, up, up!" one man cried, banging a rod against his
wheelbarrow. "Stand, one slave per floor tile. Up!"

Glancing from side to side, the captives rose to their feet.
Several of the men in togas set up a table at the back of the hall.
One by one, the captives were herded toward the table. Tall men
stood in front of Ofeer, and she couldn't see over their shoulders.
The room was so crammed her elbows banged against the
captives at her sides, her chest pressed against the back of a
woman before her, and a man pressed up behind her. The room
stank of sweat and human waste and blood.

"What's happening?" she said to Koren.

Her brother stood at her side. "By God, they're setting us all
free! And giving us a gift of a horse and castle each."

"I want a white mare," Ofeer said. "And a castle by the sea.
Do you think they're taking requests?"

Koren nodded. "Just bat your eyelashes and they'll give you
the imperial palace, gorgeous."

The imperial palace that should be my home by right, Ofeer thought. *The palace where my father lives.*

As the crowd of slaves advanced toward the table at the back, one by one, her fear grew. What would happen to her? Would she be carted off to some quarry or mine? Or sent to a brothel? Maybe assigned to toil as a galley slave, or maybe just toil in the fields? Aelar was a city of a million people, and surely there were a million ways to torment a slave here.

As she inched closer across the hall, Ofeer could hear a ruckus from outside. Somebody was shouting, and a crowd was answering. They shuffled closer, and Ofeer caught sight of a naked man—a captive from Zohar!—being escorted out a back door. Her heart leaped in fear, and cold sweat trickled down her back. What was happening?

It took hours, but finally the crowd of captives cleared out before them, the hall slowly draining. Now Ofeer and Koren approached the oaken table, guided by legionaries with spears.

Two Aelarian men sat behind the table, togas gray.

"Name!" one said to Ofeer.

"Name!" another barked at Koren.

Ofeer told them. She used the surname Sela; saying "Octavius" would no doubt earn her a lashing. The gruff man nodded and wrote her name on a slat of wood—misspelling it, she noticed, but she dared not correct him.

"Languages?" the man snapped.

Ofeer glanced around, not sure what he meant.

"Languages!" The man frowned. "What languages do you speak, and which do you read and write?"

Ofeer spoke, read, and wrote both Zoharite and Aelarian. The man wrote it down on the wooden slat, adding that she knew basic arithmetic.

"Age?"

"Eighteen," she told him, surprised for a moment to realize how young she still was. She felt infinitely older, as if a decade had passed since leaving Zohar. The man wrote down her age too, then rose and measured her height and added that as well. At her side, Koren was answering the same questions, and his own clerk was writing on a separate wooden slat.

"Any artistic skill?" the man in the gray toga asked. "Music? Singing? Dancing?"

Ofeer nodded. "All of those things. I can play the lyre and timbrel, and I can sing and dance." A hint of hope, just a small ray, filled her. Perhaps she could find work here as a musician or dancer. That wouldn't be too bad. It would be infinitely better than being sold to a brothel or mine.

The clerk nodded and scribbled it onto the slat.

"All right, off with your stola," he said.

Ofeer struggled to find her tongue. "My ... what?"

The man behind the table groaned. "Off with it! You don't expect folk to buy what they can't see, do you? Would you buy a horse without examining its teeth? Would you buy a jug of olive oil without tasting it first? Go on."

Ofeer would have done both those things, but she dared not argue back. She glanced toward Koren, and she saw that he was pulling off his tunic. "I hope there are no ladies outside," Koren said, "or I might trigger a violent auction. I'm talking fistfights."

Koren joked, but Ofeer saw the pain and fear in his eyes, saw the scars that still covered his back. His voice shook.

Ofeer looked away from him, not wanting to see her brother's nakedness. Eyes damp, fingers trembling, she removed the fine, dyed fabrics Seneca had gifted her. Hundreds of people still stood around her, and Ofeer covered her breasts with her right arm, and she placed her left hand between her legs. Her cheeks burned with shame.

Another man, this one clad in a white toga, approached her. He sported a brooch shaped as two serpents circling a staff—a physician. He spent a while examining Ofeer's body, clucking his tongue and mumbling to himself. His hands explored her everywhere—the inside of her mouth, along her spine, along the wounds on her back, even between her legs. Finally he nodded, scrubbed her down with a wet sponge, and turned toward the man behind the desk.

"She's healthy. A few marks of the whip, but nothing that would leave much of a scar. Good teeth. Good skin. No sores in her mouth, no lice in her hair. This one was raised in luxury, never lacked for proper food. The daughter of nobility, she is."

The clerk behind the table raised his eyes, scrutinizing Ofeer. "Are you healthy, girl? Have you ever had the crabs? The warts? The sores? Ever fucked a man till it burned when you pissed? I won't be selling no diseased whores in my market."

Ofeer's cheeks burned. She wanted to snap her tongue at him, to strike him, but only found herself shaking her head. Her teeth ground.

The clerk stared into her eyes, brow furrowed, as if seeking conceit. Finally he nodded and scratched more words onto the tablet. He slung a rope through the wooden slat, then handed it to a guard, who in turn hung it around Ofeer's neck. She felt like a piece of meat stamped with a price tag, but at least the wood hid her breasts.

"Step into that bucket of chalk." The guard pointed. "Both feet."

Ofeer saw that several chalky footprints led toward the back door. "Why?

The guard groaned. "All new arrivals from abroad are marked with white feet. Buyers need to tell imported from domestic. Go on."

She dutifully dipped both feet into the bucket, letting the chalk rise halfway up her shins. Imported goods.

"Now go on, out you go." The man pointed at the back door. "Next slave—up!"

Ofeer glanced back toward Koren, who wore a wooden sign around his own neck. She met his eyes, and she didn't know if she would ever see him again. Before she could say goodbye, a guard grabbed her arm, manhandled her forward, and shoved her through the doorway.

Naked but for the wooden sign hanging around her neck, Ofeer emerged into a sunlit courtyard. Wooden stairs rose before her, leading to a stage. On the platform stood a naked Nurian man, tall and well-muscled, staring around like a trapped bear. Chalk whitened his feet, deeply contrasting with his dark skin. Two guards stood by a brick wall—the exterior of the hall Ofeer had exited—helmets hiding their heads, spears and shields in their hands. An ample-bellied, balding man paced the stage, clad in a mustard toga with a red sash. He held a wooden sign like the one that hung around Ofeer's neck, reading from it.

"Kosooma of Nur!" the man in the mustard toga announced. "Age: Twenty-four. Height: six feet three inches. Speaks only Nurian, but quick of wit and can learn Aelarian within a season. The son of a warrior. Physically strong. Healthy. Has all his teeth. Excellent for physical labor."

Before the stage spread the crowd. Hundreds of Aelarians were here, draped in white togas. These people weren't as wealthy as senators or princes—most did not wear dyed fabric, nor did they sport gold or gemstones. It seemed that in Aelar, slaves were not only a luxury for the wealthy, but that even common citizens could buy them, as easily as a Zoharite back home could buy a goat or sheep.

Men in the crowd began to bid, raising their hands and calling out their offers.

"Five hundred denarii!" cried a bald man.

Another raised his hand. "Five hundred and fifty denarii for the slave!"

The auctioneer in the mustard toga kept calling out the prices, encouraging the bids. Finally he pounded a gavel, selling the Nurian for eight hundred denarii to a man in the crowd. The guards escorted the naked captive—now officially a slave—off the stage.

A guard placed a meaty hand on Ofeer's shoulder. He spoke in a rumbling voice. "Climb the stage, hand your sign to the auctioneer, then face the crowd."

Ofeer looked around her, seeking paths to escape, but thick walls surrounded the courtyard, and guards stood at every door. If she ran, they would grab her, drag her back, beat her, maybe kill her.

"Climb," the guard said, twisting her arm.

Ofeer's eyes stung, but she refused to let them see her cry. She raised her chin, squared her shoulders, and climbed the stage, leaving chalky footprints. The auctioneer stood there, gesturing for her sign. Ofeer stared at him, refusing to look at the crowd. With numb fingers, she unslung the sign from her neck and handed it over.

"Face the crowd, girl," the auctioneer said. "Go on, look at them, not at me."

Her wooden sign gone, Ofeer covered her breasts with her arm again, then turned toward the crowd. She stared at her feet. The crowd tittered as the auctioneer sighed and pulled her arms down to her sides.

"Just stare ahead and be calm," the auctioneer said, his voice softer now. "It'll go faster if you just go along with it."

Her eyes were damp. She could barely see. She stared ahead at the crowd, blinking too much, as the auctioneer read from the sign.

"Ofeer Sela!" he announced. "A princess of the desert! The daughter of a Zoharite chieftain, raised in palaces of gold, now yours for purchase! Eighteen years old. Healthy, strong, perfect teeth and flawless skin. Can speak, read, and write fluent Aelarian and Zoharite. Can sing, dance, and play both timbrel and lyre, musical instruments of the east that will astonish and delight your guests. A perfect musician or tutor. Renowned for her dusky beauty, famous among poets from her homeland." The auctioneer delivered his pitch with gusto, but Ofeer thought she detected boredom beneath the feigned excitement. "A delightful desert rose to entertain at parties, tutor children, and excite all who see her."

Ofeer wasn't a princess, and she wasn't sure her beauty was renowned anywhere outside the taverns of Gefen's port, but she dared not contradict.

"Five hundred denarii!" a man cried in the crowd, middle aged and sweating in the sunlight.

"Five hundred and ten!" Another hand rose from the crowd.

The auctioneer stepped closer to Ofeer and spoke softly. "Turn around, child, slowly, then back forward again. Let them see you. You'll fetch a fair price."

The bidding continued, soon surpassing a thousand denarii, then two thousand. Ofeer just wanted them to stop. She wanted to escape, or she wanted to die. She wanted them to stop staring at her. She could feel their eyes crawling across her, and one bidder—a tall man of about sixty years, who had bid twenty-two hundred denarii—actually stepped on stage to examine her teeth, thrusting rough fingers into her mouth.

"Twenty-five hundred denarii!" rose a cry from the crowd. The old man grunted, pulled his fingers free, and stepped off the stage.

Finally the price reached twenty-eight hundred. The bidder was a beefy, pink-cheeked man with nervous lips and soft hands. The auctioneer was about to pound his gavel, finalizing the deal, when a voice rose from the back of the crowd.

"Twenty thousand denarii!"

The crowd murmured in awe and turned toward the new bidder. Ofeer breathed out a sigh of relief—the nervous, soft-handed man scared her—only for new fear to fill her. Who was this rich man who had bid so much? That was almost the cost of a fine horse. Judging by the whispers in the crowd, nobody ever bid so much on a slave.

The auctioneer pounded his hammer. "Sold for twenty thousand denarii!"

Her buyer came walking through the crowd, wrapped in a white toga, staring at her calmly. People knelt, a great wave that swept across the courtyard. He reached up his hand, and he helped Ofeer climb off the stage.

"My desert rose," Seneca said, bowing his head. "Ofeer, keeper of her mother's vineyard."

She couldn't stop the tears from flowing. He wrapped her in a cloak, and he took her through the crowd, the people kneeling around them.

EPHER

He was walking through the streets of Beth Eloh, teaching Olive the names of the birds, when the drunken legionaries stumbled down the road, looking for blood.

"Dove!" Olive was saying that morning, pointing and laughing and hopping about. "Dove, dove, dove, dove, dove!"

She raced toward the bird, reaching out, perhaps hoping to pat it. The bird, which had been busy pecking seeds between cobblestones, burst into flight. Olive watched it fly away, then spun back toward Epher, her eyes bright.

"Dove go away."

"The dove *went* away," he said.

She nodded. "The dove went way." She flapped her arms. "Went?"

"Flew." Epher flapped his own arms like wings. "You can also say: The dove flew away."

Olive tilted her head and frowned. "What is went? How is flew not went?"

Epher tried to explain it to her, but he found himself mostly admiring her—the way her red hair, brushed and cut the length of her chin, was so smooth, and how her green eyes shone, and how so many freckles covered her face, little marks of beauty he wanted to kiss endlessly, a kiss for each one, over and over.

He had purchased her a *simlah* in the city, the common dress of Zoharites, woven of rich cotton. The fabric was white and trimmed with blue thread, a pricey dye obtained from mollusks along the coast of Kalintia in the north. He had tried to get her to wear sandals too, but these Olive had vehemently refused, discarding the pair he had purchased her. She walked through the city barefoot, her soles so thickly callused she didn't even seem to feel the heat of sunlight on cobblestones.

Or maybe she does feel the heat, Epher thought as she hopped around, racing between palm trees and down alleyways. *The woman never stands still for a moment.*

They were walking along a small courtyard, a palm tree in its center, when the legionaries emerged from the opposite street.

They were drunk. Epher saw it at once, smelled it. The three of them swaggered across the courtyard, faces flushed beneath their helms. Around them rose brick homes and shops topped with domes, a ring of stone.

Olive froze when she saw them, crouched, and hissed. Her hand reached out to grab a stone. Epher froze too, standing above her, fingers tingling. He and Olive had passed by many legionaries these past few days, but most might as well have been statues, so stiff they were. *These* men wanted trouble. Epher saw it in their eyes.

"Well, look at what we have here." One of the legionaries snorted and pointed at Olive. "A Zoharite rat with red hair."

"Ain't never seen one of the desert rats with red hair before," said his comrade.

"I like redheads," said the third man. "Back when I fought in Elania, plenty of 'em up there."

The three legionaries approached Olive, leering, staring up and down her body.

Olive stood her ground, crouched and hissing, the stone in her hand. Suddenly she seemed again like the wild woman Epher had first encountered on the beach.

"Go away!" She bared her teeth. "Go away, cunts. Fly away!"

Two legionaries laughed, but the third—a brute with crooked teeth and a scar across one eyebrow—snarled.

"Fucking whore." He reached toward her. "What did you call us?"

"Fucking whore!" Olive shrieked, raising her stone, her eyes wild. "Go away, fucking whore!"

The legionary—drunk, looking for a fight—reached for his sword. Epher sucked in air. Heart pounding, he stepped between Olive and the Aelarians.

"Forgive her, my lords!" He forced himself to hide the anger from his voice. "She's my sister. A simpleton. A mule once kicked her in the head, and she's been odd ever since. I beg your pardon." He took three silver coins from his pocket and held them out. "For your trouble, a silver each."

The snaggletoothed legionary shoved his hand aside. The silver coins clattered. "Shut your fucking mouth, rat. We're not whores you can buy with silver." He turned toward Olive and licked his lips. "Go pick up the silver coins, bitch. Go pick them up like a good rat. Take them as payment." He reached toward her. "Bet you never had Aelarian cock before."

Olive made to throw her rock, but Epher grabbed her wrist, and the rock slammed onto the cobblestones. "Come, Olive. We're going home."

He began to walk away with her, his heart hammering against his ribs, every instinct in him crying to reach under his tunic, to grab the dagger he hid there, to fight, to kill. But he had promised his mother. Her words echoed in his mind.

Epher, I know you seek more war. I know you seek to resist the eagles. But the time for peace is here.

"Where are you going, rats?" The legionary approached to block their way. "I paid three silvers for that whore. I want what I'm due."

The other legionaries approached too, surrounding Epher and Olive. One drank from a flask. "I want me a taste of her too. I like redheads."

They reached toward Olive. One man grabbed her tunic and tore it. When Epher tried to reach her, another legionary grabbed his arms, pulling him back.

Olive screamed, hurling every insult she knew. A legionary grabbed her arms, and she screamed and kicked, hitting one in the face. Blood gushed from his nose.

"Goddamn whore broke my nose!" The legionary roared and backhanded Olive, splitting her lip. "Fucking desert rats!"

The man drew his sword.

Epher reached under his tunic and whipped out his dagger.

Olive grabbed another stone and threw it.

Everything seemed to happen at once. The stone slammed into a legionary's face, and blood splattered. The sword swung toward Olive, and Epher lashed his dagger. The blade drove into a legionary's thigh, cutting deep, and the man fell. The others lunged at him, swords thrusting. Epher leaped back, dagger held before him.

Armor clattered as four more legionaries ran into the courtyard, swords drawn, blocking all exits.

Epher and Olive stood back to back, and he knew that this was it. Here was his death.

Then I die fighting.

He lunged forward with his dagger, scraping the blade across a legionary's arm. He barely dodged a sword, and Olive screamed, weaponless, and the blades thrust again, and a gladius scraped down Epher's leg. His blood splattered the courtyard. The other blades thrust, and Epher prepared for it all to end, and he only prayed that they killed Olive before they could rape her, that they killed him before they could nail him to a cross.

A buzz rose like the song of insects.

Whistles cut the air.

Stones flew from the rooftops, slamming into legionaries.

Epher gasped, looked up, and saw two young men on a rooftop, spinning slings. A doorway opened, and two other men emerged from a house, one holding a bread knife, the other wielding a meat cleaver.

"God damn rats coming out of their hole—" a legionary began. A sling stone slammed into his mouth, shattering his teeth.

Epher ran toward him and thrust his dagger, sinking the blade deep into the man's throat. The legionary's sword fell, and Olive grabbed and swung it, taking out another legionary's legs. The two city men—Knife and Cleaver—fought too, swinging their weapons against the legionaries. One took a sword to the gut, screamed, and fell. The other swung his cleaver, severing a legionary's arm. More sling stones flew, and more people emerged from their homes, armed with pans, kitchen knives, and even a rolling pin.

Another Zoharite fell, Epher drove his dagger into another legionary, and the battle was over.

Six legionaries and nine Zoharites lay dead on the street. Blood ran in the grooves between the cobblestones. A stray dog slunk up and began to lap at the grisly gift.

Epher turned toward Olive. A cut bled on her leg. "I'll get you to a healer. I—"

"Go away," she said, eyes huge, full of fear. "Epher and Olive go away. Now."

He heard it then. More armor clattering. More legionaries. He grabbed Olive's hand, and they ran. They fled the courtyard. The other Zoharites, their weapons and arms bloody, ran with them.

They raced through the warren of Beth Eloh, a hive of twisting alleyways, the brick walls close around them. The awnings of shops met above. A camel, startled, fled before them. Stone balconies hid the sun, and Epher kicked over a peddler's tin tray as he ran, scattering a thousand semiprecious stones across the narrow road. A donkey brayed, and behind him, he heard the legionaries shouting.

They split up. Two men ran down Grain Road toward the silos. Another two headed to the cemetery. Epher held Olive's arm and took her toward the marketplace. Many legionaries stood here at street corners, monitoring the vendors and shoppers, and Epher forced himself to slow down, to walk calmly, to pretend to be browsing the shops. His heart still thudded, though, and sweat beaded on his brow.

Olive glanced up at him, fear in her eyes. She said nothing. She didn't need to. Her eyes spoke more than her mouth ever could. She was afraid—not only for herself, not only for him, but for this city. For their nation.

That evening, Epher stood at the palace courtyard with his mother, with Olive, with King Shefael, with a hundred Aelarians. Together they stood at a balustrade, staring downhill at the city. Mother's eyes were damp, and Olive cursed and growled under her breath. Epher stared with dry eyes.

Prefect Remus Marcellus stepped closer to the edge of the courtyard. He placed his hands on the marble balustrade, gazing down at the city. The general who had led the assault on Gefen, who now ruled over Zohar in his emperor's name, still wore the armor of a soldier, the breastplate embossed with golden eagles, the pauldrons wide, the helmet crested. He was a towering man, close to seven feet tall.

"Do you see, Zoharites?" His eyes narrowed, and the slightest of twitches tugged at his lip. "Do you see what happens to those who resist the light and civilization of Aelar?"

Epher saw. Below in the narrow city streets, legionaries stood in the neighborhood where six of their comrades had died. They were swinging battering rams, shattering the houses that surrounded the courtyard, then spreading out, toppling more homes, leaving ruins. People were fleeing before them, but the legionaries grabbed whoever they could, beating them, chaining them.

"Six legionaries were slain," Remus said. His fists clenched. "And so six hundred Zoharite rats will die." He turned away from the city, facing Epher and his family. "If you cannot control your people, if you cannot bring order to this place, this palace too shall fall, and with it every last rat in this wretched hive. We try to civilize you. We tried to civilize Leer too. Now the great kingdom of Leer is a field of stones and skulls. If you cannot join the Empire, you will be buried beneath it."

Rage, burning, all consuming, flared through Epher. He wanted to pummel the general, to shove him off the railing, to watch his body shatter below.

But Shiloh reacted differently. She stepped toward the prefect, wrapped in a white shawl, her braid hanging out from her hood. She knelt before him, head lowered.

"Please, dominus," she whispered. "Spare us. This city has bled enough. Spare the six hundred."

Below in the streets, the legionaries were rounding people up from around the ruins. Men. Women. Children. Babies. Cries of fear and rage rose through the city.

"Rats to crucify!" a legionary cried below. "Count six hundred heads!"

"Please, dominus," Shiloh said, head bowed. She knelt and kissed Remus's feet. "Spare them."

Epher trembled with rage. How could his mother debase herself so? Had she knelt like this nineteen years ago before Marcus Octavius raped her, placing Ofeer in her belly? How long would Zohar kneel while the Empire butchered, enslaved, and raped their nation?

We are a hundred thousand souls in this city, Epher thought. *A million other Zoharites live beyond these walls. We can rise up. We can kill them. We can take back our homeland. With stones, with breadknives, with farm tools.* He dug his fingernails into his palms. *Like we slew six legionaries in the courtyard, we can slay them all.*

Remus stared down at the kneeling Shiloh. His brow furrowed, and he looked up and stared at Epher. Their eyes met. Epher stared back, fists clenched, unable to hide the rage on his face. Remus's eyes were heartless, almost like the eyes of a corpse. The prefect spoke to Shiloh, but he kept his gaze on Epher.

"Very well, Shiloh Sela," Remus said. "I will spare the six hundred ... in exchange for one life. Your son's."

"Dominus!" King Shefael said. The burly man lolloped forth, cheeks flushing. "Perhaps I can offer another lord from my court, or—"

"Please, Lord Remus!" Shiloh said, tears in her eyes. "Not him. I beg you. I've already lost a son. I—"

"Go away, cunt!" Olive was screaming at Remus, clutching Epher's arm as if to protect him. "Get lost! Get lost, whore! Fucking whore!"

Legionaries across the balcony smirked, and everyone seemed to be talking at once, and below in the city the screams still rose and the rams still swung. Through the chaos, Epher remained very still, not breaking his stare. Remus stared back into his eyes, and finally Epher saw a hint of humanity on that stony face.

Remus was smiling.

"Yes," Epher whispered.

Nobody seemed to hear him. Shiloh was still begging, Shefael was stuttering and mumbling and saying something about Epher being his dear cousin, and Olive was still shrieking curses. Epher and Remus kept staring at each other.

"Yes," Epher repeated, louder now. "Yes! I'll do this. Take me, Remus. Nail me into a cross and spare the lives of six hundred of my people. This is Zoharite pride. This is Zoharite compassion."

Remus didn't have to say anything, only to nod. His legionaries stepped across the balcony and grabbed Epher, tugging his arms behind his back, shoving Olive aside. The young woman screamed, cursed, spat, kicked, scratched, only for legionaries to grab her limbs and pin her to the ground.

"Remus, no!" Shiloh cried, stepped toward him, trying to reach him. "Lord Remus, I beg you! Take me. Take me instead."

"Epher, no!" Olive screamed from the ground. "Olive love you. Olive love—" A legionary gagged her.

"Take him to the dungeon beneath the palace," Remus said. "At dawn, he'll bear his cross for the city to see. All of Beth Eloh will hear the screams of Epheriah Sela, the Prince of Rats."

"I won't scream," Epher said. And he knew that he was lying.

As his mother cried out, as Olive flailed on the floor, as Shefael still mumbled and wrung his hands, the legionaries manhandled Epher across the courtyard. He held his head high, refusing to let himself be dragged.

"I die saving life," he said, loud enough for the others to hear. "Everyone across the Empire will see that Zohar loves life and Aelar craves death."

His mother was on her knees, crying out, tears on her cheeks. Olive stared at him from the floor, legionaries still pinning her down, love in her eyes.

Goodbye, Mother. Goodbye, Olive. I love you.

They dragged him off the courtyard, down underground, down into darkness, down into the long, cold, last night of his life.

OFEER

"Why?" Ofeer asked, staring out the window at the gardens, her eyes burning. "Why did you buy me?"

Seneca placed a hand on her shoulder. "To bring you here. To this palace. To live with me."

She wheeled around toward him. They stood in his suite, which occupied several rooms in the eastern wing of the palace. This room, brightly sunlit, was the library. Through two doors at the back, she could see corridors leading toward his bedchamber, a personal armory, and other rooms she hadn't yet explored. Ofeer remembered comforting him in the Sela library in the villa on Pine Hill, a dusty, crowded place full of scrolls in rough alcoves. This library put that old chamber to shame. Here countless scrolls stood on shelves, wrapped around giltwood rollers, topped with silver eagles, each a masterpiece. Scrolls about warfare, about plants and animals, about history, about the lineages of Aelar, scrolls of stories and myths.

Maya would love it here, Ofeer knew. But she herself had no use for these scrolls. She wanted answers. She wanted truth. She wanted to stop being tossed through her life like driftwood in a storm, to find who she was, who she could be.

"You brought me here as a slave," Ofeer said, gesturing down at her garment. She no longer wore her fine, dyed stola, the dress of a noblewoman. Instead, Seneca had clad her in a simple white tunic. Her captors had seized her eagle pendant from around her neck. Instead she wore a crude iron collar. From it hung a metal tag, like one a dog might wear, and upon it were engraved words: *I have escaped! If you find me, return me to the Acropolis, to Prince Seneca Octavius, for a thousand denarius reward.*

Seneca nodded. "That's what you are now. A slave. A slave I purchased."

Ofeer hissed and grabbed his shoulders, digging her fingernails past his toga and into his skin. "You said you'd bring me here as your princess."

Seneca raised an eyebrow. "Did I? I believe I called it 'concubine.' That you will still be, just wearing an iron collar instead of a golden necklace." He shrugged. "I took you here in my chariot of gold, Ofeer. You stood at my side—with me, a prince of Aelar!—clad in splendor, waving to a crowd of a million souls. You chose to flee that life. You chose to join the slaves. You brought this upon yourself. Be thankful that I saved you from whatever wretched scum might have bought you. I paid good money for you, Ofeer. If I hadn't, you'd no doubt have been sold to a brothel, made an expensive whore."

"And what am I now then, if not an expensive whore?"

"*My* expensive whore." He snorted. "You'd be fucking twenty men a night at the brothels."

"And you can only manage twice a night," she said, stiffly. "I suppose I should be grateful."

He reached for her breast. "I can manage three times a night. I've proven that to you."

She shoved his hand away, shuddering. She swore that she would never let him touch her again. Never. He did not know who she was, did not know they were half siblings.

I have two fathers, Ofeer thought. *One whom we share. One whom you murdered.*

His eyes narrowed, kindled with anger. "Perhaps I should have left you in the market."

"Perhaps you should have left me in Zohar," she said.

His laughter snorted out from him. "You begged me to take you to Aelar. You begged me! I hadn't known you for an hour, and you were dragging me into the cave and tugging off your dress."

Ofeer looked away from him, eyes stinging now. "I was a fool."

She meant those words. What she wouldn't give to turn back time, to go back to that day, to run—to run from him, run from this cruel prince, this twisted family, this whole twisted empire.

"So what do you want from me?" Seneca said. "To send you back? Zohar is fallen, Ofeer. Fallen! There is nothing but Aelar now. Nothing but a great empire that sprawls around the Encircled Sea."

"There is Gael." Ofeer met his gaze, chin raised. "Gael still fights."

She thought back to the battle at sea, how the Gaelian fleet had smashed into the Aelarian armada, how so many ships had sunk, how so many had died—Atalia perhaps among them.

"Then go there." Seneca snickered. "Flee this palace in the dead of night, and whore your way across the northern roads until you reach the forests, and go to the bearded barbarians, and tell them: I am Ofeer, a girl who never held anything heavier than a cock, give me a sword and let me fight with you!"

"Yours is particularly lightweight," she said.

He snorted and turned toward the window. He stared outside at the gardens where flowers bloomed and birds sang. A sigh ran through him, and his anger seemed to melt. "Perhaps I should join you there. Perhaps we should both travel to Gael and fight with the brutes. The gods know when Porcia becomes empress, there'll be no more place for me here."

Ofeer felt her own rage die down. She stepped closer to him, placed a hand on his shoulder, and looked outside the window too. The gardens sprawled between marble columns, each one topped with a statue of a god or mythological creature. Pebbly paths spread between thickets and fruit trees, and a fountain rose beyond flowerbeds.

In the distance, Ofeer could see the famous Princess Valentina, Seneca's younger sister. The girl was fabled across the Empire, famous for her kind demeanor and strange appearance. The girl was an albino, her hair milky white, her skin like a sheet.

Ofeer could see that even from this distance, and she envied the girl.

We're of an age, Ofeer knew, *Valentina and I. Both the daughters of Marcus Octavius. But while she's white and was raised in a palace, I'm dark and was raised in the desert. I would very much like to speak to you, Valentina.*

But at that moment, Ofeer looked away from the princess and looked at the prince instead.

"So you spoke to him?" Ofeer said. "You spoke to your father, and you told him what I coached you to say?"

Seneca nodded. "I did. I told him everything. Just like we practiced. That ports are what make Aelar powerful, and that I conquered the last port in the Encircled Sea. I told him that I conquered the city with blood and fire, and that Porcia merely struck a deal with a king who had already sat on the throne, essentially changing nothing. But ..." He looked down. "Porcia was convincing. She boasted of defeating Yohanan, yes, like we predicted. But she also said other things. How the lume matters more than a port, and how Beth Eloh is the fountain of lume, the place where we get our lumers. And how making deals with puppet kings is what gives Aelar its true strength, more than the might of our swords. Father seemed impressed with her. She humiliated me, Ofeer." Bitterness twisted his voice. "Everything I said, she somehow turned against me. She made me look like a callow boy, herself a seasoned leader. Father didn't name an heir, not on the spot. He'll announce his heir tomorrow. Tomorrow, Ofeer! He'll hold great games to celebrate ten years since defeating

Phedia, and there—over the corpses in the arena—he'll reveal his choice. When we spoke, he favored Porcia. I could see it in his eyes. Tomorrow, Ofeer. Tomorrow it ends."

Ofeer sucked in air and stared at a shelf. Her eyes landed on a scroll labelled *A History of Leer*. The kingdom of Leer was well known in Zohar—a kingdom that had rebelled against Aelar, that was effaced off the map, all its halls toppled, all its inhabitants slain. Should Porcia ascend to the throne, would Zohar too be destroyed, and all other kingdoms around the Encircled Sea?

True, Porcia had not destroyed Beth Eloh, if the stories were to be believed, merely turned cousin Shefael into a client king. Yet she had done this to impress Marcus Octavius. Porcia had also arrived in Gefen and tossed a severed member at Seneca. Porcia was also rumored to carve the hearts out of her enemies and feast upon them. Porcia had also dragged severed heads behind her chariots through the streets of Aelar. Such a woman, made empress, would not hesitate to plunge the world into chaos and bloodshed worse than anything Marcus Octavius had ever done. Zohar would not merely be a province under her reign; it would be a graveyard.

Ofeer shuddered. Seneca was perhaps cowardly, proud, maybe even wicked. But she could manipulate him. With the right words, some sharp and some soft, Ofeer could bend Seneca to her will. If he sat on the throne of Aelar, and she served at his side—even just as a slave—she could still wield some influence.

But Porcia? Ofeer could not even imagine what an inferno this world would become with that madwoman ruling it.

I cannot let Porcia reign. For the sake of Zohar. For the sake of my family. For the sake of the entire world, Porcia must not ascend.

She turned back toward Seneca. "So he hasn't decided yet," she said. "Not a final decision, in any case. You have until tomorrow to sway him. There's still hope for you."

He laughed mirthlessly. "What hope? What can I possibly do in the last few hours? Am I to launch a new campaign this morning, maybe conquer all of Gael by tomorrow? Perhaps bring Sekadia down to its knees before dawn? Unless you can figure out a way to do that, it's hopeless."

Ofeer grabbed him. "Do not abandon hope now. Are you a prince or a weakling? There's still something you can do— something to sway your father's mind."

"What?" His eyes narrowed and his breath shook.

Ofeer turned away from him, staring outside the window, silent.

"What?" Seneca said, louder this time, and pulled her back toward him.

She raised her chin. "I'll offer you my counsel, Seneca, but not for free. No longer. I'll tell you how you can win your inheritance. And in exchange, I want something."

"What, your freedom?"

She shook her head. "No." She stared into his eyes, refusing to show weakness. "I want you to find out what happened to my siblings. Find who bought Koren at the slave market, and buy him for a higher price. Bring him here, to serve in this palace, with me. I would not have my brother toiling in the fields or mines, not when he can be a palace slave at my side. And … my other siblings. Epher. Atalia. Maya. Pull strings. Consult with your lumer. Bring me news of them, and make sure no harm will come to them. If you promise me this, I will counsel you."

"You ask a lot." His face flushed with anger. "You ask too much."

She shrugged and turned away. "So let Porcia become heiress."

Seneca groaned. "I'll buy Koren for you, all right? I can promise you that. The boy won't be hard to find. As for the others, well, that bitch Atalia is dead. Drowned in the sea. I can tell you that already. As for Epher and Maya … I'll get my lumer to use her Sight, but I can't promise that you'll like the news." He grabbed her arm, spinning her back toward him. "Now tell me. What do I do?"

Ofeer smiled crookedly and touched his cheek. "If you cannot glorify your own position in your father's eyes, you can do the next best thing. You can tarnish Porcia."

"Tarnish Porcia?" He frowned. "How? The woman is a goddamn heroine in my father's eyes. She's strong. She's cruel. She's adored by all."

"Not by all." Ofeer shook her head, remembering what she had seen back in Zohar. "Porcia has an enemy. One who hates her more than you or I ever could. An enemy who *knows* her more than you or I ever could. Everybody has some dirt under their fingernails, even heroines like Porcia. Everyone has skeletons in their closet that, if released, could destroy them. You must simply go to the right source."

"Who?" Seneca said. "Who would have the dirt on Porcia?"

Ofeer smiled. "Her lumer. Worm."

SENECA

H e slunk through the palace at night, barefoot, barely daring
to breathe, sure that his heartbeat was so loud the entire
city could hear.

The corridor spread before him. He passed by libraries, a
chapel, a private bathhouse, armories, and the chambers of
servants. He moved toward her wing of the palace. Her little
empire within an empire. The realm of Porcia Octavius.

His older sister occupied the southern section of the palace,
the one overlooking the Amphitheatrum. While Seneca kept his
chambers mostly clean and neat, here was a grisly realm. A
deformed skeleton stood on a pedestal in the corridor, its back
crooked, its bones and skull overgrown with lumps. In a dining
room, skulls topped a table, sawed open to form mugs. The
library held scrolls of demonic incantations, and the fireplace held
bleached bones. An armory contained a host of weapons—
swords, daggers, spears, hammers, axes—all hanging through the
ribs of skeletons, the grim racks formed from vanquished
enemies.

Soon Seneca passed by Porcia's bedchamber. The door was
closed, and two Magisterians stood outside. The guards reached

for their swords as Seneca arrived, then recognized him and knelt with a clatter of armor.

"Hush!" he mouthed, mortified that Porcia should wake. If she caught him skulking here, she would slay him, he knew. She would grab one of her weapons, and she would drive it through his chest. He froze, for an instant sure the clanking had woken her. A harsh snore sounded behind the door ... then relaxed into deep breath.

Seneca exhaled in relief. He pressed a silver into each guard's hand and placed his fingers against his lips. They nodded, understanding, and pocketed the coins.

He kept walking. He knew where he'd find her. The same place where Porcia kept all her favorite treasures.

Soon Seneca reached the end of the corridor and began climbing the spiraling staircase up the tower. He hadn't been here for years. Only once, when he was ten, had Seneca dared climb Porcia's tower, seeking the curiosities within. He had caught only a quick glimpse of the collection before Porcia, a youth of thirteen, had caught him. In punishment, she had sliced him with one of these ancient, rusty instruments. He still bore the scar.

Fear had kept him from the tower since, but today Seneca would dare. Today he was a man, a conqueror, and—if he succeeded—an emperor.

After a climb that seemed to last an eternity, he reached a door. Sweat trickled down his back. His pulse pounded in his ears. The door was locked; he had expected this. He took from his pocket the key Taeer had made him. The lumer had used her most powerful magic, calling upon the Muse, one of the four pillars of Luminosity, enhancing skills in music, dance, art, and craftwork.

This key, Taeer had sworn, would open every door in the palace.

"If you lied to me, Taeer," he muttered, "I'll turn you into one of Porcia's skeleton sword racks."

His hand was clammy, barely able to hold the key. Finally he managed slipping it into the lock. He breathed out shakily as the door opened.

A shady cavern awaited him, the heart of Porcia's museum of the macabre. Her most prized possessions hid here. Shrunken heads hung from the ceiling. Glass jars contained deformed animals: calves with eight legs, lambs with two faces, snakes with two heads. Living creatures hissed and drooled in cages: the dog she had created, cutting and sewing two animals together, forming a conjoined twin; and a hairless cat with two bodies and eight legs, another creature she had made with thread and needle. In a glass case, beetles bustled over the corpse of a child, fattening off the flesh. Rusty torture instruments hung on the walls: pincers, saws, finger-crushers, hammers, sickles, helmets full of blades and screws. Paintings covered the walls, depicting medical maladies from across the world: a man with two members, a woman with a neck swollen larger than her head, a child with a pointed cranium and a hunched back, and a dozen others. Here were Porcia's most precious prizes, her treasure trove of the obscene.

Here, too, lived her lumer.

Worm knelt in an iron cage, wrapped in a ratty blanket. Two dishes lay on the cage floor, one full of water, the other with gruel.

Worm was a young woman, but she looked old. Under Seneca's care, she might have looked much like Ofeer—a pretty Zoharite with lush black hair, smooth olive skin, and large brown eyes. But serving Porcia, the lumer had withered. That black hair now hung in a tangled, oily rag. Worm's frame had dwindled, leaving her limbs stick-thin, and her eyes seemed *too* large over her gaunt cheeks. Her lip was swollen from a blow, and bruises covered her body.

"My prince!" she said. Shock, then fear filled her eyes, and she cowered, huddling at the back of her cage.

Pity filled Seneca's heart. He knelt and placed his key into the cage door, but that seemed to only frighten Worm further. She pushed herself back, covering her face with her arms, a trapped animal.

"I'm not going to hurt you," Seneca said, shaking his head sadly, torn between pity for Worm and hatred for what Porcia had done to her. "I've come here to talk." He swung open the cage door. "Come out."

Worm hesitated, staring around, terror in her eyes. He gestured for her.

"I won't hurt you," he said again, softer this time.

Trembling, Worm crawled out from her cage and knelt before him, head lowered. "My prince." She looked back up at him, eyes damp. "You should leave, my prince. If she hears I

Crowns of Rust

spoke to you, she ..." Worm glanced toward the torture instruments on the wall, then back at him. "Please, my prince."

Seneca found himself clenching his fists and grinding his teeth. More than ever before, he desperately needed to defeat Porcia, to take this empire from her. How many more girls would his sister torture? How many more limbs would she sever, how many more organs would she devour? How many millions would cry in anguish under an empire Porcia ruled?

He knelt before Worm and dried her tears with his sleeve. "What's your name?"

She stared at the floor. "This one is nothing but a worm."

"No." Seneca shook his head. "You're not a worm. You're a human. You have a real name, or did once. What is it?"

Her trembling increased. "I ... I am Worm, I—"

He placed a finger under her chin and raised her head toward him. He stared into her eyes. "Nobody will hurt you. Porcia can't hear us."

A tear hung from her chin. "Noa," she whispered. "My name is Noa Bat Seean."

Seneca tucked strands of her hair behind her ears, revealing more bruises. "Noa, I'm here to help you. I'm here ..." His voice dropped to a whisper. "To ask about Porcia."

Noa bowed her head, shivering. "Porcia treats me very well, my prince. She is most kind. She is—"

"—a cunt," Seneca finished for her. "A cruel, sadistic, bloodthirsty monster. That's who my sister is. I know it. You know it too, though you dare not speak it. Noa." He held her

279

hands in his. Her nails were bitten down to stubs. "Tomorrow at the games, my father is going to officially choose an heir. I think he will choose Porcia. If she becomes empress …"

Noa stared back into his eyes. He saw that she understood.

"What do you wish me to do, my prince?" she whispered.

He still held her hands in his; they both still knelt on the floor, facing each other. "You know Porcia better than anyone alive. Better than me, better than my father. I need you to tell me everything about her. All the sadistic, monstrous things she's done and hidden. Things that she lets nobody outside her inner circle see. I need you, Noa, to give me the dirt."

If before Noa had been frightened, now she seemed to panic. She rose to her feet, trembling, and fled to the back of the chamber. She cowered between a twisted skeleton and a suit of human skin that hung from a peg. The deformed animals in the cages, the conjoined twins Porcia had stitched herself, yipped and snapped their teeth and banged against the bars.

"I can't, my prince," Noa said. "I … please. She'll hurt me. She'll—"

"She'll hurt millions of people if she's empress," Seneca said. "And she'll hurt you more than ever, emboldened by her new position." He walked toward Noa, trapping her between his body and the wall. "Together we can take her down, Noa. We can make sure she never ascends to the throne. I promise you. I swear on my mother's grave. I will protect you from her. If I must burn half the city down, I will protect you. Nobody will know what we spoke of here, and if Porcia tries to harm you again, she will meet my blade." To demonstrate, he drew the dagger he kept hidden under his toga.

Noa's eyes hardened, and just for an instant, it felt as if Seneca were looking through a mask. That he saw a different soul peering through those large brown eyes. A soul forged of iron. A soul as hard and heartless as Porcia's.

Then Noa looked away, and once more she was trembling, and new tears flowed. She nodded and stepped toward a shelf at the back of the room. Several scrolls stood here, wrapped in velvet casings, each scroll's title embroidered onto the cloth. Seneca read a few titles: *Medical Oddities by Master Femario*, *The Dungeons of Berennia*, *The Breaking of Slaves*, *Demonic Incantations*, and other gruesome volumes on topics of torture and devilry.

Noa pulled one scroll off the shelf, the length and width of her forearm. She peeled off its velvet cover, revealing rolled-up parchment the color of jaundice. She held out the scroll to Seneca.

"It's made of human parchment," she said. "Porcia skinned several victims to make this scroll."

Seneca cringed and took the scroll from her. The parchment was soft, supple, fleshy. It felt almost like stroking a woman.

"What is it?" he asked.

"Her journal," Noa replied, meeting his eyes again, and for just another instant, he saw that different person—calculating, strong.

You're not all that you seem, Noa Bat Seean, are you?

Seneca scrolled through the parchment. He sucked in breath, and his belly curdled. He looked over the scroll at Noa.

"Is this real?" he whispered.

Noa nodded, head lowered, and nervously twisted her fingers. Her cheeks flushed. "Sometimes she made me watch. Sometimes she made me take part. She would write it all down, every time. All those … unholy, shameful things she did, made me do." She lowered her head, letting her hair hide her face.

Seneca returned his eyes to the journal, shaking his head in disbelief. As he rolled through the scroll, he kept revealing more details of Porcia's "encounters," as she called them. One page described a night in the northern garrisons, sleeping with seven auxiliary soldiers, one after another. Another page described capturing boys from a village in Gael, forcing them to pleasure her, then slitting their throats and tossing the corpses into the river. Other pages included lists of legionaries she had bedded, great orgies described in every detail. Some involved her own soldiers, others involved Worm, and all sickened Seneca.

"The acts described here …" Seneca grimaced. "It makes even the wildest nights in a brothel seem tame." Face twisted in disgust, Seneca read from one segment of scroll, written in his sister's confident handwriting. "That night, after drinking a flagon of wine, I smuggled two gladiators into the palace, brutes with cocks the size of tent poles. I took them into my mother's tomb, and I fucked them both—right atop the old witch's grave. Right with Mother's marble statue watching us. I bet the hag liked that. Someday soon, I'm going to fuck men over my father's grave too.

Maybe I'll dig up his bones and use them to—" Seneca had to stop. He could read no more. He looked back at Worm. "This has been going on for how long?"

"A few years." Noa stared at the scroll, eyes haunted. "She made me watch. Every time. Sometimes she made me take part. In the wildest orgies, with blood and sweat ... she made me take part. And she'd laugh. She'd laugh as I cried, and she'd write it all down. Afterward, to torment me, she'd make me read the scroll to her. To relive those nights. I would read and she would laugh, and then another night, it would all start again."

Seneca felt sick. Yes, he had partaken in his own nights of debauchery on occasion. He had visited brothels. He had made love to Ofeer. But those had always been tender encounters. Nights of love, not of this filth, this violence. Seneca wanted to gag ... but alongside the disgust rose elation.

This is it, he knew. *By the gods, this is it. I've got her now.*

Noa fell to her knees, weeping, hugging his legs. "Please, my prince. Please. Don't take this scroll. She'll find out. She'll hurt me. She'll know. She'll force me into chains, and she'll bring out the pinchers, and—"

"She won't hurt you ever again," Seneca said. "I promise you, Noa. But I need to take this scroll." He turned toward the door.

"No, wait!" Noa rushed toward him. "You can't. She'll know it's missing. If you take the scroll, you must take me with you."

Seneca narrowed his eyes, annoyed now. "And what would I do with you? Set you loose on the streets, where you'd starve in a gutter? Hide you under my bed like a boy hiding a stray pup?"

Those damn Zoharites! First Ofeer was begging him to save her family. Now Noa was begging him to save her. Couldn't the damn desert rats take care of themselves?

"Please, my prince," Noa whispered, tears in her eyes. "Don't place me back in my cage. Take me to the palace gates. I'll find my own fortune from there. I can work in shops. I can beg for food if I must. Anything, even death, would be preferable to that cage."

She clasped his hands in hers, and Seneca felt his blood heat. Beneath the grime, Noa was not bad looking. There was beauty to her, much like Ofeer's. If he could nurse her back to health, bring out that beauty, like a man tending to a dying rose ...

But no. Seneca shook his head. It was too risky. He could risk taking this scroll for a few hours, and Porcia would be none the wiser. He would have enough time to show this filth to his father, to stain her image. But surely, Porcia would notice her Worm missing at dawn.

He stuffed the damning parchment into his toga. He left the crimson, velvet cover behind; he filled it with another scroll, one he chose from a chest on the floor, and returned it to the shelf. Unless Porcia felt like reading her work within the next few hours, nothing in the chamber would seem awry.

"I'm sorry, Noa," he said. "Truly I am. I can't free you yet. But once Porcia falls, I promise I'll return for you. I promise."

284

She wept as he guided her back into her cage, as he locked her inside, as he walked toward the door, the scroll hidden in the folds of his toga. Yet as Seneca stepped out of the attic, he turned around once, and he saw Noa staring at him. Her eyes were dry, and she was smiling thinly.

NOA

The boy was gone. A fool. She snorted. A fool like the rest of them.

As soon as the attic door closed, Noa pulled her key out from her pocket, the key she had crafted with Luminosity. She unlocked her cage, stepped out onto the stone floor of the attic, and stretched.

Worm, they call me. She scoffed. *All conquerors, princes, and emperors end up food for worms.*

She stepped toward the shelf and lifted the scroll's crimson binding, which Seneca had left behind, stuffed with different parchment. Noa passed her hands over the velvet.

"You should have taken the binding too, boy." She sighed. "I spent long hours sewing and embroidering it. It made the scroll look so much more impressive. And you just left it behind!"

She twirled around the room. Shedding so many crocodile tears always made her want to dance. She pulled one of the skeletons off its stand, wrapped the bony arms around her, and cavorted with her cadaverous partner around the room.

"Soon, darling." Noa kissed the skull. "Soon we'll be dancing in the streets, us and all the skeletons of Aelar, a great dance macabre over the ruins of an empire."

She laughed, then slapped a hand over her mouth, stifling the sound. No. She must still be careful. Her work here was not yet done.

She returned the skeleton to his stand, closed her eyes, and thought of home.

Noa had been to Zohar only last month on Porcia's campaign. She had soaked herself full of lume, and her reserves were still strong, the magic coursing through her, giving her strength, knowledge, a warmth in the cold. She lived now in this attic, but before her, she saw the rolling dunes. The olive trees on the mountains. The city of Beth Eloh, ancient beyond measure, a place of copper, stone, gold, countless prophecies and magic.

She had only to think of those ancient brick walls, those metal domes, those palm trees rising over the desert, and she was drawing upon the lume, weaving it, luminating it. The luminescence shone in her eyes and inside her palms, framing her fingernails with threads of gold.

She pulled a sheaf of parchment from a shelf.

Human parchment, she thought and laughed. That one had come to her on the spot, and the prince had loved it, had lapped it up like the good dog that he was. She had known he would come to see her, of course. She had known for days. Foresight was among the four pillars of Luminosity, and Noa had always been a mistress of the light.

Her hands aglow, she summoned the Muse, another of the Four Pillars. It was Muse that had let lumers build this very tower and the palace around it. Muse that had raised the Amphitheatrum, sculpted the gods, inspired the music and poems of an empire. Muse that had let her forge keys from metal scraps, giving her access to every chamber in this palace. It was Muse that now flowed from her hand to her quill, writing on the parchment, forging the handwriting of Prince Seneca.

Noa read aloud as she wrote. "It was in Zohar that I first fucked my own sister, my sweet Ofeer. Yes, she is my sister! I knew it from the start. She revealed it to me in the cave, and it only made me desire her more. I know that Father would not accept our forbidden love. I'll keep it secret from him, until one day, when he least expects it ... I will stab the old goat-shagger in the back. Then Ofeer will be my wife, and her statue will rise on the hill instead of his!"

Noa laughed. Perfect. Of course, Seneca did not know the truth. He did not know that Ofeer Sela was, in fact, the daughter of Emperor Marcus, that he had thrust between the legs of his sister.

But Noa knew. Noa had the Sight. Noa was a child of Luminosity, and none in Aelar were safe from her wrath.

"It's funny, isn't it?" she asked a deformed calf in a jar. "It was Seneca who engaged in filth, not Porcia ... yet it will be my mistress who falls for impure sins."

Noa folded the piece of parchment and hid it on a shelf. For safekeeping. To be used only at the hour of need, should she choose to destroy the boy. He would be so easy to destroy.

She laughed again and slapped a shrunken head that swung from the ceiling, letting it swirl around the room, as if it too were dancing.

"They stole me from my home," she told the head. "They beat me. They chained me. They made me watch as they butchered my people. Now I will destroy them, one by one, pitting them against one another until nobody is left."

KOREN

U nder the blazing sun, Koren swung his pickaxe, chiseling away at the marble as the whips chiseled away at his back.

"A little to the left," he said. "Just … down a finger and …" The whip cracked. "Perfect."

"Silence!" The overseer snarled. "I'll flay your skin and wear it like a coat if you don't shut your maw."

Koren glanced at the man. The overseer was massive. He was larger than the slabs of marble the miners were cutting from the quarry. Sweat shone on his bald head, and blood—Koren's own blood—stained his whip.

The quarry spread around them. Koren had seen limestone quarries back in Zohar, but this place dwarfed them. Shelves of stone rose across the mountainsides, white and blinding in the sun. Hundreds of miners stood on scaffolds, hammering at the marble, then shoving wooden slats into the cracks. Hundreds more bustled below, carrying the white blocks of stone—each larger than a man—onto wooden transports. Mules tugged wagons, engineers pointed and argued, and overseers patrolled between the collared slaves, landing their whips on any man who so much as wiped sweat off his brow.

Koren had suffered more than his own share of lashes. He imagined that his back was about as ugly as the overseer's face. But he was still alive, still chiseling at the marble, not a feat to be taken lightly. Since arriving in this place, he had seen fourteen men die—crushed under stones, fallen from scaffolds, or beaten to death.

Koren kept swinging his pickaxe. He stood on a shelf of stone, a thousand feet above the surface of the world. The cliff rose even higher at his side, so high Koren's head spun. The marble ledge he stood on was narrow, barely wide enough for his feet. Whenever the wind gusted, he cringed and pressed himself against the cliff; he had already seen the wind blow one slave down to his death. He swung his pickaxe again and again, driving cracks into the very shelf of stone he stood on. All around, across the cliffs, other workers were doing the same.

"Work faster, you worms!" shouted the overseer, moving across the worksite. "Emperor Marcus is building a triumphant archway to commemorate ruling over you wretched maggots. If you don't bring him marble faster, he'll build it with your bones."

Koren doubted his bones could even build a cradle right now, let alone a triumphant archway; they felt ready to crack. A few other men worked with him, none from Zohar. One was a swarthy Nurian, his skin so dark it was almost pure black. Another was captured on the Gaelian front, a burly man with blond hair, his pale skin burning in the sun. Several other slaves were from Phedia, a realm Emperor Marcus had defeated a decade ago.

So it's possible to live a decade here, Koren thought, not sure if that thought comforted or terrified him.

Once the cracks in the marble were deep enough, Koren and his fellow slaves—all collared—shoved wedges of wood into the grooves, then poured water over the slats. The wood soaked up the water and expanded. *Cracks* sounded deep in the stone.

Whenever Koren heard those cracks, he couldn't help but wince. He kept hearing it—the catapults hurling boulders onto Gefen. Bones snapping on the streets. Houses collapsing, burying friends beneath. Whenever miners swung their hammers, Koren kept seeing Seneca swing his hammer, driving nails into Father's hands and feet.

As he labored, Koren thought about his family a lot. Thinking about them made his eyes water, made sadness swell inside him like the expanding wet wood. But he couldn't stop. He kept thinking of Atalia—lost at sea. Of Ofeer—lost somewhere in Aelar, the city that lay on the horizon, its walls only several parsa'ot away. Of Epher, Maya, and mother—back in Zohar, perhaps dead.

Finally the great marble slab—larger than a coffin—detached from the mountain. Slaves bustled around it on scaffolds, securing ropes onto the stone, then heaving it down, tugging a complex system of levers and pulleys. Perhaps the marble would form bricks at the capital, perhaps the segment of a column, perhaps a statue depicting a god or emperor. Koren would never know. He could see Aelar on the horizon, but he would never set foot in that city again. His life was here now, the life of a slave. His work continued, chiseling at another stone.

That evening, the overseers herded the slaves down to the bottom of the quarry. There the miners ate a paltry meal: some grainy bread, old cheese, and a bowl of gruel. The overseers slapped the slaves in chains, and Koren lay down to sleep on the hard ground, hundreds of other slaves around him.

He couldn't have been here for more than a few days. Yet it seemed longer, years since the tall man in the toga had bought him in the market, since guards had shoved him into a cart, since he'd been wheeled here to the quarry. Only days ago, Koren had been with Ofeer. Now it seemed another lifetime. He had been a different man then—still a man of Zohar. Now he was nothing. Only a shell. Only the last flickers of life in a dying body.

He awoke to shouts. Dawn was rising beyond the mountains, sickly gray and yellow. The overseers were moving through the camp, lashing and kicking slaves.

"Up, maggots! Up! We've got important company today. Praetor Tirus Valerius and his daughter are coming to inspect your worthless hides. Up!"

Koren blinked, still clinging to slumber. An overseer trundled toward him and drove a kick into Koren's ribs.

"Up, worm."

Koren groaned. "You keep confusing me with the slave beside me. I'm the maggot. He's the worm. Ow!" Another kick drove into Koren's belly. "All right. I'm up. Thank you for the lovely wakeup. Next time, instead of a kick, wake me up by sucking my cock."

He muttered those last words under his breath, not wishing to chance a kick to the aforementioned area. He rose and lined up for breakfast, receiving a moldy chunk of bread, a cup of brackish water, and a slab of pork so old and oily rainbows glistened on its surface.

"I don't suppose you're serving any fresh cream and strawberries, maybe some boiled eggs and cheesecake, some nice tea with cream and honey?" When the cook—if you could call him that—just returned a blank stare, Koren sighed. "Never mind. Atrophied bread and magical rainbow ham it is."

As he climbed the path up the quarry, eating as he went, Koren frowned. He kept tossing that name back and forth through his mind—Praetor Tirus Valerius. Damn it, he knew that name. It conjured images of a squat, bald man—a man from Gefen, despite the Aelarian name. But after days of hunger, labor, and the whip, fog filled Koren's mind. He could not remember more. It seemed a memory from another life.

Koren was standing on a block of marble, chiseling away at it, when the trumpets blared, and the horses rode into the quarry.

Several of the riders wore armor. At first Koren thought them legionaries; they wore silvery cuirasses, and their helmets were crested. But then he noticed the sigils on their shields— laureled eagles. These were not legionaries. Here were men of the Magisterian Guard, elite warriors who guarded Aelar and its dignitaries.

Two civilians rode here too. One was a beefy, middle aged man in a toga, wide of shoulders and bald of head, his nose bulbous, his face broad. The other rider was a woman in her twenties, her brown hair pinned above her head, releasing ringlets that hung across her brow.

Watching from the cliff above, Koren nearly dropped his pickaxe.

"Of course," he whispered.

"Dominus!" cried one of the overseers, kneeling in the dust. A few of the slaves glanced at one another, and some knelt too.

The burly man in the toga frowned from his horse. "Do not kneel, men. Rise and work!" His voice was deep and booming. "You're here to break stones and break your backs, not to bend them."

At his side, his daughter smirked. "If you keep breaking slaves' backs, Father, we'll need to find more lands to invade and more slaves to capture." She looked across the quarry. "I see a few Zoharites here. I've always liked Zoharites. Such wild creatures."

Her bald father glowered. "I've seen how well you like the savages, daughter. Those here are for me to break, not for you to toy with."

Koren found himself trembling with rage. Of course. Praetor Tirus Valerius—once Aelar's ambassador to Zohar. The bald, beefy man had spent more than one evening in the Sela villa. And the young woman was his only daughter, Claudia Valerius— the girl Epher had been enamored with.

That girl he visited the night we rode out of Gefen, Koren remembered. He had spent an hour waiting outside the city as Epher had parted from her—a girl Epher had been secretly courting for a year.

As slaves swung their hammers and pickaxes, Koren stared down from the cliff. Claudia stared up from her horse and met his gaze. A line appeared on her brow.

"Get back to work, rat!" an overseer cried, swinging his lash. The thong slammed into Koren. "Stop gawking and work." The whip swung again, biting into Koren's shoulder.

Claudia kept staring at him, frowning.

Koren inhaled sharply

Oh to hell with it, he thought.

"Claudia!" he shouted. "Claudia, it's me! Koren! Koren Sela! Epher's brother."

He cried out as the whip lashed him again. He fell and clung to the cliff as the overseer kicked him.

"Claudia!" Koren shouted again.

The overseer snarled, grabbed Koren, yanked him up, and shoved him toward the edge of the cliff. Koren dangled, head spinning.

"Shall I send him down to you, dominus?" the overseer called.

"Wait!" Claudia said. "Let him walk down. Let him live. Bring him to me."

The overseer grunted, disappointment in his eyes. He pulled Koren back onto the path, then dragged him down the scaffolding. Soon Koren was standing before Claudia and her father, both still on their horses. On the cliffs all around, the slaves toiled away, pickaxes ringing and hammers thudding.

"Claudia," Koren said, blood on his back, sweat on his brow. "There must have been some mistake. When they brought me to Aelar, they told me I could be the new emperor, but now they say Porcia might get the job. You don't suppose you could speak to the right people and still get me the gig?"

Claudia stared down from her horse, face pale, as if not sure what to make of him. Her father snorted.

"Who is this rat?" said Tirus.

Claudia spoke to her father, but she kept her eyes on Koren. "You remember him, Father. One of Jerael Sela's children."

"Is this the one you were fucking in my own house?" Tirus said.

Claudia groaned and finally looked away from Koren. "The same house where you fucked half the serving girls in Gefen? Don't patronize me, Father." She looked back at Koren. "The boy's wasted here. He's related to King Shefael. The Zoharite rats rebel; this one is a bargaining chip."

Tirus's horse nickered and spun in a circle. The beefy lord grunted and yanked the reins. "Last I heard, Jerael Sela was rotting on a cross. Let his son rot here."

Claudia glared at her father. "And your brain has already rotted, I see."

Tirus raised a fist. "Do you want me to beat you in front of the slaves?"

"I want you to listen to me," said Claudia. "You were always stubborn. Mother always said so. Think, Father. There's already violence on the streets of Beth Eloh; the Zoharites aren't yet fully cowed. The lumers say that Epheriah Sela himself killed a few legionaries only yesterday. They say that Zohar's Blade, a group of desert scum, roam the province, arming themselves, preparing for an uprising. If the rats do rebel, the province will burn. The Sela family is as close to royalty as Zoharites get. Now, if we had a Sela brother in our hands ..."

Koren's mind reeled. His brother—still alive! Still fighting! Damn it, the war wasn't over yet, and Koren was stuck here in a quarry, missing all the fun.

"I know what'll work," Koren said, looking up at Claudia. "You send me back to Zohar, and I'll talk to Epher. A moment with me, he'll forget about rebelling and switch to knitting bonnets for a living. All we demand is our villa back, maybe a few servants, a dancer or two would be nice ... oh, and Prince Seneca's head on a pike. It would look perfect mounted on our wall."

Lord Tirus rode his horse closer, and Koren cringed, expected a blow. The lord of the quarry stared down at him.

"Yes, I remember this one. The lesser of the two brothers." He turned toward Claudia. "We'll take him. He can serve wine at our table while we figure out what to do with him."

Koren wasn't enthused about serving wine, but it sure sounded nicer than mining marble.

"Perfect," Koren said. "To the wine! Which horse is mine?"

Within moments, he found himself dragging behind Tirus's horse, a chain running from the saddle to his collar. Claudia and the Magisterian Guard rode with them. Koren stumbled as the chain yanked him, coughing, dragging when he fell. Soon his knees were bleeding as he raced behind the horses. The city of Aelar rose in the distance. It would be a long journey.

But Epher is alive, Koren thought, eyes damp. *Ofeer is alive.* Even bound in chains, dragging behind his captors, beaten and bloody, Koren vowed: *I will live. I will survive this. I will see my family again.*

MAYA

She rode her camel across the desert, leading her caravan, and beheld the great city before her.

"Sekur." The wind ruffled her veil, and Maya inhaled deeply. "Capital of the Sekadian Empire. The mythical City of Gods. Heart of the desert."

Leven leaned forward on his camel, squinting at the distant city. "More like the ass of the desert. It's big, it stinks, and it's overflowing with shit."

Maya rolled her eyes. "I think it's beautiful."

Leven nodded. "Asses often are." He kneed his camel. "*Hasha! Hasha!*"

His camel burst into a run.

"*Hasha!*" Maya cried, and her own camel followed at a gallop. The rest of their caravan—a dozen camels taken from the bone-raiders—followed, raising clouds of sand. Saddlebags bounced across their flanks, full of perfumes, coins, jewels, and decorative vessels forged of gold, silver, and platinum. With this treasure, Maya would stock up on supplies, buy new maps, and head out again, at dawn tomorrow—out east, toward the distant ocean, toward the school of Luminosity she sought.

Two rivers framed the city, larger than any Maya had ever seen. Back in Zohar, far in the west, there were no more than humble streams, and even those dried up in the summer. But here the rivers gushed with fury, so wide that twenty mighty ships could sail them abreast. Irrigation canals spread out from them, feeding farmlands, orchards, and palm groves. Here was the great fertile basin of the east, a vast oasis in the desert, the cradle of civilization. It was from this arable land, the legends said, that men had first heard the word of Eloh, had traveled west and founded the land of Zohar.

My most ancient blood is from this land, Maya thought. *For we are all children of the east.*

The city of Sekur rose between the rivers and palm groves, its walls towering—perhaps even taller than the walls of Beth Eloh back in the west. They were carved of sandstone, the same color as the desert, and topped with many battlements and turrets.

Maya had seen nobody other than Leven for days now, but as she traveled the dirt road toward the city, she finally saw others. Peddlers rode donkeys, pulling carts full of amphorae, scrolls, silverware, pets in cages, and stone idols. Farmers led cattle, sheep, and wagons of grain. Soldiers walked here too, clad in ring mail, armed with bows and curved khopesh swords, the blades semicircular.

Most Sekadian men wore long, luxurious beards, deep black and curled into countless ringlets. Some men were beardless, and they wore iron collars and loincloths—eunuch slaves, Maya surmised. The women wore white dresses, cut to reveal the left breast, the hems tasseled. Some women rode in palanquins, their faces painted, their arms jingling with bracelets. Others walked afoot in the dust, leading cattle and children toward the city.

Maya even saw a few people wrapped in white robes, pale, coughing, their eyes sunken. Plaques hung around their necks, displaying words like "leprosy" and "consumption" and "possession." Here walked the ill, the dying, seeking healing in the city or an ablution of sins.

A massive gatehouse shone upon the western wall of Sekur, blue and gold. Back in Beth Eloh, Maya remembered entering ancient, crumbling gates rife with lume and antiquity—cracked, weedy structures, not much larger than a house. Yet this gatehouse could put palaces to shame. Several towers framed it, their glazed bricks the color of sapphires, embossed with golden reliefs of aurochs, falcons, and dragons. Gemstones and precious metals formed thousands of sunbursts that climbed the towers, framing their walls, leading toward golden battlements. A platinum archway rose between the towers, and a great dragon mosaic coiled above it, formed from thousands of lapis lazuli stones. The doors themselves were cedar, banded with silver and shining with jewels. When the sun hit the gates, they shone across the land, a beacon to travelers for parsa'ot around.

"Beautiful ass indeed," Maya said. "We'll find supplies here, and—Leven? Leven!"

The young thief had ridden toward a peddler's cart. Piles of wooden statuettes, copper bracelets, decorative fish with brass scales and gemstone eyes, wicker baskets full of colorful stones, and many other treasures rose here. Leven was leaning from his camel, reaching toward a silver pipe atop the pile.

"Leven!" Maya thundered.

He cringed, pulled his hand away, and rode back toward her. His eyes were wide and feverish. "I can't help it, Maya," he whispered and licked his lips. "Look around you. By God! These people ... so many peddlers, merchants, ladies with fine jewels ... this place is ripe for the taking."

"No thieving!" Maya glowered at him. "We're leading a convoy of camels laden with treasures far worthier than that junk."

"I know, I know." Leven shuddered. "It's just ... I can't help it. When a man sees treasures like this just exposed, just out there ... how can he resist reaching out to grab them?"

"Well, look at all the naked breasts around you, if you must," said Maya. "But don't you be grabbing them either. I won't be using this treasure to bail you out of prison."

The city gates were open, and many guards stood here, coated with iron rings. Beyond them spread a boulevard, a road so wide armies could march down it. Maya was used to the coiling alleyways like in Zohar, roads so narrow two donkeys could not ride abreast. This road seemed wide enough that a city could have risen atop it. Hundreds of towers rose in two palisades on the roadsides, each coated with shimmering blue tiles, golden sunbursts, and reliefs of dragons. Blue merlons topped each tower like a crown, and more guards stood between them, armed with bows and spears. Should any enemy break through the gate, they would face a long gauntlet toward the city center.

A city of wonders, Maya thought, riding down the boulevard. *A dream world. A city of beauty.*

Yet when she gazed between the blue towers that lined the avenue, she caught glimpses of another world. As opulent as the city gate and boulevard were, the streets beyond were poor. Houses stood crowded together, assembled haphazardly from old stones, no two alike. A smashed statue formed the cornerstone of one house. Another home was built from weathered tombstones, the names of the dead still engraved upon them. The city's poor huddled here, watching from rooftops and alleyways. An old man stood in but a loincloth, his ribs pushing against his skin, his arms white with leprosy. A naked child pissed in a yard among cadaverous goats. Several nursing mothers waded atop a trash heap—the hill rose taller than the houses—picking out rotten fruit and old chicken bones, collecting the meals into pouches. Flies bustled around these commoners, and the stench of nightsoil, disease, and rot filled Maya's nostrils.

Two city guards—burly men in ring mail, their beards flowing down to their belts—saw her staring at the poor. The men moved closer together between two towers, their shields held before them, blocking Maya's view. Their eyes glared from under bushy black eyebrows, urging her onward. Maya looked away.

So it is, Maya thought. *So it always is. Splendor hiding shadow. Gold hiding rust. The wonders and wealth of kings, built atop breaking backs and starving children.*

She looked back ahead along the boulevard. A full parasa away loomed the fabled Ziggurat of Sekur. Even from the distance, the building seemed massive, dwarfing the palm trees and towers before it. It was vaguely triangular, a great complex of staircases and towers, rising higher and higher, tapering into a platinum peak.

"So ... many ... treasures ..." Leven eyed a group of travelers, clad in silk and silver, holding purses. The young man was practically salivating.

"No thieving!" Maya leaned across her saddle and slapped him.

"But—"

"No!"

Leven pouted, bouncing on his camel. "Fine, but don't you forget what the scorpion did. Can't change a man's nature."

Maya glared at him. "You'll change your nature or I'll change your face with my fist."

They rode through the city, leading their camels along the boulevard. Thousands of people clogged the road with them: peddlers riding wagons of wares, farmers wheeling forth their goods, children riding donkeys, soldiers riding horses, and great aurochs—larger than any horse—with horns like spears, dragging gilded carts where sat silk-laden nobles. Farther back, past the blue towers and the hives of the poor, columned temples soared, monuments of sandstone and gold. Statues of dragons rose above palm trees, flames burning in their maws, their teeth forged of iron. Gazing at them, Maya remembered the skeletons she had seen in the desert—great beasts like whales with wings.

Dragons, she thought, staring at a massive statue of one that rose at her side. *They were real once. Long ago.*

Her mind turned toward more recent history. It was six hundred years ago—relatively recently for an ancient kingdom like Zohar—that the king of this city had marched a massive army across the desert, half a million strong. Sekadia had captured Zohar in that war, had destroyed Beth Eloh, had crushed the Temple and sent the palace crumbling down. The children of Zohar had been marched into Sekur as slaves, forced to serve the king and his people, forced to kneel before idols—maybe even before these very dragon statues. As Maya walked down this boulevard, she tried to imagine those ancient Zoharites marching here, chained and whipped, far from home. She could still feel their souls calling out from the stones.

And now it's Aelar that crushes my homeland, that enslaves my people. For three thousand years now, every generation, a nation had risen to destroy Zohar, this tiny kingdom trapped between sand and sea. The Sekadians. The Nurians before them. The Kalintians a mere century ago. The Aelarians today. Many others, going back across the millennia, empires that had risen, butchered, then vanished into dust. Maya hung her head low. *Will my people forever be trapped between empires, forever be enslaved, slaughtered, brutalized by the cruel and powerful? Will we never be a nation of healing, of peace?*

Her mind strayed to the vision she had seen outside the Gate of Mercy in Beth Eloh, that day she had entered the city with her mother, had come to see Shefael upon his throne. The lume had claimed her, and she had seen another gate, a mythical gate. The Gate of Tears, lost to history, still rising in her mind. And through that gate ... a healer, all in white, all in light, entering the city of blood, bringing peace, bringing grace.

Maya shook her head wildly, banishing the thought. That had been a mere illusion, a dream. If the Gate of Tears had ever truly existed in Beth Eloh, it was now lost, sealed up, filled with bricks, never to be found. There would be no mystical healer of light for Zohar, merely the hard work of lumers ... like the lumer she hoped to become.

"Let's find a market," Maya said, pulling her thoughts away from shadow.

Leven nodded. "Markets are prime locations for pickpocketing."

"So you better be careful." She raised her fist. "Because I intend to pound any pickpocket I find. We're going there to get supplies, that's all. Food. Water. Wine. Bandages and medicine and oil and wicks. Maps too. Enough to last me on my way east to the sea. And ..." Maya lowered her head. "And enough for your journey back to Zohar."

Yes. Leven had always meant to return to Zohar after stocking up on supplies here. When the bone-raiders had captured them, Maya had begun to think that she would die with Leven; now she realized she would live the rest of her life without him.

So what? She should rejoice! Leven was nothing but a no-good thief. He had stolen her camel! What kind of man encountered a hungry, wandering girl, and instead of offering aid stole from her? A scorpion, that was all. A scorpion who stung even the frog he rode across the river, unable to change his nature.

So why did she feel so sad to part from him?

Maya looked at the thief. Leven rode beside her, wrapped in a white robe, his hood and veil tossed back. A dark, closely cropped beard covered his cheeks. The boy was so vain he trimmed that beard regularly, even on days when only Maya was there to see.

I don't care about him, Maya told herself … yet she kept remembering that damn time he had kissed her.

Trumpets blared.

"Out of the way, out of the way!" rose a cry. "Part before Mareeshen the Magnificent, the Healer of All Hurts!"

Maya turned around on her camel and gasped.

"Well fuck me," Leven whispered, rubbing his eyes.

A great procession was marching down the boulevard from the city gates. Maya had never seen a parade of such splendor. Trumpeters led the way, blowing silver horns, while a crier rang a bell. Behind them, dancers somersaulted and jugglers juggled flaming blades. Mighty aurochs followed, draped with samite, their horns gilded and ringed with jewels. The beasts pulled a giltwood wagon, carved into the shape of a coiled-up serpent, complete with shimmering scales. Its curtains were drawn back, revealing many bottles and vials that rattled on shelves, their caps golden. Atop the wagon, on a plush leather chair, sat a corpulent man. He wore pastel silks, his mustache was thick and curling, and rings shone on his fingers. Above his seat dangled a wooden sign that bore the words: "Mareeshen the Magnificent, Healer of All Hurts! Praise him and be healed!"

"Bit showy for a healer," Maya said, remembering Master Malaci back in Zohar, a humble man in homespun.

Leven's jaw nearly hit his saddle. "So much gold in that wagon."

The trumpeters blasted a fresh fanfare. The hefty man rose from his seat on the wagon, bracelets jingling. He stroked his mustache and bellowed in a rumbling voice, "Never fear, people of Sekur! I, Mareeshen the Magnificent, shall heal your king."

Across the city, people grumbled and scoffed.

"The Priests of Elem couldn't heal our king!" one man cried out, his curled beard hanging down to his belt.

"A thousand healers from across the world failed!" shouted a woman, her headdress formed from serpents of tin and lapis lazuli. "Leave our city, fake one."

But Mareeshen only shouted louder, arms raised. "A thousand false healers have entered your city, selling perfumed water as medicine, chanting meaningless prayers to callous gods. But I have healed lepers! I have caused legs to sprout from the stumps of the legless! I have healed babes whose breath had died upon their mothers' breasts! I will heal your king, people of Sekur."

Leven frowned and turned toward Maya. "Maya, you're a healer. I saw you heal my little brother." His eyes widened, and he pointed at the ziggurat. "Do you know what this means?"

Maya stared at the towering structure down the boulevard. Twin statues of dragons rose there, dwarfing even the mightiest tree, and their eyes seemed to stare at her across the distance.

The King of Sekadia lives in there, Maya thought. *The descendant of the man who destroyed my homeland.*

"If healers have been traveling here to heal the king, they might let me try too," Maya said.

"Exactly—and once we're inside the palace, we can steal the crown jewels!" Leven licked his lips. "God, Maya. A king! I can steal from a real king! While you're healing him, I'll sneak—"

"If you steal anything in this city, even a cracker, I'm going to magically shrivel your bollocks into raisins."

Leven blinked. "But I hate raisins!"

"So you better behave."

Abandoning the market for now, Maya led her camels down the boulevard toward the ziggurat. It was a long walk, but after two months in the desert, it passed within a heartbeat. Mareeshen the Magnificent (whom Maya thought was more like Mareeshen the Mucky) reached the palace a few moments before her. He alighted his wagon with a flourish of silks. His trumpeters announced his arrival, and the heavyset healer settled in a palanquin. Bald eunuchs, collared and clad in loincloths, lifted the palanquin and began to carry it up the ziggurat's staircase. It was a long climb; hundreds of steps rose toward an archway above.

"Will you carry me?" she asked Leven. "Mareeshen's men are carrying him."

Leven snorted. "I'd sooner carry the camels."

They dismounted said camels, left them with the palace guards, and began to climb the staircases leading up the ziggurat. The sandstone dragons rose at their sides, taller than the walls of Beth Eloh. Fire burned in their eyes and mouths, casting out smoke. As Maya climbed higher, she saw that bones lay inside those stone maws, and she shuddered. Those were human bones—human sacrifice to the gods of the ziggurat.

It seemed hours that she climbed, and Maya was soon wheezing. She hadn't eaten much since leaving Zohar. Even the bone-raiders had left her only paltry supplies in their saddlebags. Maya had always been thin, but now she was downright scrawny, and the climb winded her. There were hundreds of stairs here, maybe a thousand. When she looked behind her, she could see most of the city—a vast settlement, as large as Beth Eloh, full of sandstone homes, temples, silos, towers, and bridges, palm trees swaying between them.

"Maya," Leven wheezed, crawling up the stairs on hands and knees. "Can *you* carry *me*?"

"I'm going to kick you all the way down," she said.

Finally they reached the archway upon the ziggurat's facade. It felt like Maya had climbed a mountain, yet they had ascended only half the building's height. Towers, balconies, and battlements still soared above, spinning her head when she gazed at them.

Mareeshen had already entered the archway long ago. The entrance was shaped like the mouth of a serpent, complete with ivory fangs, the eyes formed of green crystals the size of human heads. Guards stood here, tan cloaks tossed across their ring mail, their curled beards as ringed as their armor. Their spears tilted to block the passageway into the ziggurat.

"I'm a healer," Maya told them. "I've come to heal the king ... or try to, at least."

Leven nodded. "And I'm her loyal assistant. Well, more like manager." He winced as she elbowed him in the ribs. "I mean companion?"

"My servant," Maya said.

"I—" Leven began before she elbowed him again, harder now.

The guards stared at her, eyes dark. "Many have come here for years, seeking to heal our lord. Priests. Wizards. Charlatans. Physicians with ointments from distant lands. All have failed. Why should a young girl succeed when the wisest masters in the land could not?"

Maya raised her chin. "Because I'm a lumer."

That was a lie, of sorts. She wasn't yet a lumer; she wouldn't become one until she reached the sea, until she found a teacher. But she knew enough of Luminosity to heal. She had healed Leven's brother, had healed her mother's finger, had healed the stray dog before Seneca had shot him. So let these guards believe she was a mistress of magic like Avinasi. She raised her hand, summoning just enough lume to kindle her fingers, to weave strands of luminescence into a cat-sized dragon, then let them disperse.

It was enough to impress the guards. They stepped aside, eyes wide, and Maya and Leven entered the ziggurat.

They found themselves in a vestibule, the mosaic on the floor depicting thousands of serpents. Embers crackled in dragon braziers. Many people filled the room. Mareeshen was here, dabbing sweat from his brow with a purple handkerchief. Also present was a dwarf, his beard long and white, with many vials hanging from his belt. A sorceress stood beside him, eyes closed, chanting under her breath. An old man, his beard forked, held a cart full of herbs and powders. A priest held a staff around which coiled a live snake, a symbol of healing. A group of men stood in a corner, wearing beaked masks, staring through glass goggles.

"They're all healers," Maya said. "They've all come here to try to heal the king."

Leven snorted. "They've come here trying to make some money." He leaned down toward the dwarf. "Tell me, friend, what is the reward for healing the king of this place?"

The little old man raised tufted white eyebrows. He spoke in a squeaky voice. "You do not know, young man? Why, King Zamur has promised a palace to whoever can cure his ailment."

Maya had to catch Leven before he passed out.

"A palace ..." The thief blinked. "A palace!" He grabbed Maya. "God. God, Maya. God God God. Just do what you did back at the oasis! Heal him like you healed my brother. We're going to be rich! We're going to be powerful! We're going to be lord and lady of a palace!"

"*You*," Maya said, "are going to be nothing. And I'm not interested in living in a palace. My homeland is in Zohar. I wish only to learn enough Luminosity to help my homeland."

"But ... A palace! Even if it's a small palace." Leven clutched his hair. "And we wouldn't even have to steal it."

"Shush!"

One by one, guards let healers through a blue doorway into a chamber beyond. One by one, they returned into the waiting room, crestfallen. The dwarf muttered that he needed more time for his ointments to work, while the masked priests grumbled that the heathen gods of the ziggurat blocked their prayers. Mareeshen the Magnificent spent nearly an hour in the chamber, then finally emerged, silks fluttering, face red.

"I demand exclusive treatment of the king!" said the hefty healer. "I will not share my work with this riffraff." He pointed at Maya and the others who still waited in the antechamber.

"I gather your healing didn't go very well," Maya said. "Did you use the wrong sort of snake oil?"

Mareeshen blustered past her, cursing, and left the ziggurat. His guards hurried to follow.

Servants emerged from the inner chamber. They were young women, their hair long and black and curled, and their white dresses were cut to reveal their left breasts. They gestured for Maya.

"Come, healer," they said. "May the spirits give you the wisdom to heal our king."

Maya inhaled deeply. She found herself trembling.

I'm not a true lumer. How can I heal a king?

Leven took her hand in his, and he looked at her with warm eyes. She read his words in those eyes. *Because it's your nature.*

They stepped into the inner chamber together.

The stench of rot assailed Maya, overpowering. Bowls of flower petals stood on stone tables, and incense burned in bronze dragons, but the sweetness only mingled with the sickly smell, making it even worse. Maya stepped across a tiled floor, waving aside smoke. The window let in a beam of light, and the air was stifling, but it felt like no true light and warmth had filled this room in years.

On a silver bed he lay—the King of Sekadia.

Maya froze. She struggled not to gasp, not to show her shock, her pity.

Fire, she thought. *It was fire that hurt him.*

Scars covered the king, erasing his face, his hands, any semblance of the man he had been, like a wave effacing a child's drawings in sand. His ears, his nose, his eyes were gone. He had only two fingers left on one hand, none on the other; both hands curled, swollen, white. His head bloated to twice the normal size, and no hair covered him—no eyebrows, no beard, nothing but wrinkled scars. His mouth opened, a mere slit, struggling to speak.

Leven's hand tightened around Maya's. For once, he said nothing.

Maya looked at the burnt king, and along with her pity, she felt defeat. She felt hopeless.

I can't heal him. This is beyond my power.

She stepped closer to the bed. Two serving girls knelt at its sides, holding ewers of water and cloths. One girl placed a damp cloth on the king's head.

"His pain is great," the girl whispered.

The other girl lowered her head. "It's been greater of late. He moans so much. Sometimes he wishes to end his life."

Maya stood above the bed, eyes stinging.

I can't. I can't do this. His wounds are too great.

There was barely any life left here. A life twisted with pain. Maya felt it inside her—a coiling serpent in her gut, crying out, digging, constricting her. Years. He had been here for years. She knew it, felt it inside her. Years trapped in this useless body, years praying for death, trying to reach out, trying to end this life, only falling ... falling back into the agony, the endless days and nights, the bloated, rotting, unending existence.

"Hel ..." the king whispered, reaching up a fingerless hand, swollen and curled. "Hel ... me ..."

Maya's eyes dampened. She took the swollen hand in hers, and the king whimpered. She was hurting him. She gently placed his hand down, and the stench of rot spun her head. His breath rattled. He had no nose left, only two holes for nostrils. Behind her, Maya heard Leven gasp and stumble a few paces back.

How could King Zamur still be alive? How could the soul cling to such a ruin of a body? How could Maya—not yet a true lumer, only a girl—hope to heal the worst injury she had ever seen, an injury she had not imagined could exist?

"I can't," she whispered, tears in her eyes. "I'm sorry. I can't heal you."

The king had no eyes, but he seemed to stare at her, breath ragged. "Hel ... me ..."

"Please try, daughter of Zohar," whispered one of the servants. "You are of Zohar, are you not?" She pointed at the lion pendant that hung around Maya's neck. "The Zoharites are renowned for their wisdom. Please try, daughter of Eloh."

Maya nodded and lowered her head.

I don't know if I'm wise. I don't know if I'm strong. But I know that I'm in this world to heal—to heal nations, to heal the poor, to heal kings, to mend things that are broken.

She thought back to Zohar, a broken land. A land suffering under the yoke of conquerors. A land of swaying palm and fig trees that grew from the desert. A land of ancient limestone towers and archways and domes, where countless generations of sages had walked. Of pines on northern hills and cyclamens that grew along riverbanks. Of the sea that always whispered in her mind, the coast where she had been born, sunset on the waves and dawn over the hills, and chinking seashells and stones under her bare feet.

She walked there again, along the beach of Gefen, feet in the damp sand. The sun rose and fell as the world breathed, as the sea breathed, as all life breathed around her, trees and sand and stones and ancient songs. A land of light, copper, gold, myrrh,

stone, and lume. A land of God's grace. The land of her people—
a people thousands of years old—and of her family. Of candlelit
dinners under a painting of elephants. Of lying safely in her bed,
ivy and pomegranates outside the window, of her old scrolls, of
her parents, her siblings, of the light that had always filled her.

That light flowed from her now—the luminescence, the
lume she wove into magic. The glow suffused her—flowing from
her hands, her eyes, filling her, warming her. The glow of her
home. Of lume. Of Eloh. Of her life by the sea and in the desert.

Gently, she placed her hands on the burnt king.

He gasped, lipless mouth opening wide. The light flowed
from her into him. The king began to move in his bed, first
wriggling, then thrashing.

The serving girls leaped up. Guards stepped forward from
the shadows.

"She's killing him!" cried a man, drawing a sword.

"No!" Leven held the guard back. "Watch. She's helping."

"She's burning him further!" shouted another guard, raising
his blade.

"Stand back!" Leven said, pulling the man's arm down. "Let
her heal him."

The king screamed.

It was a horrible sound, inhuman, the sound of a wounded
animal, and Maya nearly lost her magic. She clung to the
memories of Zohar. The camels riding over the dunes. The
ancient towers of Beth Eloh, rising from the desert. The maidens
in their white dresses, dancing over grapes as their brothers played

lyres and drums. The waves. Golden coins and ancient jewels and limestone bricks. Light. Everywhere, light. Flowing from the Temple on the Mount of Cedars. Flowing through her. Flowing through the generations, from Adom, the father of the Zoharite nation, to Elshalom, the first king, to her mother, to her, into this king in the bed. She gave him all the light inside her, all the light of her people.

The luminescence flowed across the wounded king, hiding his form, and he calmed. He lay in his bed, and his breathing deepened. Easier breathing now. Deep, no rattle to it.

Maya took her own shuddering breath.

The light tugged at her, nearly consuming her, flowing around her. Too many memories. Too many millions of souls. Ancient feet on ancient stones. Towers rising and falling, endless years, and tribes that danced on the hills. She let it all flow out. She let it all heal him. She fell to her knees, gasping, the light draining from her, leaving her in shadows. Leaving her trembling, gasping for breath.

Leven rushed toward her. He knelt and held her in his arms. "Maya! Maya, are you all right?"

She blinked, shuddering. The world seemed to shrink. Those ancient memories faded. The landscapes of Zohar fled from her mind. Once more she was here, in the chamber of a king in a distant eastern land.

Trembling, leaning on Leven, she rose to her feet. She gazed down at the king in the bed.

Her eyes dampened, and she lowered her head.

"I failed," she whispered.

The king was still scarred, his face still gone, his fingers still missing. Maya wept for him, for her failure. She had thought that she could heal him. She had drained almost all the lume inside her. She had thought that, after healing the dog, after healing Leven's brother, she could heal this man—but she was not a true lumer.

"I'm sorry," she said. "I'm sorry, my lord. I failed. I—"

"You ... did not ... fail," the king whispered.

Maya gasped and narrowed her eyes. The king's voice was clearer now. No longer did pain twist his words. His breathing was deep, no longer rasping. When Maya dried her eyes, she noticed that his hands—though still burnt, still missing the fingers—were no longer swollen and curled. His head was still scarred, still faceless, but it was no longer bloated. The smell of rot was gone. Whatever disease had filled him, whatever pain, whatever internal fire—it had vanished under her light. He was still scarred, still eyeless, and he would never be the man he had been. But ...

"The pain is gone," the king said, voice still weak but growing stronger with every word. "I can breathe freely. I ... I can lift my limbs without pain. Help me. Help me rise from this bed. For the first time in years, let me stand up."

The king began to slowly stand. Maya held one of his arms. Leven rushed forward and grabbed the other. The servants and guards stared, eyes wide.

The king placed one foot on the floor. Then the other. Then he stood and took a step.

"The pain is gone," he whispered. He had no eyes left to weep with, but Maya heard the joyous emotion in his voice. "I can walk again. I can leave my bed. You healed me, daughter of Zohar. You healed me."

"I could not heal you fully," Maya said. "I could not bring back your eyes, your fingers, your face, could not clean off your scars."

The burnt king embraced her. "I had lost hope of ever rising from my bed, ever breathing the air without pain. I still cannot see, and perhaps I'm still scarred, but you've given me back my life. I will enter the gardens now, and I will feel the sun, and hear the birds sing, and I will contribute to my kingdom once more." His voice softened. "My spring palace lies across the river, Maya Sela of Zohar, a place of wealth, gardens, beauty. It is now yours."

She blinked. "You know my name? I didn't think that I told anyone."

"You told me your name, and of your past, and of your kingdom of Zohar—a land of peace and wisdom, a land lost to the eagles. Now live here in wealth. The spring palace is yours."

Maya shook her head. "I wish only for transport to the eastern sea. I do not wish to live in a palace, my lord, for the majesty of Luminosity shines brighter. All earth is finite, and all earthly kingdoms fade to sand, but the kingdom of Luminosity is endless and eternal."

Behind her, Leven gave a strangled sound. "But … but … Maya!"

"Are you sure, child?" asked the King of Sekadia. "You could live a comfortable life here."

Maya nodded. "I'm sure. I desire no lands, no wealth, only maps and supplies and guides to accompany me to the eastern sea. Keep your spring palace, my lord. I must reject your generous gift."

With a clatter, Leven crashed to the floor.

"Guides you shall have!" said the king. "And a hundred guards too, and a wagon and many supplies. The royal convoy will take you east. What do you seek by the sea?"

"I'm not entirely sure," Maya confessed. "A center of Luminosity, of light, of wisdom. I have a map with a symbol. It shows a four-branched candelabrum by the sea—sigil of Luminosity. But … I never learned the name of the place."

"You seek the eastern city of Suna," said the king. "Indeed, several Zoharites live there, protected under my reign, where they study the light of Eloh. The journey will take you a month, but my escorts will see you there safely."

Suna. The place I seek. An oasis of light.

Maya knelt before the king. "Thank you, my lord!" Her breath trembled, and her eyes dampened, this time with joy. "Your gift is worth to me more than an empire. Suna. The place I seek is Suna."

Leven managed to rise to his feet. "My king," the thief said, "if your palace is still up for grabs … I *did* help Maya here. Surely that deserves some credit. Maybe ... a small palace? A villa? A very nice house? Ouch!" He winced as Maya elbowed him hard in the belly.

That evening, for the first time in months, Maya lay in a bed—a real bed, the frame carved of cedar, the mattress stuffed with down. The king had given her this chamber high in the ziggurat. Candles burned in serpent sconces, illuminating frescoes depicting dragons flying over mountain and sea. The window revealed the sun setting over the city, gilding the limestone idols, the towers lining the boulevards, the columned temples, the domed homes, and the desert beyond the walls.

Leven sat beside her on his own bed, stripped down to a pair of baggy pants. In the candlelight, she could see the scars across his back—his punishment for burglarizing so many in Beth Eloh. He had trimmed his beard down to stubble, and his curled hair was just long enough to cover the tips of his ears. His skin was deep bronze, the skin of a man who had spent his life in the cruel sunlight of the desert.

Maya lay in her bed, unable to sleep, watching him.

"You should sleep," she said. "Tomorrow you'll be journeying back to Zohar. It's a long way."

Leven bit his lip. He rose from his bed, walked across the chamber, and stared out the window.

"I know you're absolutely heartbroken that I'll be leaving." He nodded. "I did warn you that I'll steal your heart."

She rolled her eyes. "Yes, heartstolen, that's me. Look how I'm weeping."

He turned back toward her. "You know, we could have lived here together. A wealthy life in Sekadia could have been ours."

"Could have been *mine*." She sat up in bed. "And I don't deserve a life of wealth. I didn't fully heal him. I have much to learn of Luminosity. I will learn across the desert, far from Aelar. In a safe place by the sea."

"Well ..." Leven tapped his foot. "Maybe I want to get away from Aelar too. Have you ever stopped to consider that?" He pointed at her. "You're not the only one who hates the Aelarians, you know. Maybe I want to go east too. Maybe I *will* go east."

She raised an eyebrow. "Your mother told you to accompany me to this city. She never said you had to walk me all the way to the sea. The king will lend me his guards."

Leven snorted. "Useless, his guards are. Couldn't stop him from being burned, could they? And I did save you already from the bone-raiders."

Now her second eyebrow rose. "If I recall correctly, *I* saved *you* from them."

"Technicalities." He waved dismissively. "Look, Maya." He knelt before her. "I know you'd be sad if I left you. And I know you'd miss me. And I know that, well ... that after getting to know each other for so long, after all we've been through, that being apart would feel so ... empty." He reached out, hesitated, then caressed her hair. "And I don't want you to feel such emptiness. So, because you insist, and because your heart is so broken, I'll keep traveling with you. To the east. All the way to the sea."

She smiled thinly. "Is it so hard, Leven? To admit you have feelings inside that shriveled-up organ you call a heart?"

"Feelings!" He scoffed. "I don't have any feelings. I'm not a girl."

She kissed his cheek. "I'm almost a lumer. I have the Sight—one of the Four Pillars of Luminosity. I can see your feelings, Leven."

She embraced him, and he climbed into the bed with her. She slept curled up in his arms, and she dreamed of home.

In the morning, they headed out—a caravan of wagons, camels, guards, and guides. They left the city of Sekur behind, heading east into the sprawling desert toward water, wisdom, and light.

OFEER

S he stood in the dark library, her mind a storm. The hour was late, but Ofeer couldn't imagine sleeping. Seneca had gone off to see Worm the lumer, leaving Ofeer alone in his chambers, this network of rooms occupying the western wing of the palace.

She brought her fingers to the iron collar around her neck, marking her a slave. With her fingertip, she felt the letters engraved there.

I have escaped! If you find me, return me to the Acropolis, to Prince Seneca Octavius, for a thousand denarius reward.

"How did this happen?" Ofeer whispered, head hung low. "I've been a fool. A fool."

She fell to her knees between the shelves of scrolls. She would have given the world to be home now—back in her true home, in Zohar. To hug them all. Her parents. Her siblings.

"I want to go back," she whispered, eyes stinging. "Please, Eloh. Let me wake up from this nightmare. Let me go back home. I promise to hug my mother so tightly. I promise to never fight with Epher and Koren and Atalia and Maya. I love them so much, and I'm so scared. I'm so scared that Epher is dead, that Koren is a slave in some mine or field, that Atalia is drowned, that Maya is lost in the desert. Please, Eloh. I'm so sorry." Her tears fell onto her thighs. "I'm so sorry for everything I've done. For yelling at my parents, for hurting them, making them cry. For running all those times to the port of Gefen. For standing among the Aelarians as they destroyed Gefen. For coming here." She sobbed. "I'm so sorry."

Rustling cloth sounded behind her, startling Ofeer. She spun around and her heart thrashed.

Valentina Octavius stood at the doorway, watching her. The youngest among Emperor Marcus's children, she was a slender girl roughly Ofeer's age. Her white hair framed a flushing face, and she nervously clutched her lavender stola—the garment Ofeer had heard rustling.

"I … I'm sorry," Valentina said. With no pigment to her skin, her blushing cheeks turned bright red. "I didn't mean to eavesdrop. I saw a light, and …"

Ofeer knelt on the mosaic floor. "My princess."

My sister, she added silently.

Valentina hesitated a moment, as if torn between walking by or staying. Finally she entered the library and gestured for Ofeer to rise. She straightened and gazed at her sister. They were of a height, but the resemblance ended there. Ofeer looked like her mother, dark and slender and sharp featured. Valentina had a softer face, rounder, gentler.

We're sisters, but we don't look alike, Ofeer thought. *Nor does she look like Seneca or Ofeer, and it's not just her colorings. Her eyes lack the ruthlessness. Porcia and Seneca have the eyes of hunters; she has the eyes of prey.*

"Are you ... Ofeer Sela?" Valentina asked.

Ofeer nodded. "Your brother told you."

"No." Valentina lowered her eyes. "I had a lumer once. She was from Gefen. Her name was Iris Bat Inet. Did you ... did you maybe know her?"

Ofeer shook her head. "No, I'm sorry, my princess. Gefen is a large city. Well, tiny compared to Aelar."

Valentina tugged nervously at her stola. Ofeer was surprised at how meek the girl seemed. An observer would be forgiven for thinking that Ofeer was the princess, Valentina the slave.

"She knew you," Valentina said. "She spoke to me often of the Sela family. I ... I couldn't help but hear you pray. I'm so sorry! I've always been fascinated with Zohar. My lumer would tell me all the stories—about the kings and queens, the lords and ladies, the beauty of Gefen, the wonders of Beth Eloh and the desert ..." Valentina sighed wistfully. "We were to visit there together."

Ofeer smiled wryly. "When you visit, will you take me with you?"

While I lived in Zohar, I comforted myself with dreams of Aelar, she thought. *Meanwhile, this one has been dreaming of Zohar.*

Valentina returned the smile. "It's strange how things change. My lumer is dead now. And Zohar has fallen. And you're here, a ..." She glanced at Ofeer's collar.

"A slave," Ofeer said.

Valentina glanced around, then back toward Ofeer. She hesitated a moment, then embraced her. "You are a great lady of Zohar, Ofeer Sela, descended of eastern nobility. I will protect you here in this palace. You have a friend here. You're not alone. I can't take you home to Zohar, but I can, maybe, help you find a new home here."

A little ray of hope filled Ofeer. She could still find some support here. Maybe not all members of the Octavius family were cruel.

Perhaps my father will be like Valentina. Perhaps he will accept me, even love me. Perhaps my dream can still come true.

"You're trembling," Valentina said. "If you can't sleep, would you like to return to my chamber? My bed is large enough for two, and we can tell each other stories of Zohar until we sleep."

"I'm not sure that Prince Seneca would like me to leave his quarters," Ofeer said. "I'm his slave now." She pointed at her collar.

Valentina snorted—a high-pitched, silly sound. "He wouldn't mind. We share everything."

"I would like that, then," Ofeer said.

They left the library and walked through the palace together, passing by columns and statues and frescoes. Finally they reached Valentina's bedchamber, which afforded a view of the gardens outside. It was a beautiful room, adorned with statues and murals, and songbirds sang in a golden cage. Candles burned in platinum sconces, and pillows topped a huge bed, larger than any Ofeer had ever seen.

They climbed onto the bed together, and Ofeer was grateful to be here, not in Seneca's chamber. When Seneca returned, he would be lustful for flesh, and he would have reached for Ofeer.

Let Taeer warm his bed tonight, Ofeer thought. *Let him never touch me again.*

"I can speak a little Zoharite," Valentina said, and now she spoke in the language of the desert, not in Aelarian.

Ofeer's eyes widened. "Did your lumer teach you?" she said, speaking Zoharite too. For many years, Ofeer had thought Zoharite an ugly, guttural language, not beautiful like flowing Aelarian. Yet now she was thankful to speak it, strangely proud of her mother tongue.

"I know a few songs of the desert too," said Valentina, and she sang them, almost perfectly.

For a long time, they lay side by side in the soft bed, and Ofeer told the princess many stories of Zohar. How she used to collect snail shells, fit little ones into big ones, then spill them all out, creating a game of snail dice. And how so many sheep would wander Pine Hill; Ofeer even made sheep sounds, and Valentina laughed. She told stories of the sunlight on the sea, and how soft the sand was, and how the seashells gleamed. She told the funny story about how Atalia had once entered the water, and how a jellyfish had stung her right on the bottom, and how Epher and Koren had laughed and laughed, and Atalia got mad and insisted it had stung her on the thigh.

"But it was right on the bottom—I saw it!" Ofeer said.

Valentina laughed. "Right on the ..." Her voice dropped to a whisper. "Ass." She gasped, as if shocked at herself, and covered her mouth with her palms.

Soon the two were giggling.

She's my age, Ofeer thought. *Yet she's still like a child. With her, I feel like a child again too. Safe.*

It was funny, Ofeer thought. For so many years, she had seen ugliness: the seedy taverns of Gefen's dregs, the beds of sweaty men, a ship of conquerors, a battle at sea, a market for slaves. She had lost so much—her country, her family. What would her life have been like now, had she been raised in this palace, the emperor's little daughter? Would she too be a blushing, giggling princess, her heart unscarred, all her memories joyous?

I could have been like her, Ofeer thought. *Like Valentina, with no pain in my heart, no nightmares to haunt my nights.*

"Valentina," Ofeer finally said, voice soft now. "I need your help. A favor."

Valentina's eyes softened. She took Ofeer's hands in hers. "Of course."

Ofeer took a deep breath. She was afraid to ask this—afraid the princess would be angry, cast her out from her bed. But Ofeer had to ask. She could not trust Seneca with this task. She needed Valentina's help.

"I came into Aelar with my brother," Ofeer finally said. "With Koren Sela. I lost him in the slave market. I don't know who bought him. Please, my princess." She squeezed Valentina's hand. "If you feel any affection toward me, help me find him. Help me find Koren. Bring him here, to this palace, to serve you instead of laboring in a mine or field."

Valentina leaned forward and kissed Ofeer's forehead.

"Of course, my sweet Ofeer." Valentina stroked Ofeer's long dark hair. "I lost my lumer. I lost Iris of Zohar, a woman I loved more than anyone. I'll save any Zoharite that I can. At dawn, I'll send forth my servants to find Koren, to buy him from his new master, and to bring him here. You and your brother will be safe with me."

Ofeer embraced her. "Thank you, my princess." Her eyes dampened. "Thank you."

Finally the princess slept, hands tucked under her cheek. Most of the candles had burned out, and only three still cast a flickering glow.

God damn it! Ofeer had to pee. Her bladder felt ready to burst. She got out of bed, seeking a place to relieve herself. She found a chamber pot, but it was cracked, and so she left the room and wandered the halls. Finally she found a lavatory, a place for the servants and slaves, but every one of the toilets was occupied. Ofeer waited, tapping her feet, holding onto her crotch, but the servants kept chatting as they expelled their waste, refusing to rise, and Ofeer felt like the piss would spurt out of her ears. She hurried down the hallway, seeking a place, any place, to empty her bladder. She considered a flower pot, but just then several senators walked by. She raced outside, trying to find a bush to pee behind, but everywhere she went there were lords, ladies, soldiers, and—

Ofeer opened her eyes.

Just a dream. She hadn't remembered falling asleep, but it was already dawn, and she still lay in Valentina's bed. Birds sang outside, and soft light fell between the curtains.

Ofeer blinked and rubbed her eyes. She wondered where Seneca was, if he had returned from speaking to Worm, if he was looking for her. Before she could contemplate the matter further, she realized the reason for her dream. Her bladder *was* indeed full to near bursting, almost painful.

Leaving Valentina to sleep, Ofeer climbed out of bed and walked down the hall. She entered the lavatory, the same one from her dream. Several toilets lined the walls, no curtains or stalls between them—the Aelarians were not ones for privacy—but thankfully the place was empty. Ofeer sat down and let the water that rushed below carry her problems away.

Relieved, she stepped back into the hallway. She tried to find her way back to Seneca's chambers—he would be furious if she didn't return to him soon—but quickly found herself lost. She wandered the hallways, feeling much as she had in her dream, struggling to find relief but winding deeper and deeper in a labyrinth she couldn't escape.

Many other people were filling the palace now—other slaves in iron collars, servants in livery, clerks in togas, and soldiers in armor. Ofeer took directions from an old scribe, and soon she found herself walking along a portico of columns, a frescoed wall to one side, the gardens to the other.

It was then that she saw him for the first time.

Ofeer froze, stared between the columns, and lost her breath.

There he was. The man she had seen carved into marble, embossed onto coins, painted on palace walls. Emperor Marcus Octavius. Her father.

The emperor wore a plain white toga today, the day he was to declare his heir in the Amphitheatrum. He stood by a fig tree, admiring the fruit. Oddly, seeing the tree filled Ofeer with a bittersweet sadness, for many fig trees grew in Zohar, and it seemed so strange to her that here, in this different land, this different father should contemplate a tree so familiar to her.

Ofeer was not afraid. Across the Empire, they told tales of Marcus Octavius's cruelty. They said that when he had returned from Leer, he had crucified thousands of prisoners along the road from Polonia to Aelar. They said that Marcus had slain the very builders who had constructed this palace, so that its secrets would never be known. They said that he fed his enemies to the lions, that he himself had murdered thousands.

So they said, Ofeer thought. The stories also said that Valentina was a ghost, a spirit who haunted these halls, moaning and cursing all in her path, and yet Valentina was kind. The stories also said that Seneca was a handsome prince and hero, yet Ofeer had seen a frightened, cruel boy.

So let them talk. She stared between the columns at the emperor. *He's my father. I need not fear him.*

She stepped between the columns and entered the gardens.

The emperor did not turn toward her. Several Magisterians stood between the columns, but here were men who had sailed with Ofeer on the ship; they knew her well, and they did not move as she approached her father. When she reached the emperor, she knelt on the grass, dirtying her tunic.

The emperor held a hanging fig, but he did not pluck it from the tree. He spoke, still facing the fruit, as if speaking to it instead of to Ofeer.

"Do you know, girl, I was poisoned once. Not long ago. I've barely eaten from the kitchens since. I come here, to my gardens, and eat the figs and apples and almonds I grow here." Finally he turned toward her. "There are poisoners everywhere. Assassins behind every column and every tree. I don't know your face. Perhaps you're an assassin too."

She shook her head, still kneeling. "Just a slave, my emperor. A new slave in this palace. I serve Prince Seneca." Slowly she rose and faced him. He was a tall man. Ofeer was not short, yet she barely reached his shoulders. "And ... more than just a slave, my emperor."

"I can see that." Marcus nodded. "You are Zoharite, yet you speak flawless Aelarian with just the hint of an accent. You're a slave, yet you have noble bearings and the healthy glow of one raised in wealth. You remind me of someone ... of someone I knew long ago."

A tremble seized Ofeer's heart. "A Zoharite, my emperor?"

He finally plucked the fig from the tree and caressed it with his thumb. "A Zoharite, yes. Funny people, you are. Proud. Stubborn. Ancient—among the most ancient around the Encircled Sea. A rich culture. It's my hope that Aelar should last for three thousand years as Zohar has."

"Zohar fell, dominus."

He raised an eyebrow. "Fell? Perhaps, yes. It's been fading for many years now. We ravaged your fleet nearly two decades ago. A civil war tore the kingdom apart. My children cracked what remained of its strength. Plucked from the tree, the fruit is to be consumed, or it rots." He bit deep into the fig. Juices ran down his chin. "And so we consume. We devour."

Ofeer took a deep breath.

I was born for now. Like a dagger. Like a dagger into the heart. Quick and brave.

"My emperor, people have always told me I look like my mother. That's who I remind you of. I am Ofeer Sela, the daughter of Shiloh Elior-Sela." She stared into his eyes, forcing down her fear. "I'm your daughter."

She was trembling now. She couldn't help it. She forced in deep breaths, refusing to look away from his eyes. Finally. Finally. After so many years of pain, of drinking in taverns, of falling asleep drunk in strange men's beds, of hating her family, of hating her homeland, of losing her family, of traveling here across the sea, of dreaming, hoping, fearing, so much fear—finally she was here. Finally she met him. Finally Ofeer had reached the great crossroads of her life. She stared, shaking, awaiting his reply.

Emperor Marcus frowned.

Slowly, he nodded.

"Yes," he said. "Yes, yes, I see it. I remember your mother well. She was a beautiful young woman then, and you are a beautiful young woman now." He stroked her cheek. "You look like her, though I see some of myself in you as well." He bit down on his fig. "Now run along, child. Return to your duties in the palace."

She blinked. She could not move. "But ... Father. I ... I ..."

He gestured. "Run along now. Back to Seneca."

"But I'm your daughter!" she blurted out, barely able to breathe. "You're my father!"

"That's how it usually works," said Marcus.

"I ..." Ofeer touched her collar. "How can I serve Seneca as a slave? I'm his sister! How can I be a slave here? I'm the daughter of an emperor." Her voice was cracking. Her soul was fraying.

Marcus sighed and watched a pair of starlings dance around a branch. "Child, the city of Aelar is full of bastards. Seneca himself probably fathered a dozen in the city's brothels and warrens. I myself must have fathered a hundred on my campaigns." He reached into his pocket and pulled out two silver coins. He placed them in her palms, one coin in each hand. "Here, take these. Buy yourself something nice, if Seneca lets you visit the city markets. But do not come to me again, child, expecting me to be a father to you. Do you understand?" He stroked her hair. "You're nothing but a Zoharite bastard slave, the daughter of a squealing whore. Never forget that, my darling, and never attempt to rise above your station again."

Ofeer stood still, staring at him, feeling the blood drain from her face. Her world seemed to collapse around her. It was all she could do to stay standing.

Shock.

She felt nothing but shock.

"Don't tell Seneca," she whispered, voice barely audible.

The emperor frowned. "Slaves do not make demands of emperors, girl. I put silver in your palms. Do not make me put nails through them next."

"Please," she whispered. She couldn't speak louder. "Don't tell him. He can't know. Can't know that he—"

She bit down on her words, and she saw that he understood.

And she saw that he would tell his son.

Seneca will know, Ofeer realized. *He'll know that I—the woman he loves, the woman he bedded—am his sister. And he'll kill me. He'll kill me like he killed Jerael. My true father. My true father . . .*

She was shaking so wildly now she almost fell. She spun around. She fled the gardens.

Her eyes stung as Ofeer raced through the palace, and now she truly felt like she were back in her dream. Only this life was worse than a nightmare. She could barely see. She ran, nearly slammed into a soldier, ran another way, lost now, delving deeper into the palace, knowing she had to flee, had to escape this place, knowing she was a fool. A fool. A fool.

Why did I do this? Why did I come here? I want to go home. I just want to go home. I want to be with you, Mother.

She knew that he would kill her. She knew that Seneca would rage, stab her, torture her, nail her to a cross, sickened with her, sickened with what he had done to her, sickened that she had not revealed the truth to him. Yet now he would know this truth. Now her life was forfeit, and she would die here, alone, far from her family, in a foreign land.

Finally she found her way to an exit, but men of the Magisterian Guard stood there, and they saw the collar around her neck, and they moved to block the door. Ofeer ran another way. She raced down a hallway, found another exit. But here too stood guards, and they blocked her passage, reaching out to her.

"Slave!" they called. "Slave, where are you going?"

She ran the other way, found another blocked door, more Magisterians. She wore a slave's collar now. She was no longer Seneca's concubine but his slave, and this palace was her prison. Trapped. Trapped like an animal. Doomed to death.

She wanted to find Valentina again, to seek comfort and safety from the princess, but she could not find her way. Finally Ofeer discovered a cellar, a little place full of amphorae, and she sat between the towering jugs, pulled her knees to her chest, and hugged her legs. She shivered, and she prayed.

SENECA

*T**oday my life's path is laid down.* Seneca walked through the palace, clutching the scroll of human skin. *Today I become heir to an empire.*

He had not slept all night, disturbed by the contents in the scroll, reading it again and again—the monstrous sins of his sister, depicting every vile sexual act he could imagine. And, along with disgust, hope—for glory, for the shameful defeat of Porcia, for a life upon a throne.

He walked down the corridor, every breath feeling significant, holy, a moment from the most important day of his life.

I will rule this palace, Seneca thought. *I will rise to rule this empire. You and I, Ofeer. The world will be ours.*

Seneca had not seen Ofeer since last night. He had not returned to his chambers after visiting Worm in her tower, his mind too stormy to sleep. He had spent the night in the Temple of Junia, goddess of wisdom, pacing the nave, thinking, planning, dreaming.

The next time I see you, Ofeer, I will be the heir to Aelar, Seneca thought.

In his dreams, he could already see it. He would emancipate Ofeer from slavery—perhaps in a year, perhaps sooner—and name her a citizen of Aelar. She would be so thankful that she would fall to her knees, kiss his feet, shed tears, and bless his name. They would make love all that day and night, and then they would marry. The whole city would come to see them ride through the streets in a jeweled chariot, a husband of Aelarian nobility and his wife, an exotic seductress of the east, a desert rose all in silk and gold.

And once Father died—it wouldn't be too long, the man was old already—they would be emperor and empress. He would show Ofeer then. He would show her how mighty he was. He would crush the rebellion in Nur, bringing Ofeer all the treasures from that land: zebra pelts and ivory and the horns of rhinoceroses. He would defeat the Gaelians too, leading the hosts himself to finally slay those bearded barbarians of the north. Perhaps, if Ofeer truly begged him, he would spare the Zoharites, let them keep living under his rule. Ofeer would be thankful for that, so thankful that she would kneel again—like she had knelt in Zohar—kiss his feet, worship him for his mercy.

"I love you, Ofeer Sela, keeper of her mother's vineyard," he whispered as he walked through the palace. "I've loved you since the moment we met on the hills of Zohar. You're my slave now, but I will make you my empress."

Seneca took a shuddering breath.

But not yet. It was premature to dream. First he had to speak to his father. First he had to secure his prize.

He knew where he would find his father this morning—the same place Emperor Marcus went every morning after feeding on fruit from the gardens. Seneca slowed his pace, inhaled deeply, and entered his mother's tomb.

The vast hall always felt like a cavern, white and austere, all in marble, colorless. Mother's statue rose there, carved of pale stone, one breast exposed, the chiseled stola flowing like real linen. Before her, so small by comparison, stood Seneca's father.

Seneca approached him. For a moment, they stared together at the great marble statue. Seneca glanced toward his father. Marcus stared ahead, and that face seemed chiseled of stone too, all sharpness and cruelty, all harsh lines, the mouth pitiless, the eyes cruel. Seneca returned his gaze to the statue; it seemed soft in comparison.

"She was a beautiful woman," Seneca said softly. "I wish I could have gotten to know her better. I—"

"Seneca, I told you not to approach me before the ceremony tonight," Marcus said. "You and your sister both know this. I am to make my decision in private, and I will not have my children campaigning to me like senators groveling for a vote."

Seneca held out the scroll. "Before you make your decision, read this. No campaigning. No groveling. Just something I think you'll find very, very interesting."

Marcus stared at the parchment. "What is this?"

"Porcia's journal." Seneca's pulse quickened, and a savage smile tugged at his lips. "Read it."

Marcus grunted and turned away. "Seneca, I told you, I'm not interested in any more—"

"She fucked gladiators," Seneca said, interrupting his father. "Two of them. Here in this very chamber, right under mother's eyes."

His heart wanted to leap out from his throat. Sweat trickled down his back. It was all Seneca could do to keep breathing.

Slowly, his father turned toward him. "Seneca, these accusations—"

"—are true." Seneca all but shoved the scroll at him. "Look at it! Read it. I took it from her chamber. It's her own handwriting. Her own signature at the bottom of each entry. And oh, she did more than bed a couple gladiators in this tomb. Much more. Something about plotting to kill you, and turning your bones into sex toys? That's in there too. And a lot more."

Marcus finally took the scroll. Frowning, the emperor began to read.

Seneca watched, laughing inside, fire burning through him. Victory. He would have victory! He wanted to dance, to cry out in joy, but forced himself to wait, silent, studying his father's reaction. As he read, Marcus's frown deepened, and his fingers tightened around the parchment, nearly tearing it.

"Even in your bed, Father," Seneca said. "With three senators, one by one—in your own bed, while you were away on a campaign."

Marcus lowered the pages. His face was harder than ever, a face of stone.

343

He's furious, Seneca knew. Glee filled him.

"Porcia is a depraved beast," Seneca said. "She beds foreigners. Slaves. She has orgies on her campaigns, in temples, here in this palace. She is perverted, Father. She—"

"—did not bed her own sibling," Marcus said.

Seneca blinked. He tilted his head. "What? Of course not!" Seneca stiffened. "Why would you ever suggest that Porcia and I would—"

"Not Porcia and you," Marcus said. "You and your other sister."

"Valentina?" Seneca took a step back, frowning, his joy curdling in his belly. This was wrong. Something was wrong. "Father, what are you talking about?"

Marcus tossed down the scroll. It unrolled across the floor. Fury raged across the emperor's face. His fists tightened.

"You come to me, son, accusing Porcia of depravity. Do you think I don't know of your slave? Of Ofeer of Zohar? Do you think I don't know that you bedded her? All the palace speaks of it."

Seneca blinked. His belly roiled. He took another step back. "Father, I ... I love Ofeer. I love her truly, as a man loves a woman. Surely there's nothing sinful in that. I know she's a foreigner. But you yourself have bedded Zoharite women, it's said, and—"

"Yes, Seneca," Marcus said slowly. "I too have bedded a Zoharite. A long time ago. Nineteen years ago, to be exact. A woman named Shiloh Sela. You met her, I believe. She looks a lot like her daughter. Like *my* daughter."

Seneca trembled. He could barely see. He could speak no louder than a whisper. "Father, what ... what are you saying?"

Marcus snorted. "Ofeer never told you. Of course not. She's a clever girl. She knew how you'd react. Ofeer is my bastard daughter, Seneca. She's your half sister. A sister you bedded. You're guilty of crimes far worse than anything described in these pages you brought me."

No.

Seneca trembled.

No. Gods, no.

"You lie," he whispered. "You lie!"

Marcus turned to leave. "Ask your lumer. Ask Taeer to use her Sight. She'll reveal the truth to you. I go to the bathhouse now, to cleanse my body before the games tonight, when I announce my heir. I suggest that you pray, Seneca, to cleanse your soul."

With that, Marcus stepped out of the tomb. Seneca remained, not realizing that he had fallen to his knees. The chamber spun around him. He fell to his side.

No. No. Lies. Lies!

"Ofeer," Seneca whispered, eyes stinging. "I love you. I love you. I ... You lied." He trembled violently. He roared. "You lied! You lied! You whore! You fucking whore!"

He leaped to his feet. Tears streamed down his cheeks. He couldn't stop shaking. Let the world burn. Let it burn! Nothing mattered now. Nothing. Nothing! Not this empire. Not the throne. Not his future. Rage. Rage! It was all he felt.

"Ofeer!" he roared. He ran through the palace, howling, shoving people aside. "Ofeer!"

He could barely see. The blood pounded through his ears. He grabbed a sword from a guard, and he ran through the palace, crying out her name, swinging his blade, vowing to plunge it into Ofeer's heart ... and then into his own.

VALENTINA

T oday.

It was today!

Valentina shivered as she walked the halls of the palace. Today Marcus Octavius planned to gather the myriads in the Amphitheatrum, to choose an heir, to promise the throne to either Porcia or Seneca.

And before that he would bathe.

It seemed such a mundane task to Valentina—to wash oneself before a grand event. Yet this day, this day to change all future days, it was a simple bath that would change the course of an empire.

Valentina stood on the palace wall, the morning cold around her. She tightened her stola and cloak around her, finding no warmth. When she gazed west, she could see the Acropolis spread before her, this city within a city, the heart of the Aelarian beast. The bathhouse. The Amphitheatrum, the great amphitheater in the heart of the Empire. The towering, golden statue of Marcus Octavius. The columned temples for Junia, goddess of wisdom; Vin, the god of wine; and Aelia, goddess of music. Great structures raised with lume, lumers stolen from

Zohar overseeing their construction. Edifices of marble and gold. Mere works of sand. Nothing but sand that would crumble in the wind.

Today it ends. Valentina hugged herself. *Today, Father, I will be brave.*

Valentina turned around, and she gazed off the wall toward the palace courtyard. She saw them there. Emperor Marcus Octavius, clad in his purple and gold toga, a laurel on his head, a tall and powerful man, handsome in a harsh, stony way. And Mingo the fool—once known as Septimus Cassius—scrawny, bearded, wearing only a loincloth, prancing around and chattering.

My two fathers, Valentina thought, gazing down at them. *My true father, and the father who raised me. A father who will live, and a father who will die.*

The fool Mingo stared up from the courtyard. For just an instant, he met her gaze, and in his eyes, Mingo vanished. The fool was no more. There was intelligence in those eyes, there was determination, there was love for her. These were the eyes of Septimus Cassius, once a senator, once the head of a great family, once the scourge of House Octavius. The bearded old man gave Valentina a single nod across the distance, then spun away and danced about again, mocking the birds, the trees, the lords and ladies of the court—once more the fool.

It was time.

Valentina walked down the staircase, off the wall, and into the palace's marble halls. Her heart trembled against her ribs like a bird in a cage, and she had to clasp her fingers to stop them from shaking.

I will be strong. I will be brave. For you, Father. For you, Aelar. For you, Ofeer, whose nation groans under the heel of my empire. For you, Iris, who cries out to me from the afterlife. For all those he hurt. For all those who suffer. I will be brave.

Down a hall lined with statues, Valentina met Ambrosia Avilius, a pretty woman with golden locks, born far in the north near the border with Gael. She was a close friend of Porcia's; Valentina had often seen the two walking together, one as cruel as iron, the other as sweet as poison.

"Ambrosia!" Valentina said, forcing a smile to her face, though her insides still churned. "I'm holding a feast at noon in the Temple of Dia." She dropped her voice to a conspiratorial whisper. "It's ten years since my father vanquished the land of Phedia, and I intend to surprise him there. Please don't tell the emperor! Not until we're all gathered." She bit her lip. "Will you and your family join me?"

Ambrosia smiled, her eyes alight. "You're so sweet, my princess! Planning a surprise party for your father!" She clasped her hands against her chest. "The love of a daughter warms my heart." She leaned closer and whispered with a wink, "Of course we'll be there."

There was very little that warmed Ambrosia's heart, Valentina knew, aside from perhaps a front row seat to see a couple sweaty gladiators cut each other down. But Valentina only nodded, keeping the smile on her face. "Be there at noon, and please don't be late. Invite everyone you know, but do not tell Emperor Marcus!"

Ambrosia laughed, no doubt thinking Valentina as silly and sweet as a toddler, and vowed to keep the secret.

Valentina nodded, and once Ambrosia had walked by, she exhaled shakily, feeling close to passing out. She steeled herself, squared her shoulders, and kept walking across the Acropolis. She approached the library, where two old men—retired generals and friends to Marcus—were reviewing scrolls and maps, reliving the battles of their youth. Valentina repeated her story to them.

"Please meet us in the Temple of Dia at noon—and remember, don't tell the emperor!"

They nodded. "Such a sweet child!" one said. "Such a loving daughter. Of course we'll be there."

Valentina nodded and turned around lest they saw the terror she felt. She left the library, and she continued her work. Through the Acropolis she walked, visiting them all—the young noblewomen who wore pastel stolas, the old soldiers, the highest echelon of Aelar. She even got her siblings to accept her invitation.

All people whom I've seen naked, Valentina thought. *Whom I've seen exposed in the baths, both their flesh and souls, flatterers and fools and soldiers and singers and priests and prefects. All those who serve him. All those I will draw away from him today, the day it all changes.*

At noon, Valentina walked down the cobbled path toward the Temple of Dia. She wore her lavender stola, pinned with the golden eagle of Aelar, but hidden in the folds of silk, she carried a secret pendant. A golden lion of Zohar. Iris's pendant.

For you, Iris, she thought. *More than for anyone, for you.*

The temple rose before her, a ring of marble columns topped with a silver dome. She climbed the stairs. She took a deep breath, and she stepped inside.

Sunlight streamed through the oculus, falling upon them all. His generals, his servants, his flatterers, all those he ruled.

Valentina's heart thudded as she stepped onto the dais, and she faced the crowd, prepared for the storm.

SEPTIMUS

" A bath, a bath, watery water for splashy splash!" Septimus danced down the corridor, pirouetting and windmilling his arms. "Time to get clean, yes dominus, wipe off all the filth, all the blood, all the shame."

Marcus grunted and kept walking, ignoring him. The emperor was nervous. Septimus knew when Marcus was nervous. There was a twitch to the tyrant's thin lips, a tightness to his hands, the faintest of frowns on the lined brow. Today was the day his heir would be chosen. Today was the day Marcus had delayed for years.

And today is the day we wash off all the filth, Emperor Marcus Octavius, Septimus thought. *Today all will be blood in the water.*

He leaped and snapped his heels together, blabbering, a crazy old loon in a loincloth, long of beard, soft of mind, a mask, a puppet, the creature Marcus thought he had created. Mingo.

You should never have taken me into your home, Marcus. You keep your friends close and your enemies closer. A dangerous strategy.

"Mingo, calm yourself," Marcus said. "I'm not in the mood for your chattering today."

Septimus nodded. "Then I must chatter onward, brave as a general plowing through his enemies. For I'm here to remind you that all mortals die, that all silence is full of endless voices."

For voices still rose in Septimus's own mind. The voice of his wife, calling to him, screaming as Marcus raped and murdered her. The voices of his sons, crying out as the legionaries stabbed them, "Father, Father!" The voice of his daughter, of sweet Valentina, laughing in the gardens, calling out "Father" too—but calling to Marcus, the man who had stolen her.

Do any of those voices still haunt you, Marcus Octavius? Septimus thought, dancing down the corridor with his emperor. *I think not. But let my voice, the voice of the fool you created, be the last one you hear, and let it torment you for eternity.*

They reached the gates to the Acropolis's bathhouse. There were many communal bathhouses across Aelar—some huge pools for thousands of commoners, others smaller and more prestigious. Marcus was fond of visiting them all, sometimes even making appearances in the great bathhouses in the city's poorer neighborhoods, letting the people see him, letting them know that even Marcus Octavius was a mortal man beneath his fine toga, one of the people.

Today he came to the Acropolis Bathhouse, Marcus's favorite and the city's finest. The gates were carved of marble, engraved with figures of fish and mermaids. Two Magisterians stood at the gates, their helmets hiding their faces, their shields in hand.

Marcus strode through the gates, not even noticing, blind to everything under his great hooked nose.

But Septimus noticed. These were not the same young guards who normally stood here. They were older officers, men who had guarded the Republic long ago.

Septimus nodded at the Magisterians. They stared back, gave him the slightest nod. And then Septimus chattered onward, dancing and singing, and entered the bathhouse after his emperor.

Here was a place of splendor. Some called it the true heart of the Acropolis. In the old days, Septimus would come here with his fellow senators and their slaves, and here—here in this water!—the true discussions were had, decisions were made, and deals were struck. Here, naked in the hot pool, had the senators governed the Aelarian Republic. Columns rose here, engraved with fish, topped with statues of the gods. Frescoes of dolphins covered the walls, and a mosaic of many sea creatures hid at the floor of the pool. The aqueduct carried steaming water in the pool, delivered from a hot spring. Many doorways led to smaller chambers—places where a rich man could pay for a massage, a barber, or a brothel girl or boy.

The Acropolis Bathhouse, even these days with Aelar an empire, was the most social of all places on these hills, more than the stern temples, more than the silent gardens, more than the somber palace. It was here that the emperor could mingle with those he ruled, from the senators who had survived the purge to the generals and to the basest of slaves. Here, naked, they were all one and the same, all just flesh in the water.

And today, this most public of all places ... was empty.

Marcus took a few more steps into the bathhouse. He paused at the edge of the steaming pool. His frown deepened.

Septimus cackled and raced across the slippery tiles. "They're not here, they're not here!" He laughed. "Surprise, surprise! Valentina has called them into the Temple of Dia! A surprise party, my emperor. Hush. Hush!" He slapped a palm over his mouth and spoke between the fingers. "I should not have spoken. Bad Mingo! Bad fool. Ruins the surprise. Mingo loves surprises, yes he does."

"I told you to cease your chatter today," Marcus snapped. "I'm in no mood for your foolishness. I only brought you here to entertain the people, yet we have this bath to ourselves." He doffed his toga and hung it on a peg. "Perhaps it's for the best. I'm in no mood for flatterers or fools today. We bathe, then we go to the Amphitheatrum, and we name our heir." He stepped closer to the pool, then lowered his head.

"My emperor?" said Septimus. "Does a melancholy weigh upon your mighty shoulders that bear the weight of an empire?"

Naked, Marcus looked at him, and there was pain in those eyes. "Mingo, I read something this morning. Something disturbing. Something that my daughter wrote, detailing acts that she ..." He shook his head as if to banish the thought. "I was hoping to see her succeed me."

"Perhaps your daughter still can," said Septimus, slyly. "You have a second daughter. Valentina."

Marcus snorted. "You'd like to see that, wouldn't you? Yes, Mingo, you still remember who she is, don't you? Deep in your broken, mad mind, you still remember. But she will remain mine. It will be Seneca who inherits my throne when I'm gone. Seneca who must bring order to this empire. And in time, I will reveal to him the truth." Marcus nodded. "I grow older, and I tire of this game. Once Seneca has received my blessing, I will reveal to him Valentina's true parentage. I will reveal that she is the daughter of Septimus Cassius, not my own daughter. At that time, I will let Seneca turn her into his memento mori, into a sniveling, broken fool, just like you are. Now come, into the bath! We wash ourselves clean."

Septimus's fury rose.

His daughter, Valentina—tortured, broken, turned into a fool.

"No," Septimus whispered.

Valentina. Precious, beautiful Valentina—debased like him. *No.*

His wife—dead, murdered by General Marcus as he crushed the Senate, a living child carved from her womb. *No.*

His sons. Stabbed. Butchered like animals, still crying out to him. *No.*

This civilization that Septimus loved, a republic of wisdom and enlightenment, reduced to an empire of vanity and bloodlust. *No.*

Marcus stepped closer toward the pool. "No, Mingo? Do you object to washing ourselves?"

"No," Septimus repeated, stepping closer. "No, Marcus. No. No. No!"

At the edge of the pool, one foot above the water, Marcus turned to look at his memento mori, confusion in his eyes.

With a roar of fury, Mingo the fool, Septimus Cassius the disgraced senator, shoved Emperor Marcus with all his strength.

The night before, Septimus had not only coached Valentina to summon the common bathers. He had not only replaced the guards with his own men—men still loyal to the Republic. He had also painstakingly coated the edge of the pool with the thinnest veneer of oil.

Marcus now floundered, feet sliding across the marble toward the water. He fell. He fell just as Septimus had planned, just as he had rehearsed with his helmeted men, and as his body crashed into the water, Emperor Marcus's head slammed onto the edge of the pool with a *crack*.

Blood splattered across the marble, and Emperor Marcus—butcher, rapist, kidnapper, tyrant—sank under the water.

Septimus walked to the edge of the pool and stared down at the sinking body. Blood spread through the water.

"For my wife," he said softly. "For my sons." His fists trembled. "For my daughter." His breath rose to a pant. "For what you did to Aelar and to the world."

Septimus's thin chest rose and fell. His head spun. Finally— finally—after seventeen years of pain, seventeen years of this charade, it was over. The puppet's strings were cut. The emperor was d—

In the pool, Marcus gave a jolt and beat his arms.

Blood gushing from his head, the emperor swam to the surface, raised his face from the water, and sucked in air.

Septimus stared for just a heartbeat, then leaped into the water.

"For my wife!" he cried, grabbing Marcus, shoving his head back underwater.

Marcus floundered, struggled, kicked, clawed at Septimus. Still the blood gushed from his head. Septimus's arms—weakened by years of slavery—trembled with rage as he held Marcus's head under the surface.

"For my sons!" he shouted.

Marcus screamed under the water, voice muffled. His fists drove into Septimus's withered frame, cracking a rib, shattering his stomach, but still Septimus held the emperor's head under the surface.

"For my daughter!"

He dug his fingers into that head, pressing them into the wound, driving through the cracked skull into the soft innards, pressing down, holding him under. Marcus still struggled. He seemed to struggle for an eternity, for far longer than any mortal man should expect to live without air, screaming, kicking, punching ...

But his blows weakened.

His arms finally hung at his sides.

Septimus released his grip.

The corpse of Marcus Octavius floated to the surface, eyes staring lifelessly, head cracked open. The emperor of Aelar, the man who had destroyed Septimus's life, who had destroyed the lives of millions, was dead.

Septimus rinsed the blood from his hands. He climbed out of the pool and stood for a moment, staring down at the corpse, then looked away.

I will never look upon him again. It's over.

He stepped into one of the side chambers, the place where barbers, masseuses, and prostitutes serviced the bathers. A basin, mirror, and razors waited here. Septimus spent a while working, shaving off his beard, cutting his hair down to a neat trim. Something resembling his own face gazed back at him—the man he had once been. A face older, deeply lined now, gaunt, haunted—but unmistakable. The face of Senator Septimus Cassius.

He left the chamber, stepping back toward the pool. He took Marcus's toga from its peg and donned it, clasping it around his shoulder with an eagle pendant. Shoulders squared, chin raised, Septimus exited the bathhouse.

"Senator Cassius!" said the guards, saluting him.

"It is done," he told them. "Now come, quickly. We gather the Magisterian Guard, and we march to the Senate. This city will soon crack and bleed. It will be our task, friends, to hold civilization together."

OFEER

Bells clanged across the Acropolis. Magisterians ran, armor clanking. Men and women cried. Senators raced down the marble halls, sandals clattering, togas fluttering. And all the while, those horrible bells, that deafening sound. *Clang. Clang.*

Ofeer panted. She raced outside onto the cobbled road and stood between the palace, the bathhouse, and the library. Everyone was running back and forth, and all the bells in all the temples were ringing. Above her, he soared—Emperor Marcus Octavius, a great statue all in gold, a hundred feet tall. Crows stood on his head, cawing, crying out with each clang of the bells.

"What happened?" Ofeer asked a pair of soldiers, but the men ran on.

A senator raced her way, clutching his ample gut.

"Dominus!" she said. "Why do the bells ring?"

The portly man ran by her, calling out for his comrades to head to the Senate.

Ofeer's head spun. She kept seeking Valentina in the crowd—her only friend here—but couldn't see the princess. Finally she caught hold of a young slave, a Gaelian girl with blond hair and blue eyes.

"What's going on?" Ofeer said, clutching the girl. "Tell me."

The slave stared back with wide eyes. "He's dead!" she whispered.

Ofeer felt a chill. "Who?"

"The emperor." The slave covered her face, trembling. "Emperor Marcus. They say he slipped in the bathhouse, that he banged his head, that he drowned in the water. They say the senators are trying to reform the Republic, and that Porcia went to summon her legions."

The girl ran off, and Ofeer stood still, for a moment overwhelmed.

My father is dead.

"Ofeer!" rose a cry somewhere in the distance, a cry twisted with rage, with madness. "Ofeer, you goddamn bastard! You knew! You knew!"

Seneca.

Ofeer sucked in air, terror leaping through her.

Marcus told him. Before he slipped and drowned, he told him.

"Ofeer, I'm going to gut you like a pig!" the shout rose.

She could still not see Seneca. Hundreds of people were rushing back and forth through the Acropolis. The bells clanged. The crows cawed.

Ofeer ran.

She raced downhill along a road, heading toward the Acropolis wall, the border separating it from the city that spread around it.

When she reached the archway that led into the outer city, Ofeer paused and gasped.

Soldiers were marching into the Acropolis. Not only the usual guards who patrolled here, but an army—hundreds of soldiers from the Magisterian Guard, marching together. At their lead walked a senator—frail, old, withered, but with square shoulders and a raised chin. It took Ofeer a moment to recognize him. It was the fool! The memento mori she had seen here in the Acropolis, a dancing idiot with a long white beard and loincloth—only that beard was gone now, and a fine toga draped across him. Behind him, the Guard kept pouring in.

"To the Senate!" cried the fool-turned-senator. "The tyrant is dead! Aelar is a republic again!"

Ofeer took a deep breath and ran. The doors were open. The soldiers kept streaming in. Nobody was paying any attention to a young slave. As the soldiers marched, Ofeer ran by them, slipping out the gates, leaving the Acropolis behind. The crows bustled above.

"Ofeer!" Seneca's voice rose somewhere in the distance.

Clang. Clang.

Caw! Caw!

The sandals of soldiers kept clacking. Seneca kept shouting. Ofeer kept running.

Outside the Acropolis, the city was a warren. Gone were the marble halls and fine columns and meticulous gardens and priceless statues. Here was a crowded labyrinth of brick apartment blocks, rickety wooden houses, roads no wider than her arm span, and a million citizens, servants, and slaves. All the city was bustling. The word was spreading here too.

"The emperor is dead!" cried a man.

"Marcus is dead!" rose another voice.

Some people were weeping, others cheering. Down the street, men were smashing into shops and looting, and one man was beating another. A dog raced down the road in terror, whipping his way through the crowd. Ofeer could no longer run; the streets were too crowded. She had to elbow her way through, and still she heard that clanging of the bells, the cawing of those crows, a din that never stopped.

She kept moving farther and farther from the Acropolis, heading deep into the maze of Aelar, this endless city, moving between peddlers, workers, scribes, slaves, soldiers, vanishing among the towering buildings, an ant in an endless hive. She felt again like she had in her dream, seeking a place to relieve herself, a place far from spying eyes and prying hands, finding no sanctuary.

Finally Ofeer made her way into a mausoleum between apartment blocks and a tavern. It rose several stories tall, the walls lined with hundreds of alcoves where the dead rested, like a great beehive for the fallen. Between the dead, Ofeer sat down and pulled her knees to her chin. She hugged her legs, shivering, alone in darkness, lost in a city far from home.

In the shadows, Ofeer found herself reading the words engraved onto a tomb before her. It was the tomb of a baby. The child had died at the age of only eleven months. As she contemplated the epitaph, Ofeer realized that she had not bled for

… not since she had met Seneca. Not since that time they had slept together in the cave on the hills.

She placed a hand on her belly, and Ofeer knew the truth, could feel it as if she were a lumer.

She was pregnant.

SEPTIMUS

He marched through the Acropolis, shoulders squared, chin raised. For the first time in seventeen years, not dancing or limping or playing the fool, not bearded or disheveled. For the first time in seventeen years, a lord of a civilization—Septimus Cassius, senator of Aelar.

Behind him marched his soldiers, five hundred men of the Magisterian Guard, their sigil a laureled eagle. For generations, the Guard had protected the city of Aelar and its rulers. While the legions fought on the frontiers of the Empire, the Guard had protected the heart of the civilization, watching that heart rot, watching a tyrant and his sadistic children wash their nation with blood. Now it would be the Magisterian Guard—defenders of the city—who returned it to righteousness.

"The tyrant is dead!" Septimus cried. "The Senate rises again!"

The bells chimed across the city. The sandals of the soldiers clanked across the flagstones.

People rushed about the Acropolis around them— priestesses, lumers, servants, slaves. The palace rose to the right on a hilltop. To the left towered the Amphitheatrum, the largest structure in the Empire, its tiers of arches gilded in the sunlight. On the highest hill rose the three golden statues: a statue of Porcia, of Seneca, and of Emperor Marcus Octavius, all in splendid armor, all watching over their domain.

These statues will soon fall, Septimus thought, *and the Octavius family will be nothing but a memory, a cautionary tale to those who would try to seize an empire for their vainglory.*

Ahead rose the Senate. A portico of granite columns formed its entrance, holding a triangular pediment engraved with the forms of past senators. Beyond the vestibule rose a great rotunda, larger than any temple in the Acropolis, supporting a massive coffered dome worked with silver. Once this building had been the center of Aelar. For five hundred years, senators here had ruled over a grand republic of enlightenment.

Then you came, Marcus Octavius, Septimus thought. *Then you, a general risen from the legions, crushed my family, bought some senators, murdered the rest, and made this building a mockery of what it had been—as you made me a mockery. But your palace will fall. The Republic will rise again.*

More senators came to join him—the elders, those who had served in the Republic twenty years ago, those who were still loyal, those who remembered the time they had reigned. Other senators—puppets of the Octavius family—stared from the sidelines. A few fled, racing into the city. Others raised their chins and came to join Septimus, perhaps still harboring some loyalty to the ideals of the Republic, perhaps simply changing their loyalties to suit the victors of the day. Soon dozens of senators were walking with Septimus, all in white togas, their soldiers marching behind them.

As Septimus approached the Senate, soldiers stepped forth—men of the Imperial Cohort. Here were Marcus's personal bodyguards, gleaned from the Magisterian Guard for their unquestionable loyalty and cruelty. A hundred of them spread out, blocking Septimus's way. Each pointed a javelin, and red crests rose from their helms. Two-headed eagles reared on their shields, wings spread, heads topped with crowns.

"Your lord is dead!" Septimus boomed. "You have failed at your duty. The Magisterian Guard, to which you belong, now serves the Senate. Lower your spears and shields, and let the new lords of Aelar step forth."

Yet these bodyguards were too well trained—chosen young, tortured, broken, their loyalty beaten into them, more loyal to their dead emperor than the Guard in which they served. They were more machines than men now, and even with their emperor dead, they would fight.

With a great cry, Marcus's bodyguards tossed their javelins.

Magisterians stepped forth, shields raised.

Javelins slammed into the wooden shields, into armor, into flesh. Several soldiers fell dead. Several senators fell too, javelins piercing their torsos.

"Cut them down, Magisterian Guard!" Septimus cried, hand raised. "Cut our way to the Senate! Fight—for the Republic!"

Roaring for battle, the soldiers charged, drawing their swords. Marcus's guards drew their own blades and ran to meet them. Swords sang. Blood washed the Acropolis. The corpses littered the road and grassy hills.

Septimus pulled a javelin free from a corpse. He had never served in the legions or the Guard, but he was a warrior of the Republic, and he would fight for it. He thrust the javelin with his men and cut a man down, moving always forward.

"To the Senate!" he cried. "The Republic rises!"

"The Republic rises!" cried his fellow senators, and they too lifted weapons, and they too fought against the remnants of Marcus's tyranny.

With blood, with death, with sacrifice, they cut their way through. They tore down the last of the Imperial Cohorts, and they stepped over their corpses, climbing the hill toward the Senate.

Septimus led the way, his toga red with blood, still holding his javelin. He climbed the stairs, passed between the portico's granite columns, and entered the vestibule. His fellow senators walked behind him, leaving the Magisterians to surround the building.

Down a tiled hallway, Septimus entered the rotunda. Here was a massive round chamber, among the largest in the Empire. Columned arches rose along the walls, and between them stood marble statues of fallen senators, those who had built the Republic. Above them rested a great ring of marble, wide as a city road, engraved with mythological scenes, showing the founding and history of Aelar. Higher up spread the largest dome in the world, coffered and worked with silver and gold, rising toward an oculus that let in the sunlight. Three hundred wooden seats stood in rings here, surrounding a stage.

Septimus walked onto the stage, as he had countless times before the fall of the Republic. He stood at the pulpit, and he looked upon his fellow senators. Some were wounded. Others were of questionable loyalty. A few Septimus knew would defend this hall with their lives.

"We will send the word across the city!" Septimus said. "We will spread the news around the Encircled Sea! The Empire is no more. The Republic stands again!"

Across the hall, the senators raised their hands and their voices.

"Hail the Republic!" they cried. "Hail Septimus Cassius!"

As they roared their approval, a flash of white caught Septimus's eye. He turned toward the doorway, and he saw a young, pale woman step into the rotunda.

Warmth and love filled Septimus's heart like melted butter.

I did this for you.

He reached out his hand to her. "Come, my daughter. Come stand at my side, Valentina Cassius."

PORCIA

S he stood in Aelaria Maritima, clad in armor, crying out for glory.

"Legio II *Stella Mare*! Hear me! Our war has not ended!"

The five thousand troops stood before her, all in armor, shields and spears in hand. The sunlight gleamed off their helmets. Around them rose the walls and towers of Castrum Aquila, the portside fortress of Aelar, a garrison between city and sea. Past an archway and boardwalk rose the masts of the fleet. At her feet lay the headless corpse of a slain senator, a traitor who had come here to raise these men in rebellion.

"Legionaries!" Porcia cried, raising her spear. The severed head of the senator dripped on the blade. "See what happens to traitors! The senators turn against us. The Magisterian Guard, tasked with defending this very city, has turned against us. They murdered my father!"

The legions were trained for silence, for perfect discipline, yet now the five thousand men cried out in rage.

"Hail Empress Porcia!" shouted one.

"Hail Empress Porcia!" they cried together.

"You fought in Zohar!" Porcia said. "You crushed the walls of Gefen, and you defeated the Gaelians at sea. You returned here as victors, yet did any honor await you? No! Your emperor instead lies slain, and the conspiring senators have turned your own brothers against you. Perhaps the Magisterian Guard—a fat, lazy force which has never fought in a campaign—has defected. But the legions still stand! We are still proud! Hail Aelar!"

"Hail Aelar!" they cried together, five thousand voices.

Porcia mounted her horse and dug her heels into the beast. The animal reared and kicked the air. Porcia shook the severed head off her spear and raised the bloody blade high.

"To conquest!" she shouted. "To victory!"

She rode out through the castle gates, emerging onto the city street. The port spread to one side, full of hundreds of ships—among them the ships that had brought this legion home from conquest in Zohar. Ahead spread the city—the greatest city in the world, the center of an empire, home to a million souls, a hive of towers, domes, temples, the glory of her family. Porcia rode, and five thousand infantrymen marched behind her.

"It will be your head on my spear next, Septimus." She licked her lips. "I can already taste your shriveled heart."

As they moved along the street, people rushed back from their way, lining the roadsides, peering from windows and balconies. Buildings soared at their sides, seven stories tall, and alleyways snaked between them.

"Traitor!" a voice rose from the crowd, and a rock flew and slammed into a legionary's armor.

Hisses rose from the street.

"Hail the Republic!" rose a distant cry. A chamber pot flew from a balcony, shattering on a legionary's helmet, spilling its foul contents.

"Fuck Octavius!" shouted a man, hidden in the crowd, and a rotten egg flew and cracked against Porcia's breastplate.

Porcia rode on. Chin raised, she turned toward her *legatus legionis*, the commander of this legion, a tall man with a scarred face.

"Burn them," she said. "Burn down these blocks."

The general stared back, eyes hard and voice gritty. "My empress, the streets are narrow, and the fire will spread quickly."

She raised an eyebrow. "We'll be protected within the Acropolis walls. Burn these rats."

The general nodded and turned to his soldiers. As they marched onward through the city, they kindled their arrows and drew back their bowstrings.

The people cried out and fled.

The flaming arrows flew. Some sank into the rickety wooden buildings of the poor, and the fire spread across the walls. Other arrows slammed into the onlookers. A child clutched his chest ahead of Porcia, falling dead, the arrow still burning. She ran over the corpse with her horse and kept riding.

"You will kneel before me, Aelar!" Porcia cried as she rode. "You will kneel before your empress, or I will burn this whole city to the ground."

The fire spread. People screamed. A man ran burning through the streets, a living torch. Enemies. Traitors. All of them—traitors! Servants of the senators. Murderers—all of them! They had murdered her father. But they would not murder her. They would kneel, or she would kill them—every last one—and reign over bones.

"They killed my father," Porcia whispered, fists clenched around the reins. "This city will bleed."

People were now fleeing before her. No more rocks were thrown. Hundreds tried to escape the legionaries, cramming into alleyways. A girl fell, trampled by the crowd. Porcia rode onward, and behind her the five thousand marched, and the fire painted the sky red.

Outside the Acropolis walls, they waited.

"The Magisterian Guard," Porcia hissed. Her grin grew, so wide it hurt her cheeks, and she licked her lips.

They stood there, thousands of them, guarding the archway into the Acropolis, topping the walls, protecting the senators within. Porcia reined her horse and raised her spear.

"Magisterians!" she shouted, hoarse now. "Marcus Octavius is dead. I am his firstborn daughter, Porcia Octavius, his heir. Join me! Join me and we will rule this empire."

They stared back, silent.

One among them stepped forth, an officer in gilded armor, a great red crest on his helmet. He held shield and spear.

"You will not pass, Porcia Octavius," he said. "With Marcus's demise, the Senate has taken emergency command of the city, until a more permanent arrangement can be decided upon. None may enter this place while the senators deliberate."

"The senators can suck my cock." Porcia snarled, dug her heels into her horse, and charged.

The officer ahead raised his sword.

Porcia steadied her spear.

Outside the gates, they crashed together. Her spear drove into the officer's shield, punching through it, yanking it from his grasp. The man spun aside, blade flying, driving into her horse, cutting deep into the flesh. The stallion screamed, blood gushing, and reared. Porcia fell from the saddle, slammed onto the ground, and thrust her spear, parrying another blow from the sword.

All around her, her legionaries rushed forth, and the battle exploded outside the Acropolis walls.

Porcia leaped to her feet, spear lashing, driving the officer back. He grabbed his own javelin and thrust, and Porcia sidestepped, and the blade whistled past her shoulder. Her horse collapsed, blood spurting, kicking and screaming as it died. The officer's spear thrust again, and Porcia sidestepped, grabbed the spear's shaft, and yanked back hard. She pulled the officer toward her, bringing him into the path of her dying stallion's kicking hooves. One hoof slammed into the officer's helmet, denting the iron.

Porcia grinned and drove her spear deep into the man's head, cutting through the skull. She tugged it back with a red shower and licked the blade, tasting the coppery blood, the brains, the glory of her victory.

"Break the gates!" Porcia cried, drawing her gladius. "Legionaries—battering ram!"

The iron-tipped ram rolled forth on wheels taller than her. This legion had fought in Zohar, had smashed the gates of Gefen. Now they faced soft soldiers—mere guards!—who had not fought in a war since Marcus Octavius had defeated the Cassius family seventeen years ago. Most of these men at the walls had never seen battle. Porcia's soldiers fought around her, slaying the senators' pets, painting the walls red. The ram swung back on its chains, then drove forward. The iron head, shaped like a true horned ram, slammed into the doors with a *crack*.

You should never have let a Cassius live, Father, Porcia thought. *You should have ended your war seventeen years ago. I will end it now.*

Two more Magisterians raced toward her, mere boys, hoping for a chance to slay an empress. She snorted as she parried one's spear with her gladius, then thrust her own spear, cutting through the other one's neck. Her gladius flew, severing the first boy's arm, then driving down into his shoulder, shattering armor. Her horse still kicked, weaker now, screams down to mewls.

The ram swung again. Again. With each blow against the gates, more wooden chips flew.

Finally, with a deafening sound, the doors shattered. As the wooden slats fell, they revealed the Acropolis beyond—and it swarmed with the senators' soldiers.

"To the Senate!" Porcia cried, leading the charge.

She raced through the shattered gates, sword and spear cutting her way through. Her brother, perhaps, hid at the back of a battle until victory was assured, but not she. Porcia always charged at the head of her troops; that was how a true leader fought. The soldiers of the Magisterian Guard ran toward her, and she cut them down. Her sword knocked back shields, letting her spear her enemies. Blood splashed her armor, coated her bare legs, sluiced inside her sandals. She licked it from her lips, and it gave her the power to keep fighting. One man crashed down before her, and Porcia knelt, driving her sword through his armor, cutting the iron, the skin, the bones. She ripped out his heart and held it above her head.

"Hail the Empire!" she cried, blood dripping down her arm.

"Hail Empress Porcia!" her soldiers roared.

They kept advancing, fighting for every step. The enemy emerged from temples. They fired arrows from the library roof. More charged from the Amphitheatrum. Hundreds soon lay dead across the hills and roads of the Acropolis, then thousands. And still Porcia fought onward.

I am an empress of blood. Of fire. Of death. I am an empress of destruction and of glorious light.

She killed all in her path, anointing her reign with blood. Thus she would earn her throne—not a gift from her father but a victory, not by divine light but by death. She had always been a conqueror.

Finally, with the sunset drenching the Acropolis in gold and crimson, Porcia stepped over the last few corpses onto the steps of the Senate.

He stood at the portico between two columns, clad in a bloodied toga, clean shaven. Her father's fool. The memento mori.

"Mingo." She spat toward him, climbing the stairs.

He stood straight and tall, taller than she had realized he was. "I am Senator Septimus Cassius, Consul of the Senate. The Empire is no more. The line of Octavius no longer rules Aelar. I strip you of all power, Porcia Octavius." He looked down at the legionaries behind her. "Men of the legions! Do not follow this woman who has led us away from wisdom. Protect this blessed Senate, which has governed the Aelarian Republic for centuries. Cast aside the folly of the Empire."

Porcia climbed another stair. "The Senate is disbanded. If you wish to live, senator, kneel now and beg me for mercy, and I will consider exiling you to die on some desert isle. Stay standing and you will die at my blade, here on these stairs."

Two more senators emerged from behind him. Then another ten. Soon hundreds of senators were emerging from within, covering the portico and top stairs, all in their togas, some wounded, all standing tall.

"Then you'll have to kill me too, Porcia Octavius," said Quintus Tatius, an elderly man who ruled great farmlands in the north, feeding thousands.

"And me," said another, a bald man who owned the city's central bank, financing Aelar's wars.

"And me as well," said another, this one short and squat, master of the city's courts.

One by one, they spoke in defiance of her. Financiers. Lawyers. Wealthy slave owners. Together they ruled this empire. They owned the courts, the masons, the farmlands, the gold.

And all were traitors.

Porcia stood before them as one by one, they rejected her. As one by one, they cursed her name.

Septimus gave her a sad smile. "Do you see, Porcia Octavius? You rule nothing. Without us, an emperor is but a helpless child. Your father understood this. It's why he let this Senate stand, why he let us continue our work. He knew that without the Senate, there is no Empire. If you slay us, you will be cutting off your own limbs. You will become no more powerful than a slave in a golden collar. You are cast out, Porcia Octavius! You are powerless."

Porcia looked behind her at her soldiers. Thousands lay dead across the Acropolis. But hundreds still remained, standing behind her on the stairs, shields and swords raised, eyes stern.

She looked back at the senators.

"You're right," Porcia said. "You control the ships, the trade, the grain, the masonry, the law, the courts, the gold, the cogs and wheels that run the Empire. But I'm not helpless." A thin smile stretched her lips. "I control the legions." She raised her voice to a howl. "Legionaries—kill them! Kill them all!"

With battle cries, the legionaries stormed up the stairs. Their swords swung. The blades cut through the senators. Men fell. Blood spurted. Corpses tumbled to the road below.

"Legionaries, stop this!" Septimus cried, standing among the slaughter. "Do not serve the usurper's daughter. You are men of wisdom, of civilization—of the Republic!"

Porcia stepped toward him. "No, senator. The legionaries are like me. They are creatures of fire and blood. They are hunters, and you are prey."

He stared at her, horror filling his eyes. He could have fled. He could have raced into the vestibule, cowered behind a chair, perhaps sought a back exit.

But he stood still, chin raised, back straight.

"I have lived, and I have fought, for the Republic," Septimus said. "For Aelar, I—"

Porcia swung her sword, slashing his throat, nearly severing his head. Blood gushed out, and Senator Septimus Cassius— Mingo the fool—crashed down at her feet, dead.

Porcia knelt. She carved out his heart, and she feasted upon the sticky red muscle, absorbing his strength. All around her, the other senators died. Some fled, only to be shot down with arrows. Others cowered and begged, only for spears to drive through them. Three hundred senators had once ruled here. One by one, they perished.

"Now the Republic is truly dead."

Porcia grinned, turned away from the portico, and stared south. From here, atop the Senate steps, she could see for miles. The amphitheater. The colossal statues of gold. The temples and libraries and palaces. And beyond the Acropolis—the city streets, the myriads of homes, the fire burning where the people had resisted her. And farther still—Aelaria Maritima, the port to the Encircled Sea. All the kingdoms around that sea were hers. Hers to rule. Hers to torment.

She raised her hand in salute. "Hail the Empire!"

Her soldiers raised their hands with hers. "Hail Empress Porcia!"

Footfalls sounded behind her—lighter than a soldier's. A soft choking accompanied it. Porcia turned around. Her eyes widened.

Her sister, meek little Valentina, was stepping out from the Senate, blood on her stola, tears in her eyes.

VALENTINA

*M*y father is dead.

She looked down at the body. There he lay. Senator Septimus Cassius. Her father. The man she loved. His neck was cut so deep his head was nearly severed.

You're no longer a fool, Valentina thought, tears in her eyes. *You died proud. A senator. A hero. I love you, Father. Always. Always.*

"Valentina?"

She raised her eyes and looked at Porcia. All her life, Valentina had thought that Porcia—this cruel, bloodthirsty conqueror—was her sister. All her life, she had feared Porcia, had not understood how two siblings could be vicious, the third and youngest so meek.

Now Valentina did not see a sister. She just saw a murderess.

"Sister." Porcia's eyes narrowed. "What are you doing here?"

She doesn't know, Valentina realized. *She doesn't know Septimus was my true father. She'll never know. Marcus is dead. All the senators are dead. Now only I know the truth.*

Porcia was scrutinizing her. Wheels were turning behind those eyes. The new empress was perhaps vicious and wild, but she was also fiercely intelligent.

Valentina looked back down at her dead father. She wanted to fall to her knees, to embrace him, to weep, to never let go.

And then I would die with him.

She forced a deep, shuddering breath. No. She could not die here today. Too many had died—the thousands lay slain across the city.

Valentina had to live. She still had a war to fight.

She stepped over her father's corpse, and she embraced the woman who had murdered him.

"Sister!" Valentina said, trembling. "I was so scared. They kidnapped me! They took me here. It was Septimus who did it. I tried to stop them, but … but … oh, thank the gods you're here. I love you, sister. I love you."

Porcia stiffened for a moment, then relaxed and stroked Valentina's hair, bloodying it.

"It's all right, little one." Porcia kissed Valentina's forehead, smearing it with blood. "They're dead now. The men who murdered our father are dead. You're safe with me, I promise. I will keep this empire safe."

As they embraced atop the Senate stairs, Valentina looked down across the burning empire.

I won't forget you, Father, she vowed. *I won't forget you, Iris. I won't forget you, all who died here this day. I promise you all: Until my last breath, I will fight. I will finish the war my father began—the war to make*

Aelar a republic again. She raised her head and gazed into Porcia's eyes. *I will fight to bring you down, Porcia.*

The new empress took Valentina's hand in hers. "Now come, little sister. Let us ring the bells of glory, and let us summon a crowd into the amphitheater. We will feed a hundred prisoners to the lions to celebrate this victory. The Empire rises from blood and fire, stronger than ever before."

EPHER

H e was hanging from chains, toes just grazing the dungeon
floor, when the devil came to see him.

Epher didn't know how long he'd been hanging here. There
was no day or night in this darkness. There was no wakefulness or
slumber, no clarity or madness. There was the pain—the pain of
his whipped back, of the joints in his arms, the cramps in his legs,
the manacles digging into his wrists. There was the stench of his
own waste, his own blood, the rot spreading through the welts
that crisscrossed his torso. There was the sound of haggard
breathing, the squeaking of rats, the clattering of chains that
tugged his arms toward the ceiling, the creaking of his bones as he
struggled to keep his weight on his toes, his heels not reaching the
floor.

And there were the memories.

The shadows wrapped around him, becoming the shadows
of night leading to dawn over the hills. The rats scurried, their
chattering becoming the song of insects. The pain across his body
became the heat of summer, sweltering, washing him with sweat,
and Epher laughed, running over the hills. He found a fallen
branch and worked at it with his knife, the small knife his father

had given him, the one with the red handle, peeling off bark and sharpening the tip into a spear.

He hunted between the pines and cypress trees, slaying invisible monsters, and Atalia roared and leaped onto him with her own spear, then cried as she fell and skinned her knees. The garden bloomed around them, and Mother brought out a bowl of pomegranates, and they ate, and Atalia was soon laughing. Lavender flowers bloomed in their villa's windowsills—Epher could not remember their names, but each blossom was formed of a hundred smaller flowers, cloying and sweet and attractive to bees, and Maya picked him a bouquet. The sea whispered in the distance, the waves rising, falling like breath. Ragged breath. Hoarse breath that sawed at his throat, and Epher tasted blood.

He blinked. His weight dropped off his toes. The manacles tightened around his wrists as more of his weight tugged his arms. He cried out—a choked sound—and pressed down on his toes again, trying to hold up his weight, to stop the chains from yanking his arms from their sockets. There were no walls to lean on. Nothing to stop the chains from ripping out his arms, leaving him alive, dangling from skin and bones, and—

Blackness spread around him, and when he sucked in breath, he was moving atop her, making love to her, to his Olive. His sweet, wild Olive with the freckled skin, the wild red hair, the huge grin, the green eyes that loved gazing at him. They made love in the heat, drenched in sweat in their little home in the city, and held each other close, whispering, tickling, laughing.

"Olive love Epher," she whispered in his memory, kissing him, nibbling on his lip, biting, gnawing, tearing into his mouth, sucking his blood.

Epher moaned, the blood dripping down his chin—blood from his cracked lips, his dry mouth.

The guards hadn't given him water nor food since chaining him here. Perhaps those guards weren't coming back. Perhaps this was not a dungeon but a tomb. A slow death, decaying alive underground. His arms creaked again. The cell stank of dry blood and rot and shit, and flies bustled on the raw wounds in his back, buzzed around his head, bit him, and—

The day was hot and lush with insects, buzzing, chirping everywhere, and sparrows singing in the trees. He was walking again with Olive through the city of Beth Eloh, this city of ancient stones, each stone a soul, each smoothed by thousands of years of feet and hands and rain and sunlight. And they emerged from the alleyways. Drunken. Stinking of sweat and cheap booze, reaching for Olive, tearing her clothes, dying on his blade. Yet more emerged. The eagles of Aelar. Legionaries in armor, great flying beasts from the west, tearing into the lions, ripping at the rank flesh like the whips had ripped at Epher's back. Tearing. Peeling off the skin.

And now he hung here. Rotting away. A slab of meat on a hook.

"But I saved them," he rasped, the hot, coppery blood filling his mouth. "I saved the six hundred. You were going to crucify them, Remus. I saved them. With my life, I saved them."

386

He hung his head low. He was ready for death, ready to vanish into nothingness. He knew that across the sea, the pagans who worshiped idols believed that all souls, after death, rose to a great land in the sky. But Epher was a Zoharite. He worshipped an older god—the god Eloh, intangible, woven of nothing, a god who did not reward or punish his children after death. Nothingness awaited Epher. An end to pain. Silence in the dark.

I'll miss you, my family. His eyes dampened. He thought of them: his wise mother, gentle yet strong, the kindest woman he knew; his brother Koren, laughing and joyous, captured in the war; his sister Atalia, fierce and noble and so afraid, taken into slavery; Ofeer, daughter of another father, so hurt, so sad, so fragile and kind beneath the armor of her bitterness; dearest Maya, gentle and sweet, gone into the east; little Mica, buried under the pomegranate tree, a light that had shone for only a day. And he thought of Olive—his love, a woman he would have married, a woman he loved more than his life, a woman he would never see again.

Tears streamed down Epher's cheeks. Now he wanted to live, if only to see them for another day, to hold them, to tell them he loved them.

He was whispering their names, remembering their faces, when the door clanked and creaked open, and torchlight flooded the dungeon.

Epher groaned and winced. The light burned his eyes. The fire came closer, and sparks flew, landing on his chest, burning his wounds. He swung on the chains, trying to look away. His sockets creaked. He struggled to keep his weight on his toes. Sweat dripped down his body, stinging, and still the fire burned.

"Well, well, still alive, are we?" spoke a man beyond the flame, a hulking shadow in the dungeon. "Good. Would have been a pity to crucify a corpse."

The shadow stepped closer, taking form in the torchlight. Even wounded, chained, maybe dying, Epher's rage rose.

"Remus Marcellus," he hissed.

Governor of Zohar. Ruler of a conquered land. The dog that had crushed Gefen and now strangled Beth Eloh in his grip.

The Aelarian general was a tall man—taller than anyone Epher had ever seen. He must have stood close to seven feet tall, but gaunt, almost haggard, as if his flesh could not find the proper way to settle over so much bone, too much skewer and not enough meat. He brought his leathery face close to Epher's, peering, scrutinizing, as if he could peel back Epher's skin with those eyes and study the map of veins and nerves beneath. They seemed almost inhuman, those eyes—the eyes of a heartless god.

"They speak of you as a hero in the city," Remus said, voice like a razor over stubbly skin, just threatening to draw blood. "They say you're a great warrior. But I see only a wretch."

"So you've come to gloat before nailing me onto the cross?" Epher could manage only a hoarse whisper, and every word hurt.

"To gloat?" Remus placed his hands on Epher's shoulders, pressing down just the slightest. Hanging from his wrists, Epher bit down on a scream as his arms creaked, the sockets threatening to pop. The manacles dug deeper into his wrists, and fresh blood trickled down Epher's arms.

"No," Remus said. "Not to gloat. To offer you a deal."

"Does this deal involve you and your brutes leaving Zohar and never coming back?" Epher rasped. "If not, I'm not interested."

Remus's face was not made for smiling, but he smiled nonetheless—a tight, ugly thing that looked more like a grimace. "You Zoharites are special people. Even when I crush you under my heel, you find a way to jest. You believe in an invisible god, even as you perish in agony. You still think you can fight, even when your hosts lie dead and rotting in your fields. And yes, Epheriah Sela. Still there are those in Zohar who fight—like cowards, slinking through alleys, stabbing legionaries in the backs with crude shivs."

"Return to us our swords and bows," Epher said, "and we'll face you in the field."

"We've already danced that dance," said Remus. "You failed at it, rather spectacularly. Rats will fight like rats—from the shadows. A group that calls itself Zohar's Blade has risen in the warrens of this wretched city. Ironic, isn't it? You call yourselves lions, yet you fight as vermin. You call yourselves children of the light, yet you hide in shadows. Since I left you hanging here, awaiting your crucifixion, these cowards of Zohar's Blade have slain five of my men."

Epher wanted to rejoice at this news. Every dead Aelarian was another vanquished enemy, another conqueror gone. Yet only fear filled him.

When I killed a few of his men, he threatened to crucify six hundred, Epher thought. *Only surrendering myself stopped him. How many more will Remus now murder?*

"What do you want from me?" Epher said. He could barely speak with the pain. He teetered on his toes, even as his feet cramped, struggling to keep holding the weight, to stop the chains from dislocating his arms. "Nail me onto the cross and be done with. Let me die in sunlight."

"Ah, see, if you die, you will become a martyr," Remus said. "Already in the city, they sing of you, chanting your name. 'Free the lion cub!' they cry." Remus sighed. "I'm not deaf to the cries of Zohar. I'll let you live, Sela. And in return, you will infiltrate Zohar's Blade, this group of fanatical rebels. You will report to me their numbers, their locations, their plans. Do these things, and I'll let you see your family again. You will see Olive again. You will live."

Lantana flowers, Epher thought, the name suddenly coming to him—the flowers formed of many smaller flowers. It was strange, he thought, how here, between death and life, in chains, in a captured city, he thought of damn flowers. Perhaps that memory—a day of spring, of family—was suddenly worth more than palaces and empires.

"So I only have to betray my kingdom," Epher said, staring at that hard, leathery face that shone in the torchlight. "I can live, but live as a traitor."

Remus pulled down harder, tugging Epher toward the floor. His joints creaked. His arms teetered on the cusp of dislocating. Remus stared into his eyes, teeth bared.

"You will live as my dog, or you will die as my bitch," the general said. "You decide."

Epher spat on his face. "I will die as a lion."

Remus stared at him for a moment longer, and finally emotion filled those dead eyes—hatred. The Aelarian pulled keys from his belt and unlocked Epher's shackles.

Epher crumpled to the floor, banging his ribs. He couldn't lower his arms, could barely bend them at all. His feet cramped, and the wounds on his back opened, dripping fresh blood. He gasped for air, only for Remus to kick him in the stomach. Epher curled up, gagging, spitting blood.

"I see no lion." Remus stared down at him, torch in hand. "I see a worm." He turned toward the door and raised his voice. "Men! Grab him! Drag him out into the sunlight. We nail him up."

Two legionaries entered the chamber, clad in lorica segmentata—the armor of the legions—and crested helmets. They grabbed Epher's arms, and he screamed in pain as they yanked him to his feet. He tried to stand, but his feet would not bend, and spasms racked his legs. He felt as if he'd been crucified already, his body unable to return to its previous form. As the legionaries manhandled him from the chamber, his feet dragged against the floor.

They took him down a corridor, up a flight of stairs, and out into a courtyard awash with sunlight. Epher's eyes burned, nearly blinded after so long in the dark. He squinted, struggling to see. Walls of craggy limestone rose around him, broken by arches. A palm tree grew from a ring of stone, and a camel flicked his tail, laden with brass pots. A cedar cross leaned against the wall.

"Give him water," Remus said. "Give him food. I want him to live for a long time on the cross."

The legionaries shoved Epher against a wall. One handed him a waterskin. When Epher shook his head, they grabbed his jaw, forced it open, and spilled the water down his throat. He sputtered and spat.

Remus watched the display, shaking his head. "Drink," he said. "Eat. Or the six hundred will still be nailed up with you."

Epher choked as they shoved the bread into his throat. He wanted to spit it out, to roar, to charge toward Remus and fight with tooth and nail—to die fighting, not on a cross.

But he couldn't let the six hundred innocents die.

For them, he thought. *This is my fight.*

He drank the water and he ate the bread.

"Good rat," Remus said. "Now lift your cross. Bear your shame through the city."

His march began. The last walk of his life, through the city of his god. Epher bore his cross, and he walked on weary legs through Beth Eloh, city of gold and blood, city of light and death.

Remus rode his horse, leading the procession. Epher marched behind, and legionaries walked farther back, whips in hand. They passed under an archway and down coiling alleyways. Houses rose around them, weeds growing between their limestone bricks. Towers and minarets and domes rose toward a pale sky, and the sun beat down, blinding, scorching. The roads twisted between the hills, and the great Temple of Eloh shone above, its light unable to heal him.

The people emerged from their homes, lined the streets, watched from their rooftops. Silent. So silent Epher heard every scrape of his feet, every ragged breath. They stared, eyes damp, hands on their hearts.

"Lion of Zohar," a veiled woman whispered.

"Bless you, lion of Zohar," said a man, reaching out to him.

"Praise Eloh," whispered a young woman.

He kept walking through the city, bearing his cross, forcing every step on shaking legs—to save them. For six hundred. Under blinding light, through canyons of stone, through a silent city of mourning and prayer.

Cemeteries and tombs rose around them across the hills, for here was not only a city of the living but a city of the dead—of three thousand years of Zoharites who had fought here, prayed here, died here. Here too would he rest—here among King Elshalom, the prophets, the freed slaves of Sekadia, here in the home of his god, in the sight of his Temple.

"If I forget you, Beth Eloh, may I forget my right arm," he whispered the ancient prayer. "If I forget you, city of gold and copper and light, may I forget all love and home."

Lumers claimed that they could feel God's grace in this city, a presence in every stone, every olive and palm tree, every breeze. They claimed that Eloh himself dwelled in the Temple on the hill, that his lume filled the streets and courtyards of his city. Epher was no lumer, but he was a man of Zohar, a lion of the desert, and here—in this grace that was invisible to him—he would rest.

Ahead he saw it—the Valley of Ashes. The place where Remus had crucified the rebels of Gefen. The place where crosses still rose. The place where Epher's life would end.

"Epher! Epher!"

No. Epher lowered his head as he walked, bearing the cross. *God, no, don't let her see me like this. Don't let her remember me as this dying wretch.*

Yet she ran toward him, tears on her cheeks. She wore the white linen dress he had bought her, and a pomegranate pendant hung from her neck. Her red hair was cut the length of her chin, and she reached out to him, weeping.

"Epher!" Olive cried.

She tried to run to him, only for legionaries to knock her back. They laughed as she fell. Olive leaped back up, elbows skinned, following the procession of soldiers, crying to him.

"I love you, Epher." She reached toward him between the soldiers. "I love you."

Epher could not reply, too weak to speak anymore, too hurt. The sight of Olive made the pain worse. He could hardly bear this cross. He fell to his knees.

Legionaries cursed and whipped him, and Epher cried out. Olive ran forward, barreling her way between soldiers, and knelt before him. She wept and kissed his lips.

"I here, Epher," she whispered, stroking his cheek, smearing her fingers with his blood. "Olive here."

She helped him rise as the legionaries laughed.

"His whore has to help him stand!" said one man.

Another Aelarian guffawed. "We're going to fuck her as you hang from the cross, boy. All of us as you watch."

Epher stood, shaking, cross on his back as Olive helped him. He took one step, trembling, toward the valley ahead—the place where idolaters had once sacrificed their children, where today Aelar crucified its victims. Several bodies still rotted there on their crosses, the crows feasting.

"I will fear no death," Epher rasped. "Not in the city of light. Not in my home. Not among lions."

They walked onward, Olive guiding his way, the legionaries around him. The city people watched from the streets, roofs, windows, praying for him, saying their farewells to Epheriah Sela Ben Jerael, lion of the desert.

The procession passed along the Road of Tears, an ancient alleyway where ancient mothers would weep for children sacrificed to Baal, when fire and iron rained from the sky.

It was there, before the Valley of Ashes, that the lions of Zohar roared.

They leaped from the roofs, tan robes fluttering, faces veiled behind prayer shawls. They landed on the street, lashing daggers, tightening garrotes around necks. Ten men, maybe more, only their wild eyes visible.

"Death to eagles!" a man cried. "Zohar rises!"

One man leaped forward, blade lashing, and tore into Remus's horse. The beast reared, neck slit open, spraying blood. Remus cursed on his horse and swung his sword. More robed men filled the alley, stabbing at the legionaries, slamming bricks onto their helmets, smashing in their faces.

"Rise free, son of Zohar," one man said, lifting the cross off Epher. He placed a dagger in Epher's hand. "Shed the enemy's blood with us."

Epher closed his fingers around the dagger. Olive grabbed a brick and stood at his side.

A legionary ran toward them.

Epher didn't even have an instant to think.

Olive roared with rage, a lioness of light, face twisted and feral. She tossed her brick, slamming the stone into the legionary's face. He fell back, cursing, blood spurting, and Epher ran toward him. He howled—not a roar of pride, not a lion's cry, but a *howl*, a torn thing, tortured, a sound of pain, a keen, the sound of a wounded animal. He howled and he plunged his dagger forth, digging the blade into the legionary's neck, shoving it down, past the shoulder blade, into the torso, digging, twisting, seeking the heart, sounding that howl as the man died.

He pulled the dagger back with a gush of blood, trembling, weak but thrumming with fear and rage.

He stared around him. The battle still raged. Remus swung his sword, tearing a man down. Three other corpses lay at the governor's feet, one with a severed arm, the other spilling its entrails. Several rebels still fought, trampling over dead legionaries, and more Aelarians raced into the alleyway.

"Come, son of Zohar." The man who'd given him the dagger grabbed Epher's arm. "Follow!"

Laughing and crying out, the rebels leaped toward a humble wooden doorway in the alley wall. They raced into a chamber, pulling Epher with them. Fifty or more clay vessels rose here, the height of men, rank with the smell of bitumen. The men raced between the amphorae, herding Epher along. Olive ran here too, teeth bared, eyes wild, holding a gladius sword she had grabbed in the battle.

"Catch the rats!" rose Remus's voice from the alleyway. "Nail them up!"

Legionaries raced into the chamber, knocking over the clay vessels. The tar spilled across the floor and washed over the Aelarians. Epher and the rebels ran toward a back door and leaped into another alleyway.

"For the light of Zohar," one rebel said, grabbed a torch from the wall, and tossed it at the pursuing legionaries.

Flames exploded, roaring through the chamber, grabbing legionaries like demonic claws. Men fell, screaming. Epher did not linger to watch the deaths. He ran, pulling Olive with him, the others running with them.

Zohar's Blade, Epher knew. *The resistance.*

They rushed down the alleyway, through another doorway, through a trapdoor under a rug, down into a tunnel. They moved through the darkness, blood dripping. Epher could barely walk; the fear that had given him strength was waning. Olive had to help him limp forward. It seemed that they moved for entire parsa'ot underground. From above, Epher could hear thumping feet, shouting men, their words muffled.

I'm alive. He limped onward. *Olive is with me.*

He squeezed her hand, and she smiled at him, tears in her eyes.

After what seemed like hours in the darkness, the men reached a shaft and climbed a ladder. Epher's arms screamed in protest as he climbed. Every rung tore at his shoulders, but he forced himself onward, finally emerging into a dusty chamber.

A curtain hid a single window. A doorway led to a second chamber. Rugs covered the floor, and three divans stood along the brick walls. A cat drank milk from a bowl, and alcoves held candles, a ram's horn, and a decorative pomegranate forged from silver. A humble home like thousands of others across the city.

The men moved about the room, checking the window, the doorway, the trapdoor in the floor. Three men went to guard the entrances, daggers drawn, while the others laughed and dropped their loot on the floor—two gladius swords, a crested *galea* helmet, a few coins, and a golden eagle amulet.

Epher could stay standing no longer. He fell onto a divan, breathing raggedly, still bleeding.

Olive glared at the men. "Get ... get ..." She gestured wildly, then tugged at her dress. She pointed at Epher. "He hurt!"

The men removed their scarves, revealing tanned, bearded faces. They were a dozen young men, some barely more than boys. The eldest couldn't have been much older than thirty. That one was a tall man, his beard closely cropped, his eyes startlingly green in his bronze face. A scar rifted one of his eyebrows, and a silver pomegranate hung around his neck.

"My cousin is wounded," the tall man said to his companions. "Fetch him some ointment and bandages. And wine too, for his strength."

Epher knew him, had fought with him in the forests of Ma'oz.

"Kahan," he said.

Uncle Benshalom's son.

Kahan Sela smiled. It was an easy smile, one that came naturally to that face, that crinkled the eyes, that revealed many white teeth.

"Welcome, Epher." He gestured around him at the humble home. "Welcome to the grand palace of Zohar's Blade, the army that will bring Aelar to its knees."

Epher's head swam. He could no longer sit up. Olive helped him lie down on his stomach, and he grimaced as she applied ointment into the wounds on his back. The pain grabbed him, tugged him, welcomed him into a cold, black embrace. He sank into it gratefully.

SENECA

He stood on the palace balcony, watching the city burn, watching the Empire crumble, watching his life destroyed.

"Hail Empress Porcia!" the legionaries below were chanting. "Hail Empress Porcia!"

Battering rams were swinging, slamming into the Senate's columns, knocking them down. Two columns cracked and fell. The triangular pediment tilted and slammed down, its statues shattering. The rotunda followed, and the great dome—largest in the Empire—collapsed. Dust flew and the legions cheered. Porcia paraded through the Acropolis, holding the severed head of Senator Septimus, while her legionaries brandished the limbs.

And I'm next, Seneca realized.

He left the balcony. He moved stiffly. He could feel nothing. He was in shock, he knew. He was terrified beyond terror, unable to think, able only to move, mindless.

He stepped into his father's bedchamber. The slaves had looted it already, or perhaps the Magisterian Guard. The drawers were opened, the chests smashed, the gems cut out from the candleholders.

Jackals, Seneca thought, taking only a little satisfaction that Porcia would find the room bare.

He shoved the bed with all his might. It screeched across the mosaic floor, tearing tiles loose. The looters, most likely, hadn't known about the trapdoor. Seneca grabbed the handle and tugged, revealing a tunnel.

He stepped into the darkness.

Perhaps Ofeer still hid in this palace. Seneca no longer cared. She had lied to him, manipulated him, then fled him at his hour of need. Perhaps Valentina still loved him, but so what? From behind the cypresses, he had seen her embrace Porcia. His legionaries, those who had fought with him in Zohar, now served Porcia too.

They all betrayed me. They'll all pay.

Tears stung Seneca's eyes. He blinked furiously.

No. No! No pain. No tears. Only rage. Only hatred.

The trapdoor led to a tunnel that delved deep under the palace. A sack of gold, a dagger, a lantern, and a vial of poison hid in a secret alcove. Seneca slung the sack across his back, hung the dagger from his belt, and stuffed the poison into his toga. He walked through the darkness, holding the lantern. The tunnel was so narrow his shoulders brushed against the walls, and the ceiling was so low he had to walk with his head bowed.

"You carved this tunnel, Father, to save your life from an invasion," Seneca said as he walked. "Then you died like a dog. Slipping on the poolside." His voice shook. "Would you have named me your heir, Father? Would you have exiled Porcia?"

He would never know the answers to those questions. His eyes were watering again.

How had this happened? Tonight was meant to be his victory. He was to become heir to an empire! To see Porcia exiled! To build a glorious life with Ofeer! Now Porcia ruled over a burning empire, he was fleeing through a tunnel, Ofeer was his sister, and all was ruin.

Seneca fell to his knees in the darkness, trapped here underground. His fingers shook as he reached for the poison. He had always wondered why his father kept poison in his escape tunnel, but now he understood.

His hand shook so wildly he couldn't open the vial. He raised it over his mouth, shaking it, trying to break off the wax lid.

Let me die. Let me die.

He was shaking too badly to drink. He tucked the poison away. Instead, he drew his dagger, placed the blade on his wrist.

A quick movement. Just a cut. That's all. That—

"No, Seneca," spoke a voice.

Ofeer!

He looked around, seeking her, but he couldn't see her. The tunnel was empty.

"You're a coward, boy," rose her voice, astral, a voice from another world. "Do you give up so easily? Without even a fight?"

"I fought!" he shouted, voice echoing down the tunnel. "I lost."

"You did not lose!" spoke the ghostly voice. "You gave up. On life. On yourself. On the empire that is yours by right."

He trembled, tears falling. "But Porcia won. She's empress now. She rules—"

"—one legion." Ofeer's voice completed his sentence. "She rules one legion. Seventy-four other legions are spread across the Empire, awaiting your command. Will you die here like a coward, leaving them without an emperor?"

Seneca pushed himself back up to his feet.

"No," he said. "No, I won't leave them. They need me. The Empire needs me. I am the victor who crushed Gefen, who defeated Jerael Sela, who completed Aelar's dominance of the Encircled Sea. I will not die here in the dark." He clenched his fist. "I will be back, Porcia, I swear this. I will be back, and then it will be your head on a spear."

He sheathed his dagger and kept walking down the tunnel. The air grew moldy, rank, spinning his head. It seemed that he walked for hours. From above, through the stone, he could hear distant, muffled sounds—voices calling out, screams, drums, bells. Seneca ignored them. He kept walking, crossing what felt like leagues, until finally the tunnel sloped upward, and he reached a wooden door.

He emerged into a dirty alleyway, the ground covered in old chicken bones, apple cores, and a couple of beggar children. Laundry hung from ropes above, and a dog was pissing in the corner. Seneca imagined his father—stern, proud Marcus Octavius, the great general—emerging into this rat hole, and the dog pissing on his leg, and suddenly Seneca was laughing. A hysterical laughter. A laughter that seized him like claws, that dropped him to his knees, and he was rolling on the ground, pounding the cobblestones, struggling for air as he laughed, as he wept.

He emerged from the alleyway to find a city of chaos. Fire rose in the distance, and smoke hid the sky. Men were rushing down the streets, barging into shops, looting, burning. A naked child wept on the street. A woman screamed in the distance and men laughed. Seneca walked down the cobbled roads between the shops, homes, and apartment blocks. He passed under an aqueduct where beggars huddled around a campfire, cooking what looked like a dog. A prostitute leaned against a brothel wall, haggard and gray-haired, her teeth stained purple with hintan, the spice smuggled from the desert. A legless man sat in a corner, dressed in rags, holding a wooden sign that read: *Lost my legs in Gael, a denarius please.*

Seneca had spent most of his life in the Acropolis, the halls of power. Whenever moving through the city proper, he had ridden a horse or chariot down the city's main boulevards. But here was a warren of narrow, twisting streets like veins in a stone giant, clogged with filth. Disgust filled him. He tossed the legless man a coin—a coin of true gold, more than what a legionary made in a month. As he passed by the prostitute, her stench nearly made him gag. He gave her a coin too and kept walking.

This is not my empire. These streets will be cleansed, I swear it. I will fix this city. I will fix this world. I will show you, Porcia. I will show you, Ofeer. I will show you all.

Night fell. He walked in darkness. It took hours, but finally—it must have been past midnight—Seneca reached Aelaria Maritima, the city's port. Some corpses of legionaries still lay here, rats already feeding upon them. Many of the ships he had taken to Zohar still docked here, emptied of troops, their legionaries now guarding Porcia in the Acropolis. Clutching his sack of gold, Seneca approached the *Aquila Aureum*—the same ship he had taken south to Zohar, a prince out to prove his worth. The same ship he had sailed back with, Ofeer and hundreds of slaves his reward.

The ship that would now win him an empire.

She was a large galley, painted red and gold, shields and oars lining her hull. Lanterns hung from her masts, glowing gold, and her figurehead thrust out across the water, a great iron eagle that had crushed the Gaelian fleet, that had sent Atalia down to her watery grave.

This ship is all I have left in the world, Seneca thought.

As he stepped closer, he saw that the galley's gangplank was lowered, connecting to the boardwalk. Five legionaries lay dead on the cobblestones, and a robed and hooded figure stood on the gangplank, gazing at Seneca. A woman's figure.

Seneca started, for an instant sure that it was Porcia. But no. This figure wore robes of silk, and jewels shone on her fingers and neck. Seneca stepped over the dead legionaries and onto the gangplank, bringing his lantern toward the figure. His eyes widened.

"Taeer?" he whispered.

His lumer pulled back her hood, revealing a dark face with painted eyelids, cascading locks of black hair, and full crimson lips. She gave him her crooked smile and reached out a hand, serpent bracelets jangling. The scent of myrrh and frankincense wafted from her, sweet and intoxicating, and an eagle pendant rested between her breasts.

"Welcome, my prince," she said. "You are late."

He narrowed his eyes. "You knew I would come here. You used the Foresight."

Taeer laughed, a tinkling sound. "I needed no Luminosity to know that you would come to me here, my prince. And I would not have you leave me behind like you leave Ofeer." She took his hand in hers. "Come, my prince, my future emperor. The sea awaits us."

She led him along the gangplank onto the deck. The ship felt so empty. Gone were the legionaries who had once manned the deck. Only a skeleton crew of sailors stood here in the darkness.

But Taeer is with me, Seneca thought, and his eyes dampened. *I'm not alone in the world.*

He upended his sack of gold, spilling coins onto the deck.

"Sail!" he told the men. "Sail and divide these among you. Leave this city. We travel south." He held Taeer's hand tightly, knowing his path. "We sail across the Encircled Sea. We sail to Nur."

The sailors pocketed their coins and scurried across the ship, raising the anchor, unfurling the sails. The galley slaves were gone; only the wind propelled the ship onward. They traveled across the harbor, navigating between other galleys, fishermen's boats, lighthouses, and columned breakwaters.

Seneca walked toward the prow and stared at the dark sea. Two lighthouses blazed ahead at the edge of breakwaters, two eyes in the night.

"Nur," he said. "The great southern savanna. A land of gold, of diamonds, of spice, of might. The land where Uncle Cicero rules great legions." He turned toward Taeer. "He's always loved me, Uncle Cicero, hasn't he?"

The lumer smiled. She had been with him since his birth—a youth captured from Zohar, brought to this empire, teaching him wisdom, teaching him the art of love.

You've always been with me, Taeer. You're the only one.

She stroked his cheek. "All around the Encircled Sea love you, my prince."

"You mean emperor," he said.

She kissed his lips. "Emperor of iron and sand, of gold and rust, of splendor and shadow. It will all be yours."

He did not know what she meant, but lumers often spoke in riddles. The ship moved onward, clearing the last lighthouses, emerging from the cove into the black open sea. They floated under stars, a single ship, alone in darkness. He placed his arm around Taeer, and her sweet scent filled his nostrils as he sailed away from home, vowing to return with fire.

MAYA

T he caravan traveled across the desert: fifty camels, each bearing a bearded warrior armed with bow and spear; ten wagons laden with supplies; and two Zoharites, a vagabond thief and a girl with light inside her.

"We're almost there," Maya said, staring east. "Almost at the sea."

For many days, she had been traveling across the desert, surviving thirst, hunger, captivity, fleeing the Aelarians who had crushed her homeland. And nearby—just a few days east from here—lay the sea. The city of Suna. The center of Luminosity she had been seeking, the only place in the world, aside from Beth Eloh, where the lume flowed.

Leven rode at her side, swaying on his camel. The beast kept trying to twist its neck around to sniff at Leven's foot, and it ended up walking in circles.

"Forward, forward!" Leven said, pointing and shaking his foot. "Stop sniffing at my feet. They don't smell that good. *Hasha, hasha!*" The thief sighed. "Stupid animal." He turned to look at Maya. "I don't know why we're traveling to the sea anyway."

She rode her own camel—an animal far better behaved. "I told you. So I can study more Luminosity."

"*Hasha*! Forward!" Leven shook his fist at his camel before turning back toward Maya. "You're already great at Luminosity. You healed my brother. You healed the King of Sekadia, for God's sake."

Maya thought back to that day—to how much light had flowed through her, nearly drowning her, a light she could barely tame.

"I eased his pain," Maya confessed. "But I left him blind, scarred, his hands still lacking fingers. I've never had a true Luminosity teacher. True lumers … their power is mighty. They say that Avinasi, the greatest lumer in Zohar, can even raise the dead. She would have returned the king to his true former self. That is the power I crave. To heal all hurts."

Leven looked at her, his eyes softer now. "And to raise the dead?"

"I don't know."

Maya stared down at her saddle. She thought of the news she had received from the king of Sekadia—that her father was dead. It seemed impossible. How could it be real? How could Lord Jerael Sela, the powerful warrior, the kindly father—be gone?

Maya's eyes watered. She remembered how, as a child, she would sometimes cry at night, fearful of monsters under her bed, and how Father would embrace her, how safe she would feel in his wide arms. She remembered how Father had always seemed as wise, mighty, and all knowing as Eloh himself. He had never been just a man to Maya but a figure of legend, both a puissant lord and a loving father.

Gone, Maya thought. *Crucified. Murdered by Prince Seneca.*

When the King of Sekadia had shared the news with her—only a few days ago in the city—Maya had refused to believe it. It seemed impossible that a man as powerful as Jerael should die. And how could Atalia and Koren be captive? Atalia was the greatest warrior in the world, and Koren was deadly with his blades. How could they have lost their war?

That news was old already, but tidings traveled slowly across the desert. Maya shuddered to imagine what might have happened in Zohar since she had left. Was Mother still alive? Had Epher escaped the enemy? Was Ofeer still serving the Aelarians?

Leven must have seen the turmoil on her face. He rode closer to her, reached between the camels, and patted her knee.

"Maya, again: I'm sorry. I know how hard this is."

Maya blinked tears out of her eyes. "In the east, I can learn how to use the Sight. One of the Four Pillars of Luminosity. Avinasi began to teach me, but ... I can't do it alone. I only used the Sight once, with Avinasi guiding me, with all the lume of Beth Eloh around me, when I gazed north and saw Porcia's armies, and the light nearly drowned me." She inhaled deeply and raised her chin. "But they can teach me in Suna, at the center of Luminosity. And then I can look to Zohar. I can learn the fate of my family. And if they're hurt, I can heal them. I can heal them all. I can ..."

... bring Father back from the dead, she wanted to say, but she dared not. In the Book of Eloh, it was written that the ancient lumers could resurrect the dead, but Maya had never heard of any lumer doing so for thousands of years. She feared this power, and yet the grief at losing Father clawed at her.

Maya looked around her. Zamur, King of Sekadia, had given her this grand caravan, worthy of royalty. Camels. Warriors. Wagons laden with fine food and wine, not to mention purses full of gold. Even live goats traveled with them, assuring fresh meat on the journey. All these the king had gifted her. Maya had come to him a ragged vagabond, and now she was wealthy. But she'd have given up all her treasures for a chance to see her family again, to bring her father back.

"All of Zohar cries in mourning," Maya said. "All the land bleeds. I must learn how to heal them all. To heal our kingdom, Leven."

He nodded, somber now, his usual smile gone. "For many years, I lived as a thief in Zohar. I stole from our kingdom, a leech sapping blood to survive. But you're right, Maya. It's time to stop being a leech."

She raised an eyebrow, a little bit of mirth lighting her pain. "I thought you were a scorpion, but you're right. Leech suits you better."

"Careful that I don't leech onto you." He squeezed her knee. "I'll suck you dry."

At his touch, Maya thought back to how they had kissed. Suddenly she wanted to kiss him again. She wanted to ... to ... .

well, to do what Ofeer did so many times. But Maya's cheeks flushed, and she only looked away from him, staring east again. She did not know the ways of lovemaking, did not know how to seduce a man. She wasn't strong and striking like Atalia, wasn't pretty like Ofeer. All Maya knew was the light of Luminosity, and it was that light she sought in the east, that light she would soon learn how to tame.

They rode onward, and the noon sun was blazing when Maya saw the bones sticking out from the sand.

A spine ridge rose ahead like a bridge, each segment the size of a chariot. Maya narrowed her eyes, trying to imagine what creature could have been so large. The camels kept riding, and soon Maya saw great claws, large as oaks, rising from the sand. The bones seemed ancient, whittled down by endless eras, pocked with holes. Ribs rose ahead like the arches of temples, so large the convoy rode between them as if traveling through a nave. Scores of these ancient creatures lay half-buried in the sand, sprawling for parsa'ot.

"What are they?" Leven asked, staring at the bones of a tail tipped with spikes, each spike the size of a spear.

Maya remembered seeing one of these skeletons in the west, not far from the border of Zohar, but that one had been smaller and alone. Here was a great graveyard of the creatures.

"Dragons," she whispered, pointing ahead.

There in the sand it rose—a skull. A skull so large Maya could have ridden her camel into the mouth. The teeth rose like columns, and the eye sockets stared, full of shadows and sand. A nest of snakes writhed and hissed in a nostril.

Leven gulped. "Thank God they're dead. Those creatures look almost as bad as camels."

The warriors in the caravan muttered and clutched the hilts of their sabers. A few made signs against evil. One man even drew his blade, glancing around nervously.

"They're dead and can't hurt us," Maya said to Urak, chief of the warriors, a gaunt man with a curled black beard.

"The men believe that the souls of the reptiles still cling to them, that these lands are cursed." Urak was gruff and scarred, a man who had fought many battles. Now he shuddered. "The *dracos* were cruel beasts, Maya of Zohar. I can smell their evil in the air."

When Maya inhaled, she could smell it too. A rancid hint on the wind. At first she could barely detect it, but as they rode onward, the smell grew stronger. A stench of oil, soot, fire, rotten meat. The bones rose all around her. The ribs towered overhead. As she rode by another skull, Maya stared into its eye sockets, seeing only darkness. Those sockets were larger than her head. She kneed her camel, riding faster. All the men now drew their swords.

A shriek rose.

Maya spun her head from side to side, but it was only the wind gusting through the skulls, scattering sand through the mouths. She let out a shaky breath. Leven clenched his jaw and drew his own sword.

"They're just bones," she told him. "They're dead. They're just skeletons."

A sudden chill ran through Maya, and she frowned. Hackles rose on her nape, and goose bumps covered her arms. Her teeth ached as if trying to flee her gums. Somebody was watching her. She felt it, knew it—a presence that twisted the lume inside her.

She raised her eyes, stared southeast, and lost her breath.

He stood there on a hill. A parasa away, too far to see clearly, so far she shouldn't be seeing him at all. A figure cloaked and hooded in black. Watching her. He had always been watching her, she realized. Memories tickled her like flickers of dreams reemerging in daylight, burning bright for an instant, then vanishing back into the murk. A shadow in her childhood, lurking behind the door. A stranger in Beth Eloh, moving among the crowd, staring at her as the city fell. The dark man. The man with the gray furrowed skin. The man in the shadows, even here under searing sunlight. Then gone again from memory like sparks from a campfire vanishing in the night.

"That one moved." Leven's voice tore her away from her thoughts. "Look, there. That skeleton. It moved."

Maya blinked. She turned toward the thief, suppressing a shudder. "Stop trying to scare me."

She glanced back toward the southern hill, seeking the figure again, but he was gone. She saw nothing but endless dunes. Had she dreamed it? Had the shadow been just a flicker of Foresight, a ghost in her luminescence?

"Maya." Leven sucked in air. He pointed his sword. "Maya, the bones, they're …"

The sand began to rumble. Slowly, Maya turned her head.

"Eloh," she whispered.

One of the bony tails was moving, trailing across the sand, its spikes rising. Across the convoy, men cursed and kneed their camels.

"Ride!" Urak shouted.

Maya dug her heels into her camel and the animal burst into a gallop. Leven rode at her side, leaning forward in the saddle.

The massive tail rose from the sand, tall as a temple's column, then slammed down onto a camel, slicing through its rider, cleaving man and beast in two. Blood sprayed the sand, Maya screamed, and the rest of the skeleton rose too.

Bony wings spread out. The spine crackled. The skull rose, swaying on the neck, and the jaw unhinged. All across the desert they rose, scores of skeletons, shedding sand, bones creaking, raining insects and serpents. The stench wafted, and the sand rose in clouds.

"*Djin!*" the men cried. "*Djin!*"

Maya knew that word.

"Demons," she whispered.

Her camel galloped. Another tail lashed, slicing through another rider. Maya tugged the reins, and her camel swerved, nearly fell, raced onward. Leven rode at her side, sword held above his head. The skeletal wings beat above. Sand flurried, slamming into Maya, cutting her skin. She narrowed her eyes to slits, nearly blinded. The shrieks rose all around her, and she knew this was not the sound of wind. The dragons were screaming. It was an ancient sound, echoing, deafening, high-pitched like steaming water fleeing a kettle, shattering her ears.

A skull plowed forward through the sand, spine rattling behind it. The jaws opened. Maya swerved an instant before the jaws closed around another camel, crushing the animal, digging through its rider. Across the desert, the Sekadian warriors were firing arrows and swinging sabers, but the weapons harmlessly cascaded off the bones.

A claw slammed down, and Maya swerved again. The skeletal foot slammed into the desert. A tail lashed across the sand like a striking serpent, and Maya tried to dodge it, but the segments whipped through her camel's legs, slicing them clean off.

The camel screamed and fell, spilling Maya from the saddle. She slammed into the sand. She stared up, and the horror pounded through her.

They flew above her now, covering the sky, raining sand. Umber clouds rose above them, and the winds roared. A hundred of them or more. Dragons reborn. Creatures of bone, of rot, of ancient vengeance. Gods of the sand.

The desert still filled them, swirling within their ribcages, flowing around them through the sky, and their wings were made of sand. The camels raced onward, caught in the storm. Above, the skeletons opened their jaws, and the screams rose to howls so loud that Maya's ears rang. The desert shook. The sky seemed to crack. The dragons blasted down their wrath.

Sand blew from the fleshless jaws, shrieking, slamming down, searing hot. A jet drove into a camel and rider, tearing them apart, peeling skin and muscle from bones. Another rider fell from his camel and ran, only for a stream of sand to slam into him, ripping him apart. An arm flew in the wind and fell before Maya, the only remnant of the man.

Maya could no longer see Leven, only catch glimpses of the others. A wagon flew overhead, slammed down, and spilled its contents. A segment of spine whipped ahead, and claws lashed down. Maya jumped aside, fell into the sand. Everywhere the desert roiled, and the winds slammed into her. Every pellet of sand was a dagger, cutting her skin, bloodying her. She closed her eyes. The sand tore at her. The shrieks ripped through her ears. The desert shook, and the sand covered her, and the screams of men died around her. She would die here, she knew. She would join the bones. She—

You are a child of light.

She tried to crawl. Something tore into her leg, digging, seeking her bones, ripping off the flesh.

You are a daughter of Luminosity.

She forced herself to open her eyes, seeing only sand, only death, only bones. A man's skull. She—

She saw the mountains.

She saw a city of light and gold and stone.

The light flared across her, filling her eyes, streaming across her body and expanding, wreathing around her, forming a sphere of luminescence.

Maya rose to her feet, arms spread out. She hovered, her toes only grazing the sand, a figure in a ball of light.

Around her, the desert roiled, slamming against her shield, trying to tear through the light, but she wove her luminescence around her, holding back the storm.

"I am a daughter of Zohar," she whispered. "I am a lioness of the desert. The sand can never hurt me."

She moved through the storm. The claws lashed at her light and fell back. Fangs and spikes cut at her shield and shattered. The sand bathed her, roaring, washing around her, and still Maya advanced, hovering through the storm as the skeletons shrieked. Through the glow of luminescence, she saw them as they had been—scaled beasts, wreathed in flame, eyes like molten bronze in smelters, creatures that had flown across this land eras ago, back when the world had been water and fire and chaos.

Leven.

Through the storm, the visions, the roaring fury, the thought rose.

Leven.

Maya held out her arms, and the light blasted out from her fingers, ten beams of luminescence, thrumming, blinding, washing across the world. The dragons fled from the light. Her beams slammed into bones, piercing them with holes, and the creatures fell back. Maya drew on all the lume inside her—all memories of

Zohar, all the waves, the dunes, the warmth of home, the love of family—weaving them all into the luminescence, into her magic. With every shred of power inside her, she cast them back until the dragons fell, the sand rained down, and the desert was still once more.

The light left her.

Maya fell to her knees in the sand.

The last sand in the sky pattered down, and the umber clouds parted, revealing blue sky. The bones lay cracked and broken, once more lifeless relics.

I cast them back, Maya realized. *I used my magic, and I defeated dragons.*

She rose to her feet.

Leven.

She took slow steps through the desert, and her elation faded. Grief seeped in instead.

Death sprawled before her.

A severed man's foot lay in the sand, the bone sticking out from the flesh. Half a head, ripped open, peered at her with one eye. What remained of a torso, shredded like red cloth, clung to the sand. Maya kept walking, unable to comprehend this horror. She had never seen such slaughter—not just death but bodies in pieces, red strips of flesh and raw bones.

"Leven," she whispered.

She walked around a shattered camel and a wagon wheel, and there she found him.

Leven lay in the sand, his legs ripped off.

Maya gasped and covered her mouth.

Remnants of bones jutted out from the stumps. The blood darkened the sand around him, still spurting. Leven's skin had gone gray, and his eyes were sunken, but he was still alive. He looked at her, tried to speak, could not.

Maya rushed toward him and knelt in the bloody sand.

"I'm going to heal you." She clutched his hand. "Cling on. Cling on, Leven. I'm going to heal you."

He swallowed and nodded, trembling, his eyes shadowed, his skin colorless.

Maya inhaled deeply and tried to think of home.

Her mind was blank.

No memories emerged.

She sucked in air and tried again, but she could not remember the land of Zohar. She knew she had come from that kingdom, but she could not recall its landscapes, its cities, the home she had lived in. She knew there was a city there called Beth Eloh. She knew she had come from a place called Gefen. But she could not remember what they looked like, could not feel the magic that flowed from them.

All my lume is gone, she realized.

She squeezed Leven's hands, screwed her eyes shut, tried again. She knew that lumers in Aelar, tributes to the Empire, returned to visit Zohar every year, to gaze upon the holy city, to resupply their reserves of lume. Maya hadn't been away for a year yet, but she had used so much of the magic, spent so much of the light when healing the king, when casting back the dragons.

Nothing.

She could not remember what the sea sounded like, could not remember the light on the stones of Beth Eloh. No memories. No lume.

Her hands could not glow, and she could not heal him.

"Leven," she whispered. "It's all right. It's all right." She pulled off her belt and wrapped it around one of his stumps, trying to stop the blood, to hold in his life. "You'll be fine. You'll get through this."

But his blood kept flowing, and she had nothing to make a tourniquet with for his second stump. He was fading fast. He was convulsing. She held him, trying to calm him, to stop his violent jerking.

"Leven, please." She looked up at the sky. "Please, Eloh. If you can hear me, please don't let him die. He's all I have from home. Please. Save him, Eloh. If not by my grace then by yours. Please."

Yet nothing but the searing sunlight fell from the sky. Leven's trembling eased. His skin was gray now, barely any blood left in him. He reached up a weak hand and poked her with one finger.

"Sting," he whispered.

His hand fell.

His eyes stared at the blue sky, lifeless.

Maya lowered her head, weeping, holding him. She knelt there for a long time, tears flowing, until the cruel sun vanished beyond the horizon, and the moon drenched the desert with silver light.

When she looked south, she saw the figure there again. She had known that she would. The man in the shadows. The master of bones. He stood in the distance, black on black, a wraith in the night. Cloaked. Hooded. Staring. And Maya knew him, knew that he had done this, knew that she would face him again before the end. But not now. Not this night, for he was patient. He was ancient. He would wait.

She looked away.

She buried Leven in starlight and moonlight. She buried him in sand, for he had come from the desert, and to the desert he returned. She sang over his grave, old songs of home—songs of Zohar, of palm trees and olive trees, of frankincense and myrrh, of turtle doves and hinds over hills. Of light and of luminescence. Maya could no longer remember these things, and the words had no meaning to her, but as she sang, she prayed that Leven's spirit would rise to the heavens, where he would forever dwell in a land of milk and honey and grace.

She walked on through the darkness, alone, navigating by the stars.

She walked all night.

The dawn rose cold and pale silver, and in its light, she saw it there in the east.

The sea.

The sunlight rose above the water, painting it all in gold. It nestled on the coast—a humble town. Several minarets and archways. A few domes. A small port and a blinking lighthouse. As Maya gazed upon it, the light of Eloh filled her, and the glow of starlight and sunlight shone inside her and around her fingers, and she wove it, just a hint of luminescence.

Maya walked toward this town by the sea, toward this new spring of lume, toward a hope to learn the ways of Luminosity, of healing, and of wisdom.

The story continues in …

Thrones of Ash (*Kingdoms of Sand* Book 3)

NOVELS BY DANIEL ARENSON

Kingdoms of Sand:
Kings of Ruin
Crowns of Rust
Thrones of Ash
Temples of Dust
Halls of Shadow
Echoes of Light

Earthrise:
Earth Alone
Earth Lost
Earth Rising
Earth Fire
Earth Shadows
Earth Valor
Earth Reborn
Earth Honor
Earth Eternal

Alien Hunters:
Alien Hunters
Alien Sky
Alien Shadows

Requiem for Dragons:

Dragons Lost

Dragons Reborn

Dragons Rising

Flame of Requiem:

Forged in Dragonfire

Crown of Dragonfire

Pillars of Dragonfire

Misfit Heroes:

Eye of the Wizard

Wand of the Witch

Standalones:

Firefly Island

The Gods of Dream

Flaming Dove

KEEP IN TOUCH

www.DanielArenson.com
Daniel@DanielArenson.com
Facebook.com/DanielArenson
Twitter.com/DanielArenson

Made in the USA
Middletown, DE
20 April 2018